Praise for *Lost*

"Zang and Knudsen infuse the investigation with intrigue by crafting diverse characters with idiosyncrasies, secrets, and mysterious pasts... it's the many tantalizing portents, clues, and seeming impossibility that makes Lost Grove shine. Balancing the central story and a myriad of characters with finesse, the authors expertly set the stage for a gripping conclusion" — *Book Life* (editor's pick)

"Zang and Knudsen skillfully introduce a massive array of characters and balance them throughout the hefty read, tucking in reminders to help the reader keep track of everybody. Despite the vast array of characters, each is fully developed and interesting...The kids are both smart and teenage-stupid in a very believable way. They banter, flirt, speak things both crass and profound—and, at their core, make up a tight, amiable group grappling with their identities at an awkward stage...Thriller, mystery, and gothic horror combine in Charlotte Zang and Alex Knudsen's LOST GROVE: Part One. It is a page-turning novel about a missing-person investigation in a small coastal town that offers depth, surprise, eeriness, and great characters." — *IndieReader*

"Satisfyingly structured, carefully paced, and packed with surprises, Lost Grove is an intriguing mystery that impeccably blends horror elements such as vampirism, telepathy and changelings, into its modern-day crime narrative. Far from gimmicky, these unnatural features add immeasurably to the story's mood, with the eerie locality of Lost Grove serving as a supernaturally charged backdrop for the investigation...In lesser hands, these tangential character arcs and plot threads might have crippled the novel's pace. However, the authors do an exemplary job of weaving these various threads into the main narrative." — *BlueInk Review*

"Marked by supernatural intrigue, the mystery novel Lost Grove reveals a town's misgivings and secrets...In Charlotte Zang and Alex Knudsen's gripping novel Lost Grove, a young woman's death reveals a web of mysteries in her small town." — *Clarion*

"Lost Grove: Part One by Charlotte Zang and Alex Knudsen is a dark dream for fans of contemporary horror...the sinister storyline laced with vicious cults, mental illness, amateur sleuthing, and divine forces makes for a multilayered and gripping read that will satisfy readers of both psychological thrillers and horror fiction."

— *Self Publishing Review* (four stars)

"Lost Grove is what would have happened if the TV show Twin Peaks (1990) had taken a more supernatural path...Because of the unraveling threads, this book can get addictive quickly. The city's lore will grip any reader's attention, and there is so much alluring strangeness going on...A paranormal mystery well worth reading, Lost Grove (Part 1) will have you questioning constantly why this creepy town is the way it is."

— *Independent Book Review*

"Reading Lost Grove: Part One by Charlotte Zang and Alex Knudson was akin to riding one of the most thrilling rollercoasters in the world. Right from page one, you are dragged into an eerie story that will send chills down your spine and have your hair standing on end...A great plot and amazing character development make this a must-read for all mystery fans."   —*Anne Marie-Reynolds, Reader's Favorite* (five stars)

"The unexpected twist of incorporating supernatural elements into what begins as a conventional thriller is a bold and successful gamble. This aspect, in particular, adds a layer of complexity and intrigue, setting the novel apart from its contemporaries...What truly elevates this book, however, is its exploration of themes that go beyond the typical thriller. The sensitive handling of death and the nuanced portrayal of the characters, especially the teenagers, are handled with a deft touch, adding a sense of realism and depth to the narrative... It is a testament to the authors' ability to craft a story that is as haunting as it is enthralling. This book is highly recommended for readers seeking a narrative that seamlessly blends mystery, thriller, and horror with a dash of the supernatural, creating a unique and memorable experience."

— *Literary Titan*

"Author team Charlotte Zang and Alex Knudsen have crafted a suspense-filled work that twists on a knife edge into plot hook after plot hook, unveiling a tapestry of dark secrets and evil deeds that tightens its grip on readers' hearts."   — *K.C. Finn, Reader's Favorite* (five stars)

"The opening scenes are so vividly described that they invite readers into a blue-grey, foggy world of utter horror, mystery and uncertainty. The unnatural, hair-raising atmosphere sets a biting tone and just enough information is given to indicate that something is not quite right which builds up the suspense...This made for an exciting and enjoyable journey through the investigation that other mainstream detective novels have yet to achieve...The overall storyline sets the scene for a captivating world with endless possibilities and that gives off Stephen King horror story-like vibes."   — *Hayley Hoatson, Reedsy Discovery*

"I could not take my eyes off the pages because of the various, quick-paced subplots that had unexpected turns. There were many different characters, each with an intriguing and distinctive past. The characters were well-developed, and there were moments when I forgot they were fictional and not actual people. This masterfully written paranormal mystery will appeal to readers seeking something different and unique in both concept and style. My mind was blown away by this story, and I am eager to read the next one."

— *Alma Boucher, Reader's Favorite* (five stars)

Also by Charlotte Zang

See all of Charlotte's books and where to get them on her website at:
https://www.charlottezang.com/

Blooding

Consuming Beauty

Lysander O'Connor

Satan's in Your Kitchen

Also by Alex J. Knudsen

See all of Alex's books and where to get them on his website at
https://www.alexjknudsen.com

The Nawie

Lost Grove
Part One

Charlotte Zang and Alex Knudsen

This novel is a work of fiction. All of the names, characters, organizations, places and events portrayed in this novel are either products of the author's imagination or are used fictitiously. Any resemblance to real or actual events, locales, or persons, living or dead, is entirely coincidental.

Copyright © 2023 Charlotte Zang & Alex Knudsen

All rights reserved. No part of this publication may be reproduced, stored or transmitted in any form or by any means, electronic, mechanical, photocopying, recording, scanning, or otherwise without written permission from the publisher. It is illegal to copy this book, post it to a website, or distribute it by any other means without permission.

Cover art and desing by Dilan Chinaka
Printed in the United States of America
First Printing, 2024

Paperback ISBN 979-8-9897962-1-2

For Leslie, Kathy, Gary, Steve, Matt, and Hagen

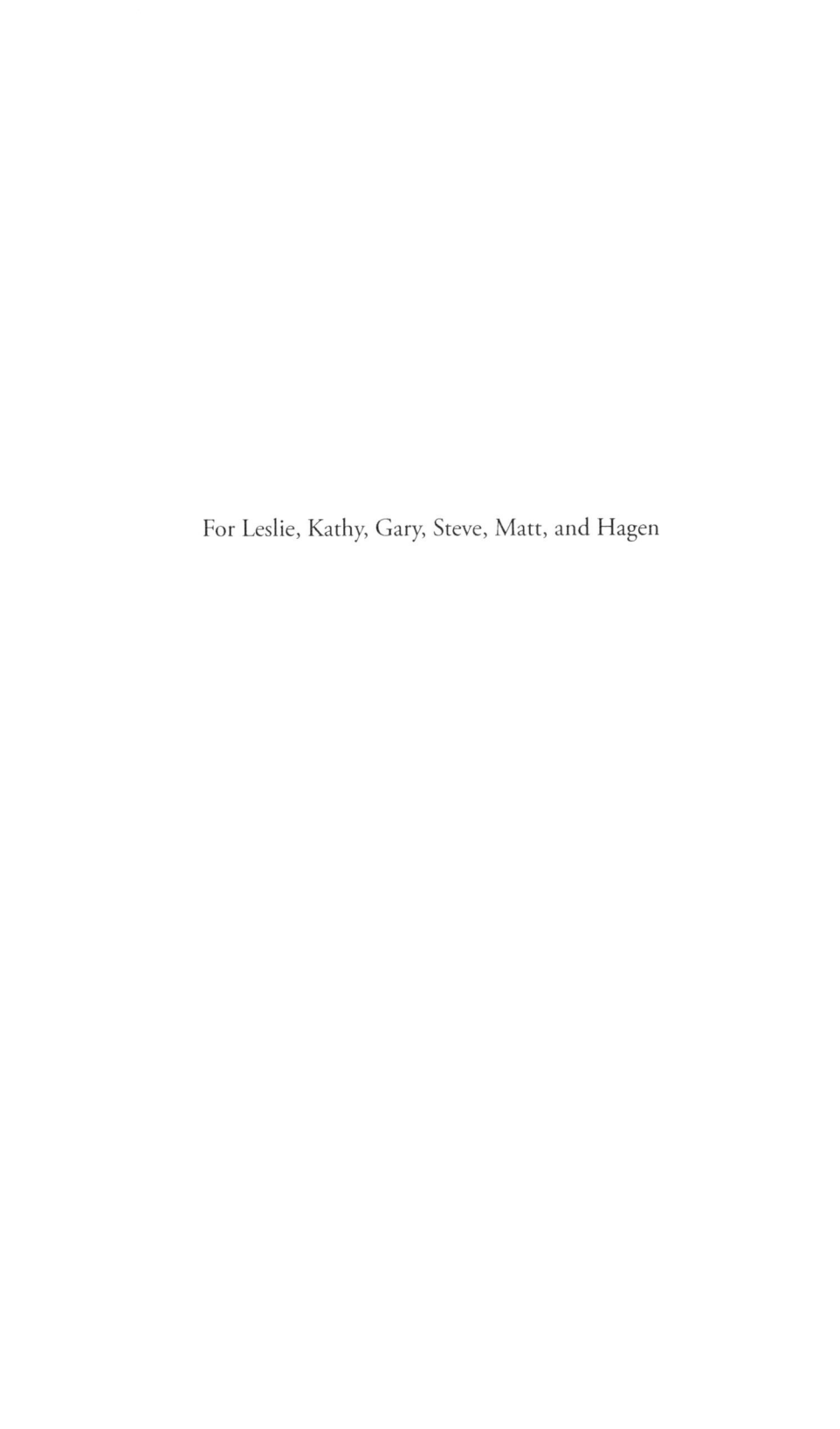

Prologue

The Wind Tastes Foul

The scent wafting down the stony shore into her sensitive nostrils alerted Mary to the human body ahead. Unlike the peculiar sea creature that had washed ashore the last time they'd had a massive storm during a full moon, a human body had a particular essence that clung to the back of her throat. It was both pleasing and gag-inducing. Involuntarily, Mary's feet slowed from a steady gallop to a walk. The pressure in her teeth tightened, a stinging pain along her gums that came with the odor of flesh. A pressing urge to move away overcame her because of the overwhelming aura of death clinging to that base level of pleasure. She should move away from the frail, pale body lying on the beach. Her stomach clenched in spasms of hunger. Instead, Mary pressed onward.

The sound of her running shoes pressing down upon the pebbles and sand rattled in her ears with each crunch of granules, the sliding screech of rock on rock. Like the commotion of an orchestra behind the curtain waiting to play, the noise became distinct before she pushed it away. The massive driftwood tree, also washed ashore during the last storm, was now surrounded by smaller chunks of wood and seaweed. The body lay in the shallow bowl of sand, like some peculiar funeral bed against the driftwood headboard.

Mary's feet came to a stop six meters from the corpse. The grey-blue of dawn painted the world in a dreamy haze. It was her favorite time, her favorite color, that intangibly transparent yet cloudy blue. Her gaze danced out to the waves at sea. Their languid roll to shore like the

Dr. Jekyll to the Mr. Hyde waves that had crashed ashore two nights ago. Mary had stood on the beach that night, her long dark blonde hair whipping her face and neck, hoping for a rogue wave and wishing the tide would pull her below. The cravings came hard and fast these days. They overwhelmed her to the point she lost reason. Mary longed to end them. Skin drenched and rain-lashed, she hadn't felt the cold or the sting that night. Not the way others would.

She played her tongue over the elongated eyeteeth, touching the tender flesh surrounding them. The carrion smell of the young woman now lying before her drew them out. Mary moved closer, lazy steps. No one else was on the beach, and no one would be for hours. And the dunes formed a natural barrier from the road. Any passing car would be too far away to notice Mary, let alone the beautiful corpse now at her feet.

"Odd," she started, "how the shade of dawn now paints your decomposing flesh."

The top layer of the body's skin was dull porcelain. Her auburn hair lacked the brilliance it emitted when she was alive. Her eyes were milky and vacant, lips a mauve blue.

Mary tilted her head, examining the corpse. "Sarah Elizabeth, what did you get yourself into?"

Sarah's body appeared freshly washed, no dirt, debris, bruises, or foreign bodies sullying her beautiful form. The position of her arms, legs, and head made it seem like she had posed for an angelic painting and then simply died. The barest sign of footprints showed in the sand, but the residual winds from the storm masked them to the point that Mary wouldn't say she could recognize them as male or female. Her gaze returned to Sarah Elizabeth, naked and blue.

"*The breeze, the breath of God, is still,*" Mary whispered, reciting the macabre Edgar Allan Poe poem that sprung to mind.

"*And the mist upon the hill
Shadowy, shadowy, yet unbroken,
Is a symbol and a token.
How it hangs upon the trees,
A mystery of mysteries,*" Mary recited.

The gravel crackled under the toes of her shoes as she bent easily over the body. A lithe grace that came from miles of running and hours on a yoga mat, exertions that abated cravings Mary could not satisfy. When she was younger, specialists said she had a form of pica, the desire to eat objects or substances that were not edible. Her eating habits had caused forms of anemia, and her desire for iron, or rather blood and raw meat, were "unsavory" habits her parents desired she abandon. Mary had always known her affliction was more than a diagnosis modern doctors could conceptualize.

The scent of the recently deceased young woman grew more intense. Mary's nostrils flared—a tantalizing sweet smell. The fragrance of death began wrapping Sarah Elizabeth in a cloak of decay, shifting a prehistoric, animalistic button inside Mary's brain. She swallowed forcefully. The desire to chew on something made the freshly dead flesh look like a raw cut of prime beef. Instead, she crouched and took up a nice flat stone from near the body. Mary placed it on her tongue, savoring the weight of it, the salty brine and metallic cool that pooled in her mouth.

Thankful for the momentary release the stone provided, Mary righted her body, standing once more over Sarah Elizabeth. Mary pushed the rock into her cheek like a piece of hard candy.

"What to do with you?" she asked herself.

Mary had known Sarah since the child was born. Now Mary knew her in death. She tilted her head back, observed the steel-blue sky, then pivoted her body to look toward town. Lost Grove was quiet and still in the early hours of the morning. Calling the police station would click over to the answering service. Mary was in no mood to deal with a switchboard operator who would ask her fifty questions.

"Time to get up, Chief Richards," she said, deciding.

Mary loped down the beach, her feet carrying her smoothly across the stony shore toward town. She'd weave through the quaint Victorian homes and stop at a modern ranch-style house on Bluff Street. Chief of Police Bill Richards and his wife would startle awake to a loud banging on their door. He would find a note pinned under a small, smooth stone, Mary's saliva already drying on the surface of it. The note would tell him to search Mourner's Beach for Sarah Elizabeth's body. At the bottom, in fine print, "Hint: she's by the pile of driftwood."

Chapter 1

Sarah Elizabeth

The shrill ringing of Sergeant Seth Wolfe's police-issued phone jolted him out of a deep sleep. The darkness in his room told him it was early. Too early. The seconds it took him to adapt to a wakeful state reminded him how quickly he had settled into the lackadaisical humdrum of small-town life in Lost Grove. During his almost twenty years as a homicide detective for the San Francisco Police Department, he only half-slept, his body always prepped to leap out of bed at any hour, mind alert. The last time he had received an early morning call in Lost Grove was two months ago, when Officer Sasha Kingsley disturbed him with news that old man Richter's sheep were causing trouble on Highway 211. With a sigh, Seth reached over and clutched his phone. He looked at the screen, and a deep frown formed on his brow.

"Bill? What's got you up—"

"Seth, we've got a 911 here. There's a—down—Mourner's Beach."

Seth blinked away the blur of sleep and sat up. His black hair was tousled from sleep and his jaw could do with a razor, though he rarely bothered with the clean-shaven look from his detective persona. He swung his legs off the bed, his bare feet hitting the cold wooden floor. "Bill, cover the receiver. It's windy as shit. All I heard was 911 and Mourner's Beach," he said, leaning on his knees and running a hand through his hair.

"There's a body. A girl. She's dead."

Seth stood, moving to the makeshift closet, a garment rack that came with the loft apartment above his father's pharmacy. "I'm on my way. Did you call Wes yet?" he asked as he foraged for fresh boxers and socks in his small dresser, holding the phone between his ear and shoulder.

"Shit, no. I called you the second I got here. I'm calling him now."

Bill clicked off, and Seth threw his phone back on the bed. Approaching forty, Seth kept his body at the same level of fitness he'd needed to place top of his class in the academy fitness test. He had a flat stomach and a chest of dark hair that was, like the hair at his temples, just starting to show sprinkles of grey. He was more lean than muscled, though a set of weights in the corner was a recent addition to his workout routine, something he had more time for since his move back. Life as a sergeant on the Lost Grove police force didn't require nearly the hours he'd put in as a homicide detective.

As he yanked on his pants, Seth's heart hammered in his chest. Adrenaline surged through him as he teetered between shock and elation, both feelings stirring up a thrill he welcomed.

Seth stomped the brakes of his police-issue Bronco as he swerved onto the sand-covered road next to Bill's Jeep. He had never needed to drive faster than 35 mph in this small town, but the synapses in his brain were popping off like fireworks, running through potential scenarios of how a dead body ended up on Mourner's Beach. In Lost Grove, a small farming town of just over 1,500 residents, the scenarios he could think up were wildly improbable compared to those from his life in the big city.

Seth jumped out of his car, wearing the still-unfamiliar police-issue jacket, and slammed the door. He'd been to this beach many times before. It was almost like an old friend, but now he was here in a new capacity: as a detective. Or rather, a sergeant acting as a detective. The title change, along with the police garb, was taking some getting used to. The biting cold had him shrugging his shoulders up to his ears as he made his way to the scene, taking care to keep an open mind. He tramped up and through the dunes. The sandy path already had multiple indents, too shallow and shifting to provide evidence if they needed it. He shoved his cold hands into his pockets, making his way through the scrub marram grass that snagged at his trousers until the vast expanse of beach revealed itself.

The ocean sound intensified, pulling Seth's gaze to the horizon. He watched the waves crest and crash at the shoreline in a familiar yet somehow foreign pattern, trying to push away the wistfulness in his chest as he took in the sight. He looked away from the horizon, torn between his past life in San Francisco and his current reality. Across the beach, the coroner's van was parked at an angle on the sloping shore. His steps became heavy as he approached what would have been a chaotic scene in the Bay Area, overflowing with flashing lights, reporters, and morbid onlookers.

Seth briefly lost his balance as the tumultuous sounds of the ocean seemed to turn off like he'd pressed Stop on a cassette player. Suddenly, all he could hear was the deafening pulse of his own heart, followed by a desperate gasp for air that seemed to go nowhere. He felt like wet cement was filling up his lungs. His vision oscillated in and out of focus as he fought for breath.

"Not a way to start a morning, Seth. No way at all. I woke up to a knock…"

A sense of déjà vu, unlike anything he had ever felt, overtook his mind, the desperate need for oxygen forgotten. The way the coroner's van sat, pointing toward a massive driftwood tree, its headlights glowing dimly in the early morning mist. The massive driftwood tree lifting from the sand, like a monument sculpted by a macabre artist, had been a morbid art installation in his mind for some time. Billowing ribbons of police tape twisted and undulated in the wind, barely hanging on to the sticks shoved into the sand. As one of them lifted, Seth knew it would snap twice more in the wind before slipping loose and sailing through the air.

Seth's gaze fastened on the centerpiece as he cautiously approached. Though he was still fifty yards away, he knew what lay in the bowl carved out by the wind at the foot of the driftwood pile. The body of a young woman was waiting for him. She'd be naked, her skin so white it was almost translucent, fingers, toes, and lips painted a cyanotic blue. Her hair would be splayed around her head like sea-foam. He already knew the way her body would fold, her limbs arranged thoughtfully, almost lovingly. One arm would be tucked behind her back, knees together, leaning to the left as if waiting for someone to come and collect her, a prince to carry her back to her bedroom and awaken her with a kiss.

"…similarities are downright eerie…"

It all returned in a flash, as if he'd just experienced this exact incident days ago. Even the way the wind licked at his clammy neck, sending shivers down his spine, was intimately familiar. The distant, crashing roar of the waves repeated like an eerie refrain from a doomsday score he had listened to hundreds of times before.

"...that sound like a plan?"

He had been here before. Not days ago. Not weeks or months. No. It was years ago. He was seventeen again, curled up in a ball of fear in a cave beneath a mountain of earth, gasping for breath as the blackness closed around him. He remembered it like it was yesterday—the moment his body transcended from that dark place and emerged here, to this very moment in time, on this beach, next to this lifeless body encircled by driftwood. It felt so surreal, yet so familiar.

He must have buried it deep in his psyche—too young to process, too otherworldly to contextualize, too mystifying to believe. What was this?

"Seth?"

Now he was hearing the same voice he'd heard in the cave. Mortified, freezing, oxygen running thin, the voice he heard now had pulled him back from the out-of-body, time-leaping experience—the voice of the man who saved his life and inspired him to become a police officer.

"Seth?"

Crawling out of his stupefied state, Seth looked to his left to see that he was walking with Chief Bill Richards, his boss, his friend, the then young man who had pulled him from the collapsed cave. Except now he was wearing a fur-lined jacket and a winter hat, not sweating in a short-sleeved beige shirt and sunglasses. How long had he been next to him? Had Bill been talking? Had Seth?

"Yeah, sorry," he uttered and coughed into a fist.

"That sound good to you?" Bill asked. He had the kind of smooth skin that belied his nearly sixty years, with a goofy but handsome face that made the chief of police approachable. Outside of his uniform, you'd never guess Bill's profession of choice was serving the community as an officer of the law. He looked more like a schoolteacher. Seth always thought Bill could have been a local news reporter, with his thick head of light brown hair and charming smile.

"Yeah," Seth replied absentmindedly.

They stopped in front of the body; Lost Grove's medical examiner crouched nearby, taking photos. Knowing precisely where he'd look first, Seth's gaze fell upon the girl's open eyes. The same auburn hair, the same parted lips, every feature distinctly recognizable, yet only in a dream. Or so he had thought. The girl's lifeless face had lingered in the forefront of his mind for months after his near-death experience, gradually retreating to the back of his mind as nothing more than an oxygen-deprived nightmare.

"You okay? You had to have seen worse."

Seth's head snapped back to Bill, registering the look on his face, the nervous way he held his body. Seth shook his head, quickly transitioning to a nod. "No. I mean, yeah, I have."

Seth had seen far worse scenes as a homicide detective: mutilated bodies, suicides from razors and gunshots, mass gang slayings, the aftermath of rape and overdoses. Still, nothing had been as unsettling as reliving an event he had experienced twenty-six years ago. This wasn't déjà vu. Seth didn't know what to call it. Perhaps there was no word for an experience like this. Seth bounced up and down on his toes and rubbed his freezing hands together. He needed to focus.

"Over the phone, all you had the chance to mention was that she was dead. Anything since to shed some light on what happened?" he said.

"Wes!" Bill called out to the medical examiner, who had returned to his van.

Dr. Wes Hensley glanced over at the men and nodded. He wore his long black hair folded over and tied up in a ponytail to stay out of his face and keep the scene clean. He had on a white long-sleeve thermal tucked into faded blue jeans and wore aged leather cowboy boots. Wes set his camera down, grabbed his medical kit, and made his way back over to the body. "Seth." He nodded at his former high school classmate.

"Wes," Seth said, admiring the collection of Indigenous bracelets adorning his old friend's wrist, the same ones he wore two decades ago. The two men had been on the same traveling baseball team growing up and now had come full circle to be working together. Although, Seth had assumed Wes would join him in San Francisco, never guessing Seth would instead return to his childhood home to join Wes as part of the Lost Grove Police Department. "What can you tell me about the body?"

"Not a whole lot at the moment. I would say she's been dead for no more than twenty-four hours. Cause of death is unclear. No apparent external injuries."

"Even with her arm like that?" Seth asked, looking down at the girl's arm twisted unnaturally behind her back.

"Neither the elbow, shoulder, or wrist are fractured or dislocated. There could be a hairline fracture, but nothing that would have been responsible for this."

Seth's brows rose. "Ya think?"

"Just sayin'," Wes replied, his arms spread out. "And I didn't want to move her until you got here."

"Appreciate that." Seth pulled latex gloves from his pocket and slipped them on. His heart was still rattling, his stomach sloshing around, threatening to contaminate the scene. The haunting familiarity of the scenario had dissipated and left him with a dizzying effect, an uneasy pressure behind his eyes he wasn't used to. Seth knelt down, looking the body over from head to toe for anything suspicious. Who was this girl? Why had he seen her before? *Focus on the scene*, he encouraged himself.

"She must have drowned." Bill broke the silence, then looked from the body to Wes. "Could she have drowned?"

"It's possible," Wes said, taking a quick glance back at the body. He was used to dead bodies, but this one stirred a raw emotion. She was a young woman who'd gone to school with his daughter. How did she end up like this? "I'll find out pretty quickly doing the autopsy if her lungs are filled with water. But if she were dead before entering the water, her lungs would be empty. Either way, it's curious that her body wouldn't have suffered any physical damage from the ocean."

Seth looked from the body to the ocean and back at Wes. "The tide couldn't possibly have brought her this far up, could it?"

"Bill and I discussed that. She's pretty far back, but considering the storm that came rolling through two nights ago, I'm not going to rule it out. And with her arm twisted behind her and her legs intertwined, it would align with the power of the tide twisting her up before she stuck to land. That being said, her hair isn't as thoroughly drenched as I would imagine it to be if she were in the water. No marine life lodged in there, either."

"Hm." Seth looked back at the young woman lying on the beach, his instinct to reach out and examine the body momentarily quelled by the fear that he might have another experience by simply touching her. He swallowed, took a deep breath, and reached over, brushing the girl's hair from her face. He turned her chin from side to side, looking at her neck, then pulled her bottom lip down and examined her gums.

"What are you looking for?" Bill asked, wishing he didn't feel so unprepared for the situation. It had been seven years since he last came upon an unexplained death, and he was far from proud of how he handled the situation. He felt like an imposter being Seth's boss, who had likely come across more suspicious deaths in a week than Bill had in his entire career.

"Clues," Seth mumbled as he carefully pulled the girl's arm out from underneath her body. His gaze went from the inside of her elbow to her wrist to her fingertips before flipping the hand over to take in her nails. He followed suit with her other hand, another pang of memory assaulting him as he noticed the delicate, feminine cursive of the word *Grace* tattooed on her wrist. Ensuring he wouldn't faint, Seth took a deep breath before standing up and taking off his gloves, eyes still on the body. "I really don't think she drowned, Wes."

"As I said, it doesn't look like it, but I've—"

"You've got to check everything. I know." Seth looked at Wes. "How many victims of drowning have you had the chance to examine?"

Wes raised his eyebrows. "Well, one in med school, and…just one on the job. Well, one that we thought drowned anyhow," he said and nodded at Bill.

Seth looked over at Bill, wondering what they were referencing.

"Same here. Or, rather, just the one I mentioned."

Seth narrowed his eyes at Bill's odd phrasing. "Well, I've had my fair share. From the Bay to lakes to bathtubs. This body would be in the best condition I've ever seen from drowning. Especially considering the violence of the ocean off this beach. No abrasions. Her fingertips are hardly wrinkled. No sand or ocean matter in her mouth."

Bill pointed at the body. "Then…what is this?"

Seth looked back at Wes. "Suicide? Overdose of pills?"

Wes nodded. "Certainly a strong possibility. I won't have details until I get the toxicology results, which could be weeks."

"I'll make sure it's not weeks," Seth offered, hoping he hadn't overstepped his bounds, considering he was just a sergeant under Bill's command. He spun around, surveying the scene and beyond. "Where are her clothes?"

Bill shook his head. "Haven't found any clothes yet."

Seth turned back to him. "Vehicle?"

"Nope. Nothing nearby anyhow."

Seth glared down at the body, processing the information. He looked back up at both men. "I'm going to take a step back from the notion of suicide."

"Why is that?" Bill asked.

Seth huffed. "Well, I think it's highly unlikely she walked all the way down here naked to drown herself or take a bunch of pills. Nearest farm is what, two and a half miles toward town? Five miles or more if you continue out around the point, away from town."

Bill scratched the top of his head and let out a heavy sigh. It was the first time Seth noticed how shaken his chief was. He'd have noticed it before had it not been for his own earth-moving experience.

"I have to get back to it, gentlemen," Wes interrupted. "I'll call you after I finish the autopsy. Likely tomorrow."

"Thanks, Wes," Bill said.

Seth thrust his hands into his jacket. "Any idea who the girl might be?"

Bill grimaced. "I told you she was a local girl."

Seth bit the inside of his lip, wondering how much he might have missed during his transcendent daze on the way to the scene. And how in the hell could he possibly explain that to Bill? He shook his head. "Sorry, Bill, I guess I was a bit…"

"In the zone? Yeah, you were laser focused."

Seth forced a laugh and a false smile as his hands started to sweat and tremble, grateful he tucked them inside his coat pockets. "Just trying to take it all in. Didn't want to miss anything."

Bill shrugged. "You're used to this sort of thing more than me. I don't think I'll be sleeping for days."

Seth nodded, assuming he would suffer similarly but for wholly different reasons.

"Her name's Sarah Elizabeth Grahams. She was off at college. I reckon this would have been her junior or senior year. I haven't seen her in town for years. Lord knows how she ended up back here. And like this," he said, shaking his head.

Seth cocked his head to the side, his curiosity piqued. "Grahams… any relation to Richard Grahams?"

Bill nodded. "Mm-hmm."

Seth's mind raced with memories of Richard from high school, his friends, his personality. "Huh. I hope he's changed. He was kind of an asshole in high school."

Bill smirked. "You guys weren't in the same year, were you?"

Seth shook his head. "Nope, he was a year ahead of me. Hopefully, he grew out of it."

"You all did. Look at where you are now."

Seth winced, feeling so far away from where he was, who he was back in San Francisco. "Yeah," was all he could muster.

"Well, I don't relish having to inform Richard and his wife, Bess, about this. They seemed like good parents to her. Such a sweet girl. Their only child, too."

Seth noticed the tightening in Bill's voice. "You alright? You want me to do it?"

Bill took a deep breath, anxiety filling his stomach from the last time he had to do this. "Nah, I better do it."

"You said she was off at college. Was it somewhere close?"

"No, which is why this is all the more troubling. I don't recall the exact college, but I remember Richard and Bess being upset that she would be so far away."

"Well, she clearly came back here for something. Find out what it was."

Bill nodded. "Had already been thinking about that. Not even a holiday or anything."

Seth nodded toward their vehicles. "I can come with you."

"Nah." Bill waved him off. He had to exert some authority before he lost all confidence. "It'd be better if we split up. You're the only one here with any experience in cases like this. Maybe start at the high school, talk to her old teachers, see who her friends were, what she's been up to since she left town, and if anyone has seen her around Lost Grove recently."

"Bill, we haven't even identified her body yet."

Bill narrowed his eyes at Seth. "I just did."

Seth sighed out a laugh, hoping Bill was joking. "Well, as much as I believe you, just make sure you go directly to Richard and…?"

"Bess."

"Bess. They both work?"

Bill nodded. "Yep. But not this early."

"Well, you better go wake them then."

"I'm on it."

"And get them to identify the body as soon as possible."

Bill nodded. "I know, I know."

Seth let out a sigh of relief. "In the meantime, I'll just tell anyone I talk to that it's regarding an ongoing investigation."

"Sounds good."

Seth looked down the beach, where two of the three officers of the Lost Grove Police Department, Joe Casey and Sasha Kingsley, were searching for evidence. Hopefully, not another body. When Seth returned to Lost

Grove, his hopes were not high for the officers he would work with. He was going from working with some of the best detectives in the country to working with Eddie Cabrera, an officer past the age of retirement who Seth knew from grade school, and two young unknowns.

In a town like Lost Grove, recruiting candidates from an academy or university was like convincing a fish to come out of the water. It was nearly impossible to match the salaries of larger towns or cities, which was almost all of them. And the opportunity for promotion was as likely as winning the Nobel Peace Prize. So, it was with wide-eyed astonishment that not only did Eddie seem to age in reverse, as lean and active as he was thirty years ago, but that Sasha and Joe were both transplants from out of state and college graduates. Their competitive desire to outdo the other in every arena presented to them, which included trying to impress Seth, gave him a much-needed boost of vitality upon joining the department.

"You gonna keep Joe and Sasha working the beach?" Seth said.

Bill followed Seth's gaze down to his youngest officers, feeling great relief that Seth had accepted the recently vacated sergeant position just three months prior. He had taken a leave of absence to come home and help his mother, Amaranth, take care of his father, Christopher, after he had a stroke. Seth had been helping at the pharmacy that his father had been running for almost four decades, making the apartment above it his temporary residence. Bill felt like he had won the lottery when Seth told him he decided to put in his resignation from the San Francisco Police Department and was willing to take on the lesser position of sergeant. Bill didn't know how long it would last, but he was grateful Seth was here now.

"Yep, they'll be at it for a while," Bill said, hoping that was the right usage of their time. "That plan make sense to you?"

Seth nodded. He had his own instincts about how he would handle the case, but he wasn't in charge. Not anymore. A fact he was still adapting to. "Sounds good to me."

Bill leaned in and lowered his voice as if a crowd were nearby. "Look, whether this was an accident or… something worse, this is going to hit the town hard."

Seth nodded. "Yeah, I know it will."

"I'm sure word will spread quickly enough, but let's try to keep a tight lid on it for as long as we can."

"Absolutely," he said, furrowing his brow. Did Bill think he was going to tell people at the local coffee shop?

"I mean, people couldn't stop talking about the boy trapped in the cave for years," Bill said with a half-hearted laugh, slapping Seth on the shoulder.

Seth swallowed down the instant rise of anxiety and forced a smile. Bill couldn't possibly know that part of Seth's soul was still stuck back in the cave after his indecipherable experience.

Bill started toward his vehicle. "And there was that incident I mentioned earlier that—"

"Bill?" Seth said, not registering what Bill was saying.

The chief turned back around. "Yeah?"

"I'm gonna give the beach another walk-through before I head into town, if that's alright." Seth wanted to take a moment to reassess the scene from the start, to make sure he didn't miss anything, which he undoubtedly had earlier.

"Whatever you need to do."

Seth waved at Bill and turned around to face Sarah Elizabeth, unease rippling across his skin in a wave of shivers.

Bill started walking. "I'll need to pull that old file. I can't tell you how goddamn similar…" He paused and looked over his shoulder to see Seth already re-examining the body. "Christ, this is not a way to start a day," he mumbled and turned back around.

Seth stared down at Sarah Elizabeth, eyes surveying every detail, desperate for something to jump out at him. A clue of any kind.

"Focus, focus," he demanded of himself. He took twenty paces back and forced himself to approach the scene from the start, with fresh eyes and solid feet on the ground. His instincts told him this girl's death was no accident.

After re-examining the body, Seth spoke with Wes again. He had nothing new to report but promised to call the moment he learned anything from the autopsy. When Seth watched Sarah's body being loaded into the coroner's van, he felt like part of him was going with her as it drove off. He looked down the coast for Sasha and Joe. They were too far away to hear Seth, even if he yelled at the top of his lungs. He'd get an update from them later. Seth looked out at the ocean. The wind, having picked up, nipped at his face and was causing waves to fight with each other like wild muskrats. He had a feeling that this was an omen of worse things to come. Seth turned away from the scene and made his way to his Bronco, well past the need for coffee.

The vibrating hum of tires and soft pattering of air through the cracked window were a meditative tune, helping Seth focus on the various scenarios playing out in his mind. Was it an accident? Falling overboard on a boat not far offshore? There was the suicide route. But the scene simply didn't fit the profile of a young woman her age taking her life. So, was she murdered? With no signs of outward harm done to her body, she could have been smothered, injected with something, or force-fed pills. But why the display?

In the four months since Seth returned to his small hometown and just over three months on the job, the most heinous crime he'd encountered was having to remove the handcuffs from a weeping, buck-naked Mitchell Roberts from his ex-wife Julie's bed. A sad attempt to win her back that had been far from successful. Even sadder was that it was the highlight of Seth's time as sergeant of the department.

Seth slowed down to take a right on Main Street and saw Mrs. Wilkes unlocking the front door to her Victorian Inn. She was wearing a long brown wool coat, black leather gloves, and had her rich chestnut hair tied up in a bun. She caught sight of his vehicle and waved wildly at him, her cherub cheeks so pink, Seth had to assume she had walked there. Mrs. Wilkes had been his history teacher in high school, retiring in her late forties to run the Inn when her mother passed away ten years ago. Seth returned the wave with a smile.

Pulling over to the curb in front of the Main Street Cafe, Seth killed the engine and climbed out, shoving his hands in his pockets, his unruly hair flapping in the wind. The scent of honey-coated croissants and fresh-ground coffee beans quelled the shivering nerves boiling in his stomach.

Seth shut his car door as a blast of cold air funneled down Main Street. He spotted Clemency Pruitt plastering a sign on the front door from the inside. Her skin was a leathery tan, and her hair was short and spiky, like silver fireworks shooting from her scalp. Her wiry frame, hidden beneath wide-legged white jeans and a mustard-yellow angora sweater, was taut with energy that added to her quirkiness. Clemency was the sister of Ben Pruitt, owner of the coffeehouse, and a breed all her own, prone to fits of uncategorical whimsy, bouts of paranoia, and belief in the supernatural.

He stepped up and read the sign: "Due to ghosts haunting our store, our computers are not working. Please be patient while we wait for the spirits to move on."

Seth's face fell as he read the sign on the cafe door. If this were yesterday, it would have brought a wide smile to his face. Today, it sent a wave of anxiety swirling around his stomach, working its way up to his chest. He opened the door, and the aroma of baking pastries, coffee beans, and wood shavings hit him. The space was small, but cozy and inviting. Rich mahogany walls, ornate furniture in vibrant shades of maroon and navy, bookcases lined with classics and vintage novels, and a bar area near the back of the room that just screamed for locals to come sip coffee and chat about their day. To one side was a glass door leading to an impressive woodworking shop, where instructors taught customers how to construct kayaks from scratch. Everything about Lost Grove seemed captured in this one space, from its warm style to its profound intimacy.

Seth recognized several familiar faces and greeted them with a nod and a quiet good morning, keeping his expression even. It was always so peaceful here, but he knew that would soon change.

He thought back to Fred Copeland's funeral, when he was in tenth grade. Fred had been a beloved member of the community and chief editor of the *Lost Grove Gazette* for almost seventy years. His father, Adam, founded the newspaper publication in 1878. He was one of the earliest settlers in the town, an immigrant from Ontario, Canada. Seth remembered the collective sadness they all shared, standing around the coffin, waiting for it to be lowered into the earth. But what had happened to Sarah Elizabeth was far worse than anything Fred had endured in his 104 years. She'd barely made it into her twenties before being taken from them, with no dignity or respect remaining. The mood in town would turn grim, and nothing could prepare them for it.

Seth stepped in line. A young man with wild brown hair that looked like it hadn't been washed in a month, wearing a wool flannel long-sleeve shirt, red corduroy pants, and orange-and-white New Balance sneakers, moved to the side, waiting for his coffee, eyes on his phone. Seth noted the Orbriallis badge on his chest as he stepped up to the counter. He was aware of the world-renowned local institute growing up but never realized just how many locals worked there. "Troubles this morning, Clem?" Seth asked.

Clemency looked up from wiping the counter. "Jacob?" she said, not so covertly nodding at the young man.

"No, the sign." Seth laughed and nodded back to the front entrance. Clemency waved her hand dismissively. "Nah, just another ghost is all. Dang computers won't work."

"Did you try restarting your router?" Jacob asked.

"It has nothing to do with routers or any kind of technology, usual?" she asked, eyeing Seth. Clemency had a way of speaking in conjunctive sentences, making it hard to tell who she was directing her words at.

"Please." Seth reached into his pocket to find it empty. "Shit," he muttered to himself. "Hey, Clem, I seem to have left my wallet at home. I can run across the street and—"

"Oh, don't you worry about that," Clemency said as she filled the portafilter with freshly ground beans and locked it under the espresso machine. "Coming back here to take care of your father, keeping our streets safe. I reckon you've earned a free one."

Seth grimaced. "Yeah, well…thanks, Clem." The bell over the front door jangled, drawing his attention.

"Ghost's again, Clemency?" Story Palmer asked in her calm, whispery voice that passed shivers across Seth's spine. These shivers, contrary to the ones attacking his body on the beach, were of the pleasant variety. Story was the town librarian, though she was far from fitting the cliche of the role. In her early thirties, she was dressed in her favorite black jeans and a shirt that looked like it came from an old sword-and-sorcery novel. She had a wild mane of dark hair clipped into a blunt bob with short bangs. Her eyes were the color of mist, drifting off of cedar boughs before turning to liquid silver as if they reflected the glow of the full moon in their depths. Silver rings adorned her fingers, and necklaces dangled at her throat. The rumor was she had an abundance of tattoos beyond the rune symbols on the knuckles of her hand.

"Good morning, Ms. Palmer," Seth said when the woman stepped up behind him, searching the depths of her fathomless satchel.

"Good morning, Sheriff," Story greeted in a singsong voice.

"Sergeant." Seth grinned, the right corner of his lip curling up.

Story shrugged before stopping her search for money and looking up at Seth. Her gaze was so direct, he almost took a step back before she slowly tipped out of his sightline, glaring at the back wall. Her brow knitted together, eyes razor focused.

Seth looked over his shoulder, but there was nothing there of note.

"Nuisance, these spirits," she said, returning to her search for money.

"Spirits?" Seth's eyes remained locked on the sea-green wall.

"Ghosts." Story pointed over his shoulder. "You saw the sign, I presume?"

"I did," Seth responded, turning back to see Story staring at him.

She narrowed her eyes as if she was trying to figure something out. "Hm," she voiced simply, and dove back into her satchel.

Seth swallowed heavily, unnerved. It was like she could see through the mask he was wearing, trying to put out the vibe that today was just another normal morning in Lost Grove.

He had met Story unexpectedly at his parents' house his first week back in town. He'd come by to bring his father to speech therapy to find the exotic woman sitting in the family room with his parents, communicating in sign language with his mother, who had been deaf since she was a child. Amaranth introduced Story to Seth as the town librarian and said she had come by to deliver a healing plant and a special homemade tea for his father. Seth told her he appreciated the gesture. When he asked if she had someone close to her who was deaf, the playful glimmer in her eyes as she replied "no" made him chuckle involuntarily. As they said goodbye, their hands clasped, and a spark ran up Seth's arm that left him feeling warm for the rest of the day. He had only come across her in passing in the months since, each encounter leaving him more intrigued.

"I've asked them nicely to go, like you suggested," Clemency began explaining to the entire store as the frothing machine whirred. "But they've come back."

"Oh, I doubt they ever left," Story said.

"Sergeant?"

Seth turned toward the familiar scraggy voice to his right. Old Tom King was sitting in a well-worn leather armchair with his legs crossed, holding his coffee with aged and callused hands. Despite being "Old Tom" by name, Seth knew Tom wasn't so old, likely in his mid-sixties now, but the man had always had a weathered face that spoke of years spent under the sun and he talked with a cadence like he had just stepped out of a 1940s western. Seth didn't think he'd ever heard anyone call him "Old Tom" to his face. It was just how everyone referred to him in conversation.

"Morning, Tom."

"They got those damned downed trees cleared off Oxburn Road yet?"

"Eddie should have taken care of that last night or early this morning before his shift ended," Seth said as he turned his attention back toward Story, watching her count coins out of a knitted change purse.

"Nope." Old Tom shook his head. "Just came through there, and them trees are still there."

"I'll make sure he gets to it tonight," Seth said as the bell rang.

"Ah, Sergeant Wolfe. I was hoping Chief Richards would be in here, but you'll have to do." Mrs. Seavert strode in, spry as the day she was born, and people had been saying she was eighty-two for a decade now.

Seth worked his jaw, attempting to release the tension of the morning. "What can I help you with, Mrs.—"

"Now, I saw the coroner's van come through here early on this morning. Don't think I didn't. Heading out toward Mourner's Beach. You tell me why I'd see such a thing as that so early in the morning, huh?"

Seth opened his mouth to reply, unsure of what he was about to say. Death didn't have working hours, and he thought it odd the early hour of the coroner's van passing through town fixated her.

"I'm respectable," Mrs. Seavert continued. "I didn't go poking my nose down there to see what y'all were up to. But I'd be well pleased to know what's got the coroner out here in our parts so early on in the morning."

Old Tom rolled his eyes. "Bella, we all know your nosy little self is just dying to get the—"

Mrs. Seavert shifted her attention to Old Tom. "Now look here, Tom. I worked on the…"

Seth drowned out the two older patrons as their argument spiraled into their usual diatribe.

Clemency pointed at Seth and spoke over the bickering. "And did I tell you about the lights I saw in the sky last night? They weren't satellites, I know what a satellite moving across the sky looks like. I meant to call in first thing to tell you, well what was I going to say anyway when that Sasha just laughs at me, she thinks she's covering the mouthpiece, but I can hear, would you like cream?"

Seth scratched his eyebrow with his thumb, longing for his detective position back in San Francisco. "I'll tell her not to give you such a problem when you call."

"Do you want cream?" she asked again.

Seth nodded at Jacob, who was busy listening to Old Tom and Mrs.

Seavert bickering.

"Huh?" He turned to Clemency. "Oh, sorry. Yes, please."

Seth shifted his weight and turned his head to meet Story's soft eyes gazing up at him from behind her dark lashes. Their eyes connected in an intense yet silent moment. It wasn't the first time he caught her holding his gaze. She had done this a few times before, and Seth was still unsure if it was simply a habit or a subtle sign she wanted to get to know him better.

"Here you are, Seth." Clemency interrupted his thoughts.

Seth nodded at Story and grabbed his double cappuccino. "Thanks, Clem. Appreciate the free one."

"No problem at all, here you go." Clemency handed Jacob his coffee, who took it and slid past Story like she contained the plague, hustling out the door.

Seth caught the hint of a grin on Story's face as he headed out, saying his goodbyes.

"Sheriff, wait." Story stopped him at the door. Rummaging through her bag, she palmed an item, sliding it into his hand. "For luck and protection."

Returning to his vehicle, Seth felt a peculiar warmth radiating off the tiny perfect acorn cradled in his hand. It was an odd gesture from the strange and alluring woman, but it fit right in line with the other unbelievable occurrences of that morning. Perturbed, he climbed back into his car and drove away.

Chapter 2

Sensorium Juvenescence

Noble Andalusian was driving himself and his younger sister Zoe to school in his used Subaru Crosstrek, the heater pointlessly cranked up. By the time the air actually got warm, they'd already be at school, living less than a mile away. Noble had thick dark hair and eyes, hidden under strong eyebrows, and full lips which seemed to draw people in. His ex said he reminded her of a character from her beloved fantasy series. He'd read parts of it and thought it was more soft-core porn than an actual story.

Noble was a well-liked eighteen-year-old star cross-country runner and track medal winner. Noble celebrated his birthday last week, but the strange and unsettling situation he encountered on his morning run after turning eighteen overshadowed the celebration. By the time he pulled up to the school parking lot, he was grateful for his sister's updates about what she was reading. It helped soothe the anxiety that had stayed with him on his morning runs ever since.

Zoe, eleven years old with a deep golden halo of hair, a gap-toothed grin and a heart-shaped face, gathered her knapsack from the floorboard and slid out of the car.

"Wait," Noble said, exiting after her and slamming the door. "Which one is she, the warrior?"

"Yeah, Litha is the warrior. She's in love with the princess of the warring kingdom."

"Right, the spy."

"Well, she was a spy for a little while. But Litha's a good person.

Anyway, she got captured and is being tortured. We'll see how she gets out of this one." Zoe whipped her bag onto her back. It was far too big for her short, thin frame. As was the faded corduroy jacket.

"Be good," Noble said as goodbye.

Zoe rolled her eyes and smiled at her brother. She was smart, too smart, and often got into trouble with teachers for innocent commentary to their lackluster lessons. "I will."

She waved goodbye and skipped away, her black Doc Marten boots thumping against the pavement like a punk rock drumbeat. They were a size too big, but she insisted on getting them and had argued with their mother until she relented. As she walked, the leather creaked with each jaunty step, and she smiled to herself, knowing that they would be perfect for kicking ass in junior high school.

Noble proudly watched his sister, not quite believing she was in junior high already. His heart ached at how unaware she was of the world around her. He felt like he'd aged a decade since he'd been her age. Noble ran his fingers through the mop of dark hair on his head, which had gone far too long without a trim, and silently wished himself back into the same blissfully naïve state as his little sister. He prayed she would never have to face what he'd experienced five mornings ago.

Noble stood in the cold parking lot of the junior high, watching his sister with an eagle eye. His thoughts raced back to Saturday morning, when he had seen something strange and unsettling that he was having a hard time making sense of. He crossed his arms over his broad chest and tucked his hands into the pockets of his plaid work coat, his shoulders hunched up as a biting wind swept through.

Living with secrets was hard enough—especially here, in such a small town where everyone seemed to know each other so well. But this secret felt like an albatross around Noble's neck, constantly reminding him of all that he didn't know about his own friends and neighbors. Who was the elderly giant who walked daily to the cemetery? Who lived in the mysterious Victorian house behind the gate guarded by golden lion statues? Was the town librarian really a witch?

"Hey, Noble!" Constance Hensley called, pulling Noble from his overactive thoughts.

His best friend since kindergarten, Stan, as her friends called her, was six feet even to Noble's six three. She walked with a dancer's grace and had high cheekbones that looked like they were carved from marble. Her golden-brown eyes sparkled under the sun, which contrasted beautifully with her rich tan skin. Her hair was flawless, black silk that shone like liquid beneath the sky.

They'd met on the ranch, where Noble's mother cared for the animals and led horseback excursions. Noble had been four going on five when four-year-old Constance loped into the paddock and climbed on top of the most obstinate horse on the ranch before anyone could stop her. Things clicked between them when Noble complimented her beaded earrings. "Those are cool," he'd said.

She'd grinned at him, revealing a toothy smile. "My grandma helps me make them."

From that day forward, they became fast friends. Their bond was unbreakable. And though Stan talked about boys sometimes, there was never any question of romance between them. Their friendship was too pure for that sort of thing.

Constance jogged across the parking lot in her cream-colored Converse, loose blue jeans, and a grey sweatshirt under an oversized jean jacket likely belonging to one of her many older brothers. She ran her elbow into Noble's arm. "Sup!"

"Hey, Stan," he said, tossing his arm around her shoulder as they made their way toward school.

"You okay?" Stan asked.

"Yeah," Noble replied. "Why?"

"You have that face."

"What face?"

Stan's face scrunched up. "The face you get when you overthink. You've had it on a lot lately."

"Have I?" Noble spoke in a casual tone, attempting to steer the conversation down a different path. Out of all the people he knew, Stan definitely had a knack for getting secrets out of him. Stan was skilled at discerning the thoughts and feelings of strangers and understood Noble even better. He was no match for her.

"You have. And I don't know what you're hiding, but it's only a matter of time before I—" Stan swung out from under his arm. "Oh shit, I got to talk to Anya about our biology homework. Anya!" Stan took off across the green.

Anya Bury spun on her heel at the sound of her name. The morning sunlight illuminated each streak of red-gold to snow-white running through her long ombre hair that fell over her fleece-lined bomber jacket. A broad smile crossed her delicate face before Stan plopped down in front of her, blocking Noble's view. His heart twisted with envy as he watched Anya. She was so lucky to have grown up on her father's ranch, learning how to tend a garden, care for animals, and live off the land. Every summer, Noble visited his mother's horse farm, and although he enjoyed brushing and cleaning the horses, it never felt quite the same as living off the land. He wished more than anything that he could experience a life like Anya and wondered if he should study veterinary science or agriculture.

Noble turned his attention to the high school entrance. His other best friend, Nate Abbott, waited for him, taking a swig of a protein shake. He was a solid five foot eleven, with medium-blonde hair and calves of steel. Not that you could see them under his tan designer joggers. Nate made athleisure look like he'd stepped from the set of a Ralph Lauren photoshoot with little effort. He had that kind of appeal, that "American boy next door" look, with his blue hoodie, white Nike running shoes and effortlessly styled hair.

"Nate," he said, coming to a stop.

"Noble," Nate greeted in return, both mimicking proper gentlemen's tones.

Nate Abbott had come to Lost Grove when he was seven, where his parents had opened a gift shop. His younger sister, Cheshire, was a full year older than Zoe. While the girls had not become great friends, Nate, Noble, and Stan were friends so fast that none of them could recall when or how it happened.

"Colder than balls," he uttered in response to the frigid temperatures Lost Grove was experiencing. "Did you run past Mourner's Beach this morning?" Nate asked as the two meandered toward the school's entrance.

The pressure of keeping a secret from his friends wasn't relenting this morning. "No, I had to take Zoe to the library to drop off books. Why?"

"Police were all over the place."

Noble cringed; his body went rigid and liquid all at once. "Police?"

"Coroner's van too. Oh, hey, Ryker!" Nate called out to their longtime friend.

Thomas Ryker Hawley jogged across the parking lot, waving. Growing up in the same house as his grandfather, also named Thomas, he'd chosen to go by his middle name. Rather, his mother had chosen it for him, naming him after the hunky hero from her favorite romance series. His stick-straight light brown hair stuck out at spiky angles under his forest-green stocking cap, which apparently was making up for him not wearing a jacket, sticking with his classic jeans and thermal look.

"Yo! What's up?" Ryker greeted his friends.

"My dick from thinking about your mom," Nate joked.

"Jesus," Noble said, wincing.

Ryker's eyes bloomed wide. "Wow. That's a new one." Ryker's mom, Audrey, was only thirty-seven years old, having had him when she was nineteen, and could pass for late twenties on a bad day. Nate had a crush on her since elementary school and often proclaimed that they would one day be together.

"You like that one? I have to admit, that shit just came to me right now," Nate boasted.

"Really…brilliant," Ryker said, shaking his head. His straight eyebrows and deep brow set over almond eyes made it look like he was far more serious than he was, though he used that to his advantage during his jiu-jitsu competitions. That love for martial arts also made him look older, with a lean, built body he spent dedicated time on. The nose that looked like it had been broken a few times added to his threatening demeanor. But, in truth, Ryker was a happy-go-lucky, salt-of-the-earth kind of kid. Which was the only reason Nate got away with his incessant mom jokes.

"You working tonight?" Nate said.

"Yeah," Ryker replied.

"Not going out with what's her name? The girl from your dojo?"

"Erin," Ryker remarked while waving at Anya and Nettie.

Lost Grove High School was not at all like the movies. There were no cliques, and minimal bullying occurred because almost everyone knew everything about each other. They'd grown up together. Everyone was friends in a town with such a small population. It wasn't like there was a divide or they weren't all friends, but Ryker, Anya, and Nettie had grown up together, just like Stan, Noble, and Nate. Ryker was the bridge friend, bringing both groups together in junior high.

"Erin," Nate said, nodding.

"Are you guys dating or…?" Noble asked.

Ryker thought about how to respond.

Nate snorted. "Don't act too enthused."

Ryker smirked, backing away toward Anya and Nettie. "I'm not putting labels on it. Maybe if you had a few friends who were girls, you'd understand that."

"Ouch!" Nate feigned offense. "Yeah, well, I'm gonna label your mom later with some of—"

Noble cut Nate off by shoving him in the shoulder.

"What?"

"Kids," Noble stated, pointing to the younger kids walking amongst them. "Can't go around shouting things like that."

"You don't know what I was gonna say."

Noble gave his friend a glaring side eye as they headed toward school. He briefly pondered if Ryker wasn't putting a label on things because he also seemed close to Anya. Maybe he had a crush on Anya and was holding out for something to come of that.

"Okay, anyway…so, what route did you run this morning?" Nate asked.

"Huh?" Noble asked.

"Where…did…you…run?" Nate reiterated annoyingly slowly, pulling open the school door and heading inside.

"I didn't," Noble responded, following.

The brief interlude with Ryker had not drawn Noble's mind from the news Nate had delivered moments before. A coroner's van had to mean there was a body. The horrible display he'd stumbled upon over the weekend was along the gully path leading to Mourner's Beach. Nate's news of the coroner's van being down there had him breaking out in a cold sweat.

"You didn't run?" Nate asked, his face contorted.

"What?"

Nate's eyes narrowed, his forehead wrinkling softly. "A, I'm clarifying that you actually didn't run this morning. B, what the hell is up with you?"

"Shit," Noble both thought and said. He should have been paying more attention to what he was saying. He moved out of the way of a gangly freshman sprinting down the hall. "I didn't, yeah, no. I'm fine. Just slept like shit last night. It was a one-time thing."

It had not been a one-time thing. The long-distance path he and Nate had mapped out for optimal training was something Noble had been avoiding. As important as it was to train on the forest paths they'd strategically chosen, Noble couldn't bring himself to run anywhere but on the road in and out of town.

"Really?" Nate huffed. "A bad night's sleep kept you from training? Since when?"

"Promise. Just a hiccup this morning."

"A hiccup? That shit won't fly with Coach Woods," Nate said, continuing the conversation when Noble wanted to drop it.

"I get it. I know," Noble said, getting agitated.

Nate held his hands up. "Look, bro, I don't mean to put added pressure on you. I mean, I'm good. It doesn't bother me. But you're the one to win it this year. You know that, right?"

Noble nodded, stopping at his locker. All too well, Noble could sense the well-intended pressure of his teammates, his coach, the school, and the residents of Lost Grove, who did an amazing job of supporting the students and their sporting endeavors.

The locker opened with a wobble, the lower left corner always sticking.

"Okay, look, everyone needs a break. Not trying to lean on you with this." Nate lowered his voice, moving closer. "I can tell you're stressed about the race, expectations. It's been getting to you this week. I don't have to deal with it because we know I won't win. You got this, buddy." Nate slapped his friend on the back.

Face hidden inside his locker, Noble rolled his eyes. He appreciated the support, but what he really needed now was for Nate's generous ego to stake claim to winning the race to take some pressure off him.

The locker door bounced fully open.

Stan smiled broadly at Noble, tipping her head. "Noble, bestie, would you please lend me your bio homework?"

"Anya didn't have it?" Noble smiled.

"She's doing it in study hour. I won't have time to copy."

Noble shook his head, rummaging in his backpack for his iPad. "I'll send it to you."

Stan opened her phone, received the Goodnote, and slapped Noble on the back. "Thanks, bro. I see you guys over here all jittery with anticipation because the entire school is already buzzing about it," Stan said, glancing up through her lashes at Nate.

Nate grinned wildly. "Do you know what—"

"No," Stan interrupted, returning her phone to her back pocket.

"But your dad—"

"My dad doesn't alert me to every call he gets. By the way, you have a highly unrealistic view of my dad's life. He's not out on homicide calls all day long. He's barely out on homicide calls, ever. The bodies come to him."

"Yeah, fine. Did he leave pretty early this morning, though?" Nate asked.

"He leaves early every morning," Stan replied.

Nate smirked. "Yeah, but, you know, earlier than that."

Stan returned the smirk. "I don't know. Unlike you two weirdos, I don't get up before the sun to pointlessly endure physical exertion."

Noble shouldered his backpack and closed the locker door, relieved for the moment to step out of the spotlight but concerned at the loud whispers echoing through the halls. The chatter was heavy with speculation about the police cars and crime scene tape visible at Mourner's Beach, as well as the coroner's van.

Did it happen again? Noble wondered, walking behind his friends heading to class. He had seen something that morning six days ago, but what? What could it mean for him?

The dilemma lingered in Noble's mind as he plodded down the hallway, filled with uncertainty.

"But, I mean, couldn't you ask him?" Nate urged Stan as the three of them stopped at Nate's locker. He had a strong interest in murder and profiling, barely keeping his grades up with a concerted effort, hoping to become an FBI agent.

"Um, no, bro," Stan replied with a growing grin. "There's, like, confidentiality. I think you would know this."

"Shit." Nate deflated, hanging his coat and grabbing his textbooks.

Stan squinted at Nate before stating, "It's verging on creepy how into this stuff you are."

"It's not creepy," Nate said, shutting the locker door with a shoulder shove; otherwise, it'd never close. "It's a passion. It's a career choice."

"Okay." Stan's lips turned into a deep frown. "Let's call it a creepy passion, then."

"Most kids don't know what they want to be when they're older. I do. You call it creepy. I call it confidence, knowing my inner self."

Stan laughed. "Right."

"I wish I'd gotten that free study approved by the school board. I could have been down on that beach right now."

"On a ride-along?" Stan huffed jovially, but her eyes had drifted toward Noble, who was remaining silent, eyes focused on the ground, the troubling crease between his eyebrows deepening. "They wouldn't let you go to an actual homicide location."

Noble flinched. "Who said it was a homicide? I thought it was just a body?"

Stan leveled her gaze at the tallest of her friends. "It is just a body. That's the point I'm trying to get across to Investigation Discovery over here. He's blown it way out of proportion."

Nate snorted, all of them turning a corner toward their first class. "Did not. It's a body. That's a big deal around here."

"It could be anything. A body from a boat wreck miles offshore," Stan started. "Or it could be a camper from the national park. It doesn't have to be as salacious as you clearly think it is."

Stan elbowed Nate into the classroom to complete the argument and followed, giving Noble a brief gaze over her shoulder. His skin had blanched to a paler white. They all swung into their seats, Stan leaning over into the aisle, resting her elbows on her lanky knees, glaring at Noble.

"What?" he eventually asked.

"That's right, what?"

Noble made a face. "What are you even talking about?" he asked, lowering his voice at the end as the classroom hushed moments before the bell rang.

"What the hell is going on in your brain? Something is bothering you, so spill," she commanded.

Nate threw them a glance over his shoulder, curious about their lowered tone. The bell rang, and Mr. Kimball closed the door the second it went off.

"Not now," Noble said as the day began with announcements over the speaker.

He couldn't put off telling her much longer. Now the question was, what would he say?

Chapter 3

A Dead Girl's Aspirations

When Seth approached the school he had attended during his teenage years, he felt a wave of nostalgia, vastly different from the beach experience he'd had just that morning. He could still remember how it felt to be walking down that same path with his backpack full of notebooks, and the awe he'd felt walking through the enormous front doors. Despite what had happened earlier, Seth couldn't help but smile as he walked down the hall toward the principal's office: the musty smell of old books, the sounds of students chatting in the classrooms, and the trophy case lined with pictures and medals hard won by former students.

The administration office was as he remembered, though some updates showed in the new age ergonomic desk chairs and slim computer screens. But the same linoleum from the halls edged up against the dark green carpet leading into the office. The woman at the front desk was no longer Mrs. Wending, which he was grateful for. Mrs. Wending was a hard woman to please, whereas the one who turned to him now smiled brilliantly. She had a cherub face, bulbous cheeks shining a brilliant pink with overly applied rouge, and she had sparkling, sweet eyes. She looked so proud, Seth wondered if she had a child attending the school.

"Hello, sir," she said.

Seth nodded, smiling politely. "Morning. I need to speak with the principal."

"Of course," she said, nodding and swirling out from behind the front desk. She was a buxom woman with a voluptuous lower half, accented by her navy blue dress. She continued smiling as she knocked on the doorframe of the principal's office. "There's an officer here to see you," she said, turning her radiant smile back on Seth. "The sergeant, actually," she corrected as she stepped back.

The man who stepped out of the office had thick, dark hair coaxed into a heavily stylized coif that sat atop his head. A manicured beard and mustache framed his serious face. He had a broad, flat nose and wore a buttoned-up vest over a bright red shirt and tie, and cuffed jeans.

"Sergeant?" he said as he made his way past the woman. He extended a hand and Seth took it, returning a firm but pleasant shake.

"Sergeant Seth Wolfe," he said in greeting.

"Principal Will Bernthal," the man said. "Come in." Principal Bernthal escorted him into a clean, sparse office, offering an empty seat to Seth while moving behind the desk to take his own. "How can I help?"

"I'd like to speak to you, and some teachers, about a former student named Sarah Elizabeth Grahams."

Will frowned as he leaned forward, placing his elbows on his desk. "Does this have something to do with all the commotion down at the beach? All the kids are buzzing about it."

"Right." Seth nodded. He forgot just how fast news could travel in this small town. People could walk past a scene like this morning in San Francisco and hardly take a second glance. "It's about an ongoing investigation. I just have a few questions."

"Of course, yes," he said. "I can't imagine Miss Grahams being a part of anything untoward. But let me pull up her records for you." His focus shifted to his computer, fingers making quick work on the keyboard. His brow creased as he leaned into the screen, scrolling down an unseen list. "Want me to print this for you?" he asked.

"That would be great, thank you."

"Sure," he said, typing more and hitting enter with a definitive tap. "Prints out in the office. I can take you around to...well, I suppose Flaherty or Young would be free right now," Will said, already moving toward the door.

Seth followed, waiting as Will walked over to the printer and grabbed the sheets of paper.

"These will be all her teachers, all four years," Will said, returning with the pages.

Seth could see the interest seething behind the receptionist's eyes as they tracked Mr. Bernthal across the room and back, flicking twice to look at Seth. Or maybe she was just admiring the view. Mr. Bernthal looked like a fit man, and he certainly inspired a rugged lumberjack aesthetic.

"I'd like to speak with the ones she had during her senior year," Seth said, taking the papers and perusing the names.

"Sure, of course." Will nodded, hands on his hips.

There was a moment's pause where Seth was certain he was going to ask more questions. It looked to be on the tip of Will's tongue to push a little more, see what he could get out of Seth, but the moment passed.

"Let me take you around. One or two of them are bound to be free during this hour."

Will held up his hand, and Seth followed. Walking out of the office, he said a thank-you and goodbye to the woman behind the desk as she eagerly peered over it, desperate to know what had prompted Seth's visit.

"So, you were clearly principal when Ms. Grahams attended," Seth said as they maneuvered down the halls. A young man carrying a block of wood as a hall pass stared at them before pushing into the restrooms.

"I was," Will replied. "She was a good kid. Excelled. Had no reason to be in my bad graces, not that many are."

"Of course," Seth said. "Did you know her well?"

Will shook his head, stopping at a classroom and peering in. "As well as any of the other students. He's not in," he mumbled before pushing off and continuing down the halls, turning left. "She was a good student. Valedictorian, not that we have those. She was top of the class."

"What was she like in the halls?"

Will looked aside at Seth, eyebrows raised, trying to recall what Sarah was like as a person. "I only really saw her with two friends. But she wasn't unpopular. She was quite friendly."

"Did you ever meet her parents?"

"Richard and Bess, yes, I know them. Good parents. I imagine they laid a solid foundation for Sarah." Will stopped and swung into a doorway, peeking inside. "Ah, good." He smiled over his shoulder at Seth and entered the classroom.

Seth followed. Entering one of his old classrooms, memories flooded back as he took in the slight changes, though there weren't many.

"Gretchen, sorry to disturb you between classes, but Sergeant Seth Wolfe is here to ask some questions about a former student of ours," Mr. Bernthal addressed the teacher sitting at her desk at the front of the classroom, wearing a lavender tie-dye kaftan dress with an open neck displaying a long bohemian necklace with gemstones and beads.

Gretchen, known to Seth as Mrs. Young, looked up from her work; recognition painted her face with a broad smile. "My, my. Seth Wolfe?"

Seth grinned. "Mrs. Young, nice to see you again." She miraculously looked like she hadn't aged more than five years. Only a few small lines around the eyes, but the same thin face, freckles dappled on her prominent cheekbones, soft full lips that Seth had a difficult time taking his eyes off during class, and the same sparkling blue eyes that displayed an inquisitive nature, always open to listening and learning. Her hair was the same chestnut brown, but whereas it was long and straight, falling past her breasts, in his high school years, it was now a fashionable shaggy bob.

"Gretchen, please. Look at you, a sergeant now with the Lost Grove Police Department?"

Seth shrugged. "So it would seem," he admitted, stepping forward to shake her outstretched hand.

"I'll leave you to it," Mr. Bernthal said. "You can come see me in the office if you—"

"I'll stop in before I leave," Seth explained.

Will smiled, waved his hands as he backed away and exited the room.

Gretchen pointed to her desk. "Give me just one moment, if that's okay? I'm just about done grading this paper."

Seth waved at her. "Take your time," he said before turning to observe the paintings on the walls while Mrs. Young wrapped up her task. The displays of artwork ran the gamut of level, style, and content, yet all were intriguing and rather well done. Pets, landscapes, abstract images, some pencil, some charcoal, and more variance of color than his eyes had seen in a long time.

Kitty-corner to the collection on the long wall was a painting that drew Seth's eyes, giving his heart a jump. It was an exceptionally accomplished painting of a woman standing on a beach clouded with mist and atmosphere. He took a step to get a closer look.

"Well, you certainly grew up to be a handsome man. I can't say that I'm surprised."

Seth spun around, startled that Mrs. Young had snuck up on him, briefly lost in the painting. "What? Oh, um, thanks," he stuttered.

"I'm sure you've heard that plenty since you've been back."

Seth shrugged, not exactly sure how to reply to the brazen comment.

"I see you're taking in your successors' work."

Seth laughed. "Successors. Yeah, I suppose they are."

"Well, what do you think?"

Seth shook his head. "I'm not really an expert, Mrs. Young."

"You can call me Gretchen, Seth; you're not in school anymore."

Seth smiled and pulled his hands from his pockets, motioning to the room they were standing in. "Well, technically I am," he said with a laugh.

"Gretchen," she said a little more firmly.

"Gretchen." Seth's smile faltered as he turned back to the wall of art. "I have to admit, I'm really impressed with these. Were we this talented when I was in high school?"

"No, not remotely."

Seth spun on his heels. "Geez. We can't have been that bad."

Gretchen gazed upon her students' work. "The youth of today are much more open, about their feelings, their sexuality, their social and political opinions. They're closer in a way to my generation, honestly. I'm not sure what happened to you early millennials."

Seth let out a dramatic sigh. "You certainly weren't this blunt when I was in your classes."

Gretchen looked back at Seth. "Perhaps time has hardened me."

"Hardly," Seth instinctively replied, immediately kicking himself.

The corner of Gretchen's mouth rose, her eyes steady on his.

Seth cleared his throat and turned around to break the moment of tension. "Whoever did this one must be your star pupil," he said, pointing at the rather haunting painting of the woman on the beach.

"Oh, no. That's no student of mine. That's a famous painter from Oregon named Tom Gregart."

Seth turned back, his brow raised. "I don't really know any painters. So, I really should get—"

"I thought you were a detective in San Francisco," Gretchen interrupted. "A little surprised to hear you're back as sergeant for our modest little police force."

Seth wondered how much she tracked her students or if he was special. He knew his mother did a lot of work with school fundraisers. "Well, I came back to help with my father after—"

"Ah, yes. I heard about that. I dropped a few dishes off for your mother over those first few days."

"Very kind of you. So, I wanted—"

Gretchen smiled. "Yes, I know. You need to ask me some questions. Perhaps we can catch up properly another time."

"Sure. That would be nice," Seth said, unsure if he had just agreed to a date.

"So, I assume this is about a former student of mine?"

Seth slid into one of the student desks to create some space so he could focus. "Indeed. You want to join me?"

Gretchen grabbed the desk in front of him and spun it around to face him before sliding into the seat. "I suppose you outrank me now."

Seth chuckled, took his notebook from his breast pocket, flipped it open, and clicked his pen. "Do you recall Sarah Elizabeth Grahams?"

"Is this about the commotion at the beach this morning?" All play had left Gretchen's voice, her eyes widening.

"At this stage, I can't say anything about—"

"Of course. It must be."

"What do you mean by that?"

Gretchen's gaze shifted past Seth. "It's all the students are talking about today. All it takes is one of them to hear something, and next thing you know, wild rumors are running through the entire school. Hopefully, it's nothing serious."

Seth measured his words carefully. "All I can say is that Sarah Elizabeth is important to an ongoing investigation, and I could use your help in getting to know her. What do you remember about her?"

Gretchen looked back at Seth. "I remembered almost everything about you and your group of friends."

Seth watched her eyes dart back and forth, running through memories, waiting for her to continue.

"I wanted so badly for her to get away. She didn't belong here."

Seth's eyes narrowed. It was an ominous statement to make as her first memory of the girl. "How is that?"

"Do you know much about her parents?"

Seth nodded. "Richard Grahams was a year ahead of us in school. I didn't know him that well. His parents lived on the same block as Tony. Old-school religious types, fire and brimstone. Whenever they heard us swearing out in the streets, they would scold us and tell us we were heathens."

Gretchen rolled her eyes. "Sarah Elizabeth was nothing like that. So wide-eyed, nonjudgmental, sweet. She was a sweet girl."

Seth felt a jab in his stomach as the image of her colorless face flashed in his mind. "So, she wasn't religious?"

"Oh no, she very much was. Just not in a way that painted everything she did or said. She didn't offend easily, like her grandparents, apparently. She didn't browbeat anyone with the Bible."

"You asked if I knew her parents. Why is that?"

Gretchen sighed. "Well, they put an enormous amount of pressure on Sarah."

Seth shrugged. "That's not uncommon, especially for kids in high school."

"Yes, but not like this. She stayed after school often to study, which is very much not common. Sometimes she studied in the library, but as time went on, she liked to study here in my room. I could sense a great deal of stress emanating from her, which I asked her about many times. It took some time for Sarah to confide in me, but she eventually opened up about how pressured she felt by her parents."

"For good grades?" Seth asked.

Gretchen nodded. "Yes, grades, of course. But also constantly needing to check in with them about where she was and what she was doing. Again, not uncommon, but I think the level at which they pressured her was severe. She didn't enjoy talking about it. But when she did, Sarah would get visibly shaken."

Seth wished he had forced Bill to let him go deliver the news to Richard and Bess Grahams with him. "Was the pressure to make sure she got into a certain college? And do you know where she went?"

Gretchen looked up and to her left. "She's at Baylor." She looked back at Seth. "Shouldn't she be at Baylor?"

"I think you might know more than me in that regard. Is that where her parents pressured her to go?"

"No, that was her choice. Her parents were not the least bit happy about it. They wanted her to stay closer to home. Part of me got the impression they didn't even want her to go to college."

Seth raised an eyebrow. "That seems a bit…counterintuitive considering the pressure for good grades."

"It wasn't just the grades or checking in constantly. I got the impression they pressured her in every aspect of her life."

Seth held her gaze. Remaining silent could serve multiple purposes. If someone was trying to recall something from the past, it was better to give them time to do so. If they were hesitant about revealing information, sometimes the uncomfortableness of silence would compel them to speak.

Gretchen batted her eyes. "Well, for one thing, she brought different clothes to school."

Seth furrowed his brow. This early picture of Sarah's home life was not flattering.

"And by that, I mean she would arrive at school in conservative clothing and then change in the bathroom into more…what, secular clothes? Skirts just above the knees, tank tops, halter tops. So sad. Her entire demeanor changed with those clothes. Every now and then, she would put on flashy makeup."

"And her parents were unaware, I assume?"

"I'm sure of it."

Seth twisted his pen, rubbing the base with his thumb. "Were there any signs of abuse?"

"Physical abuse?"

Seth nodded.

Gretchen shook her head without hesitation. "No, never."

"And you wanted her to get away. Why?"

Gretchen shifted in her chair, clearly uncomfortable under the desktop. "She asked me for a letter of recommendation to Baylor. I remember her looking at me with such desperation. Like her life depended on it. She was elated when she found out she had gotten in. I was so happy for her. Oh God, please tell me she's okay."

"As I said…"

Gretchen dropped her face into her hands. "Oh no," she moaned.

Sometimes there was no way to word things or even remain silent in a way that didn't give away the unmistakable aura that something terrible had occurred. Seth had always remained neutral when interviewing family or friends of victims, but something about being back in his hometown had his barriers down. He felt the urge to console his old teacher. He didn't. "Gretchen, did Sarah have any close friends? Best friends? I'm guessing you would know if she did."

Gretchen looked up and smiled, tears forming above her bottom eyelids. "Brigette Lowe and Jeremy Stapleton. They were inseparable."

Seth finished jotting their names down. "Lowe, Lowe…relation to—"

"Ivan, yes, that's her father."

"And are either of them still local?"

Gretchen shook her head, but then nodded. "Yes, and no. Brigette went to school on the East Coast. Davidson, if I remember correctly. Jeremy, he works at the Victorian Inn."

"With Mrs. Wilkes?"

"Yes."

Seth had to tread carefully with his next question, but he felt Mrs. Young already ascertained what had transpired. "Have you, by chance, seen Sarah Elizabeth around town lately? Or heard anyone talking about seeing her?"

Gretchen shook her head. "No. If she were in town at this time of year, I assume it would have only been for a weekend. She's going to school to be a doctor, you know."

Seth slowly shook his head. "I'm afraid I know very little about her. Which is why I'm here talking to you."

Gretchen looked down at her hands. "Right."

Seth nodded while pocketing his book and pen. "I think I have all I need for now. Thanks for your time, Mrs.—Gretchen."

Gretchen slid out of her chair and stood, her confidence diminished. "It was good to see you again, Seth."

Seth stood and shook her extended hand. "You as well." He would typically give out his card and tell someone to reach out if they could think of anything else that might help. But considering he couldn't divulge the specifics, he simply nodded and made his way out.

Gretchen turned and called out, "I hope she's okay. Would you please keep me informed?"

Seth turned back and nodded, the darkness descending upon the town already weighing heavy on his shoulders.

When Seth had passed by Mrs. Wilkes earlier that morning, he wasn't expecting a trip back to the Victorian Inn. But finding out Jeremy Stapleton had worked there since high school, Seth was now seated in the small restaurant awaiting his second round of coffee of the day. If Jeremy had seemed surprised to find a police officer showing up asking questions about Sarah Elizabeth, it was nothing compared to the shock Seth felt when Jeremey informed him he hadn't seen or heard from Sarah in over two and a half years. Seth rolled the acorn Story had given him around in his hand, wedged in his jacket pocket, pondering just how big a case this might turn into.

"Okay, here we are." Jeremy reentered the dining room, holding a silver tray with two porcelain cups, a creamer pitcher, and a small sugar dish. Jeremy was short, maybe around five-five, lean, and well put together in tight, pressed, burgundy dress pants, shiny black leather shoes (or perhaps faux leather), a formfitting cream-colored dress shirt, and a tasteful floral tie. He served the coffees and sat across from Seth at the small round table. "So, when you said Lizzy is important to an ongoing investigation, what does that mean? Have you spoken to her? Is she here in town? Did she do something?"

Seth sipped his coffee, holding his gaze steady. Jeremy was at least one person in town who had yet to hear about the commotion at Mourner's Beach. "Unfortunately, I can't say anything at this stage of the investigation. But you could be a massive help for me by answering some questions."

Jeremy swept his wavy black hair behind his ear. "I'll certainly do my best. I hope she's okay. Although I'm so not happy with her."

Seth took out his notepad and pen. "Why is that?"

"We were best friends, me, her, and Brigette. We spoke a lot during the first part of her first semester, but it got less and less as it went on. I just chalked it up to her being a study machine, which she's always been, but then she just cut us off completely after she went back for the winter semester."

"How did she do that?"

"Well, she apparently got a new phone number and refused to give it out to anyone. So, we've had no way even to get in contact with her. And she was never on social media to begin with, so it's like she doesn't even exist."

The dark irony of the statement was painful. Seth narrowed his eyes. "Why do you say 'apparently'?"

Jeremey shook his head as he stirred his coffee. "Because that's what her mother said when Brigette called her after Lizzy's number had gone out of service. She said Lizzy had threatened to change her phone number when she got back to school after winter break. Her mother assumed Brigette had it, which she didn't. She even came here to the Inn and begged me to give her the new number, which was a surprise. At least it would have been to Lizzy."

"How is that?"

Jeremy laughed. "Lizzy always thought we had to keep our friendship a secret."

Seth cocked his head to the side. "What do you mean?"

"Because I'm gay. Ooh, scary, right? She was steadfast that her parents wouldn't accept the friendship. I always told her, 'Girl, your parents know who your friends are whether you know it or not.' But that was Lizzy. She could be so paranoid about things. She always worried about her grades, didn't want to be on social media for fuck knows why, terrified she wouldn't get into college. Of course, she was wrong about all of it."

"How so?"

Jeremy continued stirring his coffee, having yet to drink any. "Well, she graduated with a 4.2 or something. She clearly got into Baylor. And Bess, her mother, knew about our friendship since grade school. We actually had an interesting talk when she showed up here. The way Lizzy made it out, part of me was nervous her mother would try to drag me to conversion therapy. But she thanked me for being such a good friend to her daughter and admitted she regretted pushing Lizzy to where she felt she needed to put distance between them."

Seth finished writing and looked up at Jeremy. "Pushing her how?"

Jeremy shrugged and finally took a sip of his coffee. "To get good grades? To go to a college closer to home? I don't know. I think Lizzy put more pressure on herself than anyone else possibly could have."

Seth was trying to gauge where the pressure was coming from. Did Sarah do it to herself, or were her parents overbearing? A mix of both seemed to paint the picture of a girl who silently struggled for years, which could lead to all kinds of mental illnesses and sporadic, even dangerous decisions. Seth turned off his profiler brain to focus on the present. "When was it that Bess Grahams came to talk to you?"

"It was after that first Christmas break, right after Lizzy went back to school. So, January 2021."

Seth leaned back in his chair. "How did Bess seem when she came in? What was her demeanor like?"

Jeremey glanced upward. "Um, she seemed genuine. She was desperate to get a hold of her. She was positive that I would hear from her and begged me to let her know when I did."

"But you didn't."

Jeremy's eyes fell to the table, and he shook his head.

"Have you seen or spoken to Mrs. Grahams since?"

Jeremy looked back at Seth and nodded. "Yeah. She actually came back a couple more times that year to have lunch and check to see if I had heard anything."

"By herself?"

"Yeah."

"Did she seem changed or different in any way?"

Jeremy took another sip of coffee. "I don't know. Maybe a bit more resigned. Like she had accepted that she wasn't going to hear from Lizzy until she was good and ready to reach out. I think it depressed her, but she did a good job of putting up a strong front."

Seth drank some of his coffee. "And have you ever seen or had contact with Sarah Elizabeth's father?"

Jeremy shook his head. "Nope."

Seth smirked and jotted down a note.

Jeremy raised an eyebrow. "Why? Do you know him?"

Seth nodded and looked up. "Yeah, I went to school with him."

"Wait, you used to live here?"

"Grew up here, yeah."

Jeremy leaned back in his chair, assessing Seth. "You must have just recently come back. I would have definitely remembered seeing you around town."

Seth smiled. "Yep. Just came back here four months ago to help take care of my parents. Wasn't planning on staying. But here I am."

"Well, welcome back then." Jeremy lifted his coffee cup.

"Thanks." Seth flipped a page on his notepad. "So, when was the last time you actually saw Sarah?"

"That first winter break. I think it was right before New Year's." Jeremy shook his head. "You've heard of the freshman fifteen, right?"

Seth nodded.

"Yeah, that was not an issue Lizzy had to contend with. She looked even more frail than usual. And tired, my God, she looked tired."

That description certainly leaned toward potential issues, prescription or otherwise. Yet she didn't look frail on the beach. "Was she ill?"

Jeremy brushed his hair behind his ear again. "She said she wasn't. She said she was fine and nothing was wrong, which clearly wasn't the case. Brige and I were super concerned for her. We knew she always had sleep issues, but she looked so unhealthy."

"What do you think it was?"

Jeremy shrugged. "We guessed it was just her usual obsessive studying. She's the type that will get so wrapped up in things that she'll forget to eat. Lizzy was determined to get a scholarship to Baylor. She was always at the library. To study, of course, but also I think to get away from her parents. Lizzy said they constantly were picking and nagging at her, and she couldn't concentrate at home. Brige and I honestly thought she never reached out with her new number because she was afraid her parents would pressure Brigette into giving it to them. That's what we told ourselves, anyhow. That's easier to believe than Lizzy not wanting anything to do with us anymore."

Seth finished writing a note and looked up at Jeremy. "I'm sorry. That must have been very difficult."

Jeremy looked down at his coffee and swallowed. "Still is."

"You mentioned the library. Do you mean the one at school?"

"Town library," Jeremy corrected with a slow nod of his head as he lifted the cup of coffee up to his face, clutched in both hands as if warming them from the cold drafts that crept through the old Victorian home.

Seth jotted a note and flipped a page in his notepad, wanting to move on to an area of keen interest. "Did Sarah Elizabeth have a boyfriend or girlfriend? Either at the time you last saw her or even in high school?"

Jeremy guffawed. "Yeah, right. With the amount of studying she did in high school? She would have never had time. And considering she thought her parents wouldn't accept me, I'm sure she thought they would be even worse if she started dating a guy. I mean, I'm pretty sure she's straight based on conversations we've had over the years, but it was always hard to tell with her."

"What do you mean by that?"

Jeremy shrugged and smiled. "Lizzy didn't exactly exude sexuality. I imagined her going through ten years of med school while still a virgin."

"So, she didn't mention anything about seeing anyone that first semester of college?"

Jeremy shook his head. "Definitely not."

Seth put a question mark next to "no dating" in his notebook. He would have guessed Jeremy would have known about such things, but then again, it was evident Sarah Elizabeth was keeping things from her best friends. From everyone. "It sounds like you still speak to Brigette Lowe. I'll need to talk to her as well. If you wouldn't mind giving me—"

"Let's just call her now," Jeremy said as he pulled his cell phone out, uplifted by the idea.

Seth waved his hand. "Really, that's not necessary. I can just call her later when—"

"Hey, bitch!" Jeremy already had his phone held up in front of his face with the speaker on.

"Hey, hoe," came Brigette's voice on the other end of the phone.

Seth sighed.

"So, I'm here with this really handsome police officer, and he has some questions about Lizzy. Say hi!" Jeremey turned the phone around to face Seth.

Seth worked the cringe on his face into a smile as he waved at the girl with straight dark hair, looking at him with a mix of confusion and worry. "Hello, Brigette. I'm Sergeant Seth Wolfe. Would you mind—"

"What's wrong? Did something happen to Lizzy? Have you seen her? Or talked to her? We haven't heard from her—"

Seth held his hand up. "I know. Jeremy filled me in. I can't say anything about the investigation at this time, but I'd like to—"

"Investigation? What's going on? Jeremy, do you know what's happening?"

Jeremy twirled the phone around. "No. You heard him. He can't say anything right now, but I'm sure she's fine." He turned the phone back toward Seth.

Seth felt like someone had punched him in the gut. These poor kids. "Look, I'd like to call you a little later to ask you some questions. Is that okay?"

Brigette's brow was knit tightly. "Sure, I guess."

Seth signaled to Jeremy to get off the phone.

"Sorry, girl, I gotta go," Jeremy said, turning the phone back toward himself. "I'll call you later. I'll try to find out what's going on. Love you!"

"Love you…"

Jeremy ended the call and set his phone down. "I apologize. I thought it might be easier, but you probably want to talk to her one-on-one."

"That's fine. Can you just give me her number?"

Jeremy picked his phone back up. "Do you want me to text it to you?"

Seth held up his mini notebook. "I'll just write it down."

Seth took Brigette Lowe's number from Jeremy and thanked him for his time. Fear had finally entered the boy's eyes as he said goodbye. He guessed Brigette's reaction had stirred something up in him. Sitting in his Bronco, Seth rolled the acorn around in his hand like a die. He considered all the new information, feeling more unnerved by the second. This case was getting stranger by the minute. He was eager to hear how Sarah Elizabeth's parents reacted to Bill's visit and knew he'd be paying them a visit himself soon.

"In the meantime," Seth said, looking down at the acorn, "time to go pay Story a visit."

Chapter 4

It's Okay, Zoe

As she exited the pharmacy on Main Street, Anya Bury shook the two strawberry milks in their plastic containers. She squinted her large aquamarine eyes against the sun's harsh glare, her pouty lips making it seem as if she took offense at the brightness. The giant glowing orb in the sky was making an exerted effort to cut the chill that had befallen Lost Grove following the unnatural storm that hit two nights ago. Scanning the sidewalks teeming with children and teens on their lunch break, Anya found Ryker sitting at a picnic bench in the courtyard of the local cafe and creamery across the street.

During the first half of her lunch break, she'd met her father, Ethan, at the feed store just down the road. They sat together on the tailgate of his old truck and shared a thermos full of warm soup. It was one of their favorite traditions. Though today, the topic of conversation was one she'd desperately been avoiding.

Her parents and teachers wanted her to attend a prestigious college. She had the grades for it, always being a student who excelled without ever pushing herself to the brink with studying. Not that she didn't appreciate the notion of college; she did. Her family could offer her further education if not for the scholarships she could get on her grades alone. The issue was her contentment. She liked her life just as it was. Anya was fond of her small town.

In all previous conversations with teachers and her parents, they never asked her if she even wanted to go to college, just assuming that was the case. Their approach disappointed her, and she had remained quiet on the subject. But with application deadlines closing in, she finally had to speak up. Anya told her father she didn't even know what she wanted to study, to which he argued many kids don't in their first semester. It took courage she rarely needed when speaking with her parents to admit she wanted to study locally and only when she was ready. She could tell her father was upset but tried not to show it.

She sighed at the recollection of the discussion and jogged across the street, settling into a spot beside Ryker. He was just unwrapping his second sandwich, the previous wrapper crumpled under the new one.

"Are you beefing up for your next jiu-jitsu competition?" she asked, handing one of the milk bottles to Ryker.

"Thanks," he replied, taking the bottle. "Not particularly for competition. Just in general. I lost weight with that flu." He twisted the cap off and gulped some of the sweet milk down.

"I noticed," she remarked. Anya cracked the cap off her milk and inserted a straw. "How much did you lose?"

"Nearly twenty pounds."

Anya's eyes expanded as she sucked on the straw. "Jesus," she said after swallowing.

"I know," he said, while tipping his chin to Noble and Stan across the street.

Anya followed his gaze and watched Noble wave, then slip inside the pharmacy with his younger sister, Zoe. Stan followed behind.

"When is the next tournament?" she asked.

"December fourth and fifth," Ryker replied. "Coming?"

"Yeah. I thought I'd written it down, but…I want to be there for this one."

Ryker laughed. "You don't have to come to all of them."

"Yeah, but I missed the last one, and you won all of your matches!"

Ryker took two more bites of his sandwich, finishing it.

Anya watched Stan exit the drugstore, a can of Coke in her hand. She paused, mid-swig, and noticed Anya looking her way. Her lips curled into a tiny smile before she gave an almost imperceptible wave. Anya smiled back as her gaze swept over to Noble and Zoe, who were also exiting the store.

To Anya, Stan was like no other person she had ever known. She was one of those rare individuals who appeared to be born ambidextrous regarding gender roles—going by the male nickname that derived from her feminine name, wearing baggy clothes that rarely included anything resembling a dress or skirt. But her nails were the most well-maintained and manicured Anya had ever seen. Her lustrous hair was thick and straight, trailing down to her tailbone, and her high cheekbones stressed the Indigenous blood coursing through her veins. Anya had something of a platonic crush on her schoolmate.

Stan said something to Noble before he looked up and met Anya's eyes. She wished she knew what they were saying.

"Yo!" Nate jumped out from the narrow alleyway between the two buildings, scaring both Ryker and Anya.

Anya jumped, a splash of her pink milk sloshing over the opening onto her hand. "Nice, thanks."

"You guys heard anything more about what happened this morning?" Nate asked as he slung his foot up onto the bench next to Ryker and perched his elbow on his knee. His voice took on that affected tone everyone noticed, both somber and excited. Anya and Stan called it his detective voice.

Anya and Ryker shook their heads.

Stan had bounded across the street, Noble and Zoe ambling after. "Can you believe this?"

"What?" Nate enthused. "What do you know?"

Ignoring Nate, Stan slid into a spot on the bench across from Anya and Ryker, addressing them. "It was a young woman they found on the beach this morning."

"A woman?" Anya asked, not quite absorbing this information.

"Fuck," Nate commented. His eyes searched the picnic area for his younger sister, Cheshire, and found her in the usual spot, alone, tapping away on her computer pad.

"I think she's a local," Stan added, voice lowered. Her heavy brown eyes widened, dark brows dropping with concern.

"Local, as in…?" Anya took a moment, her eyes flicking up to Noble. He was standing at the head of the table, taking a bottle of apple juice from his sister, who'd handed it to him when she couldn't get the top to twist off. "Like, is she from Lost Grove?"

Stan swallowed some more Coke. "I'm not sure. She could be local as in from around, or local as in—"

"We'd know her," Nate interrupted.

"What makes you say that?" Ryker asked.

Nate scouted each of the friends in his group. "You guys didn't see? Damn, okay, I saw an officer in the school today. And a source of mine said he was in with Mrs. Young."

"A source of yours?" Stan guffawed. "This is serious, Nate."

Anya quivered as a cloud covered the sun and the implication of Stan's and Nate's comments took hold.

"I am being serious, aren't I?" he argued.

Stan glared at him as she planted her feet wide and bellied up to the table, ripping open a Honey Bun. "It's hard to say," she said before taking a small bite of the sweet.

"I take this very seriously," Nate confessed.

Stan swallowed. She'd moved on from Nate's peculiar obsession. "You okay?" she asked Noble.

"What?"

"Are you okay? You've gone all green-looking."

"I'm fine."

"Wait, are you getting sick?" Nate interjected. "Is that why you didn't run this morning?"

"I am not getting sick. I'm fine."

"Cause Ryker was just sick, so…"

"I'm not sick," Noble reiterated.

Stan snorted and tilted her head, a dull expression falling over her face. "You need to fess up. What the hell's been on your mind? You said you'd tell me, so let's go. Let's hear it."

"Noble?" Zoe asked, her voice small and near his elbow.

He glared at Stan and turned to his younger sister. "What, Zo?"

"What do you think happened to the woman on the beach?" she whispered.

Noble squatted, surprised by how small she still was that he could do that and still be nearly as tall as her. "I don't know. It could have been an accident or… Zo, you don't need to worry."

"I'm not so sure it'd be an accident. Just because she's on the beach doesn't mean she drowned," Nate theorized.

"Nate! Shut up," Anya scolded.

"Dude!" Ryker admonished his friend at the same time.

"What?" Nate held his arms out.

"She drowned?" Zoe asked with wide, sad eyes.

"No, no, Zo, we don't know what happened." Noble tried to reassure his sister.

47

"Did she fall off a boat? Could Dad fall off his crab boat?" Zoe's pitch turned swiftly.

"Kiddo," Noble whispered and stood, pulling her into a hug. "Dad is fine."

"But he could fall off the boat." Her brother's shirt muffled her voice.

"I'm sorry. I didn't mean to…" Nate started and then dropped his voice to a hush, leaning over to Stan, "but like, this is crazy. Dead bodies just aren't discovered…no, bodies don't turn up in Lost Grove under shady circumstances, period."

"We shouldn't talk about this now," Stan cast a withering glare at Nate and reached over to rub Zoe's shoulder.

Nate mouthed, *Sorry.*

A soft sniffle pulled Noble's attention away from telling his friend not to worry about it. He leaned over his little sister. "Zo, hey, you don't need to cry. We'll call Dad right now, okay? See if we can get a hold of him." He pulled his phone from his pocket and hoped his father would actually answer. So often, when he left for the trips to fish king crab off the coast of Washington or Alaska, his phone was out of coverage.

The bell of the cafe door tingled so loudly in Zoe's ears she turned her head from hiding in her brother's shirt, embarrassed she was crying and so upset, and saw the town librarian walking by.

Story Palmer, clutching a parchment-wrapped sandwich in her hand, smiled at the young girl. The smile faded as she approached the group. "Are you alright, Zoe?" she asked.

Zoe sniffled in a deep breath and shook her head.

"She's upset about the…" Noble started, stopped, then proceeded, "She's afraid for our dad. He's on a crabbing run, up in Alaska, so she thinks—"

"They said it was a girl," Zoe interrupted her brother.

Story looked around the group of teenagers. Her eyes landed on the daughter of the coroner, whose subtle shift in expression showed where the information came from. "Yes, I've heard a few rumors myself."

"I feel bad. It feels so wrong." Zoe did her best to explain to Story.

Story nodded once, a subtle "Mmm" humming from her throat. She knelt down, placing her sandwich in the massive tote bag she always seemed to have, then searched for something inside. "It is wrong. To be taken at a young age is not the path most lives follow." She pulled a lock of interwoven string from her bag as she spoke. It was all kinds of colors, a sparkle of silver thread through it and another of poorly spindled wool. She moved her fingers in a practiced rhythm, forming loops and twisting strands of the string into elaborate patterns. When she finished, the colorful knot boasted an intricate Celtic design that seemed to move with its own subtle energy.

It drew Anya's attention, and a peculiar silence fell around her. She could hear the faintest of whispers, the voice of Story Palmer, the town librarian, chanting a rhyme.

What Anya heard was, "By knot of two, this spell be true. By knot of three, the spell is free. By knot of four…"

Anya looked up to find Story staring directly at her, a curious expression on her face. Her lips weren't moving, though the words continued. And just as it had come, the whisper faded, and Story was not looking at Anya; she was talking to Zoe in a perfectly normal voice, explaining why she shouldn't be afraid. Anya blinked around the group, but no one else seemed to have noticed the weird incantation.

Story smiled at Zoe, who had visibly calmed down. "Now, give me your wrist," she instructed.

Zoe held out her tiny wrist, and Story loosely tied the bracelet with pretty knots onto it.

"There, you see. Does that help to quell your unease?"

Eyes blooming, Zoe realized she no longer felt that strange burden and fear she'd been trying to overcome all day. It had come on in the night, a peculiar sense of foreboding she couldn't have characterized. But now it was gone.

Story could tell that the girl's feelings overwhelmed her. The same crawling darkness that had tried to creep inside Story's house this past night was leeching itself into Zoe's energy as well. But unlike Story, Zoe didn't know how to combat it. She'd been growing her relationship with the Andalusians, particularly Zoe, for the very reason that she could sense ancient and deep-rooted craft in their blood. She was relatively certain it came from their father's side of things, though Story had little chance of getting to know Mr. Peter Andalusian.

"It's better," Zoe squeaked, smiling.

"So mote it be." Story grinned and stood. "Good, now you have a pleasant rest of your day, yes?"

Zoe nodded.

Noble wasn't the type to gape, but his mouth was hanging slightly ajar, his right brow raised in question.

"Good afternoon, Mr. Andalusian," Story said. As she nodded her goodbyes to the rest of the group, she let her eyes linger on the one with the ginger-rooted hair. "Ms. Bury," she said. The greeting floated across the teenagers and landed only in the ears of the young woman with Fae in her blood.

Anya blinked, riddled with shock and confusion, as she stared at the back of Story Palmer heading down the street to her job at the library. The fleeting interaction overwhelmed her.

Stan took a big bite of her sugary treat, followed it with a swig of soda, and watched the town librarian walk away.

Aside from Noble and Zoe, who spent countless minutes, even hours, in the woman's presence, it was the teens' first experience as a group with the rumored witch. All of them watched her walk away, except Zoe, who played with the woven string on her wrist, smiling to herself before grasping her brother's hand and giving it a squeeze. "It's rude to stare," she instructed.

Noble snapped his jaw shut, presenting a tight smile. He always felt like Ms. Palmer pronounced their last name as if they were a rambling bunch of exotic gypsies who could read tarot cards and predict people's futures. "Still want to call Dad?"

She seemed to think about that before replying. "Text him for me?"

"I can do that," he replied, typing a text to his father.

"She is totally a witch." Nate was the first to comment.

Stan rolled her eyes. "Shut up."

Anya cleared her throat, surprised by the moment. Had they not heard the whispering coming from Ms. Palmer? More unsettling, how did the woman know her name? Maybe Nate wasn't far off the mark.

Nate tossed his water bottle into a recycling bin, missing. "She is. She stands on her lawn naked during the full moon." He walked over, picked it up, and dropped it in.

"One, you're a pervert," Ryker said.

"Two, who cares?" Stan added. "People can do whatever they want on their own property."

"Standing under the moonlight. *Naked*," Nate emphasized, returning to the table and sitting on the top, feet on the bench next to Ryker.

"How predictable," Zoe murmured.

"Jesus, this is a weird day," Nate commented.

"It's a weird week," Noble snorted.

"Yeah," Stan pronounced, elongating the word and laying her attention on Noble. "Yes, it has been a weird week, hasn't it? Perhaps you could enlighten us why that is?"

Noble closed his eyes, scratching his forehead. "Okay, look. Have any of you seen anything weird lately?"

"Define weird." Stan laughed. "The storm two nights ago wasn't weird enough? Where the hell did it come from? Oh, and let's not forget, the last time that happened, an unknown aquatic mammal washed up on Mourner's Beach."

"Yeah, only this time it's a person," Nate added.

Anya's mind snapped into overdrive. A person on Mourner's Beach? Drowned or washed ashore? Maybe it wasn't a person at all. "Maybe it's a mermaid," she muttered aloud.

"What?" Ryker asked, leaning his head down to look at Anya's face.

She popped into the conversation. "Nothing." She smiled, laughing a little.

"A mermaid?" Stan asked, having heard her the first time she mumbled it.

Anya shrugged, still holding on to her smile, hoping it would make them believe she was only talking nonsense.

"You know what, that's not that far-fetched to me anymore," Nate said, pointing at Anya. "That's weird, right? That's not normal, to be like, 'Hmm, you know what? Maybe it is a mermaid!'"

"There are the lights too," Stan offered.

"What lights?" Noble asked.

Anya laughed nervously, nodding, thrilled the subject had changed. "Yeah, Clemency Pruitt won't stop talking about them. And the ghost."

"What ghost?" Noble asked again, feeling lost in this strange conversation.

"Oh, like two, three weeks ago, Clemency was talking about this ghost in her coffee shop. The computer wasn't working, and the milk frother kept spurting to life for no reason. Coffee grinder too. Clemency says there's a ghost," Anya answered.

"That's true," Ryker said. "I stopped there this morning for a coffee and bagel, and there's a sign on the door saying, 'Bear with us while we deal with ghosts.' Paraphrasing. And so, in I go, and she rambles on about the lights in the sky."

"Yep. We've seen 'em." Stan nodded to herself.

Noble opened his mouth but lacked the words.

"So, typical Lost Grove stuff." Nate shrugged.

"Yeah. Pretty typical. Why?" Stan once again focused on Noble. "What have you seen?"

His phone alarm buzzed. "Not what you guys are talking about. Come on, Zo. I've got to get you back on time, or Mom is going to kill me."

"It's just gym. I can miss the start of gym," Zoe replied, sighing.

"I know, but the teachers don't seem to think so."

"If I was Anya, they wouldn't care. Because then I'd have been helping on my family's farm. But just because we don't have a farm, I suddenly have to be on time?" Zoe continued arguing, even though she was already walking ahead, nose back in the book she'd been reading. She took a swig of the apple juice her brother had opened.

"I've got to get her back. We'll talk," Noble said to Stan. His eyes caught on Anya's, their vibrant blue somehow piercing and strange, a trait he'd never noticed before. Her smile threw him off, the genuine happiness only slightly hindered by what he suspected was anxiety. Of course she would be anxious. He saw the same expression hiding under Stan's relatively strong facade. "See ya," he said to Anya, and it may have been the first time he could recall that he'd specifically directed a greeting at her.

Turning around to guide his sister back to school, he wondered what was more alarming, the thing he'd seen in the woods on his morning run or the dumbfounding realization that Anya Bury was so pretty.

Nate's sister, Cheshire, walked over and held her tablet up to her brother. "Did Mom put a limit on my screen time?" Cheshire was only a year older than Zoe but looked and presented herself as much older. Her blond hair was in a ponytail, showcasing her gold filigree skull earrings, already in Halloween mode.

"Yep." Nate smirked at his little sister.

"What the hell?"

"Hey, watch the mouth. You know this is why she's limiting you," Nate remarked.

"Hell? Really?"

Nate leaned over his sister. "Because you should study and do your homework. Instead, you play games and talk to weird people online."

Cheshire glared at her older brother. "They aren't weird. They're my friends."

"Sure, okay. They're probably some old perverts who get off on talking to little girls who use anime pictures as their avatars."

"They aren't," Cheshire nearly growled. "Do you know the passcode?" she asked, holding the tablet up to him.

"Fuck no."

"I can't say hell, but you can say—"

"I don't know the passcode, and if I did, I wouldn't unlock the thing. Do you know the trouble I'd get in? Do you know the shit I'm still dealing with for taking you to Buster's with me last weekend?" Nate shook his head. "Look, try to do something else. Show Mom you're not glued to that thing, and she'll cut you some slack. And also, get your grades up."

"This is ridiculous!" Cheshire shrieked, stomping back to her backpack and lunch.

Eyes wide, Nate watched his sister trudge back to her things, wondering where the little girl had gone. It seemed like she'd gotten hormones overnight. "Sorry," he said to his friends.

Stan laughed it off. "Siblings, am I right?"

Anya wished she knew. Her parents had never tried for another child. Meanwhile, Constance Hensley was the oldest daughter in a family of seven, with twins coming late to the family. They were only four to Stan's seventeen. The two exchanged smiles.

"Where's Nettie?" Nate asked.

"She has therapy on Tuesdays," Anya and Ryker responded.

"Yeah, bozo," Stan chimed in, "since like forever now."

Nate twirled his finger around his temple. Stan reached up and socked him in the arm, sending tingles up his bicep.

"Dammit, that hurt," Nate gasped between his teeth.

"Nice form." Ryker complimented Stan's loose wrist and follow-through.

"Thank my older brothers," Stan said to Ryker before turning to Nate. "You're willing to believe in a mermaid washing ashore, but still call Nettie crazy? Something is wrong in your head," Stan said, and turned to Anya. "How's she doing? Nettie?"

"Like you believe her?" Nate said.

"Fine. Usual," Anya replied at the same time. She drank the rest of the strawberry milk while standing and headed for the trash.

"You don't think a weird green dude actually took Nettie's brother, right?" Nate asked, now that Anya was slightly out of earshot.

"You'd be surprised by what I think and believe. A guy like you couldn't conceive the myriad of thoughts bouncing around in this brain."

Nate faux grinned. "All your grandmother's hocus-pocus, voodoo stuff, you mean?"

"I'm Indigenous American, you numbskull, not French Creole," Stan joked, knowing full well that Nate respected her cultural heritage and her grandmother. They all loved her grandmother. Stan twisted her mouth one way, then the other.

"It's not about belief," Ryker said. "I mean, Anya doesn't have to believe a mythical creature living in the woods took the kid—"

"There are a lot of things in the woods around here we should be cautious of," Stan interjected.

Nate rolled his eyes.

Ryker continued as Anya returned to the group. "I mean, if you'd met the kid before, you'd also see something weird happened. He was like a normal little kid."

"Yeah, but that's common for his diagnosis, right?" Nate looked between his friends but avoided Anya's eyes. "Regressive autism."

Ryker's head bounced back and forth. "I don't know. He was five. The point is, it's weird."

"So, you don't believe it was a weird dude from the forest, either?" Nate pointedly asked.

Anya sighed. "Like Ryker said, it's not about belief. She had to adapt to the change in her brother. It wasn't easy for anyone in the family."

"Right, yeah." Nate nodded, smiling.

"You're an idiot." Stan laughed. "Why do you care where Nettie is, anyway?"

"Well, she's not here and there was a body found on the beach…" Nate trailed off, hoping his friends would put the thread together like he was. "No?"

Ryker lifted an eyebrow. "You're suggesting she might have—"

"Known the person!" Nate interrupted. "But since she's at an appointment…"

Stan's eyes narrowed. "Are we missing anyone?"

"What?" Anya asked.

Stan crossed her arms, leaning back and surveying the surrounding people. "It seems like it's someone local, right? So, is anyone around town missing? Like have you noticed anyone not, you know, around?"

"Oh, damn!" Nate considered this new idea.

Stan immediately hated that she'd brought it up. No doubt he was going to go around making notes of everyone he crossed paths with now. She closed her eyes for a moment and took a deep breath.

"I haven't noticed," Anya replied. "Then again, why would I have been looking out for things like that this morning, ya know?"

"True," Ryker agreed.

Anya shook her head at the thought that she could have noted someone not where they should have been this morning. "We have to get back to classes," Anya commented, looking at the massive clock above the pharmacy.

"Let's go," Ryker said, tossing his ball of trash into the nearby can.

"I'm walking with *you*," Stan said.

"What am I, chopped liver?" Nate asked, following them all as they made their way back to school.

Stan shrugged and pointed at Ryker. "He's got a brown belt in jiujitsu."

The comment sent a shiver down Anya's spine. She'd never considered not feeling safe in this small town she loved. Like the rest of her friends, Anya was eager to know more about the woman found on Mourner's Beach this morning and how she died, but couldn't help but feeling afraid of what the answer would be.

Retrospective No. 1: Antoinetta Horne

As a young girl, Antoinetta Horne, or "Nettie" as she preferred, liked to sit at her window in her pajamas, watching the stars twinkle in unique patterns every night. She could see young people leaving their houses in whispers, their arms around each other's waists, and the old couple across the street who always took a stroll together at precisely nine p.m.

Nettie especially enjoyed watching the night-wandering woman her classmates said was a vampire. Mary was her name. She would watch as Mary stopped and observed something on the ground, bent to pick it up, and placed it in her mouth. Now and again, Nettie even saw her swallow!

The nights at her window were her favorite part of every day. That was until the first time she saw the Green Man. He was a sinister presence, and Nettie felt a chill run down her spine whenever he was around. He lived inside the small hill behind her house and seemed to revel in the chaos he caused. When she peered out of her bedroom window, his eyes seemed to dance as she watched him. And when he caught her spying, he would release a devilish grin, place his finger on the side of his nose, and wink at her like they shared a secret.

A colony of strange, childlike creatures mimicked his every move like devoted followers, skipping and prancing like demented fairies through the forest on ungainly legs. She used to think the child monsters belonged to the Green Man. Now she knew better. But that knowledge had come at a cost.

When she sat at her window these days, those little goblins were only a sad reminder to Nettie of her own lost brother George. Despite her warnings, the Green Man had stolen George and replaced him with one of those unsightly little devils. Anger had replaced the fear she originally felt when witnessing the Green Man prance through the forest. Hatred for this strange man who could steal people away with no remorse and with no one noticing. Anyone but her. She wasn't sure if she was meant to, because no one else seemed to see him. No one else had noticed his grotesquely distorted figure and his cackling laughter as he'd snatched George away.

Nettie had seen him watching her brother for a while leading up to that night. She found him on George's windowsill, contorted and strange, the nightlight illuminating his terrifying face, his features not quite right. The Green Man beckoned to George, "Come out and play," in a voice like serpents and sugar. Nettie had screamed madly at the Green Man and flung her stuffed animal at him. He only smirked and laughed, then nimbly jumped off the windowsill onto the grass. She watched him merrily walk away as her parents flew into the room, wondering what was wrong.

"What happened?" they'd asked. When she told them, all they did was soothe her and laugh behind her back, smiling at one another. "Oh, silly Antoinetta, it was simply a bad dream," they both said.

They didn't listen; they didn't believe her. Since moving to the small town of Lost Grove, they stopped worrying over things they used to. They let her walk to school on her own! They kept their front door unlocked during the day while her mother cleaned and her father was away working at the Institute. But every night, she watched the Green Man creep from the hill behind her house, and no matter how many times she tried to tell them, her parents refused to believe her. They even took her to the spot to show her there was only forest and no form of dwelling for anyone to live in.

Still, she chased the Green Man away so many times from little George's room that they finally kept the window shut and locked as if it would keep her quiet and in bed. She'd agreed it would. The next time he showed up, the Green Man scowled at the sealed window before turning to smile and wink at her before running off to commit other naughty deeds.

She thought they were taking her seriously when the man her parents called the chief of police came over to look around. She was sure the policeman would find the Green Man and arrest him. But the policeman didn't find him! Instead, he reassured her parents that no one else in town had reported a strange man walking around their houses, but the police would keep their eyes peeled for anyone suspicious. Nettie wondered if adults could even see him.

It was a mistake on her parents' part the night they left the window open. Nettie was sick with a terrible cold and was fast asleep in a medicated dreamland when the Green Man stole little George away. His chance had come, and he took it as swiftly as a bat catches a gnat in the air. But stranger still was that he replaced her brother with a replicant, a made-up boy who looked so identical it made Nettie shiver with fear. Still, the difference between George and this thing the Green Man put in his place was immediate to Nettie. One of the Green Man's little child things that danced about naked or half-clothed, things that smirked with their wide mouths and flattened heads. It was the lifeless eyes more than anything that proved it was not her brother, something her parents refused to see, refused to believe.

Nettie grew to hate the Green Man's pack of child things more and more each day she had to live with Not-George. He was disgusting. They were disgusting, with twigs and leaves and muck in their hair. They smelled of earth and rotting leaves. Nettie knew what they smelled like because one night, she snuck up on one and tackled it. She held it down, smacked it across the mouth, and demanded to know where her brother was. The little devil had the audacity to laugh hysterically. She smacked it again as it twisted with laughter, over and over. Nettie was proud when it finally stopped laughing. However, the hairs on her neck rose when she realized something was behind her, making it still. She turned around with a tough glare to see the Green Man standing a distance off, tall and lean and muscular. His eyes still danced, but with a look she thought might be pity. His brow unfurled, his distinct smile gone. He spoke in a voice like a summer breeze and fall leaves.

What he said, Nettie could not remember. All she could recall was the enchanting melody of his voice and that he allowed her to return home. She watched him for the rest of that year. Every night. He would come out, place his finger to his nose, wink, and then be off on his merry way. Yet she would always remember him differently the night his voice sang, more so than any night before or after. That night, he appeared stoic. He seemed strong. He seemed altogether good. It terrified her.

As months went on, Nettie slowly stopped watching the nighttime adventures of her neighbors. On the rare occasion she peeked out the window, Nettie would see the Green Man come out of the little hill behind her house; he and his companions would fly away into the night. Nettie would gaze upon the child-things, searching them closely in case her real brother was with them. She would look at a different one each night and study it intensely to find any trace of her little brother. But she concluded the Green Man had taken her brother somewhere else. She hoped.

Instead of listening to anything Nettie had to say, her parents took her not-brother to doctors to find out why he wasn't speaking, why he ate so little, and why he wasn't growing. According to the doctors, he wasn't growing because he wasn't eating. A stupid reason that her parents bought. But Nettie knew it was because the beastie pretending to be her little brother had forgotten how to eat. Then, suddenly, out of nowhere, the boy grew seven inches over three months. Could the doctors explain or find anything wrong with this? No. They claimed he was autistic, and Nettie had to learn all about what that meant. She hated how she had to change her life to accommodate this thing that wasn't her little brother she loved so much.

It exhausted Nettie, constantly declaring that her brother was no longer living with them, that the Green Man had replaced him. She heard the whispers around her, could sense the doubt that crept into the air. No one believed the reason George had suddenly become an eerie shadow of his former self was because one of the Green Man's monstrous creations had replaced him. But she refused to give up, and it caused a rift between her parents and the making of friends. Only the smart little girl named Anya Bury acknowledged she wasn't making things up. Anya believed Nettie because she knew there were strange things in the world. Especially in Lost Grove.

Chapter 5

Institutionalized Family Time

Nettie sat in a chair made for children and gazed out the window of the renowned Orbriallis Institute, her sleepy brown eyes drawn to the lush green landscape beyond. She absently twirled a strand of long brown hair around her index finger, wishing she could vanish from this place as quickly as her little brother had disappeared from his bedroom. Not-George still refused to speak, emitting low moans and incoherent hand gestures when he had been such a bright, conversational child. He also lacked the ability to pick up on social cues. Had never gotten the hang of eating with a fork or spoon. Of the things Nettie couldn't stand the most, it was watching him eat. George ate as if he were a feral child, using his hands to shovel mashed potatoes, chicken nuggets, and spaghetti into his mouth. The little brother she'd once known—who could converse, answer questions, and acknowledge right from wrong—was no longer present. How couldn't her parents see that? That George wasn't the same? Not even human?

Today's session was like all Tuesday afternoons. Family therapy for Nettie and her parents—Greg, who worked at the Institute, and Kim—trying to get Not-George to express himself.

Nettie glanced around the room as she pulled her phone from the pocket of her purposefully torn jeans. The floor contained a colorful array of toys for children to explore, but her gaze eventually rose, resting on the two black lenses of the cameras lurking in the upper corners of the room. Seeing them there, feeling spied upon, made her skin prickle at this supposed safe haven. The Orbriallis Institute had a lengthy, legendary past. Most notably, it had been an asylum, and then a medical research facility with a sector devoted to those with mental health issues. Rumor had it that lab experiments used to be conducted on the inmates.

She checked the time and attempted to read a series of texts from Anya. "He reacted to you last week, Nettie. Why don't you try it again?" her mother interrupted.

"No phones," Kim said and beckoned her over with enthusiasm, as if Nettie was also incapable of understanding simple commands.

Nettie leaned forward, placing her elbows on her knees. The waist of her jeans pressed into her stomach and she wondered if she was gaining weight. The way her cropped sweater hung off her shoulders would suggest she was worried over nothing. "What do you want me to say? Or do?"

"What you did last week, honey," her father added, encouraging.

"That's good. Yes, do that," said Dr. Hayman.

Nettie looked over at Not-George's shrill and annoying therapist and closed her eyes for a fleeting moment. Her Converse kept alternately tapping on the bright carpeted floor. "He reacted. He didn't interact. There's a major difference, you know."

"Can you please be present for once?" Kim sighed.

Nettie coughed a laugh.

"There's no harm in trying. Please, Antoinetta," her father added.

"No harm, right, sure. No, just eight years of doing the same shit with no result," Nettie snapped.

Kim looked fiercely out the window and then at her daughter. "You are being childish."

"Technically, Antoinetta, we have seen progress," Dr. Hayman commented. "George is interacting in his own way in a more frequent—"

"Please," Nettie scoffed.

"Nettie," Kim scolded.

"Mom," Nettie mimicked back. "What? You drag me out here every Tuesday for almost nine years. He's thirteen! He can't even eat like a normal kid. Like a human!"

"Don't yell at your mother," her father reprimanded.

"I was yelling at Dr. Hayman."

"Don't yell at him either." Greg attempted to keep his voice calm as both his daughter's and wife's pitches rose.

"You're right. I shouldn't yell at him, Dad. You should. Half your damn paycheck goes right back into this place, and fuck all if I've seen a result from his—"

"Nettie, that is enough!" Kim erupted at her daughter. "What do you suggest we do, huh?" she continued, tears welling in her eyes. "Should I just forget about my son? Forget about giving him the best life we can? You are so selfish."

"Kim," Greg warned.

Nettie's therapist, Dr. Sansa Coolidge, pulled in a deep breath from the sidelines. "The focus has shifted away from the intent of this visit. Nettie, look at me," she cooed, pulling Nettie's attention away from her parents. "Take a deep breath in to the count of five."

Nettie reluctantly obliged. She didn't hate Dr. Coolidge. In the scheme of things, she was okay.

"Good, now breathe out to the count of seven…good. Okay. Now, Nettie, there is no harm in trying what your mother suggests, is there?"

Nettie rolled her eyes.

"I realize you believe it's a waste of time, but you're already here, right?"

"Yes," Nettie agreed, nodding.

"So, I think you could give it a try."

Nettie nodded curtly, pushing up from the small chair that made her feel like a giant. George was a teenager now. There was no reason to continue to coddle him with the primary-colored plastic chairs, the brightly painted walls, and the plastic toys. Nettie walked over to Not-George, then plopped down cross-legged on the floor in front of him. She hated looking at his face. He had the same brown eyes and dark brown hair as her real brother, but Not-George had overly bushy eyebrows, a slight underbite, and had become pudgy since her parents allowed him to eat as much and as often as he wanted. They also dressed him in overly baggy grey sweatpants and a tattered purple sweatshirt. It was almost as if her parents wanted him to look unsightly.

Nettie reached over and snatched a toy from the toy bin. She looked down and reeled back, noticing the toy was a grotesque, old-time hand puppet with a beaked nose, beady black eyes, and a green felt hat. It reminded her of the Green Man, heinously exaggerated. She slipped the puppet over her hand.

"Hello, boy who isn't George," Nettie began.

"Nettie," her mother hissed.

"Mrs. Horne, we have to let Nettie express her feelings as well," Dr. Coolidge corrected.

Nettie stared at Not-George's face. Again, she manipulated the puppet, pitching her voice in a nasal whine. "Don't I look familiar? Like someone you know?"

Not-George's head tilted up, rolling his eyes upward to look at the puppet.

Nettie turned the puppet this way and that, and flicked her fingers so the hands and arms opened and closed. "There he is, my old friend. You *do* know who I am! The Green Man has come to take you back. Give him a hug." She opened the puppet's arms wide, shoving it toward Not-George.

"Nettie, that is enough!" Her mother snatched the puppet from her hand. "I'm sorry, but no. No, I can't do this. I can't keep indulging her fantasy." She stood, dropped the puppet to the floor, and, holding up a hand, silenced Drs. Coolidge and Hayward, exiting the room.

Nettie glanced at her father, and he replied with a look of resignation, a lackluster attempt to scold her, as he'd used many times before. Nettie and her mother argued practically every Tuesday, which had created a cold, unspoken crevice between mother and daughter. That crevice had become a canyon.

Not-George leaned forward and looked down at the puppet. "Baa baa la Rah-nch," he said with words diluted and slurred like he was trying to speak from a dream.

Nettie's eyes widened in surprise. The damaged imposter had never uttered a word before, and what just came out of his mouth was more than a grunt or a moan. He actually tried to say something. She pushed to standing and stumbled backward as her heart pounded in her chest. The room seemed to spin around her as an icy chill ran down her spine. She could feel goosebumps popping up on her arms and a sickening flutter deep in her stomach. His voice, the gargled words, had triggered something inside of her that made every nerve stand at attention.

Dr. Hayman bolted over and squatted down. "What was that, George?"

Her father swooped in, kneeling at his son's side. "George, what do you want to say?"

Usually Not-George's eyes were dull and witless, but as Nettie stared in disbelief at the imposter, his eyes shifted and burned with a maniacal glint that made her draw back. His slowly curling lips pulled up into a wide, evil grin that only widened as he caught her eye. He started to laugh softly, then louder and harder. His snickering escalated to a full-blown cackle.

Nettie reached across the space between them and slapped Not-George across the face. The sharp crack resonated against the stillness of the room, and all eyes were suddenly on her.

"Antoinetta, what is wrong with you?" her father admonished, turning to look at Not-George's face.

Nettie fled, her feet barely touching the soft carpet as she charged out of the therapy room. Her heart raced, and her head felt hot with rage. All she wanted was to get out of the Orbriallis Institute as quickly as possible. She stomped down the stairwell, thankful they were only on the fourth floor of the towering structure, and burst out the door to the lobby. She sprinted toward the exit, the marble tiles gleaming beneath her feet, eventually pushing through the heavy glass doors that separated her from freedom. Nettie dashed across the parking lot to the family car, ripped open the trunk, and yanked out her bike. Without looking back, she pedaled hard and fast, feeling a sense of liberation with each revolution of the wheel until she reached school.

Chapter 6

Witchy Bibliognost

Seth ascended the maroon-painted concrete steps to the Lost Grove Public Library. The building had a domineering facade, a weight as if it was built to stand the test of time, which he supposed was true. The library that stood today, modeled in the Classic Revival architectural style, was built after the Great San Francisco Earthquake in 1909 on solid concrete foundations.

He paused for a moment, a wave of nostalgia washing over him as he remembered his last visit here. It must have been during his senior year of high school when he had done research for his final history paper. Memories flooded him of that time when he had pored over books about Roald Amundsen, the Norwegian explorer who was the first to reach the South Pole. Amundsen and his story attracted Seth because he thought Antarctica was the most exciting place a man could explore. There was no shortage of treacherous lands to traverse in the world, but something about your boat getting stuck in ice and potentially freezing to death hit a primal nerve in Seth's heart. That Amundsen perished attempting to save a fellow explorer who crashed at sea was the type of heroism Seth wanted to emulate in his life and one he could identify with.

Seth smiled halfheartedly as he remembered how that ill-fated dream had ended with him getting infamously stuck in a cave—something he hadn't thought about in detail for over ten years, until now.

As he landed on the top step, Seth wondered how his current state of mind might be different if Bill had saved him twenty minutes earlier than he had. He was certain that his focus would be sharper. But was there actually something in the memory, or rather the absurd time travel, that could somehow prove helpful in this bizarre case? Brushing aside the bewildering thought, Seth pulled open one of the massive, glass-paneled front doors, painted maroon to match the steps, and stopped mid-stride. Close-open-close-open. Something was missing, different.

"A squeak," Seth mumbled as he entered the library. Much like the student desks at his old high school, the building felt smaller despite his unchanged height. The smell was familiar: wood, aged paper, a hint of vanilla, but the fresh remnants of a sweet floral candle and the spice of cedar and incense were new. Story wouldn't be burning either in here, would she? Matches, a lighter, a burning wick, all significant violations, or at least heavily frowned upon, in a building filled with paper. Would he have to give her a citation? He didn't spot anyone behind the front desk, a glorious wooden structure with hand-carved corbels under the overhang, the rich wood polished to a dull shine.

Seth stepped further inside, noticing how his eyes had been tricked, how space seemed to shift around the shelves as they ventured deep into the dark depths of the building. He tapped his knuckles on the counter, inclined to wait, when the soft patter of footsteps made him turn. Story Palmer stepped out from the aisles of books, her boots gently clipping on the marble floor. A knit cardigan had replaced her coat, and the soft, warm light glinted off her jewelry. Her appearance caused Seth's breath to catch in his throat.

"Hello, Sheriff," Story said, coming to a stop in front of him.

Seth shifted on his feet. "Story, hello. And it's—"

"Sergeant, I know. But Sheriff just seems to suit you better. You carry that gravitas with you. More so than Bill, no offense against the man."

"I don't know about that," Seth said humbly, though unable to disagree.

"Were you a sheriff before you came back here from… Where was it you worked? San Francisco?"

Seth cocked his head to the side. "Yes. But, um, no, I was a detective. Did I tell you where I had worked?"

Story shrugged. "You must have. Or someone mentioned it; you know how this town is."

"I do."

She quietly snapped her fingers. "Your mother must have said. Detective…" Story looked up, stretching the word out, and then nodded back at him. "That makes sense."

"How so?"

Story pursed her lips and considered. "The seriousness. The aura of dogged determination."

Seth narrowed his eyes. "That's a lot to gauge…and from what?"

"I just said. Your aura," she said with a laugh.

Seth smiled at her throaty giggle that wasn't at all obnoxious, more endearing. "Indeed, you did."

"Would you like to sit down somewhere to talk?"

Seth batted his eyelids. "And how do you know I'm here to see you?"

"Well, I doubt you're here to see Becky," Story said, glancing past Seth's shoulder.

Seth looked behind him to see a young girl, likely still in high school. She wore a button-up under a loose-fitted sweater, oversized glasses, severe hair pulled back into a chignon. He felt she was trying to look older than she was, or perhaps more studious. He also wondered where she'd come from. Minutes before, there hadn't been a soul in sight. "Nope, no need to speak with Becky."

"Over here." Story headed deeper into the library to one of the small study areas containing two tables and four chairs, all of which had seen wear over the ages.

Seth trailed Story to the furthest table, taking off his coat and hanging it over the chair's back before sitting. Two tiny vintage stained-glass lamps sat in the center of each table. Story pulled the bronze chains to turn them on; their glow created a magical tone. He pulled out his notebook and pen and looked up at Story. Her eyes met his, the subtle glow from the lamps twinkling like kaleidoscopes in her irises.

"I'm assuming the body found at Mourner's Beach was a recent student."

Seth pursed his lips as he tapped his pen on his notepad. "Why would you assume that?"

Story smiled, her hands folded in front of her. "Most people who frequent this fine establishment are students or older residents. And if you're here to ask me about whomever the victim is, I imagine it would be someone with whom you think I might have formed a relationship. Or, at the least, came here often enough that I would have picked up on habits, seen who they hung out with."

"Mm-hmm." Seth was getting the distinct impression he wouldn't get much past the enigmatic librarian. "We don't have a confirmed identity of the victim, but anything you can tell me about Sarah Elizabeth Grahams would be beneficial to our investigation."

Story's playful expression fell ever so slightly, but enough for Seth to notice. She brought her hands up in front of her and started twisting one of her rings, her glare dropping to the table. "Yes, I can do that."

Seth waited, falsely assuming she would follow that up with information. "What's the first thing that comes to your mind about her?"

Story closed her eyes and conjured a memory, a vision of the young girl's face, her full lips, button nose, long auburn hair leaning more red than brown, and eyes filled with a mixture of innocence and inner turmoil. She opened her eyes, still staring at the table. "Une petite ingénue, une dédié eleve, solitaire, perdu," she said.

Seth's lips parted, and his mouth opened softly, releasing a small click as his tongue met his palate. The pen in his hand hovered over his notebook. "And that would be?"

"French, sorry."

"You speak French?"

"Oui," Story confirmed. "My native language. I thought your mother… I'm from Nova Scotia."

"Oh." Seth shifted in his chair.

"Sorry, let me, um," Story continued. "It's been years, but I can still clearly see her face. Her eyes. She was in here more than anyone else has been since I took over as head librarian, and the next closest student her age would be a mile off. So I was more familiar with her face than maybe any other in town. She studied hard, like it really meant something to her. She was sweet and genuinely kind."

"That fits with what I've heard. Did you speak with her much? Get to know her at all?"

Story's mouth parted as she looked up at Seth but hesitated a moment, her eyes narrowing. "Not so much, no. Not in what you might consider a typical way."

Seth splayed his hands out, pen in hand. "Elaborate on that one for me?"

"You're a detective. I imagine you discern plenty from close observation. Enough to learn things about people without really getting to know them."

Seth smiled. "That makes sense. So what did you intuit?"

Story grinned despite the melancholy behind her eyes. "That's the perfect word. I intuited that Ms. Grahams was determined, focused, lonely. Lost. She seemed unhappy."

"Unhappy how?"

"Well, as I said, she spent an abnormal amount of time here. She clearly had no desire to be home with her parents."

Seth noted the past tense. "Did she do anything besides study when she was here? Was she on her phone a lot? Or with friends?"

Story tilted her head and glanced upward. "For a moment, I couldn't recall if I ever saw her with a cell phone. But I do remember seeing her with her head down and the glow from her phone on her face. That was rare though, predominantly studying."

"Okay, and friends? A study group?"

Story looked back at Seth. "No, always by herself."

Seth slowly nodded and then jotted down a note. That could explain why Story felt she was lonely. "So, what did she study?"

"Besides schoolwork?"

Seth's head bounced left and right like a metronome. "Yes… maybe. That or anything she seemed particularly fixated on regarding schoolwork."

Story's eyes drifted just past Seth's. "She'd request books from other libraries. Things on neurology, the mind, insomnia." Story pushed the sleeves of her cardigan up, revealing one arm covered in geometric floral tattoos, the other only partially so.

Seth noticed them, the detailed craftsmanship of each one. "Is that what she planned on studying at college?" he asked.

Story nodded and looked back at him, noticing his eyes shoot back up from her arms. She felt a warm rush of blood course through her chest. "I believe so, yes. The research seemed extracurricular to her schoolwork."

"Did she ever give you any reason? I mean, you two must have had at least a few conversations."

"Sure." Story nodded some more. "But she never gave me a reason she wanted to study neurology, or if that even was what she planned to study. She'd take out books on psychology, too. Well, let me rephrase that; she never took out books. She only read things here. I kept a small cart at the front with her books on it, so I didn't have to log them in and out every day."

Seth furrowed his brow. "She never checked out books?"

Story shook her head. "I gathered she didn't want her parents, or maybe her friends, to know what she was reading."

"The books on neurology, insomnia?"

"That's right. The rest of the books she read were ones from school she brought with her."

"Do kids still use textbooks anymore?" Seth asked.

Story let out another throaty laugh. "I see a lot of computers and tablets, but yes, there are still textbooks in existence."

"Was she in here literally every day?"

"Figure of speech." Story smiled.

"Got it." Seth returned her smile and jotted down a note. "She came back home for winter break in December 2020, the year she started college at Baylor. Did she stop in to study at all? Or say hello?"

Story looked away to the tall, lead glass windows, their wavy distortions giving the outside trees a sense as if an artist painted them. She took in a breath. "She didn't stop in here to say hello, no."

Seth glanced up, not lifting his head from his notepad.

Story wrung her hands. "She came by my house."

Seth's head rose, brows tight. "Had she ever come to your house before?"

"No."

"How did… Forget it, everyone knows everything here. Why did she come to visit you?"

Story placed her hands back on the table and looked directly at Seth. "To ask me for something."

Seth pushed his notepad to the side and gave Story his full attention. "What did she ask for?"

Story sighed. "I'm assuming you've heard by now, in your, what, four months as of yesterday, isn't it?"

"Four, yes," Seth responded, eyelids flickering closed. Was she that astute, or was she a stalker?

"Yes, so, you must have heard that some people think I'm a witch." The edges of Story's lips twitched in the threat of a smile.

Seth's head pulled back. "No…I don't really think so."

"Well, they do."

"And why would they think that?" Seth asked; the small acorn in his pocket felt like it was burning a hole in his thigh.

Story offered him a tight smile. "Sarah came to my house and asked if I'd make her something to quiet her mind. She wasn't sleeping well."

"She thought you'd…do what, exactly?"

"Cast a spell. Make her a potion," Story explained. "I did, of course."

Seth's eyelids fluttered. "A potion?"

"I made her a tea. Chamomile, lavender, valerian root, poppy, and a touch of lemon."

"So, an herbal remedy?" Seth asked for verification.

Story gave the slightest of nods. Getting into the details wasn't in the cards for today. She couldn't rightly explain that she did, in fact, cast intentions into the tea when she made it for Sarah or that she did the same when she brought his father, Christopher, the tea mix to help him recover quicker.

"Did you talk about anything during this visit?"

"I didn't ask too many questions. Something was clearly troubling her. I wanted to help."

Seth tapped his pen on the table. "Do you have any idea at all what was troubling her? Besides sleep issues."

Story sighed. "I wish I did. I'm guessing I'll wish I had asked the questions I'd wanted to."

"And what were those?"

Story looked down at the table, whispering to herself.

Seth dropped the line of inquiry. "Right, and that was all you saw of her when she was home visiting?"

Story looked back up. "I saw her around town with her friends. But, yes, that was my only interaction with her."

Seth grabbed his notepad back and scribbled a few quick notes. "Her friends were?"

"Jeremy Stapleton and Brigette…I can't recall if I ever heard her last name. But Jeremy I know because sometimes I'll get a glass of wine at the bar at the Inn after work."

Seth looked up to see what those words might imply, but Story was fussing with her sweater now. "Thinking back to when Sarah was in high school, did you sense that she might have a relationship with someone?"

"Romantic relationship?" Story asked, brows slightly raised. "Yes."

Seth's eyebrows knit together. Jeremy had been definitive in his declaration that Sarah never dated, but Story's quick response said otherwise. "Did you see her with someone? Around town or…"

Story shook her head. "No. She was head-down studious when she came in here."

"So, how do you know she had a boyfriend or girlfriend?"

"You can just tell when a girl is into someone."

Seth tipped his head in a sideways nod. "I'd love to know that secret."

Story smiled. "Don't you?"

Seth paused. "I don't…do you have any idea who it could have been?"

"No clue."

"Okay then." Seth pocketed his notebook and pen, getting the distinct impression that Story Palmer was having difficulty processing that Sarah Elizabeth was likely deceased. He didn't need to press her any further tonight. "If I think of any other—"

"Yes, of course. Perhaps during non-library hours."

Seth rose and grabbed his jacket. "Sure, of course. I didn't mean to take too much of your time."

Story smiled and rose with him. "You didn't."

Seth nodded. "Well, thanks nonetheless." He turned to walk off.

"Do you still have it with you?"

Seth chuckled and turned back to her, pulling the acorn from his pocket. He held it up and twisted it in the air.

Story nodded in approval. "Very good."

Chapter 7

Baa Baa Black Sheep

Anya pulled her knit stocking cap down, using her hip to push the doors of the school open to exit. Try as they might, the teachers had a tough time making the day appear normal. Too much of everyone's attention was on what little they knew about the person who died. The police officer being at the school so soon had everyone leaning toward thinking the body was that of a student. Most likely a former one, as everyone in their current class seemed to be accounted for.

Anya had racked her brain to think of who still lived in town, or nearby, that it could be, but came up with very little. Or at least very little to suggest they could be the person found dead on a beach. Few people swam at Mourner's Beach. Occasionally, there were a few surfers, maybe a little wading in the shallows, but swimming? The waves broke too close to make it a good beach for vacationers. Tourists didn't come to Lost Grove for the beaches. They came for the quaint Victorian atmosphere, the proximity to national forest preserves, and a relaxing trip into small-town life.

She pulled her bike from the stand, wishing now more than ever that her father would complete the fixes on the baby-blue Chevette he'd been restoring for her.

"Hey," Nettie said, pulling her own bike from the school rack.

"Hey. Feeling any better?" Anya was grateful for the distraction of Nettie's family drama.

"I don't know. No?" Nettie responded.

Anya offered a kind smile to her friend as they rode their bikes out of town toward her family farm. Though Nettie's father wanted her home, given the news around town, he wouldn't institute any punishment if she disobeyed. Ethan, Anya's father, would drive her home after dinner. Besides, Nettie needed to unpack her feelings and thoughts to her best friend and address the creepy, sickening sensation that Not-George had communicated something to her. She needed to figure out what he meant by his mumbled nonsense.

As they pulled into the pea gravel drive of the Bury farm, Anya asked, "Are you sure it was cognizant words?" She dismounted, sweeping her feet over the bike seat as it slowed.

"I've thought about it all day. I'm telling you, I know he meant something by it. He's just such a complete idiot and never speaks. He's forgotten how to form actual words. Like…" Nettie paused, pondering how to verbalize her frustration, failing to do so.

They pushed their bikes across the gravel courtyard toward the Bury barn. They didn't use it for livestock anymore. The Burys had fashioned it into a workshop for building and carving. Inside, wood shavings were scattered across sealed cement like leaves across a meadow. Her father's latest piece of work, restoring a massive antique armoire, was hardly visible in the dark depths of the barn.

Nettie set her bike by Anya's, clicking the kickstand down and pulling her backpack up on her shoulders before continuing. "So he's said something, but no one can make sense of it. I know he said something," she whispered.

"And then he laughed?" Anya asked, shutting the barn doors and heading toward the house. The pea gravel crunched loudly under their boots. The little pebbles sounded different in the winter, sharp and cruel, whereas in the summer, the sun made them sound like little stones tumbling together, soft percussions that were pleasing to the ear.

Nettie nodded, following Anya toward the gorgeous white Victorian farmhouse. It was the nicest farmhouse in Lost Grove, looking freshly painted, or rather, it looked like they had dipped it in creamy white chocolate, the color of the fresh milk from their cows.

"Was it like he was teasing you?" Anya asked, heading up the lush grass lawn toward the back door. Movement drew her eyes to the left. Her father, with his brown disheveled hair and full beard, was ambling toward them from the feed shed, dressed appropriately in workman's jeans, a long-sleeve flannel, L.L.Bean boots, and a black down vest. Anya paused.

"It certainly felt that way," Nettie responded, waiting beside her friend.

"Hey, kiddo," Ethan said, wrapping his daughter in a one-armed hug. In the other arm, he was lugging a fifty-pound bag of feed for the chickens. "Hey, Nettie. Did you guys have a good day?"

Anya cast her father a wide-eyed glare.

"Aside from the news. Okay, terrible question." Ethan kissed her on the head and walked toward the coop. "Oh, hey, have you seen your mother?"

Anya looked toward the house. "No. But we just got here. Why?"

Ethan smiled, walking backward on his way to complete his farm errand. "She's not been home for a few hours is all."

"Dad!" Anya's stomach flipped with concern. "When was the last time you saw her?" she called after her father.

"A few hours is all. She probably went for a swim," he responded, pausing.

"Why would your mom go for a swim? Today of all days?" Nettie asked for only Anya to hear.

Anya half turned to her friend and then focused back on her dad. "Are you going to check?"

Ethan nodded. "Yeah, I'll check. Let me just…" He trailed off, eyes squinting past the house across the pasture toward the distant line of trees. "Never mind. There she is."

Anya turned. Her mother was walking up to the pasture fence with a lighthearted stride, her long blue dress billowing in the wind. She launched herself onto the wooden top rail and swung both legs over in one effortless motion before quickly hopping down on the other side.

The girls met her at the steps leading up to the small back porch.

"Hi, baby," Leith, Anya's mother, greeted her beloved daughter.

Leith's smile was broad and inviting, like a sunbeam on a rippling lake, and her mid-length dress hugged every curve of her damp, slender frame. She seemed unaffected by the crisp autumn air brushing her skin.

She tucked a loose strand of Anya's hair behind her ear and opened the door, ushering the girls inside. "You should have called to have your father pick you up."

"You went swimming?" Anya asked instead, with a touch of annoyance.

Inside, the mudroom was warm and smelled of dirt, dust, and a hint of her father's aftershave. Leith kicked her tall black rubber Wellington boots off, noticing how Nettie looked at her quizzically. Anya slipped her shoes off, noticing the way her friend was eyeing her mother. While it wasn't abnormal to Anya, Leith's now vibrant copper, dripping wet hair would be the opposite of what Nettie was used to seeing. Usually, Leith's hair was stark white.

Leith waved her hand through the air, brushing her daughter's comment aside. "I needed a brief respite from the news of what happened today. It had my mind spinning over all sorts of things, and I simply could not stay in that mindset. So much easier to disconnect back in the wild. Do you guys want a snack?"

Leith maneuvered through the doorway and around the kitchen island of the family home. While much of the house remained the same through generations, renovations had been made and were most evident in the soft hues of grey-and-white cabinets and the sleek stainless steel appliances. Ethan had done a stellar job restoring all the furniture in the family home; every piece was an exquisite antique. He'd outdone himself with Anya's suite on the third floor, though. It featured a warm, inviting color palette and a dizzying spiral staircase that led up to a widow's walk.

"I can reheat the soft pretzels I made; whip up a quick cheese dip?" Leith suggested, already pulling things from the cabinets.

"That sounds great, but you don't have to," Nettie replied.

"Mom?" Anya whispered, leaning closer to her mother and casting a smile at Nettie while helping her mother pull a sheet pan from the cabinet and line it with parchment paper. "You're completely ignoring the fact that you're soaking wet and your hair is—"

"Darling." Leith stopped her, hair dripping water on her daughter's face. "It can't be helped. Now," she said, turning to Nettie, "are you staying for dinner?"

Nettie smiled. "I was planning on it if that's okay."

"Of course it is. And then Ethan will drive you home after. I won't have you riding your bike home that late. I don't like that you rode them out here as it is. Your parents were okay with you coming over?"

"Not…not really. Dad wanted me home, but I just didn't. I wasn't…"

Leith stayed quiet, her gaze fixed on the task of making them food. Though Anya shared almost everything with her mother, Leith wasn't about to tell Nettie that she knew all about the therapy sessions. She also knew all about the little boy that was not her brother. Leith had seen the not-children and the Green Man once, and only once. She'd chased him off her part of the woods, revealing her vicious, aggressive side typically only used to fight off large predators and hunt fish. If you looked in the right place, Leith was pretty sure the Green Man would still wield the scar from their encounter.

Leith hadn't told her daughter the truth about the Green Man's existence. Not that she needed to. Anya already knew enough about her mother and where she came from to accept Antoinette Horne's story about her missing brother.

She slapped a healthy pat of butter into a pan, grabbing flour and cream from the pantry and fridge. "How was everyone at school?"

"Weirded out," Anya replied.

Nettie nodded, though she kept looking between Leith and Anya, expecting some kind of explanation about the swim and her mother's changed hair. "It's creepy."

"It is, isn't it?" Leith spun to the melted butter, tossing flour in. "If you girls want to talk about it or anything, you know I'm here for you."

"We know, Mom," Anya said.

"I…" Nettie started, paused, then continued, "Where do you go swimming?"

"Oh, sweetheart." Leith leaned across the island and patted Nettie's hand. "Not Mourner's Beach. No, I swim in a pond in the woods down that end of the field."

Anya's stomach clenched, knowing Nettie would know how out of the ordinary that was.

Everyone in Lost Grove had heard the stories of how, deep in the woods, things shifted and changed without warning. They'd all heard the stories of eerie events that happened in the woods—disappearances that defied explanation, strange lights, and otherworldly sounds.

Ethan's younger sister Emily had been taken by the woods many years ago, but he'd also found his wife within them. People whispered about how it seemed luck was fickle inside those trees.

A confused smile painted Nettie's face. "You swim, you go…you go in the woods down there? Aren't those the cursed woods?"

Anya saw her mother's shoulders rise as she stirred milk into the pan. When she turned, Leith wore a smile. "I do. But do not go into those parts of the woods. The warnings are true. There are too many dangers inside."

"But how do you—"

"I know my way," Leith interrupted. "Some woods, as harmless as they may seem, just aren't the same as other woods. Be it, I don't know, bogs, quicksand, strange sounds, toxic natural gasses…those kinds of things can disorient people."

Leith went back to making the cheese dip for the soft pretzels.

"Do you think that's what could have happened to the girl?" Anya asked to pull the conversation in another direction.

"That would make sense. She wouldn't be the first to go into the woods and end up lost in a completely different location," Nettie said.

Anya put the pretzels on the baking sheet and slid them into the oven. "That's different."

"Is it?" Nettie countered. "That little boy was found in the bushes right on the search team's path. He said a bear took care of him. And what about that guy? He was like a professional. Hadn't he climbed Everest or something?"

"I don't think it was Everest," Anya noted, trying to recall.

"But he was a seasoned outdoorsman. He was camping in Devil's Cradle State Park when there was that fluke winter storm. He tried to go for help for the rest of his camping team, went off the path cutting through, and ended up barefoot, disoriented, and thirty miles from where he was going. Not to mention…" Nettie let the words drop, though her hand was outstretched toward the back door.

They didn't talk about Emily Bury except in fond memories. Never once of how she went walking up toward town to catch her older brother's baseball game and showed up three days later in the estuary leading into the Pacific. The last person to see her was an old man driving past as she was taking a shortcut, heading through the cursed woods that ran like a splinter through downtown Lost Grove.

Leith took in a deep breath. "It's possible. She could have been a camper—"

"No, Mom, she wasn't," Anya interrupted.

Though her mother continued stirring the pot, she looked over her shoulder at her daughter. "What do you mean?"

"An officer was in the school today talking to teachers."

The spoon stopped stirring, and Leith's brow wrinkled in worry. "You mean it's someone local?"

Anya shrugged. "Why else would an officer come in to talk to teachers?"

"Well, that's awful. I hadn't heard that."

"I've been trying to think of who it might be," Nettie said.

"Me too," Anya concurred. "Did you think of anyone?"

"That's rather morbid, don't you think?" Leith mildly scolded. "You girls shouldn't be thinking about things like that."

"But it's happened, Mom. So it's not like we can't think about it. I mean, I literally can't stop thinking about it."

Leith brushed her palm across her daughter's cheek while moving toward the refrigerator. She grabbed the fresh chicken, tofu, and soy sauce and, moving back to the island, said, "I hope it's not like that other poor girl. What was her name?"

"What other poor girl?" Anya asked, beating Nettie to the punch.

"Kelly, that was her name. You girls were about nine, so we hid it from you as best we could."

"Wait, I remember that," Nettie exclaimed.

"The whole town paid their respects. I didn't want to drag you there with us, but it was what it was," Leith explained to Anya. Her daughter had that squinched-up, questioning expression. "I had you play outside for most of it. You just popped in to show your face, and then I sent you out."

"My mom made me sit respectfully inside. I remember asking her who the girl was."

Leith set down the knife she'd been using to clean the chicken of any remaining fat. "It's terrible rehashing this. Kelly Fulson, she was around, gosh, twenty-two? I don't recall her actual age. Her body came ashore on Jonathan's property. You know where the road dips down and his cattle love to eat the grass in that valley?"

Anya nodded. Jonathan was a rancher living next to the coast and Devil's Cradle State Park. Like any in the area, cattle or milk cows, everyone who raised cows knew each other. Anya had known Jonathan Baume and his wife, Christine, all her life.

"He was down there rounding them to come back up to the house when he noticed her. He and your father talked at great lengths about it. Jonathan just couldn't get that out of his mind. The look of her. He was pretty torn up about it. Even Christine talked to me about it. Said she'd never seen her husband look as white as he did that day. All the things he's endured on their ranch…"

"How'd she die?" Anya asked.

Leith met her daughter's gaze. "They never found that out, really. Now, go on up to your room while I finish the pretzels and start dinner."

Anya's feet shuffled up the stairs, her hand lightly gripping Nettie's arm. She opened the door at the top of the landing and stepped into her room. The patchwork quilt draped over her bed was a kaleidoscope of colors, from mauve to sage green, rich marigold to honeyed tan. Her grandmother had made it with fabrics that were in the family for generations. It smelled like home, like a pinch of nutmeg and a spoonful of vanilla.

Antiques were everywhere—velvet curtains hung heavy over the windows, covering gauzy cotton ones that had been there since Anya's great-great-grandparents built the homestead. A four-poster bed made of white oak covered a threadbare Persian rug. Under a dormer window was an antique desk, which framed a view of the driveway and the enormous live oak tree that shaded the front yard. But modern touches lurked—a laptop sat on the old wooden desk, a TV with an ornately carved frame hung on the wall, and the giant beanbag chair overflowed with soft fabric.

Nettie plopped into the massive beanbag chair, dropping her bag to the floor. A deep grunt escaped her.

Anya put her bag on the desk, pulling out her iPad, books, and notebook. "This just keeps getting weirder."

"You're telling me. I totally forgot about that girl, Kelly." Nettie played with her hair, watching Anya move across the room and plop herself onto her bed. "Did your mom dye her hair?"

Anya inwardly cringed. "Must have."

"What, she did it today or something?"

Anya shrugged. Years of being the only one in on the secret of her mother's true nature weighed heavily, and yet she had to remain silent. She wished someone could understand why her hair was so soft and bright without a salon's help, why her eyes glowed with an uncommon hue, why she felt so deeply connected to the environment that surrounded her. But these were secrets, secrets that weren't hers to tell.

"It looks so natural," Nettie commented.

"I guess. Look, I can't…I don't want to think about this girl anymore. Let's talk about what the heck happened to you today. Give me a breakdown. What do you think is going on?"

"Okay, so I told you about the puppet…"

"Yep," Anya confirmed with a succinct nod.

"Not-George looks up at me, makes full-on eye contact, and says, 'Baa baa la ranch' or 'Baa baa la rain itch.' And I just knew. I knew it was saying something to me. Then it started laughing. At me." Nettie gestured to herself. "I don't know what the words mean, but they mean something. That was the first communication like that, ever, and I'm telling you, I can just feel it. There's something behind it."

"Okay, yes. Right. So, okay…" Anya plotted inside her mind, licking her lips in thought. "You get the puppet, you're all like, 'Hey, remember me, the Green Man, your old friend!' and it's all like…"

"Ba ba la ranch," Nettie said. They sat in silence for a moment. "I know, it's like, what the hell could that actually be? But it's something. It could have been bol bol. Bol bol la ranch…maybe."

"Do you think it was referring to the puppet?"

Nettie pondered that a moment before answering, "As what, though?"

Anya shrugged, grimacing, "As in his name?"

"You think he was saying the Green Man's actual name?"

"Or the puppet's," Anya said and then launched into an explanation, seeing her friend grow annoyed by that comment. "You've said the Institute is weird about your not-brother. He, it, gets an unusual amount of therapy, and most of it isn't even around you or your parents."

Nettie squinted her eyes, directing them to the ceiling.

"I think you're right. It's suspicious that it spoke, and it must mean something, but if it's as dense as we think it is, we have to think in the same disconnected manner it might." Anya made sure to use the correct pronouns for Not-George, if you could say *it* was a pronoun.

Nettie suddenly crossed her legs and leaned forward, excitement sparkling in her eyes. "I don't want to say anything major, and most of this is probably just all to do with the weird urban legends surrounding Orbriallis, but I can't tell you how creepy they are. The place, all the cameras. Why are there cameras in the treatment rooms? Isn't that against some law?"

Anya toggled her head left to right. "Not sure. You'd think so. We could ask Stan to ask her dad. He'd probably know."

"You text her," Nettie stuttered at the knock on the door.

"Here's a snack, girls," Leith sang, bringing in a small platter of fine china carrying four soft pretzels and a silver dish of bright orange cheese sauce.

It wasn't intentionally fancy. The Burys used all the hand-me-down china and silver from the family daily. There was so much of it from the generations; it seemed a shame and a waste not to use it. Leith set it on the floor between them and snuck back out.

Anya sprung down from her bed, crossed her legs on the floor, and ripped one of the chewy, warm pretzels into smaller pieces, dipping it in cheese. Chewing, she reached back onto the bed and grabbed her phone, shooting off a text to Stan about patients' privacy practices in mental hospitals. Nettie was digging into her own pretzel.

After another bite, Anya asked, "Could he be reciting some creepy childhood rhyme? All I can think of is Baa baa, black sheep."

"Possible."

"Because, I'm just thinking, maybe it's not so much about what he said, as it is about that he can say something. Maybe?" Anya swiped another dollop of cheese onto a chunk of salty bread.

"I'm willing to entertain that." Nettie chewed. "But I think it's something more."

Anya thought for a moment, contemplating this conundrum like a mathematical problem. There were many interpretations, and Nettie had so far suggested he could have said baa, bol, ranch, and rain itch. She wiped the salt from her fingers and grabbed her laptop.

"The only way to go about this is to be systematic. We need to write down all the possibilities of what he could have said. Baa, bah with an *h*, bol, ranch, rain, itch. Maybe he said range? Maybe he said pa? Maybe he said puh? Am I right?"

Nettie nodded. She wanted to believe she'd heard him correctly, but his voice was so mumbled she could be sure.

Anya grabbed a google sheet and started making columns, typing alternatives in each. "So, we put down any of the things it might have been, then we go through and see if something comes together."

"And if that doesn't work?"

Anya paused in her typing, thinking about how to solve this riddle. "Then we shoot in the dark. But for now, let's try a scientific method."

Retrospective No.2: Mary Germaine

Mary's face was a simmering storm cloud as she trudged through the forest. Her parents had known it would rain, yet still dragged her out on this trail, and now Mary's feet were soaked and freezing. The dampness from below was like an icy caterpillar making its way up from her ankles to her thighs. And despite the extra-large raincoat, the chill still seemed to penetrate her bones.

To get back at them, she'd done exactly what they'd warned against: she wandered off. Their constant need to volunteer, dragging her along to help clean parks, beaches, highways, and this godforsaken forest—it always infuriated her. Maybe if they realized she was missing, it would jolt some sense into them and make them regret being so pushy.

Mary trudged through the moss-covered forest floor of the towering redwoods, the faint sound of drizzle echoing in her ears. Her fingers were turning numb from the cold, rubbing against the rough bark and mud as she climbed over fallen tree branches. Suddenly, the rain stopped, and rays of sun poked between gaps in the canopy above, casting a gentle light on Mary's face. She glanced around, trying to make sense of her surroundings, and realized she was lost. Taking a deep breath to calm her racing heart, she began following her own footsteps back through the forest. Suddenly, a loud squeal jolted her and made her jump.

Mary's eyes darted from side to side, searching for the source of the desperate cries. The sound reminded her of the human screams from the horror movies she had snuck downstairs to watch with her parents late at night. Her heart raced as the noise became more anguished and intense.

Curiosity drove her forward toward the pitiful crying. Cautiously, she traced the source of the sound deeper into the forest, through thick moss and patches of wildflowers.

Suddenly, she stopped in her tracks. Just ahead of her lay a small animal, writhing around in agony on the ground. Its tail was short and banded like a raccoon's, and Mary thought for a moment that it might have more than four legs. It reminded her of the ferrets in the pet shop back home—the way they loved to wrestle and play together. But this creature wasn't playing; it was obviously in terrible pain, and Mary felt a sharp pang of sadness as she watched. It flooded her mind with images of alien creatures coming to Earth to skin animals alive and then leave them to die, exposed and vulnerable to bacteria and infection. She shivered from both fear and cold.

Mary tentatively took a step forward, the twigs and leaves crunching under her boots. The creature stopped moving. She watched the ribs move in and out, which was also strange because it seemed to be two animals breathing at opposite times.

She could feel the tension in the air as she whispered softly, "Shh…" A ripple seemed to move over the animal's body like an invisible string had been wound around it and pulled tight. Mary kneeled down to get a closer look and realized it was tangled up in some netting, just like the birds that got caught in her grandmother's badminton set.

Mary gingerly stepped closer, her boots squelching in the muddy grass as she crouched next to it and pulled her hands into her raincoat, expecting the animal would react poorly to her intervention. She reached out with both hands and clutched at the animal's slim body with the cuffs of her jacket, feeling tiny bones beneath its matted fur. The creature twitched and spun around with lightning speed, baring its teeth and releasing an eerie scream that made Mary fall back onto her butt.

Its face was malformed with matted fur and raw flesh. Tiny, razor-sharp teeth protruded from the mouth at awkward angles from a jaw that appeared dislocated, the tongue a hideous swollen purple red. A pungent, sour smell wafted off the creature as it hissed, lunging toward her.

Mary released a startled shriek and scrambled backward, terror gripping her heart like an icy hand. The creature replied with a shrill, inhuman cry that sent shivers down her spine. Why had she been so foolish as to follow the screams?

The animal thrashed around, clawing at its own hind legs before finally breaking out of the net. It scuttled closer to Mary on too many thin, spindly legs.

"Go away!" Mary shouted, kicking frantically at the air. The monster hesitated, then darted forward with a loud screech. In sheer panic, Mary kicked her foot out and caught the beast on its side. Startled by the contact, it shuddered and ran off into the underbrush until it was gone from sight.

Mary stumbled through the woods, her breath ragged and erratic. Pain shot through her right hand like a lightning bolt, and she quickly brought it to her face, dark blood dripping from between her fingers. She shuddered again as the cold dampness of the soil seeped into her pants.

Her left hand remained shaking as she pushed her raincoat's sleeve up, revealing a deep red gash with four puncture wounds clearly visible in the center. She gasped when she noticed a few teeth marks in between each fang mark—the animal had bitten down hard enough to penetrate her thick rubber raincoat. Fear and confusion coursed through her veins as the coppery smell of blood filled the air around her.

She winced as the warmth of her own blood seeped through her fingers, saturating the sleeve of her shirt. She heard footsteps and looked up to see her parents racing toward her, their faces etched with worry. They frantically helped her to the car and drove to the hospital, passing strangers who gawked at them like they were mad. Once inside, the nurses questioned her constantly, wanting to know every detail about what kind of animal had attacked her. After a few long hours in the emergency room and multiple injections later, she received permission to go home.

Seven months later, they moved to Lost Grove. The rare home had come up for sale, and her parents, who adored the natural surroundings and access to the lost coastal beaches, pounced. They had to outbid another couple and went a little over what they were comfortable with, but it was an indulgence they were happy to make. A month after that—when they'd fully settled in—Mary began to notice the changes in herself.

She'd developed an unusual hunger. The sharp smell of crayon shavings would cause her mouth to water. Every day on her walk to school, the smallest pebbles scattered along the sidewalk drew her attention. She imagined their cool, metallic, briny taste melting on her tongue. She had accidentally swallowed her mother's pearl earring after she'd slyly rolled it around beneath her tongue for hours without realizing it. As the initial shock wore off, she finally accepted that deep down, she'd wanted to swallow it.

One day, it all came to a head. Mary trudged downstairs, a heavy exhaustion settled into her shoulders. She had managed to finish her homework without any prompting from her parents, who seemed disinterested in any aspect of her life outside the four walls of their home. She could smell the raw meat before she even entered the kitchen, and it made her stomach churn uncomfortably. Her mother was bustling around the kitchen, sprinkling parmesan cheese over each meatball she rolled between her palms with an expert delicacy, the moist, squishing sound amplified in Mary's ears. A burning sensation erupted in her gums, followed by excruciating pain radiating from her two top eyeteeth. Before she could stifle it, a gasp escaped through clenched teeth.

"Mary," her mother said, jumping, "don't scare me like that. Don't make such noises unless you're dying, really. It's overdramatic."

Mary moved forward without thinking, grabbed one meatball from the aluminum tray, and shoved it in her mouth. The sensation was glorious, the texture scintillating, explosions of flavor that took over her tongue. Iron, earth, salt. A deep moan rolled out from within her before she realized what was happening. Out of nowhere, her mother's tight grasp grabbed her jaw and forced open her clenched teeth, pulling out some of the raw meat.

"What on earth is wrong with you?" she scolded.

Mary licked her lips.

"Go upstairs. Go to your room!" her mother ordered.

Mary did as instructed, retreating to her room and worrying over the ramifications. She heard her mother's hushed voice explaining the incident to her father when he got home from work, then felt their footsteps coming up the stairs to talk to her.

They talked about her acting out because of the move and how she wasn't happy leaving her friends, but it wasn't her choice to make. They were the adults, and they made these kinds of decisions. Lost Grove was a one-of-a-kind place to live.

The second time Mary defied her parents, it was on purpose. Her stomach felt so empty, and the tantalizing smell of grilled burgers wafted in the air. She inched closer to the grill, where she saw a raw burger sizzling over the flames. She grabbed it off the flames, shoveling raw meat into her mouth. Her father reached out to slap it from her hands but ended up connecting his palm with her face instead. The group erupted in gasps as Mary stood firm and defiant.

Fury rose within her, so she marched up to the picnic table and grabbed three corn-on-the-cob holders from their plates. She could feel one scraping down her throat but welcomed the familiar taste of iron and metal flooding her mouth. Horrified, Mary's parents rushed her to the emergency room for another stomach operation.

After several visits with specialists, they discovered Mary had pica—an eating disorder characterized by an overwhelming compulsion to consume nonfood items such as dirt, safety pins, and nails.

Mary understood that feeling. She could imagine all of those things with their cold metallic taste, the earthy flavor that permeated the raw meat she so desired. When her first menses came at seventeen, Mary took the bus up to Eureka and paid handsomely for a gallon of fresh blood from the butcher. She had to do more than pay him monetarily, but she didn't care. Mary found a secluded place on the beach and drank the blood, feeling her body come alive with each gulp.

Her parents thought it would pass. She'd learned to hide it, learned to fend for herself. She also realized, over time, that the doctors weren't at all right about what she was suffering from. Sure, it was a kind of pica, and she had blood issues, but the transformation of her jaw, the sensitive hearing, the overly perfect eyesight, even the way her flesh seemed to divine minute shifts in the weather. Mary always knew it was more. She had haunted libraries and scoured the web for answers, but all the experts and internet sleuths she consulted could not identify what mysterious creature she'd encountered in the woods that fateful day.

Chapter 8

Let Me Explain

Noble pulled out his phone, his eyes flickering over the texts he had exchanged with his father—still no response. He eyed the teenager behind the cash register: Jake, a classmate from school who wore a bored expression on his round, blemished face. Noble heaved a sigh and stuffed his phone back in his pocket, thankful that Zoe had bounced back from her earlier breakdown; kids were resilient like that.

"$20.77," Jake said, swiping his greasy black hair out of his eyes, only for it to fall right back over them.

Noble nodded, already sliding his card into the machine. He punched in his PIN, waiting for the command to remove his card.

"Crazy news today, huh?" Jake offered.

Noble nodded and removed his card. "Yeah, man."

"Do you think it's someone from school?"

"No, we would have heard something by now."

Jake handed Noble the receipt. "Yeah, probably. I saw that cop guy—"

The sliding doors whooshed open, giving off a slight squeak that never seemed to go away no matter how much Brady, the owner of the local grocery, tried to fix it.

"Noble!" exclaimed an older gentleman, stepping into the store and approaching him.

Noble turned to see his dad's friend, Paddy, a few shades shy of stumbling over his own two feet. Patrick Kipp, nicknamed Paddy, had black hair he kept buzzed close to his scalp and earth-brown skin representative of his Indigenous blood. He was about five foot ten, with thick-set shoulders and corded, muscular arms. He had a beaked nose with a mushed quality due to too many busted noses in his youth.

"Hey, Paddy," Noble said.

"Hey, Paddy," Jake added.

Paddy lifted a hand in greeting toward Jake but focused on Noble, who stepped away from the checkout with his bag of groceries. "Your dad left early this morning."

Noble nodded. "Yep."

"Ah, well…"

Noble waited for him to say more, but Paddy just patted his pockets and surveyed the store.

"Here to get some bread," Paddy said, pointing toward the aisle.

"Okay," Noble said, trying not to laugh. He could smell what he guessed was whiskey on Paddy's breath, not that he'd ever had any. Most of his friends weren't interested in drinking yet, save for Ryker and Nate, who snuck a beer here and there.

"What'd you get?"

Noble nodded toward the bag. "Mom needs cream for the morning, and Zoe needed cereal with loads of sugar, you know."

Paddy stuck his hand in the bag and peeked in. "Lucky Charms. Those fuckers are delicious."

Noble couldn't help but laugh a little now. "They are, yeah."

"You don't eat any of that, though, do you? Lean and healthy track star!" Paddy wobbled back, extending his arms wide to match his smile.

"Not usually."

"Good." Paddy leaned forward now, peering into the bag once more. "And some juice. That for you?"

"All of us."

"I might get some juice," Paddy said, finally sauntering into the store.

"Sounds good," Noble said, turning for the door.

"See ya 'round, kid." Paddy waved. "Oh, hey," he called, stopping Noble from leaving. "You okay? You need anything?"

Noble smiled at the gesture. Paddy was always keeping an eye out for the Andalusian family while Noble's father was away. It was clear that these two men shared a deep connection from their time serving in the military together. He felt a sense of brotherhood between them.

"Nah. We're good," Noble replied.

"Okay. You let me know," Paddy said, waving again and heading down the bread aisle.

"Will do. See ya later," Noble said and stepped outside, nearly running into a petite woman with thin grey hair hanging limply to her shoulders. "Oh, sorry," he said, meeting her eyes briefly before looking away quickly.

She smiled politely, about to apologize for bumping into him, but when she looked up and noted who she'd nearly run into, the smile faded from her face, and her lips thinned into a hard line.

"Sorry," Noble repeated quietly, taking a slow step backward as he remembered the moment from a couple of years ago. He'd been here with his dad, and this same woman had stared hard at his father and said, "You shouldn't feel right showing your face around town. You shouldn't feel right walking by me like I mean nothing to you when you know what happened to my baby girl!"

The memory came back quick and fierce, and though the woman had already moved on, Noble hesitated a moment on the sidewalk before heading toward home. He had never thought much about what the woman had said, being only ten years old. But something about the woman's face now, still hard and angry, coupled with what she said all those years back, gave Noble an extremely uneasy feeling. A chilly breeze blew down Main Street, scattering dry leaves across his path. He stuffed his free hand into his jacket pocket.

He kept his head down, starting his walk home as he remembered the woman's harsh words from when he was a child, wondering what she meant about her daughter. The sound of metal clicking against metal pulled his attention out of his thoughts. Four houses down, Mary Germaine exited her front yard with her running gear. Noble's heart kicked into his throat as he stopped in his tracks. It had been five days since the morning Noble last encountered Mary, five long days he had been harboring a secret that had been eating away at him, the clarity of which was still a mystery.

It was early Saturday morning, just before dawn, when Noble had left home for his daily run. He wanted to get it in early so he could drive up to Ross Ranch with his dad to help at the stables. The size of Lost Grove didn't afford many options for routes, but that morning he chose the one he traveled least, the one that curved around the ocean inlet into the forest. Having heard rumors and stories his whole life as reasons not to go into parts of the forest, mainly from Stan, his senses were always on edge when traveling this course.

Not that Noble believed in tales of wendigos, wormholes, and giant owl women, but a part of him feared what truths these stories spawned from. The factual news reports and photos of strange deer creatures and unidentified ocean life were enough to open the mind about what bizarre possibilities hid in the depths of Lost Grove.

That morning, headphones on, Noble rounded the corner from the ocean into the woods when his eyes caught something at the furthest stretch of the road at the precipice of the forest. It was just bright enough from the rise of dawn to make out some detail. What he at first assumed was a large animal came into focus to be a person, Mary Germaine. She was crouched, sitting high on the balls of her feet, her back hunched, head dropped low over something she held in her arms. His pace had slowed to a stop, and he'd slowly shuffled to his right onto the road to see what she was cradling. Thin, pale limbs came into focus, a small foot, a tiny hand, the soft swirl of hair on a small head. She was holding a child.

Panic flowed into him, his brain making sensible suggestions. The last image to register of the distant scene—the one that had plagued his mind ever since—was the blood. Not just on the body, dripping from the neck and down the naked, slim shoulder and arm of the child, but around Mary's mouth. Noble gasped audibly as he stumbled to the side of the road, scrambling to hide behind a tree. He thought he had gone unnoticed, but then Mary's head darted in his direction. She looked shocked and afraid, but also fierce, as if she were ready to defend herself. It was too far away to be sure. Noble hoped she hadn't locked eyes on him, but as he slowly backed away, her eyes tracked him.

Noble turned and ran at top speed back home and hadn't mentioned a word to anyone since. More than once, he had considered walking down this very street to confront Mary, hoping she would tell him something logical, anything that didn't involve her drinking blood from a child's neck. Perhaps this was precisely why he had unconsciously taken this route home.

Mary froze mid-stride at the sight of Noble Andalusian. She'd been living with a duplicitous feeling: wanting to stay far away from the boy and needing to speak with him to clear the air. If that was even possible. That she needed to fabricate the truth didn't make the task any easier. There was simply no way that he could understand who she was. What she was.

Mary cautiously held her hands out. "Noble, I think we really need to talk."

Noble swallowed down the fear at what he might hear fall from her mouth. "I agree with you. We should talk."

The coldness in the boy's voice pierced Mary's heart. She looked left and right at her neighbors' houses. "Maybe we can go inside—"

"Your house? I don't think so," he replied, hoisting up the bag of groceries.

"I promise I can explain everything. If we can just sit on my front—"

"I'm good right here."

Tears welled up in Mary's eyes. She damned herself, not wanting to show weakness. Weakness that might indicate guilt. She held her breath and emotions in as she inched toward Noble. She kept her voice low. "Okay. I understand why you might be—"

"Wary to be near you? I'm sure you do," Noble said. The arrogance in his tone was so unfamiliar his head actually recoiled.

Mary nodded, her gaze falling to the ground. "Yes, I can understand… not knowing what you saw or the circumstances that led me to be…in that position."

Noble let go of the tension in his shoulders. The pain in Mary's voice, on her face, was palpable. He reminded himself that he swore he would give her a chance to explain what had happened. And really, he didn't know Mary, despite seeing her around town since he was a child.

Noble motioned toward Mary's house. "Did you want to sit on your front porch?"

Mary looked up, her cheeks wet from tears. She nodded. "If that's okay with—"

"It's fine. Let's just"—Noble paused and shrugged—"get this over with."

Mary nodded and turned back toward her home, opening the gate and allowing Noble to walk past her. She left the gate open, not wanting the boy to feel locked in.

Noble walked up to the front porch and set the groceries down, almost laughing at himself. He had acted like Mary was a physical threat to him, and here she was in tears, so meek with her movements and gestures. He sat down and motioned for her to join him. "I'm listening."

Mary sat down a few feet away and glanced up at him. "I was on my morning run, just like you, and I…I saw this, this…boy lying on the side of the road, half in the grass leading into the woods. He was covered in blood, and…"

Noble grimaced. "What…how did—"

"It was from an animal, but—"

"An animal? What kind of animal could…I mean, where was he bleeding from?"

Mary motioned to her neck and then her midsection. "There were gouges, scratches, huge scratches, all over. The blood was mainly coming from its neck. But more was—"

"Its? What do you mean 'its'?"

Mary shook her head vigorously. "His…the boy's…I can't imagine what kind of animal could have made marks so…so vicious, so deep. I've thought about it all week, a lion, a wolf, a cougar…"

Noble furrowed his brow. "A lion?"

"I don't know, Noble," Mary pleaded. "All I'm saying is that the marks were so deep that…it had to have been something like that."

They'd had a few cougars in the area from time to time, but most of them stayed deeper in Devil's Cradle State Park. "Okay. And…you what?"

Mary looked down at the ground. "I checked to see if he was still alive. I checked for a pulse in his wrist and neck…and then I tried to give him CPR," she lied, knowing full well that the thing that looked like a boy was long gone.

Noble wrinkled his nose. "CPR?"

Mary looked directly at Noble. "I didn't…have you ever come across a dead body before?"

Noble swallowed heavily.

"Well, I hadn't, and I didn't know what to do."

Noble motioned toward her. "Why didn't you… Did you call the police? Chief Richards?"

"Do you run with your phone?" Mary asked.

"Yeah, I listen to music while—"

"Well, I don't. So, I did what I did. And I tried to give him mouth to mouth, which is why I had…" Mary pointed to her mouth and threw her hand out, frustrated. Frustrated and ashamed at the one major fabrication she knew she had to tell. In her greatest moment of weakness, pressing her mouth to the neck of the not-child and sucking in the fresh blood was something no one could understand. No one but Story Palmer.

Noble sat with the information, playing back the morning in his head. It lined up, yet something still felt off to him. His eyes darted back and forth. "Okay, I get that. But, then what?"

Mary narrowed her eyes at the boy. "What do you mean?"

"I mean, you checked his pulse, gave him CPR, whatever. So, was he dead? And then what did you do?" Noble could feel his heart rate rising.

"I…" Mary shook her head. "I knew it was dead the moment I saw it, but I just didn't—"

Noble jumped to his feet. "It! Why do you keep saying 'it'?"

Mary stood up, motioning him to keep his voice down. "I didn't—"

"Just tell me."

Mary dropped her gaze, contemplating at a rapid pace the ramifications of what she was about to say. She looked back up and stepped in closer to him. "Noble, it wasn't a child. It wasn't even human."

Noble took a step back. "What?"

"There are…out in the woods"—Mary pointed over her shoulder—"these things run around at night, led by their—"

"Whoa, whoa, whoa." Noble held a hand up. "What the hell are you even talking about?"

Mary moved toward the boy again. "Have you not seen them? Have you not heard others talk about them?"

Noble was so thrown off course he didn't know what to say or do.

"Has not a single friend of yours told you they saw something in the woods that didn't look right? Wasn't right?"

Noble gazed inwardly, the question igniting a memory. It was Nettie. He remembered when they were all younger, Nettie tried to tell them that someone had stolen her brother. Stole him and replaced him with a…not-human? Was that what she said?

"They did," Mary said, her voice dropping. Relief washed over her. She hadn't been wrong to speak it.

"I remem…I don't. It doesn't matter," Noble stuttered and looked back at Mary. "Did you even call the cops? Ever?"

"Noble, you're not listening. They're not right. They smell of wet, rotted plastic. Their eyes, there's nothing behind them. Their fingerprints, Noble, they're not formed all the way. The skin is—"

"I gotta go," Noble said, spinning back to grab his groceries.

Mary ran over to him. "It was an animal that killed it, Noble."

"I don't care." Noble headed for the open gate.

"There was nothing to call about. It wasn't…the boy wasn't a boy."

Noble spun around after passing through the gate. "Mary, look, I don't think you're a bad person. You've been nothing but courteous to me ever since I've known you."

Mary stopped, her skin tingling from the scent of the worked-up boy.

"I don't know what happened. I don't know what you're talking about, that there are little children-things in the woods that aren't really children. But I believe you weren't responsible. We're good. Okay?"

Mary bit her cheek hard. Hard enough that blood flowed over her tongue. Sadness returned to her as her nerves quelled. "I'm sorry I frightened you."

"It's…it's fine. I don't know what I…"

"I know what people say about me." Mary's eyes again welled up with tears.

"I don't care what anyone says about anyone. Believe me," Noble stated assuredly. "But I'm going to go now. I have to get home."

Mary nodded, her eyes meeting his. "Thank you."

Noble nodded back. "Sure. It's cool. We're cool."

Mary watched as the boy hurried down the street. Would she wake up in the middle of the night to Chief Bill Richards pounding at her door? Oh, the irony. Or would she wake up in peace, go for a run, and maybe even see Noble crossing her path and smile at him?

Would he smile at her?

Chapter 9

Filling the Board

The office of the Lost Grove Police Department was a modest wood building that might be mistaken for a roadside motel if it had more doors. Quaint as it was in size, it was more than enough for the squad of five, with rotating volunteers throughout the year.

Dusk had fallen, and with it, the temperature had dropped even lower. Seth entered through the front door, take-out dinner in hand, eager to start putting the pieces of the case together. The recently polished linoleum floor of the small waiting area squeaked under his boots. No one manned the small reception desk tucked to the left of the door. Flyers about local events, missing pets, fall burn schedules, and missing people filled the corkboard to the right. Seth always looked over the faces as he came and went, memorizing their contours. He was curious about the one for a young woman, blonde and with a brilliant smile that sparkled through the inkjet print on cheap copy paper, but had yet to ask why they had a flyer for a missing person from the state of Oregon on their board.

Seth made his way into the bullpen, which consisted of three desks. Two sat facing each other, the other tucked toward the right wall facing into the bullpen. Facing each other at the adjoining desks were their two youngest officers.

Joe Casey was a relatively recent graduate, having just crossed his one-year mark with the team. He stood maybe five foot five with his boots on, had sandy-blonde hair perpetually under his police-issued baseball hat, and a slim body that looked as if he never learned how to survive on anything other than hot dogs and ramen. He had a cleft chin and was attempting to grow a mustache, though that wasn't working out for him so far. What Joe lacked in physical stature, he made up for with an eagerness to learn and follow through with tasks given to him with enthusiastic zeal. If it weren't for the earnestness in his eyes, one might think his agreeable demeanor was mocking sarcasm.

Sasha Kingsley served as a polar opposite in just about every way imaginable. She towered over Joe at six feet even, had a muscular physique that spoke to years in the gym, tattoos covering her neck, perhaps elsewhere, and her skin the color of rich cedar. Sasha was, in fact, scathingly and proudly sarcastic, but also sharp, quick-witted, and a genial ball buster. She'd been with the department for five years, and from what Seth had seen over the past three months, he believed she was the strongest of his officers. She was serious about her job and routinely studied up on cases from all over the country. Sasha liked to pick his brain about cases in other cities and what the life of a homicide detective was like. Seth gave her two years before she was off to a bigger city and bigger position.

Both were busy writing up their reports for the materials collected at the beach as potential evidence. Seth gave them a nod in greeting. The most seasoned officer by decades, Eddie Cabrera worked the graveyard shift and wouldn't be in for several hours.

Behind the bullpen stood the chief's office. The sergeant's office was beside it, with windows looking out onto the parking lot, though Seth spent little time occupying it. He preferred to be in the bullpen with the rest of the team. The San Francisco Police Department was like living off a busy interstate with its constant, audible buzz. It was a sound Seth hadn't realized he enjoyed until he spent some time inside LGPD, which, more often than not, was silent save for tapping keys, creaking chairs, and jangling keys. Sitting amongst the three Lost Grove officers was a meager substitute, but it was better than the deafening silence of a closed-in office.

"Seth!" Bill called, waving at him from his office doorway. He held some photos in his hands.

Shortly after leaving the library, Seth got a text from Bill letting him know that Sarah Elizabeth's parents positively identified her body and that he had surprising news.

Seth held up his finger. "Be there in one minute."

Bill nodded and moved back into his office.

"Sasha, Joe, how'd the rest of the afternoon go?" Seth asked, dropping the takeout on his desk.

"I guess about as well as it could, considering how the day started," Sasha replied, eyes fixed on her computer screen as she typed.

"You handled it well," Seth said.

"You think I wouldn't?" she asked.

Seth laughed. "I had no doubt. You turn up anything at Devil's Cradle?"

"Yeah, a lot of fucking trash," Sasha replied. Seth had asked her to search the campgrounds and park for any abandoned vehicles, camping gear, or clothes. "I swear if I ever catch anyone just throwing shit on the ground, I'm going to taser them."

"Just entice them to make an aggressive move at you first."

Sasha grinned and continued typing.

Seth walked over and stood next to Joe, who was glaring at his computer screen.

Joe looked up at him, adjusting his hat. "Hey, Seth. I was just doing some research on—never mind. We didn't find a whole lot out there. The beach was actually pretty clean. Only thing I found was a lighter and a sandal. Sasha found a used condom," he said, pointing at her.

"Fucking disgusting," Sasha replied.

Seth glanced at her. "Did you bag it and—"

"Of course. Sent it in for testing right away."

"Good."

"But I bet you've seen much worse in all your years as a detective," Joe commented.

"Here we go." Sasha sighed.

"Within days on the force." Seth chuckled.

Joe had a proclivity to look up to Seth like he was some sort of superhero and follow him around like an obedient bloodhound. Seth admired the boy's tenacity and work ethic, seeing a younger version of himself.

"So, what is it you're looking into?"

"Agh, I don't know." Joe motioned toward his screen. "I was just seeing if there were any similar cases along the coast."

Seth leaned on the desk, looking at the screen. "Dead bodies of nude young women found on a beach?"

Sasha looked up. "Creep."

"What? That's literally what we found," Joe defended himself. He looked up at Seth. "I know. It's stupid."

"Not at all. Good instincts. Start broader, though; search 'dead body on beach' and set your search parameters for the last year or two. Then narrow it down from there if you find anything interesting."

"Awesome, thanks!" Joe nodded as he started typing in his new search.

"Yay, Joe's learning," Sasha exclaimed.

Seth patted Joe on the shoulder. "Keep looking. Let me know what you find. Sasha, you heading to Ross Ranch tomorrow?"

"First thing in the morning."

"Great. Call me if you find anything."

"Will do."

"Oh, have one of you printed out the transcript of the call we got this morning reporting the body?"

Sasha and Joe exchanged a quizzical look.

"What? It's not a big deal if you haven't; just print it up and bring it into Bill's office for me," Seth said, taking a step in that direction.

"Um, Seth?" Joe said sheepishly.

"What is it?"

"There wasn't really a…"

"Jesus," Sasha said and looked up at Seth. "There was no call. Didn't Bill tell you?"

Seth swallowed hard, images from his catatonic walk toward Sarah Elizabeth's body flashing in his mind. "Clearly not," he said, probably, yet unknowingly, lying.

Sasha shook her head. "Well, he was pretty shaken up when we arrived, so I'm not surprised. He got a note. Someone pinned it on his front door, knocked, and then ran for the hills."

Joe pointed at Sasha. "Yeah."

Sasha sneered at him. "Nice input."

Seth's lungs compressed around his heart as if he were being suffocated by a sumo wrestler. A note? Who the hell would leave a note? If Bill had mentioned it to him, which logic would dedicate he had, Seth had just spent the day going through his interviews blind. "You're telling me that someone stumbled upon Sarah Grahams's body, drove over to Bill's house, left him a note, and then left? Did they sign the note?"

Sasha shook her head. "Nope."

Seth looked over at Bill's office, electrons firing through his brain, racing to piece together this information.

"They could have walked."

Seth turned back to Joe. "What?"

Joe adjusted his hat again. "You said 'drove over to Bill's.' They could have walked."

"Wow," Sasha replied.

"What? People walk."

"Yes. Yes, they do, Joe."

Seth nodded, turning away from the bickering duo, and walked as slowly as he could to Bill's office. How was he going to approach this? Risk asking Bill why he hadn't told him about the note when, in all likelihood, he had? For that matter, what else could Bill have told him he didn't consciously process? Seth needed to pull himself together and start acting like the detective he'd left behind in San Francisco. There was already a preponderance of mysteries in a case hardly twelve hours old.

Seth walked in and shut the door behind him. Bill stood in front of a crime scene board, pinning up a photo.

"Hey, Bill."

"Seth. Looking forward to hearing about your day," Bill said as he stared at photos of Sarah Elizabeth across the board: high school class photos, family photos, and photos of her lifeless body on the beach. "I got these up here like you asked me to. There are dozens more crime scene photos, but I thought it would be good to see a broader picture of her."

"No, that's good."

"Plus, I brought another board in here just in case," Bill said, motioning to the portable dry-erase board next to his desk.

Seth crossed his arms as he examined the photos. The ones from the beach instantly filled him with anxiety. He was used to the setup, photos of a victim living and dead side by side. He had a strong will for detachment, but it never stopped him from seeing the loss of human life and understanding the effect it could have on the victim's circle of family, friends, or coworkers. However, there was no way of mentally or emotionally detaching from Sarah Elizabeth after what he had experienced. Twice.

"Why isn't the note up here?" Seth asked, taking a calculated risk.

"Oh, I…" Bill walked over to his desk, rummaging through folders and paperwork. He pulled a crime scene bag from under a stack of old files with the note sealed inside. He brought it over to Seth, handing it to him. "Sorry, you said photos, so…"

Seth grabbed the bag. His brow furrowed as he noticed the lavender paper and fresh ink, not yet reading the message. "Why is this still here?"

"I, um…"

"This should be at the lab, being scoured for fingerprints, fibers. We should have copies."

Bill scratched the back of his neck, arching an eyebrow as he looked up at Seth. "You told me to keep it here, Seth. I asked you if you wanted me to hold on to it so you could examine it. You said that sounded good."

Seth sneered, directed inwardly at himself for such a colossal fuckup. "Sorry, I guess I should have known you meant to keep a copy."

Seth shook his head. "No. It's my fault, Bill. I was too focused on the body." Which was true enough.

"I can have Joe run it up there now," Bill said, stepping toward the door.

"Hold on. Let's have a look at it together while we have it." Seth finally brought the note closer to his face to read.

You'll want to bring the forensic team to Mourner's Beach.
There's a body.
It's Sarah Elizabeth Grahams.
Hint: She's under the massive driftwood, near the dune grass.

"'Hint?'" Seth verbalized while his heart beat heavy. He looked up at Bill. "This is highly unnerving."

"I know it."

"This is worded like a game. I mean, Bill, who, A, wouldn't call 911? And B, leave you a hint?"

Bill shook his head. "Hell if I know. Been driving me crazy since that knock woke me up."

Seth squinted, looking back down at the note, rereading it, taking in the penmanship, the choice of lavender paper. Seth looked back at Bill and held the note up. "This was either left by the killer—"

"Killer? We don't even know if—"

"Or by someone with a seriously sick sense of humor."

Bill nodded. "I won't argue with that."

"Either way, it's someone who likely knows more than we do at this stage." Seth started pacing, his adrenaline going through the roof. He was so angry with himself, he wanted to punch a hole in Bill's wall. All the wasted time. Focus. "Clearly, it's someone who knew Sarah Elizabeth. That's got to narrow it down some."

"Definitely does. But I don't think it's someone who went to school with her. The way it's written doesn't come across as…youthful, I guess."

"I agree," Seth said, looking back at the note.

"Plus, I can't imagine too many around her age would know or care where I live."

"But you must know the people who do know where you live. You've been sitting with this all day, Bill. Do you at least have an idea of who might have written this?"

Bill threw his hand in the air and sighed. "Seth, I know every single person in this town, most of them well. This could be a hundred different people."

"Well, we're going to have to start knocking on the doors of those hundred people."

"We haven't even put out a press release yet, much less—"

"I know. Once we're at a place where we're confident in releasing Sarah's name."

"Won't be long before it spreads, anyway. Richard and Bess will probably talk to someone, and you've been asking around about her."

"Even more urgent for us to gather what we have, what we know, and come up with a concrete plan of action."

Bill nodded.

Seth handed Bill the evidence bag. "Have Joe make multiple copies of this and then get it directly up to the lab."

"You got it."

"Bill." Seth stopped him. "Where are the rest of Wes's photos?"

Bill crossed over to his desk and grabbed a manila folder and handed it to Seth. "Here ya go."

"Come right back with the copies," Seth said, grabbing the folder.

"On it," Bill said, and quickly exited the room.

Seth ran a hand through his hair and let out a quiet yet weighted exhale. Somehow he had managed to tiptoe around dropping the ball, as inadvertent as it was. The lost moments on the beach ate away at him like a vulture pulling pieces of flesh from a dead coyote. The unearthly feeling of seeing Sarah's body, the driftwood, floating toward the scene, came flooding back through his body. Seth shook his head, willing his mind to focus on the case and not allowing the experience to overtake him once again. Whatever he had gone through could wait. Sarah Elizabeth deserved answers.

Seth marched over and grabbed the other board Bill brought in and rolled it over next to the one filled with photos. Opening the folder, he began slowly leafing through them. He looked up at the board and moved the family photos and the class photos over to one side, clearing the room for more crime scene photos. He grabbed the small disc-shaped magnets and added five more photos to the board. Photos that spoke to him. Photos that told him there was a clue waiting to be discovered.

Bill walked back into the room and shut the door. He joined Seth at the board and handed him one copy of the note. "Here's a copy. Joe's on his way now. Said he would text us to confirm it was dropped off and in the proper hands."

Seth looked over the note again before placing it on top of the folder he was holding and refocusing on the photos. "Thanks, Bill."

Bill surveyed the added photos. "You see something?"

Seth took a step back, shoving the folder under his arm. He studied the way Sarah Elizabeth's body was found, her legs together, bent casually to the side, the one arm twisted behind her back. Her other arm, bent at the elbow, forearm lying horizontally away from her body. Seth narrowed his eyes, leaning in.

"What are you looking at?" Bill asked as he stepped up next to him.

"There's something about the way she's laid out. It bugged me at the time, but I couldn't say why," Seth said, knowing full well why. His brain had been scrambled, his focus nowhere near where it should have been.

"Can you now?"

"It looks posed."

Bill leaned in closer. "You mean…"

"Yes, like someone displayed her like this on purpose."

"So, what is it that looks posed to you?" Bill inquired.

Seth pointed to the main overhead photo of her body. "You had originally thought her body was twisted up because of the ocean."

"Yep."

"I gave it some thought as well, but as I said there, I don't think she drowned, and I think we'll find that out as soon as we hear from Wes."

"Well, I—"

Seth tapped the photo, his finger on Sarah Elizabeth's legs. "So, why are her legs placed like this? Even if this was a suicide, her body being in this position doesn't make sense. It's almost like whoever put her here was being…respectful by not having her legs spread out."

Bill winced at the thought. "I sort of get that, but she is still naked."

"And look at her left arm," Seth continued. "I was so focused on the arm bent behind her back I didn't notice what this looked like."

"Like it's broken?" Bill guessed.

"No, like she's pointing. Someone could have even tried to extend her pointer finger here, and it could have just curled back in like this."

Bill scratched the side of his face. "Okay, but for what purpose?"

"To tell us something," Seth said. He leaned back from the board and held up the copy of the note. "Just like the note."

Bill sighed. "I don't know."

Seth paced once again. "The note, the body…this is all something a serial killer would do."

Bill guffawed. "A serial killer? We don't even know if this is a—"

"A murder? No, not yet. But what do we know so far? We know someone knocked on your door and left you a playful note regarding a dead young woman on the beach. Sarah Elizabeth was naked, splayed out in a bizarre pose. No clothes, no car, miles away from the nearest house."

Bill held up his hands. "I know. I agree, it's beyond suspicious, but until we hear from Wes, we can't assume this was a murder, much less a serial killer."

Seth handed Bill the folder of remaining photos and the copy of the note. "No, we assume nothing. What we do is start working the case. And that starts here." Seth grabbed a black marker and stepped over to the blank dry-erase board. He turned back to Bill. "You said you had surprising news. What is it?"

Bill's eyes lit up, clearly excited to share what he had learned. "Richard and Bess say they hadn't seen or talked to Sarah Elizabeth in over two years. They say she hasn't been back to Lost Grove since January, two and a half years ago."

"That actually lines up with what I heard."

Bill almost looked disappointed. "I'll be damned. From who?"

"One of her best friends, Jeremy Stapleton."

Bill pointed to his left. "The kid that works over at the Inn?"

Seth nodded. "That's right. He has no clue what happened. The way he tells it, she just cut off communication. With her parents, with him, and with her other best friend, Brigette Lowe, out of nowhere. I'm gonna talk to her tomorrow. I also spoke with a teacher she was very close to, Gretchen Young—"

"I know her well. She taught both of my girls."

"And Story Palmer—"

"Huh. Everyone knows her."

Seth cocked his head to the side, not sure what to make of that remark. "And no one has seen Sarah Grahams since that time." Seth wrote her name in the top left corner, underlined it, and wrote 'Not seen in Lost Grove since Jan. 2021.' Seth turned around. "So, where has she been?"

"In Texas. At Baylor."

"Yet we found her at Mourner's Beach this morning, and she's currently at the morgue with Wes in Eureka. How did she get here? When did she get here?"

"Drove?" Bill guessed.

Seth turned around and wrote 'Missing Clues' next to Sarah's name, underlined it, and wrote 'Missing vehicle.' He turned back to Bill. "That's certainly a strong possibility. Did you get the make and model of her car from her parents?"

"They said she didn't have one. They drove her to the airport after that winter break. Doesn't mean she didn't obtain one."

"Good. So, we need to look for any abandoned vehicles, run the plates, and see what we come up with. We also need to ensure that every vehicle parked on the street or in a driveway belongs to the residents living there."

"We can have Joe and Sasha split up first thing in the morning and get on that."

Seth held up his hand with the marker. "One of them. I have a feeling we're going to need the other one planted at their desk making calls. For starters, we need to get in touch with everyone who knew her at Baylor. Teachers, counselors, roommates, friends. When was the last time she was in class? When's the last time someone saw her there?" Seth wrote 'Last known whereabouts' under 'Missing Clues.'

"Makes sense."

"And to that point, we need to get her bank records. Tracking money is the easiest way to track a person's movements. Did you ask Richard and Bess about money? A monthly or quarterly allowance, anything like that?"

Bill shook his head. "Didn't come to mind at the time."

Seth looked back at the board and wrote 'Track money' under the

'Missing Clues' column. "Two and a half years is a long time. I can understand why her friends, and certainly teachers, wouldn't go down to Baylor to see her. But why the hell didn't Richard or Bess just fly to Texas to go see her?"

Bill shrugged. "I didn't press them too hard, Seth. Didn't seem like the right time."

Seth turned back to Bill. "So, how did they take the news, then?"

Bill stuck his thumb in his belt and let out a sigh. "Before I brought them in?"

"Yeah."

"About as well as you might expect."

"I've seen a gamut of reactions, ranging from stone-cold denial to utter hysteria, so fill me in."

"Well, they were devastated. Richard, in particular, was inconsolable. Bess had to do most of the talking. Said they had been worried sick about her for years."

Seth's eyes narrowed. "Again, why didn't they fly down to ensure she was okay?"

Bill shrugged.

"How long would you and Linda have waited to go see Stacey or Rachel if they cut you off?"

"I get you."

"How long?"

Bill puffed out his cheeks as he imagined the scenario. "Two weeks? Give or take."

Seth nodded and wrote on the board as he spoke. "Here's what I learned today, a throughline if you will. On the positive side, she seemed universally well liked, intelligent, highly motivated, kind. No one had a bad thing to say about Sarah. On the other hand, Gretchen, Jeremy, and Story all say she didn't get along with her parents, that she felt heavily pressured by them, that she wanted to get away."

Bill groaned. "Look, I know all high school kids don't get along with their parents, but Richard and Bess are good people."

"People close to them would have sworn that Jeffrey Dahmer and Ted Bundy were good people."

"Jesus, Seth. What are you trying to say?"

"All I'm saying is that appearances can be deceiving. People tend to present themselves how they want to be seen, not always who they are.

Did you know that Sarah Elizabeth would go to school dressed a certain way, conservatively, and change into different clothes in the bathroom?"

Bill frowned. "What?"

"Mrs. Young is a very observant teacher, and Sarah felt close enough to her to confide in her. She said that Sarah got visibly shaken when talking about how her parents pressured her and how they constantly checked in on her, wanting to know where she was at all times. The picture painted of their relationship was not a good one. That the Grahams didn't bother to go check up on their only daughter, even if just to confirm she was alive and well, for over two and a half years is suspicious."

"They could have followed her on social media," Bill argued.

"And that's another thing," Seth said, pointing the marker in the air. "We'll need to verify this, but according to Jeremy, Sarah had absolutely no social media footprint."

Bill reeled back. "None? Not even Facebook?"

"Not Facebook, not Instagram, not TikTok, nothing. Jeremey was her best friend. He said she never wanted to be on social media." Seth made a note of this on the board to verify the social media claim.

"What? I can't even keep track of all the sites or apps or whatever Stacey and Rachel are on. I can't imagine anyone Sarah's age not being on all that stuff."

"If I had to guess, it would be because she didn't want her parents stalking her." Seth turned around and wrote 'Suspects' on the top right side of the board, underlined it, and wrote 'Richard and Bess Grahams' underneath.

"Now hold on, Seth. You can't possibly think her parents would have something to do with…her death. Just because they didn't get along—"

"Right now, we've got very little to go on, Bill. And until we find actual evidence that points us in a specific direction, anyone who arouses suspicion in this case is a suspect. We follow every lead we have. And unless Wes comes back with suicide as a cause of death, which I don't believe he will, we'll be investigating Sarah Elizabeth's death as a homicide. And statistically speaking, of murder victims, over fifty percent are killed by someone they know, and nearly twenty-five percent by family members."

Bill found it difficult to argue against someone with Seth's experience. The young man he had once saved from suffocating in a cave had spent the last two decades investigating homicides, suicides that looked like homicides, and the reverse. Bill had a single suspicious death case under his belt in that amount of time, and that was seven years ago. "I'll follow your lead on this, Seth."

Seth smiled. "You're still the boss, Bill. So, if you feel like something—"

"Agh!" Bill waved him off. "I'm not stupid enough not to listen to you. I'm lucky you're here for this. We all are."

"Tell me about your conversation with the Grahams. What did they say about this whole cut-off in communication? How'd it come about?"

Bill stepped over to his desk, set down the folder of crime scene photos and the copies of the mysterious note. He picked up his notepad and ran his fingers over his notes. "Bess said Sarah came home for winter break on December 12, 2020. They picked her up from the airport. Said she looked sick, too thin, and that she was having issues with insomnia, something she had apparently been dealing with for a while."

"That fits pretty well with what I heard." Seth wrote 'Insomnia' under Sarah's heading on the board.

"They felt she had changed since going off to Baylor. They admitted there was a lot of tension between them when she came back and that they got into several arguments."

"About what?"

Bill read through his notes and jabbed his finger at the pad. "Well, shit. I guess what you said about her changing clothes at school might not be such a surprise. One thing Bess mentioned was how she dressed, the amount of makeup she had on. She had apparently got a nose ring and that small tattoo on her wrist we saw."

"Grace," Seth stated, the word, the calligraphy, still etched into his mind.

Bill nodded. "Yeah, apparently, that was new."

"I can't imagine it surprised them she might rebel or change."

"No. Bess said she expected Sarah would become her own person. What they weren't expecting was how disrespectful she acted toward them."

Seth raised an eyebrow at Bill. "Which comprised what?"

Bill ran a finger down his notebook. "Raised her voice at them, used profanity, wore short skirts to the dinner table just to spite them." Bill looked up at Seth. "Their words, of course."

"What else did they say about that winter break? And how it ended?"

Bill looked back at his notes. "Well, Bess claims Sarah threatened them and that her actions were becoming violent."

"Violent? What exactly did they classify as violent?" From what he'd heard today, Seth would not have pegged Sarah as being capable of violence toward anyone or anything.

"She said Sarah's tone of voice was filled with rage, that she slammed doors, and one time threw her cell phone at her bed—and this is where the threat comes in—saying she was going to get a new phone number and her own service plan if they didn't leave her alone."

"Leave her alone in what way?"

Bill looked back at Seth. "They didn't specify. I imagine just in general."

Seth wrote 'New cell phone' under the 'Missing Clues' heading and 'Personality change' under 'Missing Clues.' "Well, I'd like to see if Sarah was referring to something more specific."

"What are you thinking?"

"I think her parents were domineering when she lived under their roof; Richard and Bess felt like they were in control. With Sarah halfway across the country, they had no control whatsoever. I'd like to know if that loss of control caused them to behave or act more severely. To have pushed Sarah to feel she had to threaten them, had to shut them out."

"Hm." Bill narrowed his eyes and nodded. "Well, you're the psychology major; you can ask them tomorrow when they come in for their official interview and see what you can suss out."

"I plan on it. What I can't figure out, for the life of me, is why she would also shut out her best friends. By all accounts, they were inseparable. The principal and every teacher I talked to said they hardly saw them apart. And I didn't get the sense from Jeremy that anything negative ever happened between them."

Bill let out a heavy sigh. "I don't know. It's all very strange. I would have to agree with you. I can see why she may have wanted to distance herself from her parents, but why the friends?"

"I'm hoping maybe I hear something from Brigette tomorrow that sheds some more light on it. Maybe something happened between them that Jeremy didn't want to share."

"It's possible."

"Did you ask Bess and Richard if Sarah had a boyfriend or a girlfriend that they knew of?"

Bill dropped his notebook by his side. "That didn't come up. Sorry."

Seth shook his head. "It's fine. We can press them tomorrow. It's just that…Mrs. Young was positive that Sarah wasn't in a relationship with anyone. She even asked her about it, wondering if that was a source of contention with her parents. But Sarah laughed it off, saying she might have time for such things after college. She was studying to be a doctor."

"They mentioned that. Seemed rightfully proud."

"And Jeremy thought the idea of Sarah having a boyfriend or girlfriend was hilarious. He said she never would have had time."

"So, what's your point?" Bill asked.

"Well, Story Palmer was positive that she was seeing someone."

Bill rolled his eyes. "Ms. Palmer. Okay, she saw Sarah Elizabeth with someone she believed to be a lover?"

"No. She didn't see Sarah with anyone. She just has a hunch."

Bill sighed. "So, her best friend and her favorite teacher don't think there was a lover, but Story Palmer does. I'd say her best friend knew her better."

Seth scratched the back of his neck.

"But you're not so sure," Bill said with a sigh.

"Story has been right about a few hunches before."

Bill let his hands fall to his desk. "I don't need reminding of that, thank you."

"She told you Burt was gonna try something with his ex—"

"I know, I know."

"Think of it this way, Bill. If she had a lover that no one seemed to know about, that could explain why no one knew she was back in town."

"Fair enough."

Seth wrote 'Mystery lover' under 'Suspects' and turned to face Bill. "Anything else of note from her parents?"

Bill lifted his notepad and eyed the rest of his notes. "Nothing that we haven't gone over. But there was something I wanted to share with you." Bill walked back to his desk and swapped his notepad for a file thick with papers. "Now, I tried bringing this up at the beach this morning, but you seemed miles away."

Seth looked up and swallowed the lump rising up his throat. "Sorry about that."

Bill waved him off and lifted the file. "There was this case from back in 2015, where a young girl from town, Kelly Fulson, was found dead. Washed up on a beach just north of Mourner's on Jonathan Baume's property."

Seth scowled, mainly at himself. What else had he missed on his mind-bending trip toward Sarah's body? "What happened?"

Bill handed him the file. "Don't know. Never did solve what happened to Kelly, what caused her to be there. Worst part was, she was pregnant."

"Jesus. Was she local as well?"

Bill nodded. "Yep. Was a terrible ordeal. Her parents, Henry and Molly, were beloved in the community. Still are."

Seth narrowed his eyes. "Names sound really familiar, but I can't place them."

"They have a farm just out past Richter's. I'm sure you've seen them around town. At any rate, it was just an awful time. It shook the whole town. It doesn't even seem like that long ago that people got over it. Obviously, her parents and Kelly's younger brother never will. Christ, I feel like I'm reliving it all now. It's gonna be shit once word spreads about Sarah."

"I bet the fact that it's an open case isn't helping."

Bill looked up at Seth. "You think I don't know that?"

Seth held his hands up. "Not how I meant it, Bill. I know nothing about the case."

"I know. I'm sorry. It's just always sat heavy with me. I sure as shit hope this case doesn't turn out the same way."

"We'll make sure that it doesn't."

Bill nodded. "Glad you're here, Seth."

Seth smiled.

Bill threw his hands up. "Anyhow, I can't see how there would be any correlation between that case and this one, but I wanted to dig it back up, just in case."

Seth nodded. "No, that's good. Long time ago, but you never know."

"Oh, here, before I forget." Bill retrieved a sheet of paper from his desk and handed it to Seth. "This is the press release. I kept it vague. Let me know what you think."

Seth grabbed the paper and read the statement out loud. "'Lost Grove Police responded to a call Thursday morning—'"

"Thought best to put it like that."

Seth glanced up. "I would have to agree. We don't want to tip our hat to anything at this point."

Bill nodded.

Seth continued reading. "'…at 5:45 a.m. reporting a body spotted at Mourner's Beach. Police confirmed the person, a young woman, was deceased. No details about the death are available at this time. Police are currently investigating.'"

"Well?"

"Remove 'a young woman.' We don't want to give any information about the sex or age."

Bill frowned. "Right, right."

"And you can cut the bit about no details being available. Just say that we're investigating. We'll have to release another statement in the next couple of days, which will contain more specifics. And, if we're lucky, a cause of death." Seth handed Bill back the statement.

"Thanks, Seth. I'm not used to having—"

"I know," Seth said reassuringly.

"Okay, then, I'll make those changes and send it over to the *Gazette*. Then I'm going to head home to have dinner with the wife. Gonna be a long day tomorrow."

"Sounds good." Seth moved out of the way so Bill could grab his jacket.

"Let me know how the interview with Sarah's friend Brigette goes. I have a meeting first thing tomorrow with Mayor Sumner to fill her in and come up with a plan for a press release."

Seth stepped out into the office ahead of Bill. "We gonna release it tomorrow?"

"Tomorrow night or Saturday morning, I imagine. Would sure like to find out more before we do."

"Hopefully, the autopsy will shed some light on things."

Bill walked past Joe and Sasha. "Good work today, you two. Don't stay too late."

"Goodnight, Bill," Sasha called as he stepped out the front door.

"See ya," Joe meekly called out after that door had closed.

"'See ya,'" Sasha mimicked him.

Seth laughed as he sat at the desk opposite them and grabbed his sandwich. He hadn't eaten a thing all day. After the episode on the beach, his nerves had gotten the better of him. He unwrapped the sandwich and stared at it as Sarah Elizabeth's lifeless face flashed back in his mind. Would he dream about her tonight? Dream about the cave? Would he even be able to sleep?

"You okay, Seth? You need some water or something?"

Seth looked up at Joe, not realizing how long he had been looking down at his sandwich.

"God, shut up, Joe," Sasha said, her face twisted up.

"What? I was just trying to help."

"Help what? He's fine."

"I'm fine," Seth said.

"He looked like he might be sick," Joe offered.

Sasha looked over her shoulder at Seth. "Are you going to be sick?"

"No, honestly, I'm fine," Seth lied.

Sasha looked back to Joe. "He's fine."

Joe shook his head.

"You sound like such a little bitch when you do that," Sasha said as she typed away at her computer.

"Do what?"

"You know what."

Seth laughed and forced himself to take a bite of his sandwich.

Chapter 10

Gemini Rising

Constance "Stan" Hensley eyed the newcomers sitting together on the bleachers on the other side of the racetrack during their allotted Physical Fitness hour. Stan did not believe in physical fitness. She got enough exercise wrestling with her brothers on a daily basis. Instead, she had a small packet of sour gummy worms she intended to consume while getting to know the two new students who had joined their midst.

"New students" was not a term heard often in Lost Grove. Once in a blue moon. And these two were different. The girl hadn't uttered a word all morning, even having teachers stumped by the note she handed them at the start of each class. What that was about, Stan intended to find out. But there was more; something was off with the boy too. Stan prided herself on being able to read people pretty well, and these two were giving off some majorly intriguing vibes.

Even now, she watched the boy laugh with whom she assumed was his sister, even though the girl hadn't uttered a word or turned to face him. And he wasn't holding a phone. They'd been doing things like that all day. Maybe they had escaped from the mental ward at the Orbriallis Institute and were giving it a go at Lost Grove High. Stan tossed her bag of gummies in the air, catching it with one hand as she stood up and headed across the track-and-field stadium.

"Hey, watch out, Stan!" Calvin Jasper said, stumbling to a stop as Stan passed in front without bothering to avoid him. She specifically chose not to get out of his way because he was wearing too-short shorts and a tank top. Who did he think he was fooling? Most of her fellow students brave enough to be running the track on this frigid afternoon were wearing leggings and sweatshirts. "They're looking for you on the set of *Baywatch: The Next Generation*, Calvin!"

"What?" he yelled back, genuinely perplexed.

"Bozo," Stan mumbled to herself as she trekked over the bright green field, approaching Rebecca Osterberg and Makaila Sullivan kicking a soccer ball back and forth.

"What are you doing out here, Stan?" Rebecca called out.

"Rude!" Stan replied with a sly grin.

"You know what I mean."

"Don't exercise-shame me, Osterberg."

"I so would never do that," Rebecca said and kicked the ball over to Makaila.

Stan took two quick steps and intercepted the ball, booting it in the opposite direction.

"Stan!" Makaila whined and ran after the ball.

Stan crossed the far side of the track and climbed the bleachers with a casual tempo, stopping in front of the enigmatic duo. "Hey."

The boy smiled and pointed out to the field. "Hey. You're funny."

"Thanks!" Stan said and turned to the girl. "Hey, what's up?"

Instead of any form of a reply, the girl's eyes darted around like she was looking for a way out.

"Like a deer in headlights," Stan muttered to herself as she gazed skeptically at the girl with her Lauryn Hill, Fugees-era Afro and hazel eyes. She was wearing a huge, comfortable-looking overcoat that looked like it was made out of her grandmother's quilt. She turned back to the maybe-brother, who looked more stylish in his ripped black jeans, bright white tennis shoes, and maroon hoodie with a black jean jacket over it. "Is she okay?"

"She's fine," the boy answered. He had long, thick, dark brown hair tucked behind his ears, the shape of his eyes more almond than the girl's round ones. "She doesn't talk."

The girl looked up at Stan.

"So it would seem," Stan replied after waiting for the girl to correct him. She dropped onto the cold metal and pulled out her bag of gummies. "Want some?" she asked, offering the bag to the silent one.

The girl hesitated but then grabbed a couple after looking up and catching Stan's warm smile. Stan aimed the bag over to the boy, who didn't waver before grabbing a small handful.

"I'm Stan, by the way. Constance, but everyone calls me Stan."

"Cool," he said through the sticky gummy. "I'm Emory, and my sister is Ember. Graff. We're the Graff twins."

"Twins? Damn, I should have picked up on that. I've got twin baby brothers." Stan settled between them, resting her elbows on the seat behind her and kicking her feet up on the one in front. Her feet wiggled back and forth, the three of them consuming the sour sweets in awkward silence. Like herself, every student passing on the track looked up, wondering about these two but not finding the confidence to ask. "So, do you guys feel like an oddity in a zoo yet?"

WHAT DOES SHE MEAN BY THAT?

Emory struggled to keep the flinch from his face. His sister's concern roared inside his head, her thoughts part of his own, intruding on his reply. *I doubt she means anything by it. Maybe you could try some control. Don't shout inside my thoughts like that.* Emory cleared his throat, a warning to his sister. "You mean all the people who keep staring at us but not talking to us?" he asked Stan.

Sorry, Ember whispered into her brother's mind.

Stan tossed a gummy at one runner, who had slowed down to stare. "Keep moving, Daryl!" She turned to Emory. "Yeah. Stupid right? But we don't get new people in town very often, and we certainly don't get new students. I don't think I've seen one join our class since…Eric Dunifer in fifth grade. So, yeah. What brings you to the quaint Victorian village that is Lost Grove, anyway?"

What are you going to say? Ember asked.

What should I say?

I don't know. Not the truth!

Why not the truth? That's easier than a lie. We'd have to maintain that—

You want them to think we're nuts?

They could find out just as easily elsewhere. The trial was public. Emory nodded toward the horizon, realizing he was taking a moment too long to converse with his sister before responding. "That."

Stan looked in the direction he'd nodded, then back at him, brow raised.

"We're going to the Orbriallis Institute," he replied.

"Oh shit," Stan said, taking a moment to observe Emory. She hadn't expected her thoughts to be so on the nose. "Medically or mentally?"

"What?"

Don't say, Ember urged.

"Are you going for medical issues or mental ones?" Stan expounded, curious if the girl's inability to speak had something to do with it.

Emory hesitated, but Stan just kept looking at him, waiting. She took one moment to turn to Ember, who quickly looked away before pressing her attention back on Emory.

"Mental," Emory finally replied.

"Huh," Stan murmured, digging in for another gummy and biting it in half. Maybe she had her grandmother's sixth sense after all.

A town this small, we're going to be ostracized. Ember's defeated thoughts came through. *I knew it would be worse here. I knew a small town would be worse. We're the only kids of color here, and now they know we're batshit. This couldn't get any worse.*

Stan motioned toward Orbriallis. "It's a world-renowned facility. Probably one of the best places if you need treatment of either kind, really. When'd you guys get here?"

Quit talking about the—

Emory's eyes darted toward his sister. *Will you stop? You're supposed to be learning to control your thoughts. All you've done is sit inside my head and let me know every single thing on your—* "We've been in Lost Grove for a couple months now." *—mind. Just chill. Focus. She's nice.*

Stan looked at him, eyes narrowed. "Really? But you guys just…"

"Yeah, we, um, you know, just needed some time before we got back into school."

Stan nodded and looked back out to the track, letting that topic go. One of them didn't speak, and they were receiving treatment at the Orbriallis. It wouldn't be too far-fetched to think they were recovering from trauma.

Stop it, Emory!

It's fine. I didn't say anything. Just chill.

Ember took in a deep breath.

Emory felt the ebbing sensation of Ember leaving his mind like an invisible string unraveling with each thought she released.

Having been twins since birth, the Graff siblings had shared an unexplainable bond that transcended language, giving them the ability to communicate without speaking. They could sense each other's feelings and emotions, knowing when the other was hungry or sad. But as they grew older, this powerful connection became more than just understanding one another; it gave them the power to influence other people's thoughts and manipulate their responses.

They used this newfound talent playfully at first, getting away with begging for a large pizza or convincing their parents to let them stay out late with friends. It had even saved Emory from being caught after a summer party—though it caused him to be sick instead. He pushed his mind too far in manipulating his parents' thoughts and ended up paying for it.

Emory glanced over at Stan, focusing on her thoughts.

…wonder if they're reading my mind now. They're definitely weird. Like right now, why the hell did he just snap his attention to me? Weird twin shit, just like my brothers. I bet they…

Emory's heart raced with fear. A rush of adrenaline coursed through his veins as Stan's words popped into his head. They were tinted green and smelled faintly of cinnamon.

He glanced over at Ember, who was blissfully unaware of the shared thoughts. He knew they had to be careful being in such a small town where people paid attention to even the slightest details.

His heart raced faster as he remembered the last time someone "discovered" their talents, a flashing memory that made his stomach flip, his skin prickle with goosebumps and sweat.

"So, what do you know about the Orbriallis?" Emory asked, trying to divert her thoughts away from himself. He lifted his hand to point at the tower tucked into the mist, surrounded by cedars, pines, and redwoods. It stood out like a beacon of glistening chrome and glass, twinkling amongst the deep evergreen foliage juxtaposed to the grey fog that clung to the forest every morning and night. It was an eyesore and a marvel of architecture. "And was that always a part of it?"

"The tower?" Stan asked.

"Yeah. It seems like…really out of place." What Emory wanted to say was that it was overbearing and haunting. He didn't like the way it sat amongst the boughs of redwoods, looking down on the town, watching. Outside, it had the same watchful presence as when he'd been inside. Cameras followed them down the halls, recorded their reactions, watching, always watching.

"No shit," Stan blurted.

Ember laughed.

"She laughs!" Stan gently slapped Ember with the back of her hand, not noticing the smile it brought to the girl's face. "So, the original building is actually nice. They added on that ridiculous tower in 1986,

'87, no, I think it was '86."

Emory wiped his hands together, brushing off sugar dust from the sour candies. "Yeah, the older part is actually pretty cool. It has that creepy gothic thing going on."

Stan assessed him out of the side of her eye. He had a sense of humor, which was nice. "Anyway, it's not like a big deal to be going there. I mean, you aren't locked up, right?" She elbowed Emory and laughed.

Ember pursed her lips, grateful this new friend didn't know how close they had come to being locked up.

"Nettie has been seeing a therapist there since she was eight. No, nine." Stan shrugged, ripping a gummy worm in half with her teeth.

"Nettie?" Emory asked.

Stan pointed across the green to Nettie and Anya, who were meandering around the track. "See the one with the copper-and-white ombre hair? The one next to her with the long brown hair, that's Nettie. They're part of our tight group of friends."

I wonder why she's going there. Ember made herself intentionally known in her brother's mind. It was different this time. She had control, like when she worked over her parents or teachers.

Emory asked, "What's she going there for?"

Stan shrugged. "Her little brother is a changeling. She thinks so anyway. I mean…" Stan itched her nose, leaning back to rest her elbows on the bleacher behind them again. "He could be, for all I know. One day, he was a healthy five-year-old. The next—he wouldn't talk, eat, nothing."

"For real?"

"For reals, yo," Stan emphasized, snapping her fingers in the air.

Stan felt Ember tap her and turned to see the mute girl pointing down at her phone. Stan leaned down to read it. The text typed out in a note said: It's thought that children with Down syndrome were mistaken as changelings because they act so differently from normal infants.

"I thought you said she doesn't talk," Stan turned to Emory.

"She doesn't."

"Right." Stan pulled out her phone, quickly creating a contact for Ember. She turned back to the girl and handed her phone over. "'Kay, give me your number."

Ember's cheeks warmed as she hesitantly grabbed Stan's phone. *Do you think she likes girls?*

Emory sighed. *Just shut up and type in your number.*

Stan glanced over at him, wondering what had annoyed him, but he was looking away from them both. She furrowed her brow as she felt the softest touch on her shoulder. She turned around to see Ember pull her hand back and then extend her other hand with Stan's phone.

"I'm not made of glass, ya know," Stan said and grabbed her phone. She smacked Ember's thigh with the back of her hand again. "Just hit me. I've got three older brothers, too."

Ember giggled again and then nonchalantly backhanded Stan's shoulder.

Stan smirked. "That's a start." She opened her camera and held up her phone. "Smile. Or do something stupid."

Ember lifted her hands, put her fingertips together under her chin, and smiled.

Stan snapped the photo. "Look at you coming out of your shell being all cute," she said and then started composing a text for her.

Oh my god! She's totally into girls!

Emory looked over at his sister and smirked. *Don't get your hopes up.*

"He didn't have Down syndrome," Stan started. "Doesn't have it, I should say."

"Who?" Emory asked.

"Nettie's brother. The changeling."

"Oh, yeah."

"Who knows what it is? I think the doctors claim it's some form of autism, but Nettie says that's bullshit. I mean, he was a normal little dude for years, then one day—" She snapped her fingers, not successfully. She tried again but still had no success.

Ember and Emory both laughed.

Stan stared at the Graff twins, taking in their similarities and differences. They were peculiar, secretive, but Stan sensed something special about them. She could almost feel the warmth of their energy radiating from them as they spoke.

She sent Ember a gif of Mike Myers from *Wayne's World* that said, "Are you mental?"

Ember laughed and texted back: What do you know about the institute? "Ha!"

Emory jumped, startled by Stan's outburst of laughter. "What?"

Stan jutted her thumb toward Ember. "She asked what I've heard about Orbriallis." She looked back and forth between the two. "You mean, you guys haven't heard the stories yet?"

"Stories?" Emory asked, his brow arched toward his hairline.

Stan dropped the bag of gummies to her side and rubbed her hands together to get the sugar off. She looked up, and her eyes opened wide. "Yo!"

Nate was approaching them, taking the stairs of the bleachers three at a time. "Hey, how's it going?"

Noble was behind him, going at a more normal, two-stairs-at-a-time pace. Both were sweating from running.

"Nate, Noble, good sirs, meet Emory and his dear sister, Ember," Stan introduced them.

Noble extended his hand toward Emory. "Hey, good to meet you. Welcome."

Emory shook his hand. "Hey, man, what's up?"

Nate planted his foot on the step above him and leaned his forearm on his knee. "Yo, yo, saw you guys earlier."

Stan laughed. "What the fuck are you doing? About to give a lecture or something?"

"Shut up. I'm tired out, but don't feel like sitting."

The Graff twins both laughed.

"Hey, your dad had to have told you something by now, Stan," Nate pressed.

"He hasn't, and can we just not talk about that right now?"

"Why not?"

They must be talking about the body at the beach, Ember said to her brother.

For sure. I wonder who Stan's dad is.

"Nate, just leave it," Noble protested. "That's all you've talked about for two days now."

Nate guffawed. "Well, yeah! This is some serious shit, dude. And I'm going to get to the bottom of it, with or without Stan's information, which I know you have!"

Stan extended her middle finger in response.

"You do that," Noble said and turned to Stan and the twins. "So, what were you guys talking about when we interrupted?"

"We're just getting to the good stuff," Stan replied, sitting up straight. "The Power Twins want to know about the Orbriallis Institute."

Emory exchanged a quizzical glance with his sister. *Power Twins?*

Do you think she can tell? Oh crap, could she be like us? Ember shifted in the bleachers.

Nate smiled wickedly. "Oh, man! So this is—"

"Okay, wait, wait." Stan stopped them, holding up her hands.

"There's this nursery rhyme and everything," Noble said offhandedly to Ember.

She smiled, looking around the group.

"Do you even remember it?" Nate asked.

Noble turned to his friend. "Nah. Parts of it." He started humming the stanzas, trying to remember the words. "Little Lina was her name."

Nate leaned forward. "Yes! 'Skin of diamonds.'"

"'Mouth of sores,'" Noble and Nate continued. "'Little Lina stayed indoors.'"

"I always remember something about a dress and—" Stan started.

Nate chimed in, "'Little Lina, dressed in lace, went outdoors without a face.' I love that part. Amazing."

"Sounds fucking weird." Emory laughed.

The kids laughed along with him.

Stan began maliciously rubbing her hands together. "Okay, let's get you guys inducted into Lost Grove lore. The story of Geiger Orbriallis," she said theatrically, spreading her hands across the air in front of her.

"Oh." Emory leaned back. "Okay. I see where this is going."

"No, dude, this shit is weird. It's a thrilling tale," Nate said, holding his hands out to Emory and Ember like, *Wait for it.*

Stan squinted at Nate. "'A thrilling tale?'"

"Yeah. It's creepy. It's good. So—" Nate began before being interrupted by Stan.

"Wait, let me do this because you'll just fuck it up," Stan started. "Are you ready?" she asked the twins.

They nodded, eager to hear these tales from their new classmates.

"Geiger Orbriallis grew up in Germany, where he fell in love with his first cousin, Ilsa Müller. And against the family's wishes, they married before the war. Geiger enlisted, as every able-bodied man did, and they exchanged many letters while he was serving. It was extra nerve-racking for Ilsa, waiting for the war to end because her husband was working as a spy for the Allied forces.

"When the war ends and rumors start spreading that Geiger was a turncoat, friends, neighbors, and even relatives turn on them. Their home gets vandalized, and they get the worst rations at the store. Geiger said, 'Why don't we move to America?' and Ilsa, who wasn't overly fond of the idea because she loved her home and her country, finally agreed.

So they moved to San Francisco and eventually ended up here in Lost Grove.

"Now, it wasn't an issue during the war, as they had barely seen each other, but it became apparent that Ilsa was having trouble conceiving a child and carrying it to full term. They went through dozens of false hopes and stillbirths, losing child after child. This affected Ilsa deeply, and she wanted to give up, when Geiger convinced her to try one last time.

"Ilsa barely left the house during her pregnancy. She stayed in bed most of the time, traumatized that she'd lose another child, like all the others. At seven months, she went into labor. It was long, intense, and painful, but at last, with a final push, the Orbriallises heard their child. But what a miracle is to some might be a curse to others.

"It wailed and screamed with gurgling, watery lungs. And when Geiger saw the child, he gasped in horror. Her lip was cleft in two, skin shredded and pulling apart into diamond-like sections, and her head was malformed and ovoid. He thought for sure it wouldn't survive and tried to take it away from Ilsa before she even saw it. But Ilsa demanded she see the baby, and she cradled the little girl in her arms, cooed at it, and named her Lina.

"Every morning, Geiger was sure this would be the day the child would die, but it didn't. And though the child pushed on and kept living, Ilsa seemed to fade. She withdrew into long moments of stillness, holding the baby to her breast in the rocking chair. Her color was sallow and pale, and it took great pains for her to walk from one room to the other.

"So when he woke one morning to the babe's cries, to find Ilsa the one deceased and not the monster in her arms, Geiger fell into despair. He was certain she had died of the shame it had burdened her with, having carried their incestuous creation to term, which made him loathe the monster his wife had named Lina and thought to rid himself of it altogether. He ran a bath and placed the infant in it, pushing it down into the water. The ripples as the baby wiggled drew his attention, and as the water shifted, he saw that the child, Lina, could be beautiful if only he could make her right.

"Having studied as a doctor in Germany, he put his training to work. First, he bought a place to conduct his experiments and named it the Orbriallis Institute. He experimented on his daughter with many fluids and ointments…and skin. Pigs went into that place at an alarming rate, their skin used as grafts to perfect the mangled and torn flesh of Lina.

"The townspeople watched as Geiger went from a man who put care into his appearance to a wild, frantic one who didn't comb or cut his hair. They thought he was grieving, burdened with raising a deformed child. But Geiger didn't even think of Lina as his child anymore. She had become something other, a thing he needed to perfect. But nothing was working, and Geiger was growing desperate.

"That's when the children started disappearing. Geiger couldn't cure his daughter, so instead, he'd have to rebuild her from the inside out, and there was only one way to do that. He needed new hair, eyes, teeth, skin… bones. So Geiger took up a new routine of spending a vast amount of time walking along old Foxglove Run. It's a path that runs alongside the grade school, and he would sit and watch the children playing, picking the best of them. His victims.

"The first to go missing was Susie Kane."

"It's always Susie, little Susie Something," Nate interjected.

Stan ignored him and continued. "She was playing at a friend's house before they sent her home for dinner. She never made it home.

"Second was Billy Tudor."

"There's always a Billy!" Nate guffawed.

This made Ember giggle because she also thought the names were painfully generic.

Stan went on. "Billy had the bluest eyes. Everyone always commented on them. He and his mother were at the farmer's market when he disappeared from her side.

"Five children were lost that summer."

"It's always summer!" Noble and Nate commented in gleeful exasperation at how cliche the tale was.

"Shush," Stan said and continued. "At the end of August, Geiger went to the local funeral home. He bought a small coffin and buried his daughter in the town cemetery next to his wife. The town felt sorry for the man, having lost his wife and daughter, but what they didn't know was that she had died from complications of the latest experimental surgery. If she hadn't? Who knows how many more children would have gone missing?

"But the thing is, on foggy nights, when the light at the top of the Orbriallis tower shines like a beacon through the mist, they say you can expect to see Lina walking in a black veil, all grown up, haunting the streets of this town. She pays a visit to all the houses of the children that shaped her, stopping at each one and watching the happy family living inside." Stan finished in the spooky, lowered voice of a campfire tale.

Emory bit down on his bottom lip to keep from bursting with laughter.

"Isn't that story the shit?" Nate exclaimed.

"But it's not true. None of it," Noble said. "Total bullshit."

"You're bullshit," Nate retorted.

Stan choked back her laugh, attempting to keep her voice conspiratorial. "You mean you haven't seen her, Noble?"

"Okay, right, sorry. 'Oh guys, I've totally seen her walking the streets,'" he said, miming spooky hands.

Ember giggled more, and Emory laughed, finding himself drawn into the simple exchange between these friends, feeling his sister soften and let down her walls. These kids felt genuine in a way he'd never known. Back in San Francisco, every move, every word he uttered, was calculated to fit in with the elite social class his mother and father had put them in.

He admired what his parents had achieved, but hated the fallacy of everyone around him. These kids were so far from that he almost felt a twang of homesickness for a childhood he'd never known. Almost. There was still so much he and his sister had to protect, to hide. But damn, he wished he could let his guard down fully, tell these kids who he was, what he could do.

Stan looked down at the text she had just gotten from Ember: Okay, so how much of this is true?

"So, is any of that actually true?" Emory asked.

Stan laughed at the pair. "Those are facts, man," she whined, as if the question had wounded her.

"Nowhere close," Noble jumped in. "Before Geiger got there, it was just a hospital that no one used. The US government purchased it in 1947, after the war. It was originally called Her Mother's Mercy Hospital before Geiger took over and rebranded it the Orbriallis Institute. Now, Geiger was, in fact, an ally, and he was, in fact, a doctor, a psychologist, and he was, in fact, married to his first cousin, Ilsa Müller. And the reason he and Ilsa moved here was to run the hospital under government orders—yes, Nate, I see you—to run experiments around psychological warfare; Jesus, go ahead." Noble handed it over to Nate.

Nate buzzed, shuffling forward on the bleachers. "Do you guys know anything about MK Ultra? No? Okay, so after the war, many countries started experiments on how to strengthen soldiers. Not that Marvel, supersoldier stuff. Ones who had the mental toughness and could run like machines without fatigue. Okay, so maybe a little like Marvel. They had Geiger doing that sort of thing up there. Experiments with psychedelics."

"Yes, okay, let's not fall into the urban legends again of the Russian Sleep Experiment," Noble interjected. "They studied brainwashing, how far they could push a human being and their body. They wanted to know how an entire country had fallen under Adolf Hitler's spell."

"I get it." Emory nodded. "Like, how did Jim Jones convince nine hundred people to off themselves?"

"Exactly!" Nate roared. "Just like Double J."

"Are you fucking kidding me right now?" Stan stared wide-eyed at Nate.

"What?"

"I'm pretty sure no one ever called him that," Noble added.

"You don't know that."

Stan rolled her eyes and then looked down at another text from Ember. Stan read it aloud. "'Does the government still run Orbriallis?'"

"Are you asking me that?" Nate interrupted.

"No, idiot. I was reading a text from Ember."

"Huh? Why is she texting you? She's sitting right there."

"She doesn't talk," Stan and Emory said in unison.

Nate looked over at Noble, confounded.

"Don't look at me like I know what's going on here."

"To answer your question, Ember"—Stan loudly diverted attention—"no, I don't believe the government still runs it."

"Yes, they do," Nate argued.

"They might," Noble added.

"If they do," Stan started, "they're silent partners at this point. Now the wacko Neil Owens is in charge."

"Wacko?" Emory asked for all kinds of reasons.

"He's the one who built that dope tower," Nate explained.

"It's hideous," Stan argued.

"It's fucking awesome! Look at it!" Nate pointed, eyes maniacally wide.

Noble looked at Emory. "The whole town kind of thinks he's a little extreme, that he pushes the boundaries too far. But the advances they're coming up with may be worth it. They've got the highest success rate for helping people with fertility issues. They created that biologically engineered skin all hospitals use for burn victims now. And they're working on some major breakthroughs in giving children, people born deaf, the ability to hear."

"Among other things." Nate waggled his brow at Ember.

She smiled at him, daring herself to look at his thoughts.

...a cute smile. I wonder why she doesn't talk. I wonder how rude it would be for me to ask. Nice body, amazing...

Ember left before hearing more. Heat rising from her neck up her cheeks. Emory noticed how she'd hopped into his thoughts, felt her block him, and moved away like the buzz of an insect hovering nearby. But that all played in the back of his mind. Instead, his focus was on why the judge had ordered them to seek treatment specifically at Orbriallis, and if there was more to all the tests they'd been putting him and his sister through recently. Hearing the history and horror stories about the Institute, true or not, had Emory on edge. He looked back at all they had been through these past two months with a fresh set of eyes.

The bell signaling the end of Physical Fitness hour startled Emory out of his thoughts.

"Let's go, assholes!" Nate yelled as he went bounding carelessly down the steel steps.

"You're going to break something before our next meet!" Noble shouted after him.

"Never!"

Emory looked over at Ember sitting next to Stan, the two laughing while continuing to text one another as they stood up to head back to class.

"Good to meet you!" Noble yelled as he followed behind Nate, glancing back at Emory.

"Cool. You too!" Emory yelled back. He got behind Ember and Stan as they headed down the stairs and burrowed his way past his sister's surface feelings of titillation for their new friend in search of what she was feeling about the Orbriallis. Just as he got there, Ember blocked him out. But he had gleaned just enough to latch on to her one overriding emotion: fear.

Chapter 11

Religious Ephemera

"Hey, you've reached Brigette. I can't talk right now, so just leave me a message or shoot me a text. Have a good day!"

"Hello, Miss Lowe. This is Sergeant Seth Wolfe of the Lost Grove Police. We met briefly yesterday. I'd like to speak with you about Sarah Elizabeth Grahams as soon as you have a few moments. You can call or text me at 707–555-1604 with a time you're free to talk over FaceTime. Thanks." Sitting in his rarely used office, Seth disconnected and looked through the window into the bullpen to see that Joe had arrived. He stood, pocketed his phone, grabbed his jacket and keys, and stepped out into the main offices.

"Morning, Joe."

"Morning, Seth. I got you a coffee," the young officer said, pointing to the extra to-go cup on the corner of his desk.

"Appreciate that." Seth grabbed the cup and took a tentative sip, knowing how scorching hot Clemency made her cappuccinos.

"Enough time to cool down?"

Seth nodded. "Perfect. Gonna be a long one. Did you come across anything in your search for similar cases?"

Joe shook his head. "Nothing relating to bodies washed up on a beach. So I moved on to looking for girls who have gone missing from colleges in Northern California and Oregon over the past couple of years. Any students, actually, but focusing mainly on females."

"Even though Sarah Elizabeth went to college in Texas?"

"But she ended up here. Was from here. So…"

Seth nodded. "Makes sense. Any hits?"

Joe pointed to his computer screen. "Fortunately, or unfortunately, depending on how you look at it, I've got a small list going. There are three so far: one from Cal State Sacramento, one from San Jose State, and one from Notre Dame de Namur, a small private college in Belmont, not to be confused with the Fighting Irish in Indiana."

"Thanks for that," Seth said with a slight grin.

"I'll email you the full list when I'm done searching."

"Good work. Look, I've got to head out for some more interviews at the high school. I need you to put that search to the side temporarily. Our number one priority now is establishing Sarah Elizabeth's last known whereabouts, so I need you to contact Baylor and get in touch with her teachers, roommates, friends, anyone you can. Create a log of the last time and place each and every one of them last saw her."

Joe had walked to his desk and was scribbling notes on his notepad. "Got it."

"Whether you finish up with that or hit a wall, the next thing will be getting access to her bank. Call her parents, tell them it's imperative they cooperate. They should be able to get direct access to her accounts in this scenario, whereas we would need to—"

"Get a court order, right?"

Seth nodded. "That's right. If you get any pushback from her parents, let me know right away."

"I'm on it."

Seth raised his cup of coffee. "Thanks again for the coffee."

Seth was just turning into the high school parking lot when his phone vibrated with a call from Brigette. He wheeled into the first empty space he found, then pulled out his notepad and pen. With a deep breath, he answered her call.

Brigette's face appeared on-screen, her straight dark hair in a sophisticated bob with pieces tucked behind her ears, which elongated her face, making her look almost girlish.

"Good morning, Miss Lowe," Seth greeted her, placing his phone on the dashboard holder and going through the steps to activate the FaceTime record feature on his iPhone.

"Morning, sir," she replied. Her voice was shaky, eyes wide and glittering with apprehension. "I was on my way to class when I got your message. I thought…I just thought it'd be best to call directly." Brigette was sitting outside on what appeared to be a park bench under some tree shade.

"I appreciate that. I need to—"

"Something happened to her, didn't it?"

Seth took in a breath. "Just so you're aware, I will be recording this call. I have some questions I need to ask, and since you are her best friend—"

"Was," Brigette quickly said. "I was. I haven't heard from her since she went back to school after our first winter break, just like everyone else."

"Like everyone else?"

"Her parents, everyone. No one's heard from her since she left for the spring semester that first year. Jeremy said he told you about it. And she never joined social media. I've searched so many times." Brigette paused and focused her eyes on Seth. "Is she alright? Is she dead? Please, just tell me."

Seth's breath caught in his chest. His stomach plummeted as he imagined the horror that Sarah's parents must have gone through when they identified her body. He knew it was only a matter of time before word got around and everyone would find out what had happened; he was sure half the town already knew by now, even without an official press statement being released.

"I'm afraid she's deceased. I'm sorry."

Brigette sucked in a sharp breath, her eyes widening and filling with tears that threatened to spill over. She nodded, pressing her lips together as if to contain her pain.

"Miss Lowe, do you have reason to believe she would come to harm?"

"No, why? Why would you ask that?" she snapped.

"Because you pretty quickly surmised something had happened, that she was dead."

Brigette took a shaky breath in. "I mean, why wouldn't I? Who gets a call from a police officer about a high school friend unless something bad happened? And Jeremy called me last night and said a body was found on the beach. Was that her?"

Seth held in a sigh of exasperation. "It was. Her parents identified her body yesterday."

"What the fuck!" Brigette let out a muffled cry into her hands, obscuring the camera from view. Tiny glimpses of treetops and a grey sky flashed in the screen's corner between her fingers and sobs. After a moment, she sat back up and wiped away tears with the back of her hand. Her arms trembled as she attempted to keep the phone still. "What happened to her? Why was she there? Why was she back home? Was she at her parents'?"

"That's exactly what I'm trying to determine, and I could really use your help."

Brigette closed her eyes and let out a long sigh before opening them and nodding.

Seth shifted in his seat, propping his notepad on his knee. "When was the last time you spoke with Sarah?"

Brigette shook her head. "It was the last time I saw her, over Christmas break. We didn't talk nearly as much as we used to during that first semester. She kept saying she was overloaded with schoolwork, which made sense. She was pre-med, and if you knew Lizzy, that would never surprise you. But when she was back…it was different. She was different. She was so skinny! At first, we thought it was just because of her obsessive studying, but…I don't know, it was like she looked at us differently, she—"

"I'm sorry to cut you off, Brigette, but to be clear, when you say 'us,' you're referring to…"

"Jeremy. She didn't have any other close friends there. We were it. We were…" Brigette closed her eyes, trying to compose herself, a tear falling down her cheek.

"Take your time."

Brigette wiped her cheek. "I mean, I know she was having a hard time adapting to college life. She said she felt out of place, that she couldn't really connect with anyone. But that didn't seem too crazy to me because I felt the same way. It was something we talked about when school started, our freshman year. At least at the start."

"I get that," Seth agreed. "Going from Lost Grove High to San Francisco State University was an enormous shock for me as well. The entire world got much bigger overnight."

Brigette nodded. "Yeah, exactly. Jeremey said you were from Lost Grove too, so you know. But it was something else with Lizzy. It was more than trouble at school. Something was really wrong with her when she came back that break. We both knew it, but…I don't know. I was worried that maybe…I asked her if anything happened to her. You know, like at a party or at someone else's place."

Seth narrowed his eyes. "And did something happen?"

Brigette shook her head. "No. I don't think so. She's not the type of person to put herself in a situation like that."

"Sometimes that has nothing to do with it. But you don't think that was the case?"

"The way she was acting…but she said no. I asked a lot. Like, I bugged her about it. I wanted to be sure she had every opportunity to tell me, so I kept asking. But she always said no. It was frustrating because she just wouldn't talk about whatever was going on. She was just like…walled up. She kept saying she was fine, no matter how hard we tried to reach her. We should have done something, said something to someone else."

Seth had done his fair share of interviews with grieving family members and friends of the recently deceased. He saw their tears and heard their stories, felt the weight of their sorrow, and watched helplessly as they tried to make sense of an inexplicable loss. "Miss Lowe, I sincerely doubt there's anything you could have said or done that would have changed what happened."

"You don't know that." Brigette sniffed and wiped her eyes. "Goddamnit."

Seth tapped his pen on his notepad, giving her a moment. "Can you tell me what Sarah was like? Before college."

Brigette let out a gentle laugh. "She was my best friend. I mean, she was everything. She was the sweetest person I've ever known. She had, like, a genuinely pure heart. And I mean that; how many of us can honestly say…God, I can't imagine how she ended up…" She pulled her lips into her mouth, chin quivering.

"It's okay; take a deep breath," Seth suggested in a soft tone.

Brigette pinched the bridge of her nose and inhaled slowly. "I don't know what else to tell you. I mean, there's, like, nothing negative to say about her. She didn't judge anybody. Ever. Even if she maybe should have," she said, laughing.

Seth held up his hand. "I know this might sound a bit crazy considering what you just told me, but I have to ask. And I need you to really think about it, hard. Did she ever have any kind of trouble with anyone? At school, her church, in town. Or did anyone ever have an issue with her?"

Brigette smiled and opened her mouth to reply but stopped and looked down toward the ground. "I honestly can't think of anyone at school. I don't go to church, so I don't really know a lot about who went to hers."

"Any issues with a boyfriend at all?"

"A boyfriend?" Brigette huffed. "When would she ever have time for a boyfriend…no. She was determined to get a full scholarship to Baylor so she wouldn't have to rely on her parents. I'd say if she had trouble with anyone, it was them."

Seth felt a twinge in his gut. "Why do you think that is?"

Another shrug as she wiped her nose. "It was the way they wanted to control her, the way they fawned over her like she was a gift. Like she was Mother Mary reincarnated. No joke, they were crazy over her, but not in a good way, if that makes sense."

Seth imperceptibly nodded. "So, you'd say her family life was troublesome?"

"Yeah," Brigette said, like it was common knowledge. "She was terrified of them."

Seth leaned in closer to the phone, his gut tingling. "How so?"

"They were just so fucking controlling, you know. She had to check in with them all the time. We couldn't be out for more than two hours without Lizzy calling or texting to let them know where she was and what she was doing. They gave her a curfew like she was ten fucking years old. And she would get so nervous if she was even close to being out past that time. And if it were up to them, Richard and Bess, Lizzy would have worn baggy pants and a turtleneck with a loose-fitting sweater over it every day. Anything to hide that she had a great body."

Seth flinched, recalling the image of Sarah Elizabeth's lifeless body in his mind.

"Did you know she had me bring cute clothes to school for her to wear?"

"I actually did hear that she changed clothes after getting to school."

Brigette's brow tightened. "From who? Jeremy?"

Seth shook his head. "No, from one of your teachers."

Brigette looked down for a moment and then back up. "Mrs. Young?"

"That's right."

Brigette smiled. "I always had a feeling she knew what was going on. She seemed to give Lizzy extra care and attention. Like she knew she needed support or something. She was a good teacher."

"She was," Seth quickly agreed.

"Huh?"

"She was my teacher once upon a time as well."

Brigette squinted, her eyes darting back and forth. "How old is she?

I mean, she doesn't seem much older than you."

"I'm sure she would love to hear that. Let's go back to Sarah's parents. Were there any other reasons she was afraid of them? Did they ever physically hurt her?"

"No, nothing like that. I mean, they loved her, but…they were just too much. I was honestly so fucking happy when Bess called me that spring semester after the break, asking if I had her new number. I hated that I didn't have it, but to know she cut off her parents…I was proud of her. Which is honestly why this is so confusing. Why would she be back home? It's been sticking in my fucking mind, like, why? I wish she'd…I just don't know what I ever did to make her pull away from me." Fresh tears percolated, and then she covered her face with one hand.

Seth's heart ached for Brigette; the roller coaster of emotions on display was painful. "I don't know anything about your relationship with Sarah, but as you said, it was everyone. Not just you. I'd be willing to bet it had nothing to do with you or Jeremy. The whole situation is very mysterious, and I plan on figuring out what happened."

Brigette nodded and then looked up, wincing. "I don't know if I really want to know…but what happened? Like, was it bad?"

"I truly don't know yet. We're still waiting on the autopsy. But I can tell you it didn't appear, at least from the outside, that she was physically harmed by herself or someone else."

Brigette flinched back. "Herself? Never in a million years."

"It's rare that anyone close to—"

"Nope," Brigette cut him off. "If I can tell you anything with one hundred percent certainty, it's that Lizzy would never, ever, even think about harming herself. She was grateful for the life she was given. She said that often, and it was as genuine as anything anyone could claim and mean. And all she wanted to do was help others. She was ready to dedicate her life to that purpose."

Seth nodded. Suicide was already far down on his list of what happened, but it was good to hear Brigette's declaration. "Okay, fair enough. I believe you knew her as well as anyone."

"I did," she replied quietly, another tear falling down her cheek.

"Is there anything else at all that you can tell me about Sarah that might help me understand more about her? Any physical or mental issues that she dealt with?"

Brigette wiped a tear from her cheek and thought for a moment.

"Well, she had major sleep issues. Like, she either couldn't fall asleep, or she'd wake up in the middle of the night and not be able to get back to sleep. And she'd have these really strange visions. She only told me a few of them. I messed that up, making fun of her once. So fucking stupid." Brigette looked away from the screen.

Seth grimaced as if a rank smell just wafted through the window. *Visions* was typically not a word used lightly or incorrectly. "You said visions. Do you mean dreams?"

Brigette shook her head. "No, like when she couldn't sleep. She said that she had these, like, really intense visions, and she was hyper-awake. They were focused on specific people. She didn't know them but felt like she did. And she said she felt like…no, she knew they needed her help. The visions traumatized her. I know that doesn't make sense, but I don't know how else to explain it."

Seth swallowed heavily. This proclaimed sensation Sarah Elizabeth suffered from felt eerily familiar. He suddenly felt hyper-aware of his heart beating and tried leveling out his breathing.

"Sorry, I wish I could help more. I want to."

Seth quickly snapped out of it and batted his eyes. "No, not at all. Everything you said has been extremely helpful. You mentioned you messed up once. What did she tell you that prompted you to make fun of her?"

Brigette sighed. "She told me about this one vision. I think because it really shook her. I mean, like, she told me about it because she had to talk to someone. She was distressed by it but also…what's the word I'm looking for? She was excited by it? There was a part in the vision where she saw what she thought might have been a divine being."

Seth's hairs rose on his forearms.

"She'd been asleep when she woke up and was thrust into this vision. I think that's how it happened. I don't know, I shouldn't have made fun of her. I'd know more to tell you now." Brigette shook her head.

"What do you think she meant by a divine being?"

Brigette took in a deep breath, looking off screen and into her memories. "So, this vision was dark. She felt panic and pain and was helpless to move or do anything. Sarah was afraid, but then the pain and fear went away when this being arrived. Sarah told me it was ethereal, that it shimmered or something like that. And she said she felt snow or feathers, something soft and comforting. I laughed and…I guess I kind of poked fun at her spirituality, her religion. Maybe I thought it was a joke. Or wanted to believe it was a joke would be more like it. So stupid, I can't even really recall what I said. I just remember she was upset, and I apologized, but she never told me about any more visions after that."

Seth scratched his face with the back of his pen. This added a whole new wrinkle to the case, the possibility of some form of mental illness. "Did these visions ever come on during the day?"

"I mean, I guess it…I don't know. Like, did I ever witness one?"

Seth tilted his head from side to side. "Yes. Or maybe you heard about her having some kind of episode?"

Brigette shook her head slowly. "No. Nothing like that."

"And she never had one of these visions when you had a sleepover or—"

"We never had sleepovers. She wasn't allowed to," Brigette interrupted.

Seth processed this information in a much different capacity than any other information he'd taken during a witness statement before. Brigette's reaction to Sarah Elizabeth was the exact reason he knew he couldn't explain what he'd gone through to anyone else, much less Bill. "Was there any part of what she told you about her visions, this particular one or others, that you did believe?"

Brigette shrugged. "I don't know. I guess I believed that she believed it. I mean…" She pursed her lips, looked down at her lap, then back up to the screen. "Lizzy was really into that stuff. Like, she believed in that part of her religion. The goodness of it, I guess. I think that's what made her so, well, to be honest, so naïve."

Seth scribbled notes on his pad and looked up. "And her religion, was this something she shared with her parents? Or something they pressured her into?"

"I mean, her parents are super religious, but I think in a different way than Lizzy. I assume they were responsible for, I don't know, getting her into it. Isn't that how it happens with kids, usually?"

Seth nodded. "Assuming we're talking about Sarah at a very young age, yes, that would typically be the case. I think how much a young person holds on to that is much more complicated. Did Sarah ever tell you anything regarding her parents and religion? Anything that seemed…I don't know, extreme? Or did you get the sense…" Seth trailed off, seeing Brigette deep in thought.

"You know, there was something," Brigette started, her eyes shifting back and forth. "I remember her telling me when we were younger. How did she…"

Seth waited patiently for the girl to find the memory, sensing they had stumbled on something important.

"I don't think I thought it was serious at the time. I mean, we were like seven or eight, so none of it really would have made sense anyhow. But she told me that her parents thought she could communicate with God."

Seth felt goosebumps ripple up his back. "In the sense of praying?"

Brigette shook her head. "No, no. Lizzy told me that her parents believed she could, I don't know, like literally talk with Him?"

"And…did Sarah say that she could?"

"No," Brigette said, waving her finger back and forth. "She actually specifically said that her parents were wrong, that they didn't understand. But they kept asking her to do it. Like they needed something? Fuck, I don't remember all of it, but that just popped back into my head when you asked."

Seth realized he was biting on his pen, a habit he had broken years ago. This whole interview had taken a bizarre turn he wasn't expecting, and it piqued his instincts with a potential new line of thought. It would have to wait for now. "That's great you remembered at all. Was this something still going on when you were in high school?"

Brigette let out a soft moan as tears rose once more. "Oh my God, what happened to her?" She dropped her head into her hands.

"I don't mean to press you, but—"

"It's okay," Brigette quickly replied and shook her head. "I'm sorry. Um, no, she didn't mention anything like that specifically. About her parents, you mean?"

Seth nodded.

"Yeah, no. She never mentioned anything about that since we were young. But that doesn't mean it didn't continue. Jesus, now I think back on it…Obviously, her visions were ongoing. Look, Lizzy had her own connection to religion. I don't think anyone could have impacted what she believed. She was steadfast, secure. I don't know how to explain it."

Seth closed his notepad. "I understand."

Brigette swiped another tear from her cheek. "Sarah was…she was a good girl. She was a good person. She was like the Madonna, right? That depiction of her? You see this beautiful, serene-faced woman who appears chaste and—" Brigette stopped, bowing her head.

Seth gave the young woman time to gain control of her emotions.

"She reminded me of those statues," Brigette said, face still tilted into her lap, picking at the tissue crumpled in her hand. "Like she was a martyr."

Retrospective No.3: Sarah Elizabeth—Child

Sarah Elizabeth sat cross-legged on the plush-carpeted floor of her bedroom, shuffling two tiny porcelain people together. Her strawberry-blonde hair curled around her temples and at the ends, a quirk she liked, though her mother would insist on cutting the summer length back to hang at her shoulders before school started. Her room was painted sky blue, with fluffy clouds on the ceiling. A small desk sat in front of the window, and two tall bookshelves framed them, her books neatly ordered, as were the toys she kept on the shelves. At the foot of her bed, which was swamped in the fluffiest down comforter she'd ever seen, was her favorite item in her room: a large black traveling chest that held all her dress-up costumes.

Sarah set her figurines at the entrance of the miniature church made of mahogany by her father. Saturday was always special; it meant no interruption of chores or school for hours while she built an imaginary world around her. Plastic animals greeted her from their places, standing tall. On the opposite side, she could peek in to see the aisles, nave, and altar that were tucked away within the wooden walls. Her Lite-Brite sat plugged in off to the side with an orange sun glaring brightly off the black paper underneath. She felt connected to her parents every time she made something new on her Lite-Brite—they said they remembered playing with one just like it when they were her age.

At seven years old, Sarah Elizabeth could barely contain her excitement for the coming school year. She recalled fondly the playground adventures, art projects, and nature walks her classmates had enjoyed together in first grade, especially when Mrs. Rutherford brought out her pet snake from the glass tank. Most of them were too terrified to touch it, but not Sarah Elizabeth: she loved animals no matter how strange or slimy they might be. And nothing compared to spending five days a week with her best friend Brigette, who'd become like a sister to her, even if her parents only allowed her to come over once a month to play at their house.

"Do you want to play with the tigers today, Mary?" She bounced the male figurine up and down.

Sarah shook the female figurine back and forth. "No, Joseph. How many times do I have to tell you that tigers are dangerous?"

"Not this one. He's as nice as a cat." She walked the man toward the tiger.

Sarah dropped the woman and grabbed the tiger. "RAAR!" She propped the tiger on its hind legs and wiggled it at the man.

"Oh no!" The man ran back toward the woman.

She picked the woman back up. "See, I told you. You never learn, Joseph."

Sarah Elizabeth dropped both figures and grabbed a white-and-brown horse. As she started galloping the animal toward the model fence that went with her toy barn, Sarah's body went rigid. Her hands cramped, her back arched, and her head tilted back between her shoulder blades. Her eyelids fluttered, her eyeballs rolling back into her head so only the whites were visible. Sarah's mouth was slightly ajar, and her underbite jutted out as saliva accumulated on her bottom lip.

Everything you…done…very bad way

Sarah snapped out of her trance, her breath hitched in her little lungs, and a chill ran up her spine. An eerie whisper seemed to linger in the air, like someone had spoken just before she awoke. The room felt unfamiliar and strange, until her eyes landed on Angie, her beloved baby doll, perched atop the pink, frilly pillow on her bed.

"Was that you?" Sarah Elizabeth asked in astonishment, jumping to her feet and running toward her doll.

As Sarah rounded the foot of her bed and took her first stride toward her pillows, her body contracted like a snail touching salt. She collapsed onto the side of her bed and fell to the ground. Once again, her eyes rolled back into her head, her hands and arms tightened against her chest like she was pretending to be a bunny rabbit, and her mouth opened and shut with a hard crack from her jaw.

Children…immune…disease

Sarah's body relaxed as she took a giant inhale of breath, her eyes settling back into place. She rolled over to her knees and used the mattress to pull herself to her feet. She leaned on the bed and grabbed Angie, looking directly into the doll's sparkling green eyes.

"What are you trying to tell me?" she asked her doll.

Sarah Elizabeth climbed up on the bed and swung her feet around to hang off the side as she sat Angie on her lap, facing her. Sarah had many conversations with Angie over the years but had never clearly heard her voice until today. It surprised her that Angie's voice sounded much older than the baby's voice she had imagined. She sounded all grown up. Sarah wondered what she would sound like when she grew up. Would she sound sweet like Angie, or harder and more serious like her mother?

"How old are you really?" Sarah asked her doll. She lifted Angie's arms up and down, waiting for a response, when her body once again tensed. But this time, it was more subtle and under control. Her hand squeezed tighter around her doll as her head started tilting back. Then, just as her eyes rolled back into her head, they reversed forward, her head lifting back up along with them. Sarah's eyes glared ahead with a layer of glaze over them, thick as motor oil.

Do not be afraid, Sarah Elizabeth…that is what I'm asking…

Sarah's eyes opened wide as she listened to the new, unfamiliar voice.

She heard her father speaking as she made her way down the stairs with Angie held close to her chest.

"'What to me is the multitude of your sacrifices?' says the Lord. 'I have had enough of burnt offerings of rams and the fat of well-fed beasts; I do not delight in the blood of bulls, or of lambs, or of goats.'"

Her father always seemed to be the one talking. Even when they had their best friends Brian and Christina over for their study sessions on Saturdays.

"Now, Brian, you've argued in the past, the meaning in this is clear: God does not want animal sacrifice. And you've also raised the point of vegetarianism, which I think is quite intriguing. Yet, as we see in other verses, Genesis 15:9, for example…"

Sarah Elizabeth started humming quietly as she approached her parents and their friends, fueled by confidence and excitement. She caught her mother's eyes first, who was sitting in a chair facing her. Sarah's father was standing with his back to her, and Brian and Christina were on the couch, staring up at him, listening.

"Hey, sweetheart, what is it?" Bess asked her daughter.

Sarah Elizabeth locked eyes with her mother, though she could feel the gaze of the others fall upon her. "Angie talked to me," she said proudly, if not a little defiantly.

"That's nice. Can you go back upstairs now? It's not quite time for lunch."

Sarah drew her eyebrows together and pulled her bottom lip in under her two buck teeth. Her mother said she'd grow into them.

"Who's Angie?" Christina asked, looking from Richard to Bess.

"Her doll," Bess answered.

Sarah held Angie up. "My doll."

Richard walked around the couch and squatted down to speak with his daughter. "What did you and Angie talk about?"

Sarah Elizabeth squeezed Angie back into her chest. "It was hard to hear her."

"Did you want to tell her something?"

Sarah shook her head. "She was trying to tell me something."

Richard smiled and tousled her curly strawberry-blonde hair. "Do you want me to come up and play Lite-Brite with you?"

"Richard." Bess drew his attention. "We're right in the middle of—"

"I know," Richard said, looking back over his shoulder at his wife. "It would just be for a few minutes."

"Go ahead, Rich," Brian added in. "We've got it. I can pick up from where you left—"

"But then he spoke," Sarah proclaimed.

All heads turned back toward Sarah Elizabeth.

Bess perked up, sliding to the edge of her seat. "What did you say, honey?"

Brian turned to his wife. "He?"

Richard's brow furrowed. "Who was 'he,' sweetie?"

"He was strong. He knew everything," Sarah responded.

Bess looked over at Christina, sensing the mood in the room shift. "She's never been like this before."

Sarah scrunched her nose up, annoyed at how her mother was talking about her. She looked back at her father. "He said the baby will be healthy."

Richard's face paled. He felt his jaw go slack, falling open.

Christina reached over and grabbed Bess's hand. "Praise."

"It's a sign," Bess responded.

Richard looked over his shoulder. "Bess, let's not jump to—"

"We've been praying for this, Richard." Bess let go of Christina's hand and walked over to her daughter, crouching down, pulling her attention away from her father. "What else did He say to you, honey?"

Sarah looked at her father, unsure if she should say more.

Richard glanced about the room, his brow furrowed with concern. He could feel the weight of his daughter's gaze as his eyes traveled back to her slight frame, studying her carefully as though it would be the last time he would do so. "It's okay, sweetie. You can tell us if you want to. But only if you want to."

"Richard." Bess quickly glared at her husband before looking back at her daughter with a smile. "There's no reason you can't tell us, Sarah. We're your parents."

Sarah closed her eyes and repeated the first thing she heard. "He said, 'Fear not, Sarah Elizabeth.'"

Brian jumped to his feet. "Luke 1:26. The Annunciation."

Richard whipped his head toward his best friend. "Brian, hold on just a second. That's a little extreme."

Christina grabbed her husband's hand. "Do you really think it is?"

Richard looked at his wife. "Bess, we've got to leave this alone."

"No!" Bess said, standing to her feet. "We cannot just ignore the Lord answering our prayers, Richard."

Richard sighed, turned to Sarah Elizabeth, and put a hand on her shoulder. "Honey, why don't we just go up—"

"What else did he say?" Bess jumped in. "You tell Mommy."

Sarah Elizabeth felt her face getting warmer. No one was listening to her. They didn't understand. "He talked to *me*!"

Bess nodded. "I know He did, Sarah. He chose you as a vessel to—"

"Bess, stop!" Richard turned to her, trying to keep his voice under control.

Bess pointed her finger sharply at her husband, her eyes saying everything. Then she turned back to her daughter, her face flipping as quickly as a light switch to pleasantness. "I'm so happy He talked to you, darling. Just tell me what else He said."

Sarah looked down, twisting Angie's arms. "The baby will be a miracle," she muttered.

Bess's hand clasped over her mouth.

Brian shook his head. "Unbelievable."

Christina stood up and grabbed hold of his arm.

Richard rubbed his brow. "Okay, that's enough, my love. Time to go upstairs." He grabbed his daughter's hand and stood to his feet.

"I'm finally going to have another baby!" Bess wailed. "Richard, we're going to—"

"It's not yours, Bess!" Sarah screamed.

Everyone in the room simultaneously recoiled.

Bess's eyes almost came out of her head as she raised her eyebrows at her daughter. "Sarah Elizabeth, I am your mother! You will—"

"No!" Richard held his hand out toward Bess as he wrapped his other arm around Sarah.

"It's my baby!" Sarah Elizabeth roared, tears cresting over her eyelids as she stared defiantly at her mother.

Richard looked down at his daughter, chills surging through his heart, breath stuck in his chest.

"It's not your baby, Mother! He said it's mine!" She turned and pulled her father along with her as she made her way back up the stairs.

Chapter 12

Mondegreen or Nonsense

It's been a weird morning, day... A body was found on mourner's beach. It may be something bad has happened to them. Everyone is talking about it. Whole town is freaking out.

    Zo is terrified. She's somehow got it in her head the person drowned. Now she's having a panic attack that something will happen to you. Can you call?

    I'll call tonight.

Noble slipped into the school library, the door creaking behind him as he stepped onto the threadbare carpet. In the dark silence of the room, his phone's blue light shone up on his face like a beacon. He read the same text message again, but something about his father's response unsettled him. Why had he not reacted to hearing there was a dead body on the beach?

When his father called late last night, their mother, Julie, had spoken with him for only a few minutes. He hadn't exactly taken much notice of the conversation. The one he'd had with Mary Germaine still had him pondering her explanations against his half-seen experience.

But this morning, as he and Zoe jumped into his car and waved goodbye to his mom, the conversation between his parents jumped to the forefront of his thoughts. It was all he could think about on the short drive through the small town. His mother had said something like, "Yes, it's all over town... I'm not sure. Some are saying it's a young woman... Mm-hmm, I've already told her not to worry about you. Are you going out tomorrow?" She laughed at something he said, then looked at Noble before saying, "He's under pressure. Want to say hi to Dad?" She lifted the phone off her shoulder.

"Hi, Dad!" he'd said.

"He says hi and 'you've got this,'" Jolie had told her son. "Hmm? Oh, I don't know. You know Bo won't put her down. We'll keep an eye on it. Wrap the leg. She'll have a nice retired life…"

A brief mention of the significant event of the day and nothing more. Their conversation turned to the ailing older trail horse they'd been treating all summer up at the ranch, and then they said their goodbyes. It was a perfectly normal conversation, save for the fact that his father had displayed no interest or worry about a dead body on the town's beach.

Noble rubbed his forehead in confusion, trying to make sense of his thoughts. He wasn't sure if he was just overreacting, because his nerves were already on a razor's edge, and yet he couldn't shake the feeling that his parents were hiding something from him.

He clicked the phone screen off, shoving it into his pocket, and surveyed the quiet library. It was an architectural feat, carefully crafted with ingenuity by an eccentric architect who had worked in the district for years. The high-arching entrance tunneled into a round room with large archways along the side walls. A light shone from the oculus on the ceiling in a way that reminded him of Grand Central Station's Whispering Gallery. Despite its beauty, low-wattage bulbs cast only minimal light over the wooden desks and bookshelves. Still, it had its allure, though most kids preferred the more modern, brighter atrium off of the cafeteria as a place to mingle or study. So it surprised Noble when he heard a soft whisper in his ear, "Top off with ranch."

Shifting his backpack on his shoulders, Noble walked further into the library, following the sound of the disembodied voice. At a table toward the back, Anya Bury was laughing to herself—in a library voice— twirling a pen between her fingers. Her lilting laughter briefly interrupted his thoughts, like a breeze through his mind.

Noble approached and gently cleared his throat. "Top what with ranch?" he asked.

Aquamarine eyes leaped from the table to meet his. "Oh, crap. You scared me," she said with a smile.

"Sorry," Noble said. He moved to the table, pulling out a chair to have a seat. "I just thought I heard a ghost say, 'top it with ranch' but, turns out, it was you."

Anya laughed. "I could see a ghost haunting our school."

A smile split Noble's face, one he couldn't contain. "So, what are we topping with ranch?"

"I don't know. A puppet?" Anya waved the pen between her fingers, distracted, and focused on the notebook beside her.

Noble looked from Anya to the notebook, taking a brief peek at the organized columns of random words printed in elegant calligraphy. "Huh?"

Anya looked up, meeting his eyes. It was almost as if this second glance registered she was talking to a real person. She shook her head and blinked. "Sorry, um…" She paused, tapping her pen on the notebook. "I'm trying to see if I can make a logical phrase or word out of this," she said, circling a random selection of letters at the top of the page. Then she spun it to face Noble.

He leaned over and read them, "Ba Ba La Rain Itch. Is it a puzzle? Like a game?"

Anya shook her head. "No, not really. I'm not sure if they'll even make sense."

"Mondegreen," Noble stated.

"What?"

"Mondegreen. They're misunderstood or misinterpreted words. Like when you hear something else in the lyrics of a song. Say, instead of hearing 'there's a bad moon on the rise,' you hear 'there's a bathroom on the right,'" Noble explained, pushing the notebook back toward her. "Or something like 'these if hill wore.'"

"What's 'these if hill wore'?"

"The civil war," Noble said with a hint of a laugh. "That's more what you're trying to do, right? Find out if these syllables make a word or words?"

Anya pursed her lips, a smile alighting in her luminescent blue eyes. "I didn't know you were so into wordplay."

Anya's expression when she smiled mesmerized Noble. Her eyes lit up like a pair of brilliant stars, watery and bright, and her cheeks dimpled as her mouth formed the perfect shape. Her hair cascaded in waves, shifting from copper to pale blonde to near white at the tips like sunbeams had kissed them. He remembered when they first met in kindergarten with Ms. Ryans, Anya wore it very short in a Charlize Theron–style bowl cut that didn't show off her unique coloring as prominently. It was honestly the first time, sitting this close and in such a quiet and personal atmosphere, that he could fully take in how pretty she was. Not classically pretty, more like a fantasy painting of a strange, ethereal fairy.

"We played Mad Gab a lot when I was young," he explained.

"Ah. I don't really know that game. Now I kind of wish I did." Anya pulled her legs up under her.

Noble bounced his knee under the table, contemplating why their paths were always on the same plane but rarely intersecting. He'd always liked Anya. He still recalled her tenth birthday party on her family's farm, riding horses and camping outside on their property. So why hadn't he done more to get to know her before, when right now, all he could think about was how much he'd like to know her better? "It might help to run it through a text-to-speech system."

"Hm, haven't tried that."

Noble reached around to his backpack, pulling his tablet from inside. It woke, and he tapped into a search engine, pulling up a free text-to-speech app. He typed in the words, then scooted closer, turning the screen toward her and turning up the volume. He tapped the play button.

The words came out in the voice of a female AI, awkward and nonhuman. Both their eyebrows were knit tight, concentrating on the sound coming out.

"Wait, let me switch it to a male voice," Noble suggested, making changes and then playing it again.

Eventually, Anya shook her head. "Not sure if I'm hearing anything that makes sense."

"Yeah, me neither." Noble set his tablet on the table. "What's this for? Class or something?"

Anya opened her mouth, then hesitated.

"It's cool if it's personal," Noble said. He pulled his tablet from the table.

"No, it's not personal. It's just weird."

Noble couldn't help but laugh. It came out like a flood he couldn't control. "I get that."

She wondered what he meant by his comment, the awkward release of laughter. "You okay?" she asked facetiously, laughing at his burst of laughter.

Noble ran a hand through his hair. "Yeah, sorry. It's just been a weird week."

"I guess you guys have that meet coming up. Everyone keeps talking about how you're going to win and all…"

Noble's eyes narrowed briefly, then he nodded. "That's been…yeah, there's some pressure there."

"Oh." Anya second-guessed what was bothering him. "Or do you mean the body on the beach?"

Noble tilted his head.

"Or none of those things." Anya half laughed. "I just—"

"No, it…it's kind of all those things."

A moment of silence lapsed between them.

"Do you remember how Nettie used to say her brother wasn't her brother?" Anya blurted.

He did. He'd thought about it a lot since talking to Mary on her porch. The fact that Anya was bringing it up made his flesh prickle.

While the details of her childhood story were foggy, he recalled her mentioning her brother being replaced by something else. "Kind of? I know you guys are close, so you probably know more about it than me."

Anya settled into the poorly cushioned chair. "Well, yeah. He was five when he was"—she paused, smiling and shaking her head before continuing—"taken. Do you know what five-year-olds are like?"

"I know what my sister was like."

"Okay, so you know. Nettie's brother spoke, as in he talked in sentences. He ate like a normal kid. And then, overnight, he was… What was he?" She thought it over. What words could she use to express the change without divulging an entire family history? "He couldn't talk, didn't talk. He ate with his hands, like a toddler, like an infant."

"But he's ill, right? Like he—"

"Yeah, doctors diagnosed him with regressive autism. For a while, they thought it might be Sanfilippo syndrome. I only know all this 'cause—"

"'Cause of Nettie, right?"

"Right. Anyway, it doesn't talk. He hasn't talked," Anya quickly corrected. It was one thing to call Not-George an 'it' around Nettie, a whole other thing to say something like that in front of Noble, who didn't know as much about Nettie's refusal to call the thing living with them a human.

Noble's gut clenched, his whole body tensed as if waiting for the starting gun to go off. Why had Anya just used the word *it*? Just like Mary Germaine had slipped on multiple occasions.

"Some grunts or noises now and again, but…yesterday in therapy, he said something to Nettie," Anya continued.

Noble tried to wrangle his thoughts. Where was this going? Why did he feel like he needed to listen? He looked down at the notebook and took a deep breath as he would at the starting line before racing. "That's what he said?"

"That's what she said it sounded like. She was playing with him. That's part of the therapy, trying to interact with him, and she had this puppet. It was one of those old-school ugly ones."

"Punch and Judy type deal," Noble said, nodding along.

"And…" She let out an exasperated breath. "She thinks maybe it—he was finally trying to say something."

"Why would he be trying to say something now? I mean to say…" Noble pulled his lower lip in, dragging his front teeth across it. "I don't get why this would be… You know you called him an 'it'?" He couldn't let it drop.

Anya looked down, played with her fingernails, and in a hushed voice said, "Nettie doesn't like calling Not-George a 'he.'"

"Not-George?"

"That's what she refers to him as."

"And why doesn't she like calling him a 'he'?"

Anya glanced up and around the room. "She doesn't think Not-George is a real person. A human."

Noble's lips parted. He wanted to laugh, but after his discussion with Mary, hearing this from Anya felt like someone had punched him in the gut. "Are you serious?"

Anya slid the notebook toward herself, an action that had Noble suggesting she was about to pack up and leave. He didn't want her to.

"Wait, I mean—"

"I feel bad telling you this. It's her story to tell," Anya said. She capped her pen, slipping it into the backpack on the chair beside her.

Noble concentrated on what he could remember from their childhood, what Nettie used to tell them. "She, uh, Nettie, she said her real brother was taken, right?"

Anya nodded. Noble had always struck her as a fair person. Or maybe it was simply that he had his own set of worries. "Yeah," she finally replied.

"You believe her?"

Slowly, Anya nodded. "I do, in a way."

Noble's leg jostled under the table. "And there were others, right? Like, little fairy children or—"

"Changelings. That's what she saw. Not children, but goblins or, yeah, fairy things, I guess. That's the folklore. Why are you asking?" Anya was cautious but curious why Noble had taken a sudden interest.

Noble's leg was bouncing even faster now, matching his beating heart. What were they even talking about? And why did he have a growing feeling, worry, that it was real? "Have you ever, um, seen these other not-children she says she saw?"

Anya shook her head. "No. But—"

"I'm not—" Noble started, cutting her off. He offered a smile. "I didn't mean to interrupt, but I just wanted you to know I'm not asking for proof or…I know what kind of bizarre shit there is out there, in the weird part of the forest. We all do, right?"

"We do. Yes." Anya kept her eyes down on the table. She knew precisely what kind of weirdness surrounded Lost Grove, at least one aspect of it. Her mother was one of those weird things, but she'd never dream of telling anyone the truth of that.

"Sorry. I'm not trying to pry. It's just that…I could help. If you wanted."

Anya smiled, nearly laughing. "King of Mad Gab."

Noble couldn't help but smile. "Something like that. I mean, hey, you have no experience in the word game world from the sounds of it."

Anya looked up, meeting his eyes. "Very true. And I'd like that, thanks."

The bell rang, causing both of them to stir, particularly away from one another. Noble had forgotten how close he'd moved to sit next to her.

"Cool," he said, standing. "I'll text you if I come up with anything."

"That would be awesome," Anya said, pushing her stuff into her bag.

Noble had turned to walk out but suddenly twirled back around and pulled out his phone. "Wait. I, um, do I have your number? I have to, right?"

Anya looked up, her cheeks with a hint of rose in them. "Um…" She pulled out her phone.

"Oh, here's a group text," Noble said and showed her his phone. "This is your number, yeah?"

Anya nodded. "Yep."

Noble held his finger on the number until it prompted him to add a new contact. How on earth did they not have each other's names programmed into their phones? He shook his head as he sent her a text. "There, I just texted you."

She looked down at the incoming text and read it out loud, "'Hey, I'm Noble.'" Anya laughed.

"Okay, gotta run to class. See ya!"

Anya's gaze lingered on Noble as he headed toward the doors, and she wondered why it had taken her so long to really look at him. His eyes were wide and sincere—almost too trusting for his own good. Her first crush had been on him, when they were both ten. He'd toured the horses around her birthday party like a seasoned jockey, and the animals seemed to look over their shoulders to make sure he was still with them. She saw something in his eyes that day—an old-soul kind of sadness. Smiling softly, Anya thought maybe that crush wasn't such a distant memory after all.

Chapter 13

Autopsy

Seth tried not to eviscerate the speed limit as he took the last turn to get back to the station. His mind had been racing with possibilities from his conversation with Brigette when Bill's text came through on his phone. In it, Wes had finished the autopsy and needed to see them urgently. The throb of adrenaline in his veins made him want to push the gas pedal, but Seth had to remind himself he wasn't back in San Francisco doing his best Steve McQueen impression from *Bullitt*. The next death in Lost Grove coming as a result of the reckless driving by their new sergeant would not be a good look.

Seth pulled into the parking lot, happy to see Bill outside waiting for him. He swung his Bronco around and stopped next to the chief of police.

Bill opened the door. "I'm eager to hear the big news from your talk with Ms. Lowe," he said as he climbed in and shut the door.

"Did Wes tell you anything?" Seth asked, pulling out of the lot on nearly squealing tires.

"Not a thing. Said he needed to see us both."

"That means it's not straightforward."

"I figured." Bill grinned at Seth's driving. "You could put on the flashers, ya know."

Seth took his foot off the gas pedal. "Not exactly an emergency."

"Compared to what we usually get calls about, I would say it qualifies."

Seth laughed but resisted the urge.

"So, I take it nothing much from the other teachers you spoke to?"

"All the same stuff. Sweet girl, smart, driven. Most of them haven't seen her since graduation."

Bill shrugged. "Not a whole lot there. What about boyfriends? Anyone see her with a boy?"

Seth shook his head. "Nope. Brigette, in particular, thought the idea of Sarah having a lover she didn't know about was hilarious. Said she'd never have the time."

"So, unless we learn something about a college boyfriend, we can cross that off our list."

"Well…I don't think that's a good idea."

Bill held a hand out. "I'd love to hear why not."

"For starters, two and a half years with no one speaking to her leaves ample time for her to have been in a relationship, if not multiple. And they wouldn't have to be at college."

"Fair point. So, what's the big news then?"

"Brigette said Sarah Elizabeth had serious sleep issues that would often keep her up, wide awake. This backs up what her parents mentioned about her insomnia, but the one thing Brigette added was that when Sarah lay awake at night, she had visions."

Bill frowned. "Visions?"

Seth nodded, knowing he could just as well be speaking about himself. "Not dreams. She was adamant about that. But very clear visions. Visions of people that she had never met but felt like she knew intimately. She said she knew they needed her help, and her inability to do anything about it traumatized her."

Bill slowly turned to Seth. "Um, I'm not really sure what to make of that."

Seth nodded, pushing the gas as they left Lost Grove proper and merged onto the highway, leading them to Eureka. "What's the first thing that came into your mind when I said Sarah had visions? Don't judge it, just answer."

"That she was crazy," Bill admitted.

Seth pointed a finger in the air. "Exactly! Now, we don't use that terminology anymore and for multiple good reasons, but hearing about these visions brings mental stability into question. Was she diagnosed, treated, medicated? Or did she keep her visions a close-held secret?"

Bill narrowed his gaze. "So, you think that has something to do with how she ended up back here on the beach?"

"It's just another avenue to pursue, and a significant one. Here's this girl that everyone describes as studious, sweet, determined, but also changes clothes at school, puts on makeup that she takes off before she gets back home. One of her best friends, Jeremy, mentions nothing about these visions, and her other best friend, whom she confided in, hears stories of visions. And even more, Brigette said that in one of her visions, Sarah believed she saw a divine being."

Bill shot another look at Seth. "A divine being? Like an angel or something?"

"It's possible. Brigette said that she was having a terrifying vision, that she actually felt pain and felt helpless to do anything until this being showed up. Sarah said it shimmered and then she felt snow or feathers, something soft and comforting."

"Feathers? Sure sounds like an angel."

"Well, whatever it was, it brought her a sense of peace."

Bill raised his eyebrows. "So, you believe she saw an angel?"

"No. No, I'm not saying that. But I believe Brigette believes Sarah believed it. And if Sarah truly believed she had that experience, I would say that's a significant piece of information about her psyche. And it's not just her I'm concerned about. I'm concerned about the psyche of her parents."

"What do Richard and Bess have to do with that?"

"I think quite a bit. Brigette told me that when they were younger, Sarah told her that her parents believed she could talk to God."

Bill tilted his head. "Like praying?"

"That's what I said. No, like actually converse with Him. But Sarah told Brigette that her parents were wrong, that she wasn't talking to God. But they kept pressing her to speak with Him. I couldn't get much more than that; it was a foggy memory for Brigette. But it would seem that Richard and Bess were maybe trying to use their daughter as a conduit to communicate with God. To tell him something, find out something, I don't know."

Bill slowly nodded. "Like people who believe that God is telling them to burn down a school? Something along those lines?"

Seth grimaced. "Sort of? My point is, she could have been suffering from a serious mental illness all her life. And instead of getting their daughter help, they thought she was communicating with God. She could have had borderline schizophrenia, which could explain her visions and why she, out of nowhere, cut off her friends and family. It could be part of what led to her being in a situation that got her to where we are today. It could explain why no one would know she was back in town."

"Well, I don't like the sound of that. Guess we'll have to keep that in mind when we talk to them."

"Agreed. And of course, this could all change when we hear what Wes has to tell us."

Bill nodded. "And there's that."

Seth followed Bill into the pinkish-beige edifice that served as the coroner's public administration building. The door, which looked like they hijacked it from the high school gymnasium, opened with moaning protestations and creaks. It seemed like the old hinges abhorred this unseasonable cold as much as the townsfolk. The inside was bare and industrial, an unwelcoming series of browns, whites, and beiges that felt depressing and dull. Only the tiled linoleum floor possessed any color, though the pattern left much to be desired.

Bill waved a brief hello as they passed the mouse of a man at reception and made their way down the hall toward Wes's office. Bill rapped his knuckles on the doorframe. "Wes, you ready?"

Wes looked up from his desk, already removing a pair of reading glasses. He dropped them onto the table with such carelessness Bill imagined he went through multiple pairs a year.

"Gentlemen," Wes greeted them. He rose and pulled on his lab coat, offering a quick handshake. "Any questions before we head in?"

"Nope," Bill said.

Seth shook his head.

"Alright then," Wes said. With a wave over his shoulder, he headed down the hall with the officers trailing after.

Seth stuck his hands in his pockets, feeling his chest constrict, fighting to take a breath. He'd been at hundreds of autopsies during and post-operation in his years as a detective, but revisiting the body of Sarah Elizabeth Grahams felt like entering quicksand. He couldn't afford to have another episode, not in front of Bill, not when they were on the precipice of discovering vital information in a case Seth felt in his bones was about to become a lot more complicated.

Wes pushed open the door and entered the autopsy room.

Bill held his hand out to hold open the door and looked back at Seth. "Let's see what we can learn."

Seth gave him an over-assured nod, which felt fake even to himself.

He stepped past Bill to see Sarah's body on the stainless steel operating table, uncovered and already sewn back up. Wes stepped up next to her, snapping on his second latex glove. The chill of the room felt as if they'd stepped back outside into the frigid fall. Fluorescent lights eliminated any room for shadows to creep and painted the men in a poorly looking hue.

Wes picked up the clipboard with his notes, reviewing them briefly in a manner to give the officers time to adjust and take in the body on their own. Seth let out a sigh of relief that seeing Sarah again didn't besiege him with a flashback or a sensation of floating on air. He spotted a look of apprehension on his old friend's face as he came further into the room.

Bill stepped up closer to the table. "I hope you've got some answers for us, Wes. Because all we've run into are more questions."

Seth walked over to the far side of the table, noticing Bill's reticence to look at the body.

"Well, I've got a host of findings for you gentlemen, but I'm afraid most of them will lead to more questions, some of which baffle even me," Wes said, stepping over to the foot of the table. "It's something like *A Tale of Two Cities*."

Seth raised an eyebrow at Bill.

"Go on," Bill said.

Wes motioned to the body with his clipboard. "So, on the outside, we have no signs of injury. Nothing to suggest a confrontation. Clean nails, no ligature marks, no blunt trauma, no abrasions. Honestly, her body is practically untouched on the surface."

"So, like I thought, she was never in the water," Seth said.

Wes held up his hand. "There's a remote chance she was in the ocean, but I agree, it's highly unlikely. There was no water in her lungs, which means she didn't drown. If she were to have been in the water, she was dead beforehand. That being said, her body is in far too good of condition for me to believe she was in the water. That and there was no trace of salt water in her hair."

Seth looked at Bill, then back to Wes. "So, someone placed her body on the beach."

"That would be my assessment, yes."

"What about suicide?" Bill asked.

Wes shook his head. "We can rule that out for a myriad of reasons."

"The other city, as you say?" Seth prompted him.

"Yes, her insides." Wes stepped around to the middle of the table, directly across from Seth. He paused for a moment and then wiped his brow.

Seth noticed a slight tremble in Wes's hand and that he almost instantly looked paler. "Jesus, what is it, Wes?"

Wes motioned to Sarah Elizabeth's belly and looked up at Seth. "She was pregnant."

"I beg your pardon?" Bill felt his heart kick over, then start back up.

"Fuck," Seth muttered. The Kelly Fulson case jumped to the forefront of his mind. He looked over at Bill. "This is an eerie fucking coincidence."

"Just what I was thinking," Bill said and looked at Wes.

"Kelly Fulson?" Wes guessed.

"I mean, we talked about it yesterday, but I would never have thought…"

Wes sighed. "It was a long time ago. And I will say this. There is one major difference regarding the pregnancy."

Bill pointed to Sarah's body. "That we couldn't tell. She can't have been pregnant for more than—"

"No, that's not it," Wes jumped in. "The reason we couldn't tell, aside from a slightly distended belly, which could have just been how her body was, is because she already had the baby. So to speak."

"What?" Bill gasped.

"What do you mean, 'so to speak'?" Seth asked at the same time.

"Well," Wes started and wiped his head again, the sweat now apparent to Seth. "I have to warn you both. This is where things get…well, quite frankly, really fucked up."

Bill and Seth exchanged nervous glances.

"I'll assume neither of you has heard of a symphysiotomy or a pubiotomy?"

Both men silently indicated they hadn't.

"I heard about it in med school, but I had to look it up to be sure of what I was seeing. Both are essentially medieval operations to remove a baby from the uterus during difficult, obstructed childbirth."

Seth's stomach clenched.

Bill winced. "I'm not sure I want to know."

"You don't." Wes shook his head. "They're very similar operations, and I use that term loosely because in modern times…it's barbaric. A symphysiotomy is a severing of the cartilage between the pubis and hip bone. Whereas a pubiotomy is sawing through the pubic bone itself."

"Jesus Christ," Seth turned away from the thought, rubbing a hand down his jaw.

Bill covered his mouth.

Seth turned back to Wes. "Which one was done to her?"

"Both," Wes stated.

Bill dropped his hand as his eyes widened. "Wait, is the baby—"

"No," Wes jumped in quickly, "there was no baby in the uterus. When I checked, I…" Wes set his clipboard down next to the body and brought his hand to his chin.

A swell of anxiety filled Seth's chest. He had never in his career seen a medical examiner so flustered or distressed by their findings. He looked over at Bill, whose face had gone ashen.

Wes cleared his throat. "My apologies. I've just never seen anything like this in my life. Disturbingly, it would appear they ripped the infant out of her body."

Bill brought the back of his hand to cover his mouth.

Seth looked down at Sarah Elizabeth's body. "I don't understand. What does that mean?" he asked, looking back up at Wes.

"The umbilical cord attached to a baby connects to the placenta, which is attached to the wall of the uterus. Forgive the anatomy lesson—"

"It's fine. Go on," Seth said.

"But it's important to my findings, and I think it will be paramount to your investigation. The placenta typically comes out shortly after the woman finishes giving birth to the child, in the third stage of labor. There are several potential complications with the placenta that can be quite dangerous to the mother and the child if they're not detected or dealt with properly. There is a placenta abruption where the placenta dislodges from the uterine wall before delivery. This can cause bleeding and prevent the infant from getting the proper nutrients."

"Okay…" Seth let the word linger, wondering where Wes was going with this.

Wes pointed to the lower area of Sarah Elizabeth's belly. "And then there's placenta accreta. This is when the placenta grows too deeply into the uterus wall, which can be life-threatening. It appears this was the case with Sarah Elizabeth. The placenta was no longer inside her, but the wall of the uterus was…badly torn apart."

Bill spun away from the table and ran around the room like a chicken until he found the stainless steel wastebasket behind Wes, where he dropped to his knees and vomited.

Wes looked at Seth and raised his eyebrows.

Seth let out a long exhale through pursed lips. He had seen his share of violence and its aftermath but had never heard of anything so vile. He looked past Wes to see Bill wiping his mouth with his sleeve as he stood fully up.

"Sorry, guys," Bill started as he rejoined the men at the table, "I just…"

"It's alright, Bill." Seth reached over and patted his boss on the back of the arm. "Do you want to step outside? I can fill you in if—"

"No. No, I'll be fine." Bill pointed at Wes. "Go on."

Wes nodded. "Right, so, the area that was torn was so vast and so damaged that the blood loss most certainly would have killed her. If she wasn't dead already."

"You haven't determined the cause of death yet?" Seth asked.

"I've got two theories, neither too pleasant."

Bill closed his eyes and took in a deep breath.

"She either died from severe blood loss stemming from the combination of the symphysiotomy, the pubiotomy, and the placenta being torn out—"

"Fucking Christ," Seth muttered.

"—or, considering the amount of stress put on her body and the inhuman amount of pain she must have gone through, she could have died from a heart attack. Or a combination of both. I don't know. We still have to wait for the toxicology report to come in. Still, I can't fathom it will tell us anything that would overshadow this. This poor girl was mutilated."

The sounds of a sniffle drew Seth's attention over to Bill, who was squeezing the bridge of his nose, tears surrounding his fingers.

"I've just… This sort of thing doesn't happen here." Bill dropped his hands and opened his eyes. "Christ, I've got two daughters."

Seth was at a loss for words.

Bill looked at Wes. "Sorry, I know I'm not the only one with a daughter."

"It's okay," Wes said. "It's barbaric and truly fucked up. Constance isn't much younger than Sarah. I can't help but think of her and what I…"

Seth turned away from the table and paced while Bill and Wes stood in painful silence. "I mean, why on earth would something like this have been done?"

Wes cleared his throat. "Well, I can't speak to why these procedures were done, but historically, it was to save the infant's life."

"There's no way this was performed at a hospital. Is there?" Seth turned to look at Wes.

Wes shook his head. "There's no way a practicing physician would have done this. They would have performed a cesarean if she were in a hospital."

"Right, not an active doctor. But a professional, someone trained, would have had to do it, right? It's not as if a person off the street would know—"

"No, it would be someone with medical training, no question about that. I just can't comprehend that any employed professional would resort to these procedures. Not in a hospital. Not in this country."

Bill's head snapped back. "Would any professional perform such an operation these days? In any country?"

Wes shook his head. "To my shock, and I think this is why I recalled this from med school, it was uncovered that hundreds, if not thousands, of both operations were performed in Ireland from the forties through the eighties."

"In God's name, why?" Bill gasped.

"From what I read, it seems it was driven by Catholicism, women's duties of motherhood and such."

Seth's head snapped toward Bill, brow pinched, the notion of Sarah Elizabeth's parents forcing her to communicate with God dancing through his mind.

"Now, there's no documentation that they have done these procedures since then," Wes continued. "Obviously, now the cesarean section is the much safer alternative, but that wasn't always the case. But why they were still performing symphysiotomies or pubiotomies in the eighties is beyond me."

Bill ran his hand through his hair, trying to process just how far their case had leaped in a manner of minutes.

Seth stepped back toward the operating table. "So someone, or some people, in where we're assuming is outside of any hospital, performed this…operation, surgery, torture, I don't know. And then they, what? Cleaned her up, drove her out to Mourner's Beach, and dumped her body there?"

Wes held his hands up. "I don't know. That's for you to figure out. But, yes, something along those lines."

Seth looked at Bill. "All the more reason to get to the bottom of the note left on your door."

Bill nodded. "I'd say so."

Seth's eyes dropped to Sarah Elizabeth's body, his mind racing down various avenues of where to go from here. "Oh, fuck." Seth looked up at Wes with wide eyes.

"What?" Bill asked, voice shaky.

Seth's eyes narrowed. "Is there a chance the baby is still alive?"

Wes took in a heavy breath and let out an audible sigh. "As horrendous as what happened to Sarah Elizabeth is, there's no reason to believe that the baby isn't alive."

Bill looked at Seth. "Mother of God."

"I assume you've spoken with her parents?" Wes asked.

Bill nodded. "Yes, I talked to them yesterday informally. And they made no mention of Sarah being pregnant or a baby."

Seth looked back at the examiner. "We're taking their official statements later this afternoon, but Wes, who are we looking for here? And what are we charging them with?"

Wes pursed his lips in thought. "Well, as I said earlier, someone with medical training, to be sure. It could be a practicing surgeon, but I'm highly skeptical of that notion. So this would leave us looking at either a surgeon in training or a retired surgeon. And of those two, I would lean heavily toward the older of the two based on the era these procedures were done."

Seth nodded. "I'm with you on that."

"As to what you're looking to charge them with? Involuntary manslaughter, based on the fact they were likely trying to save the child's life. But you've also got the fact that they abandoned Sarah Elizabeth, tried to make it appear no physical harm was done to her, and may or may not be in possession of that child."

Seth started pacing again. "So, involuntary manslaughter, tampering with a corpse, destroying and concealing evidence, and possible abduction of an infant. Great."

Bill shook his head. "So, what the hell are we telling her parents?"

Seth thrust his hands in his pockets as he looked down at the pale face of Sarah Elizabeth. He couldn't fathom any parents being involved in such an act. But then again, there was the scene at Golden Gate Park in San Francisco that had completely altered his view of what a parent could do to their child. It was one reason he didn't hesitate to return home to help his parents.

Seth stopped pacing and looked at Bill. "We don't tell them shit to start. We need to know what they know and if they're hiding anything."

Bill narrowed his brow. "You can't possibly think they had anything to do with something like this."

"I don't think anything yet, Bill, but we have to at least look at it as a possibility." Seth turned to the medical examiner. "Wes, this means you can't reveal any of this to them. Not the baby, not the surgeries, nothing hinting at the cause of death. If they're concealing knowledge of this, or if anyone else is, we can't risk this information leaking and tipping the responsible party off."

"I haven't scheduled a time to talk to them yet," Wes said. "You just let me know the how and the when."

"I'll call you after we interview them and keep you up to speed."

Wes nodded.

Seth turned to Bill. "Let's head back to the station and plot out how we're going to go about these interviews. Because this changes everything."

Bill scratched his head. "I don't have a clue how to go about—"

"Yes, you do. We just need to be on the same page."

Without a hint of confidence, Bill nodded.

Chapter 14

Richard Grahams, Loving Father

Peeking out the blinds in Bill's office, Seth noted the Grahamses waiting for their formal statements to be taken. The delay to their interviews was an intentional act but also a necessary one. They had obtained an avalanche of new information since they were last in the office and needed to sift through it to ensure they missed nothing speaking with the Grahamses.

Seth walked back to the whiteboard, where Bill was standing, his notepad in one hand, marker in the other. He spoke out loud as he wrote, "We've got visions…a divine being…mental stability to check on…a missing baby…"

"I still just can't believe it," Bill muttered.

"The list of suspects now expands to not only who performed the procedures that took Sarah's life but anyone who had knowledge of her pregnancy, which obviously includes our mystery father."

"Sarah Grahams, of all people."

Seth wrote 'Cult' under the 'Suspects' heading.

Bill scowled. "A cult?"

Eyes still focused on the board, his mind shifting pieces around, connecting dots, Seth said, "No one has seen Sarah Elizabeth for almost three years. If she got a new phone number, no one knows what it is. She reportedly has no social media presence. She somehow got pregnant without anyone having a clue. Barring hearing back from anyone at Baylor, Sarah Elizabeth has been a ghost. So, where the hell has she been?"

Seth turned to face Bill. "There is a decent chance, based on what we heard from Brigette, that Sarah was suffering from some form of mental illness. All of these signs point to a possibility of her falling in with some sort of cult. And based on her seeing divine beings—"

"Angels," Bill said.

"Whatever the case, I would have to guess it would be a religious cult. Cult leaders, typically white males, look for susceptible young women as their prime targets, those open to radical theories, ideas off the beaten path. Is it likely she was in a cult? No, probably not. But ask yourself this: Knowing everything we do thus far, would it really shock you if that's what we found out?"

"All things considered, I guess not." Bill let out a long exhale. "Jesus. Serial killers? Cults? Is this how your cases always work?"

Seth chuckled. "Not all of them, no. But do you see what I'm getting at?"

"We have no idea where she's been for well over two years, so anything is possible," Bill responded.

Seth smiled and nodded, then set the marker down in the small tray at the bottom of the whiteboard. "And right now, we have the opportunity to see if any of these"—he tapped the board—"can be confirmed or taken off the list."

Bill walked over to his window and peered out at the Grahamses. He looked back at Seth. "Do you still suspect them?"

Seth joined Bill at the window and lifted a blind. Richard's left leg was bouncing up and down, and he flicked his wrist up at that moment to look at his watch. "Do I suspect either of them performing a symphysiotomy or a pubiotomy? No, I don't. Do I think they had a role in Sarah's psychological issues? I think it's highly likely. There's a big bridge between those two things, but I mainly want to find out if they've really had no contact with their daughter since January 2021."

"Shall we get to it, then?"

"I think we've kept them waiting long enough," Seth said as he headed toward Bill's door. The Grahamses' appointment had been set for two p.m. It was now three p.m. A nice long time for their moods to sour or their fears to kick in.

"Richard. Bess," Bill greeted the Grahamses, seated next to each other in the station's waiting area. "Thanks for coming in."

"Of course. Anything we can do to help." Richard stood and offered his hand to the chief of police. Richard was tall, just under six feet, and thin, if not athletic. His hair typically appeared darker, styled with thick hair product, but in his current untethered state, it was an ash brown.

Bess remained seated, eyes red and swollen, her blonde hair pulled up into a frazzled bun. This was the first time Bill could recall seeing her with no makeup on.

"I think you know Sergeant Seth Wolfe." Bill motioned back to Seth.

"Richard." Seth stepped forward and extended his hand. Aside from his hollow eyes, it looked like Richard had aged well. Seth had always thought Richard had a face that would have lent itself to being cast as a snide, bullying kid in an eighties film, but in the decades since, his face had softened and filled out. He now looked like he would be cast as the amiable neighbor who offers words of wisdom to his troubled friend.

"Seth." Richard met his hand for a brief handshake. "This is my wife, Bess."

Bess looked up at Seth and nodded.

"I'm sorry to have to see you under these circumstances, Richard. And meet you." Seth nodded at Bess. "My condolences to both of you."

"Thank you," Bess offered meekly.

Bill stepped back and held open the waist-high saloon doors leading into the bullpen. "If you want to follow me back, we'll try to make this as quick and painless as possible."

Arriving at the first room, Seth turned to face the parents. "Richard, if you'd like to step into room number one, we'll start with—"

"What do you mean, room number one? I'm not leaving my wife alone," Richard protested.

"You won't be leaving her alone. She'll be with me and Bill."

Richard looked at Bill. "What's the meaning of this?"

"No meaning at all," Bill stated. "We need to get individual statements from both of you."

"Why do we need to be separated for that?" Bess asked.

"Well, it really wouldn't be individual, then," Seth said plainly. "This is not an uncommon practice."

"Uncommon for what? Our daughter just died. Why would you separate us? At a time like this?" Bess turned into Richard's arm and began weeping.

"It's okay, honey," Richard said, giving Seth a stern glare. "Honestly, is this necessary?"

"I'm afraid it's very necessary," Seth replied. "Especially given the scenario. Neither of you has seen or spoken to your daughter in over two and a half years."

"What's that got to do with it?"

"Memories from that long ago can vary. Greatly. And the best way for us to get the clearest picture of who Sarah Elizabeth was, and what happened leading up to the last time you saw her, is by individual interviews."

Bess peered at Seth from Richard's arm. "You don't trust us to tell you the truth? How could you—"

"That's got nothing to do with it," Seth cut her off, keeping his voice low and calm. "I'm sure you each had your own special relationship with Sarah. And we need to hear that, unfiltered."

"What does that even mean?" Richard asked.

"Look"—Bill held his hands up—"we have a lot of unanswered questions surrounding your daughter's death, and this will be the most helpful way for us—for all of us—to get some answers."

Seth nodded at Bill and looked back to the Grahamses. "I promise you; we want to solve this case as quickly as possible."

Bess patted Richard's chest and let go of her grasp on him. "It's fine, Richard. We all want the same thing."

"That's right," Bill assured them.

Richard rubbed his face with both hands and sighed. "Yeah, okay. However it's done."

"We appreciate it," Seth said, opening the door to Interview Room 1 "Richard, if you could step in here."

Bill motioned to the back of the station. "Bess, I'll walk you to room number two. And can I get either of you some coffee? A Danish? Got some fresh from the bakery."

"From this morning?" Bess asked with a sneer.

"Just coffee, then?" Bill attempted, stepping backward toward the other room.

"This is Sergeant Seth Wolfe, along with Sheriff Bill Richards of the Lost Grove Police Department. The time is"—Seth checked his Bulova watch, an indulgence piece crafted for the demands of the lunar environment for an astronaut on the *Apollo 15* mission—"3:08 p.m., Friday, October 8, 2023. We are taking the official statement of Richard Grahams regarding the death of his daughter, Sarah Elizabeth Grahams. Sarah's body was found yesterday morning at Mourner's Beach somewhere between four a.m. and five a.m. Mr. Grahams, please state your full name for the record."

"My name is Richard Allen Grahams," he said through clenched teeth. "And why do I feel like this is an interrogation?"

"Probably from TV," Seth replied. "You would typically hear this official rhetoric when a seedy-looking suspect is being interviewed. But you're not a suspect. We don't even have the toxicology report back yet. And we would say the same thing if we were interviewing a child."

"It's the truth," Bill added.

The interview room was warmer than the rest of the building. The walls were painted a shade of white that wasn't glaring, and had royal blue sound-deadening panels on the walls. A camera in the upper corner of the room glared down on them, recording to a hard drive on the server in the back storage closet that also acted as the evidence locker.

Richard ran his hands through his hair. "I'm sorry. I'm just… It's been a nightmare. All of it. I don't even… It doesn't feel real. I don't want it to. I can't imagine life without her," he said, sucking in his bottom lip and biting down on it.

"I am truly sorry, Richard," Bill said. "You know I've got two daughters of my own, and I can't even imagine."

Richard nodded.

"Do you need a moment?" Seth asked.

Richard shook his head. "I just want to get it over with. All of it."

"Okay, then."

Bill cleared his throat and looked down at his notes. "Okay, Richard, you earlier stated to me that neither you nor your wife had any contact with your daughter in…how long was it?"

Richard sighed. "It's been…it had been…two and a half years, almost three."

"When was the last time you spoke with her? That's maybe an easier way to put it."

Richard stared past both men. "When we took her to the airport. To go back for her spring semester. Her freshman year. So…January of 2021."

Seth cut in, "You said, 'we took her to the airport.'"

Richard looked at Seth, waiting. "Is that a question?"

"Just trying to establish who the 'we' is."

"My wife. Who else would it be?"

Seth shrugged. "One of her best friends, a relative."

"Bess and I drove her to the airport so she could fly back to college."

"What day in January 2021?"

Richard rubbed his forehead. "Um, it was right after New Year's. I'm pretty sure it was a Wednesday. Wednesdays have always felt weird to me since then." Richard pulled out his phone. "Can I…"

"Of course."

Richard scrolled through the calendar on his phone. "Yes, it was January 2, a Wednesday."

"Thank you," Seth said as he jotted in his notepad.

Bill leaned in, his forearms planted on the table. "And why was that the last time you spoke to Sarah?"

Richard closed his eyes. "Because she got a new cell phone plan of her own. A new number. And she didn't tell us what the number was."

"Why wouldn't she give you her new number?" Seth asked.

"Because she thought we pestered her too much," Richard said, opening his eyes. "She didn't like being bothered when she was still living with us, and she certainly didn't like it while she was trying to study at college. Not that I…"

Seth narrowed his eyes. "Not that you what?"

"Nothing. I don't know."

Seth tapped his pen on his pad and then wrote a quick note. If he were to guess, it sounded like Richard was about to say it wasn't him that bothered her all the time, which would point to Bess. "So, you and your wife dropped her off at the airport; I'm assuming this is what, Oakland International? Sacramento?"

"What?"

"Which airport did you drop her off at? If this was the last time you saw her, which at this point sounds like the last time anyone saw her, we need to know where that is."

Richard winced. "Oakland."

"Great." Seth jotted down the location. "Should be easy enough to pull her flight records with the date and location. We'll get Joe on that, yeah?" Seth glanced at Bill.

"Sounds good."

Seth looked back at Richard, trying to discern whether the look of pallor on his face was from genuine pain or fear of them verifying the flight. "What was the goodbye like? Did you already know she was going to get a new phone number when you dropped her off?"

Richard swallowed. "It wasn't good. The whole winter break was… very tense. She threatened to get a new phone number, but we didn't find out until she was back at Baylor."

"How long until you found out?"

"Um, a day or two. It happened very quickly."

"Day or two," Seth repeated to himself as he jotted it down in his notepad. "Did you or your wife try calling her and get a message that her old phone was no longer in service?"

Richard stared at him, brows drawn into a tight knot in the center of his forehead.

"How did you know she got a new phone and plan?" Bill prodded.

"We tried getting a hold of her but, yeah, it was disconnected."

"And was it you or your wife who made that call?" Seth asked.

Richard shrugged. "I honestly don't recall."

Seth scribbled in a quick note and looked back up toward Richard. "When Sarah first went to college, did she fly there? Or…"

Richard shook his head. "No, I drove her. Her best friend, Brigette, came along as well."

"Bess didn't go?" Bill asked.

"No. She said it was going to be too difficult for her."

Seth picked up a hint of what he perceived as annoyance in Richard's voice. "How was that trip?"

Richard smiled, staring down at the table. The smile slowly faded as tears welled up. Richard gripped his temples and started to cry.

Bill looked over at Seth, who held a hand up, telling him to let it play out.

"I'm sorry." Richard wiped his eyes. "I feel like that's the last time I saw her. Really saw her like she always was. Happy, smiling…she was so excited to start college. She and Brigette were singing the entire ride there." He laughed. "It was just like how I imagined it would be. Helping her with her luggage, watching her and Brigette decorating her room. Everything felt so…promising."

Seth gave Richard a smile. "How was that goodbye?"

Richard stifled a moan, his face constricting, tears once again falling. He sucked in a deep breath and slowly blew it out. "It was perfect. She hugged me and held on for…so long. She told me she loved me and would miss me. And that was it. I left full of hope."

"You said you left. Did Brigette not drive back with you?"

Richard shook his head. "No, she stayed there for a few days and then flew back here before she headed off to college herself."

"So, you said the goodbye you had with Sarah after that winter break wasn't good. How was it different from the one just months earlier?"

Richard huffed. "Night and day. I…I don't know where my girl went. She could hardly look either of us in the eye. Pouting and angry like I imagine a lot of teenagers are, but never Sarah. Not until that break."

"Were you the one driving to the airport that day?" Seth asked.

"Yes."

"And were there any hugs goodbye? 'I love yous'?"

Richard slowly shook his head. "Nothing like that. She just…got out and stomped away."

Seth observed Richard, his eyes still glued to the table. "Richard, I need to understand something here. What you told Bill, what you're telling me now, is that you dropped Sarah off at the airport on January 2, 2021 and simply never saw or talked to her again? For over two and a half years?"

"Yes," Richard answered with a sigh of exasperation.

"And that was it? You didn't attempt to track her down? Write her? Maybe go—"

"Of course we tried."

"How?"

"How?" Richard flipped his hand in the air. "We checked every social media site there is. We checked her friends' pages to see all of their connections in case she was using a nickname or a different name."

"Did Sarah have any nicknames?" Bill interjected.

"Lizzy. That's what Brigette called her."

"Any others?" Seth asked.

"Not that I know of."

Seth tapped his pen on his pad again. "And how else did you try to contact her?"

Richard shook his head. "I mean, Bess went to talk to her friends here in town and begged them to give us her new phone number, but they swore they didn't have it either."

"And who were these friends?"

"Well, Brigette, like I said, and her other best friend works—"

"Brigette Lowe goes to college in New York," Seth interjected.

Richard paused, his mouth still open. "I know that. And she comes home to visit her parents. For holidays, in the summer. She comes by our house every time to ask us if we've heard from her. Just ask her."

Seth narrowed his eyes. "You sound resentful."

Richard fell back in his chair. "Wouldn't you be? We gave her everything. Supported her in everything she wanted to do. We gave her a living allowance, so she didn't have to work while she went to college. And she just cut us off. Yet we still continued to put money in her account. And nothing. Just complete silence. Like we meant nothing to her. Like her friends meant nothing to her. It devastated Brigette and Jeremy."

"Jeremy," Seth stated. "Was he the other best friend you were speaking of?"

"Yes."

"Did he come to your house as well?"

Richard shook his head. "Bess went to see him at the Victorian Inn. More than once. She said he was in tears."

Seth nodded as he wrote in his notepad.

Bill shifted in his chair. "So, what happened, Richard? Or what do you think happened?"

Richard wiped his eyes and pinched the bridge of his nose. "I don't know. I really don't. But she was different when she came back that winter break."

"You keep mentioning that. Can you give us more details, specifics?"

Richard leaned forward and dropped his eyes to the table. "She was like a completely different person. She was unhinged, fidgety. She paced all the time. Cursed."

"As in, she swore?" Seth asked.

Richard furrowed his brow. "What else would it mean?"

"That she was cursed. Bad luck."

"No, that's not what I meant."

"How she acted, how she spoke. These were completely new?"

"We had literally never heard her curse, or swear, in her whole life. That break, it was like it was second nature to her."

"Well," Bill drew out the word, "I think most kids change when they go off to college. I know Stacey really came into her own after freshman year, and I'm sure that Rachel—"

"Did you recognize them?" Richard asked.

Bill narrowed his eyes. "I'm sorry?"

"I don't think you understand what I'm saying. I'm not talking about kids growing up or figuring out what they want to do. Sarah was different," Richard spat. "Her weight. I mean, she was gaunt like a supermodel, hollowed cheeks, bony elbows and knees. The look in her eyes was different. The way she talked. She argued and yelled at us at every turn for seemingly no reason. She slammed doors, threw her phone, stormed out of the house. Her entire demeanor had changed. It was like she was possessed."

Seth leaned in closer to the table, a chill running down his spine. "I'm not trying to read into or manipulate your words, Richard. But 'possessed' is a rather vivid description. Did you talk to Sarah about mental illness?"

Richard slowly shook his head. "I mean, there were clearly some mental or emotional issues troubling her. We asked her if she wanted to talk to someone, but she didn't want to discuss anything with us."

"And none of these things happened before? She never went through a phase like this in high school?"

"No," Richard firmly stated. "Ask anyone that knew her. She was the sweetest girl: respectable, calm, patient. She had a perpetual smile on her face. She was kind to everyone."

Seth nodded. "That matches the image I've gotten from everyone I've talked to thus far. What else had changed in her?"

Richard lifted his hand up and dropped his forehead into it, his hand trembling. "Everything. It was like she was doing everything to spite us. She got her nose pierced and got a tattoo and threw it in our face like it was something we would even be upset about."

"And it wasn't?"

"No," Richard said, his lip curling up. "Look, Seth, we may have gone to school together, but you know nothing about us."

Bill sat up. "Richard, I don't think Seth—"

"It's fine, Bill," Seth interrupted, keeping his eyes on Richard. "You're right, Richard. I don't know you. I only know what I've heard from talking to her friends, her teachers, and people around town."

"What does that mean?" Richard asked, straightening his back.

Seth held his hand up. "It doesn't necessarily mean anything. I'm just trying to get a picture of Sarah Elizabeth in every aspect of her life so we can figure out what happened to her, why she disappeared from everyone's life for so long, what led to her death, and why. Let me ask you this. Is there anything she did that upset you or your wife when she came back that winter break?"

Richard huffed. "I mean, it was all upsetting. Everything I told you, except for the nose ring and tattoo, upset us. She…she stopped dressing like herself, and that was something she vigorously threw in our face."

"And this consisted of what?" Seth asked.

Richard shook his head. "Look, I know we were maybe too hard on her in certain aspects of her life growing up, but it was only to protect her, to nurture her into becoming a strong, self-confident person. I was… maybe too strict about what she wore and how she presented herself. It's just…I know how boys are at that age. Maybe because I was a stupid one myself. I just didn't want her to feel she needed to present herself in a way to get attention."

Bill nodded. "That was definitely one of the hardest things for me as a father of two girls. Hard to not want to protect them, to step back and let them be themselves."

Richard grimaced, his head dropping. "Yes, I realize that, Bill. Thank you."

"I didn't mean anything negative about it. Just saying that I understand."

Seth tapped his pen on the table harder than before. "Back to the point. How was it she dressed differently? And in what way did she throw it in your face?"

"I'm sure you can imagine from what I just told you, but she wore very little. Short skirts, T-shirts, and tank tops with…with no bra on." Richard looked up at Seth. "That's not something a father wants thrust in his face."

This was a whole new facet of Sarah Elizabeth and her apparent downward spiral Seth hadn't heard. He could sense the genuine regret and pain Richard was feeling.

"During these times, would you say she was more vehement toward you or your wife, or was it equally distributed?" Seth asked.

Richard shrugged. "It felt equal. She just seemed mad about everything, upset with anything we said or did, any mention we made of her health, a mild glance at her outfit of choice would set her off."

Seth lifted his notebook, referencing it as he spoke. "The picture you've painted of Sarah Elizabeth during that winter break is that of someone exhibiting erratic behavior, and by all accounts, that was not her persona before she went off to college. You described her as being fidgety, pacing, her eyes being 'different.' I'm sorry to be blunt about this, but these are all signs and symptoms of potential drug use or, in certain cases, withdrawal. Do you know if that was the case or a possibility?"

"No, I can't…" Richard sighed as he sat up. "I don't know. We didn't find anything like that. And we looked. We didn't know what was happening, but the first time she stormed out of the house, I didn't know what else to do. I looked through her bags, her drawers. Bess looked in every room and every drawer and cupboard, like…I don't know. But we found nothing. She told us she had been having major sleep issues. Apparently, for a long time, dating back to junior high. She blamed us for that as well. 'How did you not notice?' she screamed. How were we supposed to notice something like that if she never told us?" Richard asked Seth.

Seth shook his head. "I can't say. But it sounds like she was clearly going through something or dealing with something that was greatly affecting her. Did she mention anything alluding to that? Anything about her first semester of college? Maybe something that happened to her? It was a rather short timeframe for such a shift in her personality."

"Of course we asked her that. More times than she cared to hear it, but we persisted. All we got was that she couldn't sleep, and she couldn't focus. And it seemed like maybe she was having issues connecting with friends there. Or making friends, I guess. But she wouldn't confide anything in us. Nothing real or specific."

"Richard," Bill said to grab his attention. "Even though she didn't want to talk to you about it, did you try to get her help? Professional help from a doctor or a therapist?" Bill asked, almost scolding.

Seth glanced over at Bill, narrowing his eyes.

"Of course we did!" Richard shouted. "You think we just threw up our hands in defeat?"

Bill held up his hand. "No. That's not what I'm saying. It just seems like she—"

"I know how it seemed, and yes, we tried. But she resisted everything we suggested or tried to do."

Seth wasn't happy about Bill reacting emotionally, but Richard's response brought about the perfect opportunity for Seth to get to the one thing bothering him most about the Grahamses' story. "Richard."

"What?" Richard shifted his attention to Seth.

"We know you cared a great deal for Sarah. And it must have been challenging to go through that time over winter break. Which makes it even more difficult for me to believe that you had no contact with your daughter in the two and a half years since then."

Richard's nose flared as he sighed. "Well, we didn't."

"Okay, so you don't have her new phone number. That's an issue. But are you telling me you didn't try calling the school to get a hold of her? Reach out to her professors or her roommate via email or social media?"

"I…" Richard stuttered. "We… Look, she made it very clear where she stood, and she did not want us to contact her. We didn't want to push her further away."

Seth narrowed his eyes. "How could you possibly push her further away than having no contact with her at all? For years?"

"We didn't just give up. We tried all those routes over time but didn't get any help from anyone."

Seth looked at Bill and let out a stifled laugh before looking back at Richard. "You've said that twice now. That you didn't give up. Did it ever cross your mind to, I don't know, maybe fly down to Texas and see her and make sure she was okay? Drive down? Take a train—"

"No, it didn't!"

Seth raised his eyebrows. "It didn't cross your mind? You're saying you never even talked about the option of going directly to her? It's not like you didn't know where she was. Assuming the school, roommate, or teachers you say you contacted confirmed she was still going to classes."

Richard dropped his shoulder and sighed through his nose. "We hoped that by respecting her wishes, over time, she would get through whatever grudges she was holding against us and come back. Or call. Or…" Richard shook his head and dropped it into both hands, elbows planted on the table.

"Okay then." Seth took in a deep breath. "Did you at least know she was back here?"

Richard looked from Seth to Bill. "What…what do you mean?"

Bill tilted his head to the side. "Well, she was, and I'm sorry for bringing this up, but we found her body at Mourner's Beach."

"I know that. But, no, of course we didn't know… Was she back?"

Bill frowned.

Richard looked at Seth. "We still don't even know what happened. Do you guys have any information yet? Why don't you tell me why she was here? Did someone hurt her, or…"

"We don't have all the answers yet," Seth said. "We don't know why she was here or how long she was here. And we still have yet to determine the cause of death and what led up to it. This is why we're asking you these questions. If you want to know what happened, we need your help."

"Of course, we want to know what happened," Richard snapped and then shrunk back in his chair. "She was…my baby girl."

"We know," Bill said.

"Okay, moving on," Seth said. "If Sarah wasn't staying with you, do you know who else here in Lost Grove she could have been staying with? Even if she was only back in town one night before we found her."

Richard looked at both men. "I have no idea. If it wasn't at the Lowes', or Jeremey's parents' house, or maybe Jeremy has his own place now, I don't know, then I don't have a clue."

"Do you or Bess have relatives in town?"

Richard huffed. "My mother is here in town, but she's living at Lashley Senior Care Center."

"Okay. And you can't think of anyone else she could have been staying with?"

Richard lifted his hands in the air. "No, I…maybe a teacher or someone from church that she was close to that we didn't know about. I assume you guys are looking into this."

Bill nodded. "Of course we are, Richard. And I promise that we'll go knocking door-to-door if we have to."

"Good."

Seth flipped through his notepad and looked back up. "What was your daughter's relationship like with her boyfriend in high school?"

Richard's lip curled up. "She didn't have a boyfriend. Who told you that? Where are you getting your information from?"

"Your daughter was, by all accounts, a charming, friendly, intelligent girl. Are you telling me she didn't date anyone throughout high school? Boy or girl?"

Richard's jaw clenched. "No, she didn't date anyone. Boy or… You don't know anything about my daughter."

"Richard"—Bill grabbed his attention away from Seth—"you've got to know that we're the last ones to know, as parents. Linda and I had no clue Staccy's best friend Julie was actually her girlfriend for—"

Richard slammed the table. "Sarah was not… We would have known if she was seeing someone. She would have told us."

Seth laughed. "You just told us that she didn't confide in you, Richard."

"I…that was after she went off to college, Seth," Richard hissed.

"So, you don't know if she was dating anyone at Baylor?"

"What did I just say?"

"That your daughter didn't tell you things."

Richard glared at Seth, his breathing heavy through his nose.

"Did you ever talk to Sarah about birth control?"

Richard guffawed. "What kind of… Do you think a teenage daughter would come to her father to discuss birth control?"

Seth shrugged and looked at Bill.

Bill nodded, looking at Richard. "Linda and I talked to both of our girls about birth control, sex, all sorts of—"

"That's enough," Richard snapped. "What's your point? Why are you asking me about birth control? What's that have to do with my daughter showing up…dead on a beach?"

Seth ignored the question as he flipped over a page in his notepad. He looked up. "Now, Richard, we've got a very specific question to ask, and much like how we started the interview, this is just protocol. Where were you this past Wednesday night between the hours of eight p.m. and midnight?"

Richard's mouth fell open, overdramatically Seth thought. "I was home. With my wife. Drinking tea while she watched TV. Then we went to bed."

"What time did you go to bed?"

"Some time after ten, like ten thirty, probably."

"What were you watching?"

"I don't know. She was watching some show about home renovations. I was reading."

Seth nodded. "What were you reading?"

"What?"

"You said you were reading. Were you reading a book, or…"

Richard threw his hands up. "I was reading a book, a John Grisham book, if that has any bearing on anything."

Seth shook his head. "Nope." He looked over at Bill and gave him a slight nod.

"Richard." Bill looked up, brows drawn together. "I'm just trying to wrap my head around something here."

Richard tore his eyes away from Seth and looked at Bill. "What?"

"You don't have any other family in Lost Grove besides your mother?"

"No," Richard drew out the word, brows pinched.

Bill looked down and over to Seth. "And you swear she didn't have any relationships in town."

"No intimate relationships," Seth clarified.

"Yes, that's right," Richard answered.

"Right," Bill said and looked at Richard. "So, Seth and I are wondering, we've been struggling to figure out…just where on earth the baby could be."

"What!" Richard yelped and then looked back and forth between the two men. "What on earth are you talking about?"

Retrospective No.4: Cleo

There was something wrong with this situation. Cleo knew she shouldn't be here anymore. The restlessness had been building over time. Yes, time, that's what it was, and it was now unbearable, suffocating. The oscillating light, dark-bright-dark-bright, had awoken her yet again. But this time, a heinous shriek accompanied it. The sound jolted her heart, so much so that she could feel, see her chest pumping up and down.

The foundation shook with urgent violence. Cleo gripped at the walls, trying to keep her balance. She was being moved yet again. Faster than ever before, the passage of time between luminance and darkness rapid in its succession, and with it, the pressure on her skull and chest. Stumbling, flipping, sliding, the shackles ensuring her imprisonment, tangled around her neck and leg, tripping her. Cleo reached down, gripped the chain, and tugged, anger and frustration taking over. The restraint gave more than it ever had before. She yanked again, even harder. Another piercing bolt of pain. Behind it, the wave of a howl that clawed into her. But Cleo pressed through it. This was her time, and escape was dire.

Finally, coming to a stop, Cleo regained her balance and kicked the chain from her foot. What was it with the constant relocation? What would her surroundings be when she chose the right time to procure her freedom? More cries and commotion permeated the walls. The overabundance of visual and auditory stimuli had Cleo on edge, ready to pounce at anyone or anything that dared to impede her mission. She banged her head against the wall, not for the first time but certainly the hardest. Again and again, and again, and again, she butted her head against the wall, tugging at the chain.

Then she felt an incredible weight upon her body, a pressure, unlike anything she had ever felt. Her prison was closing in around her. Her heart flipped and somersaulted in her chest in a panicky rhythm. Too fast, too fast. Disorientation overtaking her mind, her bearings lost, Cleo toppled over and passed out.

A stinging sensation jolted Cleo from her momentary lapse of consciousness, her arms flailing and head jerking in response. She opened her eyes to a razor-thin stream of light so vivid she had to squint to focus on what it was. The combination of cool air and radiating glow invoked a primal instinct that sent blood surging through her veins, pumping wildly from her heart. It was her way out, her liberation.

Before Cleo could ready herself, something gripped her from behind and started violently trying to shove her forward. She felt pressure from all sides as the intruder pushed her headfirst toward the light. A noose tightened around her throat, clenching her esophagus. The chain that kept her imprisoned, determined to keep her, to hold her close, and never let her go. She clawed wildly as it cinched tighter around her neck. It was no use trying to unravel it. But to pull it free from the wall, where she'd already made headway, that was what she must do.

Cleo kicked and squirmed and bit at anything in her way. The pandemonium outside her prison was of no concern to her. She drowned out the shrill bellows as she fought off the closing darkness at the edges of her eyes. Her numb fingers got a hold of the chain keeping her from the warm, inviting sliver of light, the light to freedom, and she pulled. Her natural strength was nothing she had needed to rely upon before, but it came swiftly and without fail. A tide of viscous fluid accompanied a haunting scream, a sound unlike anything Cleo had ever heard.

As quickly as she felt the warmth surrounding her, an icy chill from the opposite direction washed over her. Once the dual sensation had passed outside her body, Cleo felt a duplicitous feeling of her own. The noose around her neck loosened. Cleo could move, freed from the walls of her prison. But that freedom came at a price, as she suddenly found it nearly impossible to breathe. Cleo, fading in and out with the shifting shadows and brightness, positioned herself toward the light. The coldness crept in faster than she wanted, more quickly than she could understand. Even though the chain was loose, it wouldn't let her gasp in any air.

Finally, before the blackness could overwhelm her, Cleo thrust her arm out and felt the most exhilarating sensation in her life, unadulterated freedom. Nothing was impeding her fist, her fingers, just a refreshing tickle of…air, breeze, oxygen? The moment of elation was short-lived, as a foreign object clasped onto her hand. Cleo's reaction was immediate and violent. She dug her fingernails into the soft, forceful object with such ferocity that it disappeared from her grasp.

Her lungs screamed for the freedom of the air that passed across her fist. Her body weakened, and the strength she had only moments ago was disappearing at an alarming rate. Cleo gripped the outer wall of her cell to pull herself free, but the momentum was leaving her. She couldn't muster the power to get free. A frigid, metallic instrument sliding past her body, sending shivers over her skin, startled Cleo out of her desire to rest. An amalgam of hope and fear gripped her heart as the breach she had crested opened wider, the chilly breeze racing up her arm. Before she could react, yet another contraption, reflecting the light from the open air beyond, drove past. Back and forth, the slick object skidded across her body, creating a reverberating sluicing sound, distracting her from her halted goal.

An abominable crunching noise was followed by a sharp crack and then another warm rush of red liquid flowing past her body and out of the fissure. As the metallic taste seeped into her mouth, Cleo's entire being was wrenched from her stronghold. The explosion of light, discord, and stinging air evoked the inception of an experience Cleo had never had.

Her eyes blinked and batted against the harsh light. Something was telling her to take a breath, but her body refused to do it. An unfamiliar sensation of force clamped around her chest, her back, fervently pressing and rubbing. A thin instrument was shoved up her nostrils, suction pulling at the slime of blood stuffed inside. Cleo's lips parted, and oxygen flowed into her lungs. The pressure, the wall, gone at last. The dark clouds around Cleo's eyes blinked away, and light flooded into them, revealing her new world and new freedom.

Chapter 15

Bess Grahams, Doting Mother

Seth Wolfe strode down the hall toward Interview Room 2, his boots tapping on the linoleum in time with the beat of his heart. He held a steaming mug of coffee in one hand, its scent mixing with the faintest hint of sweat, carbon paper, and fear emanating from Interview Room 1. The answers he received from Richard Grahams stirred his suspicions. None more so than Richard's forced shock at hearing about the baby, which felt rehearsed and telegraphed, as if he was just waiting for the subject to be broached.

Seth had come into the interviews with Sarah's parents with an open mind, as he did with all interviews. He was ready and willing to believe that they, in fact, had not had contact with their daughter in almost three years. Richard's grief was palpable and genuine; there was no denying that. But Seth had caught just enough hesitation and shifting of the eyes during some of Richard's answers regarding the last time he saw her and the time since to set off his bullshit detector. Something about dropping her off at the airport and the failed attempts at tracking her down didn't add up in Seth's mind.

Now, with one interview in the books, Seth had the information he needed in order to potentially catch Richard and Bess in any falsehoods or contradictions in their stories. He put stars next to the answers he received from Richard that would prove most likely for a slipup, if there were any. His tactic for his interview with Bess Grahams would be different, more aggressive. He needed to remain in control of the situation and not let Bess follow any storyline she may have planned in her head.

Seth opened the door to the second interview room. The grieving mother racked with tears only an hour prior was not the same woman who greeted him now. No surprise there; even in her sorrow, Seth had sensed something false about her mourning, something too calculated, as if it were a performance rather than a genuine outpouring of grief.

Bess Grahams glared, steely eyed, at Seth. "How dare you leave me sitting here for this long."

Seth looked around the sparse interview room. The room was the same as the one her husband was in, pleasant white walls with sound-deadening panels in an emerald green. "It's a private space. Would you have preferred to wait in the lobby?"

"Yes, I would have."

Seth shrugged and sat down across from her. "You could have said so."

Bess's mouth dropped as she let out a grunt. "What took you so long? I thought we were just coming to give statements."

Seth sipped his coffee and nodded. "Mm-hmm."

Bess narrowed her eyes and looked toward the door. "Where's Bill? I don't want to talk to you."

"He'll be here. And I'm afraid you don't have a choice. I'm leading the investigation into the death of your daughter."

"And what have you found out? I hope you have some answers," Bess said, glancing down at the table and then back up.

Seth took out his notepad and clicked his pen open. "And we hope your answers can help lead us to the answers you're looking for."

"What's that supposed to mean?"

"It means that we have a lot more questions than answers and I'd be willing to bet you knew your daughter better than anyone else," Seth said, not sure he believed it.

Bess leaned back and gave a dismissive flick of her wrist at Seth. "Can we just get on with this?"

Seth leaned forward. "You know, Mrs. Grahams, we're investigating your daughter's death and potential murder. I would think you would want to take as much time as needed to assist us."

The corner of Bess's mouth drooped. "What do you mean 'murder'?"

Seth held Bess's eyes for a concentrated moment before speaking. "We're not ruling anything out at this stage, and to say we found her body under questionable circumstances would be an understatement."

Bess opened her mouth to speak but then shut it, leaning back into her seat.

Seth reached over and started the tape recorder to his left. He glanced at his watch. "This is Sergeant Seth Wolfe of the Lost Grove Police Department. The time is 3:53 p.m., Friday, October 8, 2023. I am in the room with Bess Grahams, mother of Sarah Elizabeth Grahams, taking her official statement regarding her daughter's death. Mrs. Grahams, please state your full name for the record."

Bess rolled her eyes. "Bess Francis Grahams."

Seth jumped right in. "How long had your daughter been back in town?"

Bess froze with her mouth open.

"It's a straightforward question."

"What are you talking about? Back in town when?"

"Before we found her body."

"I have no idea. Bill must have told you we hadn't—"

"Seen your daughter for almost three years. Yes, I heard. The problem is, I'm having a really difficult time believing that."

Bess looked to the door once more, then snarled, looking back at Seth. "How dare you question the veracity of what I say?"

"Mrs. Grahams," Seth commanded, instilling a hush in the room, the sound of the ticking clock over Bess's head suddenly prominent. "I've investigated nearly a hundred homicide cases, and in nearly every single one, I have to deal with bereaved parents, children, or friends of the deceased. And you know what every one of them wants?"

Bess had slinked back in her chair, the tension in her face slipping.

Seth lowered his voice but kept it pointed. "They want to help us find out who did it. And thus far, I haven't gotten that impression from either you or your husband, and I'd like to know why that is."

Bess's bottom lip started trembling, prompting her to take a deep breath. "You have no idea how difficult the past few years have been for me. I devoted my entire life to Sarah. I gave up everything I loved to ensure we gave her the proper support, tutelage, and love as she grew into a young woman. And then, the moment she leaves home, she tossed me away like I was nothing. A nuisance. So, I'm sorry if I don't come across like every other derelict you dealt with in the city, but I was shunned by my own daughter, and it hurt!"

Seth kept steady, his only move a single blink while he waited.

Bess sat up straight in her chair. "I do want you to find out what happened to my daughter. And if someone is responsible, I want you to bring that person to justice. So, yes, I will answer your questions, Officer

Wolfe, but don't you dare raise your voice at me again."

"It's Sergeant Wolfe. Okay, Mrs. Grahams." Seth glanced down at his notebook and clicked his pen. "When was the last time you saw your daughter?"

"The day I drove her to the airport in January 2021 to return to Baylor."

The answer came quickly, but it was the first misstep the Grahamses made. He jotted down the note and looked up, expression unchanged. "What day exactly?"

Bess closed her eyes as she responded, "January 2, 2021."

"And which airport was that?"

"Oakland," she replied quickly.

"And when was the last time you spoke with her?"

"The moment she shut the door and walked into the airport. After that, she got her own phone plan, changed her number, and didn't bother to give it to us. I'm sure you've heard."

Seth nodded. "I have. How did you find out she'd picked up her own phone plan and disconnected the previous one?"

Bess gazed along the top of the table as if it held the answer. "I don't know. We must have tried texting or calling her."

Seth jotted down a note as he asked, "And when did you find out? How soon after she returned to school?"

"I don't recall exactly, but probably a week or so. Both Richard and I were a little browbeaten. We weren't exactly sure how to reach out, not to mention what our daughter's reaction would be."

"Is it possible she just blocked your numbers?"

Bess snorted. "And those of her best friends, too? No, she disconnected her previous number and plan."

"When she left for college, she was on her own plan, or was she on a family plan?"

"She was on ours. I think I checked it and found out she'd removed herself from the plan."

Seth nodded, then turned to his notepad, scribbling in a memo. "What was the ride to the airport like?"

"It was awful. Hours of tension with hardly a word said."

"Did you try to talk to her?"

Bess shrugged. "Maybe twice. The silent treatment had already gone into effect days before going to the airport, so I didn't persist. She made it painfully obvious that we pressured her and annoyed her for years, despite the fact she never mentioned it until she came back for winter break."

"And was that aimed more so at you or at your husband?"

Bess narrowed her eyes. "At both of us."

"Are you guessing?"

"What?"

Seth tapped his pen on his notepad. "You hesitated and sounded unsure is all."

"What does it matter who she was angrier with? And what does that have to do with her death?"

Seth forced a sigh of frustration. "Here's the thing. Every case with a suspicious death, whether it appears to be a murder, a suicide, or is wholly unclear, which is the category your daughter's case falls into, is a puzzle. The problem is that you don't have all the pieces yet, sometimes none at all. So, every bit of information is vital because it could be the missing piece that helps us start to put that puzzle together. And sometimes the seemingly most insignificant piece of information doesn't become clear until much further down the line."

"Okay," Bess muttered, her arms crossed.

"The information we have now is that no one who knew her well, at least those who we've been told knew her well, including you and your husband, has had contact with Sarah in over two and a half years. That's two and a half years of information I don't have to base my case off of. So, I'm going to need every last bit of detail of her last known movements."

"Then you should ask her roommate."

Seth glanced down at his notepad and then back up. "And her roommate is who?"

"You don't have that information yet?"

"No. That's why I'm asking."

Beth shook her head. "Allison…something or other."

Seth laughed. "You're telling me that your daughter went off to college and that you spoke for at least three months before she cut you off, and you don't know her roommate's name?"

The door creaked open, and Sheriff Bill Richards entered with a cup of coffee.

"Oh, how lovely that you took all the time you needed to get here, Bill," Bess said, words dripping with sarcasm. "Did you drive into town for that?"

Seth leaned over to the recorder. "Sheriff Bill Richards has entered the room."

Bess sneered at him.

Bill lifted the cup up and smiled. "Apologies, Bess. I had to wrap up the paperwork for your husband's interview."

Bess raised her eyebrows and nodded. "Great. We were just discussing my daughter's decision to sever the lifeline to her parents when she returned for her spring semester."

Bill sat down and exchanged a glance with Seth. "Okay."

"And we were at the point where I asked Mrs. Grahams who Sarah's roommate was, to which she replied"—Seth looked down at his notes—"'Allison something or other.'"

Bill looked over at Bess. "You don't know her roommate's name?"

Bess opened her arms. "It's Allison…Terry. Terry."

Seth nodded. "There we go."

"Don't you mock me," Bess warned.

Bill stiffened in his chair, sensing a very different mood in this interview.

"Did you ever reach out to Allison Terry to get a hold of your daughter?"

"No. I reluctantly respected her wishes."

Bill frowned. "Didn't you at least want to hear if she was okay from someone?"

Bess slowly turned toward Bill. "What do you think? Of course I did! I tried to find her on social media. I talked to poor Jeremy and Brigette, who she also abandoned for Lord knows what reason. The last thing I wanted to do was call the school or track down her roommate so they could go to Sarah and tell her, 'Your parents are trying to get a hold of you.' If you had seen the mood she was in, her state of mind, you would have known it just would have angered her more."

"So, you never called the school?" Bill asked.

Bess stared at Bill, her face unmoving. "No."

Bill shifted in his chair and looked over at Seth.

Seth let out a heavy exhale. "Okay. I mean, that's a long time to go without talking to your only child. Did you and your husband at least talk about going to see her? Flying, driving—"

Bess scoffed. "Of course we talked about it. We considered it many times. But we took the high road and gave her the space she wanted."

Seth nodded, jotting one misstep down after another. "High road," he repeated and then looked back up at Bess. "So, I'd like to go back to where we got off track. Your daughter was clearly back in Lost Grove, for how long we don't know, and if she wasn't staying with you, I'd like to know where you think she could have been staying."

Bess shook her head. "I just can't believe that she would have been staying here."

"Yet we found her body on Mourner's Beach."

"I didn't mean…I'm saying that I have no idea where she would have been staying. And I find it hard to believe she would have been back here for any amount of time without someone seeing her."

"Do you know the Lowes?"

Bess tilted her head to the side. "Brigette and Sarah have been… had been best friends since they were infants. Of course I know them. And no, there is no chance they would have let her stay there without informing me."

Bill leaned forward. "Even if Sarah was in a really terrible spot and begged them not to tell you?"

"Yes, even then."

"I know Richard's mother is over at Lashley's being cared for, but do you have any family in town? Or even nearby? Up in Eureka, maybe?"

"I do not. And if there was anywhere at all I thought she might stay, I would obviously tell you. You think I like not knowing what happened? Or why?"

Bill shook his head. "No, not at all. And I promise you we're doing all we can to find out."

Seth finished writing in his notepad and looked up at Bess. "Mrs. Grahams, how often did you talk to your daughter during that first semester?"

"Not often. Maybe once every other week for the first couple of months. Then we didn't hear from her for a solid month and a half. She said she was overloaded with studying for tests, that she was behind, and every time she spoke to us, it threw her off and set her back even further. I guess I should have seen it coming."

Seth narrowed his eyes. "Seen what coming?"

"How she behaved when she came back for winter break. She was clearly agitated with me well before then."

"I noticed you switched from discussing her demeanor toward 'us' to just you."

Bess sighed. "Yes, it was more geared toward me. It always has been. Not that she treated Richard with any respect that winter break, either."

"Why is that? That it's always been directed at you?"

Bess sneered and waited a moment to reply. "Because I've always been the one that needed to set and enforce the rules, to motivate her to work hard for her grades, anything that required stern discipline."

Seth clicked his pen on and off. "I haven't got the impression that Sarah did much to butt heads with anyone. At least not before that break."

Bess laughed. "Oh, she had her ways, believe me. Kids like to present themselves as one thing. But behind closed doors…"

"So, were you surprised by the way she acted toward you when she came home for that winter break?"

Bess's eyes widened. "Nothing could have prepared me for the way she acted, the way she presented herself when she returned home. It was honestly like a different person inside her body. And even her body had changed."

Seth wrote the word *possession* again in his notepad. First Richard literally mentioned the word and now Bess saying it was like someone else inside her body; there was something here that needed to be explored. "Could you elaborate on that for me, please?"

"For starters, she completely changed her attire: short skirts, loose-fitting tank tops, no bras, for Heaven's sake. She had gotten herself a tattoo, which I was honestly fine with, given the message. But she strutted out of the airport toward the car in one of these ludicrous outfits, clearly meant to shock us. I mean, it must have been thirty-five degrees out."

Seth tapped his pen on his notepad, considering what he was about to say. "Did you know that when your daughter was still at Lost Grove High, she would, at times, change outfits when she arrived?"

Bess's mouth parted. "What do you mean?"

Seth could tell instantly she had no idea. "She asked Brigette to bring different clothes to school so she could change into them. Clothes more toward what you're describing, but not as extreme from what I've heard."

Bess looked down at the table, shaking her head.

Seth waited patiently for her to make the next move.

Bess brought her hand to her eyes and wiped them before sitting up and attempting to present a strong front. "I did not know that."

Seth nodded. "You mentioned you butted heads long before she left for college but that she was like a different person when she came back that winter. How did her demeanor differ on this return?"

Bess sighed. "She used to express her displeasure with me in silent ways during high school: a glare, refusing to answer questions. She used to hum when she was angry with me, almost in a sarcastic, cheerful way. It was the polar opposite when she came back. Everything was yelling, screaming, grunts, stomping, throwing things. It was more how I might have expected a teenager to act. Sarah was…she was off-kilter."

"Was it consistent?"

"Her being off-kilter? There weren't any happy days or moments of levity, if that's what you're asking."

"Did she express why? Any reasons?"

Bess's eyes fluttered. "School. Grades. Missing deadlines, which I would never in a million years have predicted. She said she had gotten so stressed out that she wasn't sleeping. And she clearly wasn't eating with how sickly thin she was."

"And where did all of this stem from?" Seth asked. "Whether she told you or if you had to guess."

Bess glanced up at the ceiling. "It was so predictable. Of course it was all our fault. Pressuring her, pestering her—she must have used that word a thousand times—things that made no sense to blame us for, she did."

"Like what?"

Bess looked back down. "I don't know. Thinking back now, it all felt like a storm. It had obviously been building for longer than I realized. I never knew about the clothes." Bess took a heavy breath in through her nose. "I shudder to think how else she decided to rebel against us."

Seth squinted his eyes; his attention perked. "Like what? Drinking? Drugs? Promiscuity?"

Bess closed her eyes, took another deep breath, and opened them back up. "I don't know. I suppose it's possible."

"Did she mention anything at all about new friends, a boyfriend, a girlfriend?"

"No one specific."

Bill leaned forward. "What about any groups? A sorority? Something she might have got wrapped up in?"

Bess shook her head. "She mentioned nothing of that nature. I didn't get the impression she had made many new friends."

"Why do you say that?" Seth asked.

Bess shrugged. "The times we spoke, all she talked about was her classes and studying, nothing regarding classmates or school activities or a crush."

"I have to ask. With how you described her, how she acted, what she said about sleep issues, her being off-kilter, did you think she needed professional help?"

Bess looked at Seth. "Of course I did. You think that all just sailed over my head?"

Seth shook his head. "I don't know. Did you bring her in to see a doctor or anything that break?"

"I tried. Believe me, I tried. I told her I was going to drag her in to see a doctor. She told me I was the one that needed to see a doctor and that she'd like to see me try."

"Did you try?"

Bess pointed at Seth. "I tried everything I could short of making Richard drag her into the car. Not that he would have. But I tried. I didn't like how she was acting, but I was highly concerned for her health."

Seth nodded as he wrote in his notepad. He looked back up and held his hand up in the air. "Now, just for the record, this is something we ask every person we interview; where were you this past Wednesday night between the hours of eight p.m. and midnight?"

"Home."

The answer came too quickly for Seth's liking. He held her gaze, waiting for her to make the next move.

"What? Do you want a play-by-play? The only night we are out that late is Friday when we go to Lost Grove Pizza Company."

Bill leaned back in his chair. "If you could let us know what you and your husband did Wednesday night, that would be a big help, Mrs. Grahams."

Bess narrowed her eyes. "Well, Bill, we went to bed at around ten thirty p.m. Before that, we relaxed in the living room watching television."

"What did you guys watch?" Seth asked.

"Are you joking?" Bess's hands balled into fists.

Seth shrugged. "Just curious."

"*Downton Abbey*. Are you happy?"

"We love that show, too," Bill said, smiling.

Bess shut her eyes, letting out a long breath through her nostrils before batting her eyelids back open.

Seth flipped a page in his notepad and jotted down a note. "Let's get back to Sarah Elizabeth."

"Yes, let's," Beth said.

Seth looked up. "Did your daughter date at all when she was in high school? Even if it was nothing serious?"

Bess shook her head. "No, she never made the time. I even encouraged her to meet people at youth group. I thought it would be good for her to meet someone decent before going off to college."

"Did you ever suspect she could have been seeing someone but trying to keep it a secret?"

Bess laughed. "Like her secret best friend, Jeremy?"

Seth couldn't help but let the corner of his mouth creep upward.

"Sarah thought she was being so stealthy, the way she tried to keep him away from us. As if we would have turned him away because he was gay."

"You wouldn't have?" Seth asked.

Bess made a face like she had taken a bite of a lemon. "You think just like her. We're old and religious and out of touch, so we must despise the LGBTQ community. We don't live in the Stone Age, Sergeant."

"Good. My apologies. From what I've heard, your daughter was devoutly religious as well. Why would your views have differed?"

"Isn't every generation like that? When we're young, we all think our parents understand nothing we're going through, that they hold on to archaic beliefs. She loved debating the Bible with us. 'You have to understand how this adapts to our lives now,' she would say. Like we were incapable of grasping such a concept."

"Did you tell her that?" Seth asked.

Bess laughed. "Sure, we both did. That didn't matter, though. She would listen to what we had to say but then give us this look of skepticism, like we were simply saying things to appease her."

"Were you?"

Bess tilted her head back. "Yes. No. Who cares? Are we really getting into the semantics of the Bible here? Is that going to help us figure out what happened to my daughter?"

Bill leaned forward. "Well, Bess, you need to understand that every bit of information—"

"Right, the puzzle pieces. I know."

Bill's head jutted forward and then he looked at Seth, bewildered.

"Before we leave the subject of religion," Seth said, "I have to ask you something, Mrs. Grahams. Did you or your husband ever try to use your daughter to speak with God?"

Bess's eyes widened, and Seth could see her skin visibly flush, mainly on her neck. "What on earth are you talking about?"

"Just a bit of information we came across in our many interviews since yesterday."

Bess started gesticulating with her hands before finding the words to speak. "That's a preposterous accusation. Where did you hear such a thing?"

"You know we can't reveal that," Bill said.

"So, is that a yes or a no?" Seth asked.

Bess's chin jutted back. "No. That's… Do you mean praying? Of course we encouraged her—"

"No, no. Quite specifically, to speak with God. To obtain information."

"That's lunacy."

"I would have to agree with you," Seth said. "So, did you?"

"No! What would such a thing even have to do with her…passing away?"

Seth adopted a pained expression and glanced over to Bill before looking back at Bess. "From all accounts, the last time anyone saw Sarah, over that winter break, she was mentally unhinged, had issues with insomnia, and had lost a lot of weight. I'm very concerned with her state of mind at that time. And a lot of factors could play into that, and her parents trying to force her to speak with God could be one of them, especially if it was at an early age."

Bess shook her head. "Whoever told you that is making up salacious stories for no other reason than to hurt us. I won't have it."

"Okay then, we'll move on." Seth flipped a page in his notebook. "Mrs. Grahams, did you ever speak with Sarah about birth control?"

Bess narrowed her eyes, her body regaining a sense of composure. "Of course I did. It's called abstinence. They talk about it in the youth group at our church. They give out chastity rings. Cheap things, but it's the symbol that counts."

"And she wore one?"

"She did."

Bill popped in. "Was she wearing it when she came back home for winter break?"

Bess took a measured breath. "No, she was not."

"Did you ask her about it?"

"It wasn't the primary thing on my mind, as I'm sure you can imagine by now."

"Yes, I certainly can," Seth started. "And now, considering your stance on birth control, how would you have felt if she had come home from school and told you she was pregnant?"

Bess winced and then let out a short laugh. "I…I can't even fathom what I would have done or said. I would not have supported an abortion, I can assure you of that."

Seth nodded subtly. The mention of pregnancy had thrown Bess off track again. Her eyes were dancing all over the place and her voice faltered, the pitch rising.

Bess grimaced as she shook her head and flipped a hand in the air. "Something like that would have ruined her life. Everything she had worked so hard for would have gone up in flames. She was studying to be a doctor, you know."

Bill nodded. "We do."

Seth leveled his eyes at Bess. "Would you have taken care of the baby?"

Bess swallowed. "Perhaps."

Seth looked over at Bill.

"What?" Bess asked, the word barely escaping her throat.

Bill took in a deep breath and looked directly at her. "Bess, do you know where the baby is?"

Bess hesitated for the slightest of moments. "What on earth are you talking about?"

Chapter 16

Where's the Baby?

Bess Grahams's agitated voice reverberated off of the cream walls and plain tile floors of the Lost Grove Police Department's Interview Room 2 as Seth and Bill calmly excused themselves and left. Closing the door on her demands for an answer to their last question drowned her out, but just barely.

They sauntered across the bullpen, Bill glancing over to the two rookie deputies, Sasha and Joe, with a gesture of assurance. With brisk strides, they entered Bill's office.

Seth entered, moving toward the whiteboards that lined the walls. He scanned the photos, the keywords, putting together all the information from Sarah's parents' interviews. Bill closed the door carefully, trapping them in an oppressive silence.

"Well," Bill huffed. He adjusted the waist of his pants.

Seth started condensing the photos on one board to make room for more notes. "I'm not buying their story. How about you?"

"Something seems off. Could we chalk it up to emotions? Stress?" Bill shifted further into the room.

"I wouldn't." Seth wrote 'Inconsistencies' as a new heading. "The parts of their stories they had concrete answers for came across rehearsed."

"Rehearsed?" Bill sat on the edge of his desk, folded his arms across his chest. "I mean—"

"Their answers were either too spot on or widely variant," Seth interrupted, turning to face Bill. "Their replies to our questions, even though we phrased them differently, came out almost identical. For example, when we asked them how Sarah changed, they both rattled off the same three things: short skirts, tank tops, no bra. At least Bess did a job of calling out how ludicrous it sounds for their daughter to go around wearing outfits like that in the winter."

"I didn't catch that." Bill rubbed a finger under his nose to stifle a sneeze.

"On her attitude, they both commented that she was yelling, stomping, throwing things."

"Maybe she was."

"Yes, maybe she was, but it's the choice of words and the way they both said them, in order. Both of them said these things in the same order. And let's get into the holes in their story." Seth turned back to the board and wrote 'Wednesday, October 6' under his new headings.

"I don't think mixing up what they watched on TV two days ago counts as conspiracy."

Seth offered his chief a half smile. "It's not just the television show, it's the manner in which the night progressed. Richard says she was watching TV, and he was reading. Bess is saying they watched TV together. Not only that, they messed up their specifics. A home renovation show and *Downton Abbey* aren't commonly confused."

"No, I suppose not."

"Okay." Seth wrote 'Trip to the airport' on the board. "Let's start at the top. When did they say they'd last seen their daughter?"

"January 2, 2021."

"Yes, taking their daughter to the airport. Only Richard said 'we' and Bess said 'I,' and later Richard said he was driving, and Bess said, 'I drove her to the airport.'"

Bill released a snort, his small stomach jolting with the noise. "Mind like a steel trap."

"Sixteen years in homicide," Seth said offhand. "Now think of this, Bill. The last time they saw their daughter. The last time. The last time we, as people, see someone close to us, especially if you know it's going to be a long time, don't tend to fog up those memories. Do you remember the last time you saw your mom and dad before they passed away?"

Bill nodded. "Oh, yeah. Every detail."

"Do you remember the temperature that day, what you ate, any smells?"

"Quite a bit," Bill said, feeling a swell of emotion for departed parents.

"Something is definitely off about that final day they saw her. We need to get Joe on the flight manifests for all flights from Oakland to

Dallas on January 2. It shouldn't take long. And I think there's a decent chance we won't find Sarah's name on those lists."

Bill moaned. "I don't know about that. They'd have to know we can find that information pretty damn easy."

"People grasp at things when they're cornered. And it's not just the ride to the airport and to-be-confirmed -flight. We asked them both when they found out the phone had changed. Richard said a day or two and that Bess made the call. Bess said it was about a week and was unsure if it was a text or a call, then claims she confirmed it with their provider that she'd removed herself from the family plan. That one bothers me. And the other thing that bothers me is Richard saying they tried to get a hold of her, called the roommate, called the school. Bess says they didn't make those calls."

"Hm," Bill grunted.

"And what was up with the roommate? She obviously knew Alison Terry's name, so why, even for a moment, pretend that you don't?"

"I didn't understand that one."

"Again, it's easy enough information to find out, but it's like she's trying to stall us."

"Stall us from what?"

"Finding out anything that might implicate them, that might make bigger cracks in their stories."

Bill rubbed his forehead and sighed.

"You've already made comments and mention of this," Seth said, "but as a parent, even if you'd had a verbal argument, things were said, would you really go two and a half years not tracking down one of your daughters? Even on the sly? Just to see they were well?"

Bill looked up and met Seth's gaze. "No, I wouldn't. But maybe that's not in the Grahams' nature. They're churchgoing types. Maybe what they said, letting Sarah come back to them, was what seemed right to them."

Seth raised his hand and pointed at Bill. "Agreed. And what if she did come back to them? In trouble, with a child growing in her womb? The thing is, Bill, we asked both of them point blank who she'd stay with if she was back in town. They both said no one. There is no one else in this town for her to stay with."

"What about Jeremy?"

"That kid didn't have a clue why I'd come to see him Thursday morning. He'd have to be Laurence fucking Olivier to pull off how out of the loop he was."

"I'll take your word for it." Bill's head popped up. "Hey, I thought you weren't going to bring up the talking-to-God business."

"I wasn't."

"What changed your mind?"

Seth shook his head. "All the talk about how she'd changed, became a different person, was 'possessed' in Richard's words. It kept gnawing away at me. And you saw her reaction."

"I did. I'll admit, Bess seemed shaken that you knew that."

"She all but confirmed that they did this to her as a child. And we have no clue how long that went on for. Brigette said she didn't hear about it again, but that doesn't mean anything."

"So, how does this play in?"

Seth shrugged. "I'm not sure yet, but I have a feeling we'll find out down the line."

A brief silence fell between them.

"Bill," Seth said, drawing his chief's attention. "They know something about that baby. Richard acted like that person who finds out you're throwing them a surprise party but doesn't want to hurt your feelings, so they act like they didn't have any clue. Bess, well, you heard her. She's overplaying it on the other end. Making demands we tell her what's happened, why we'd ask that question. But it's all anger and no fear or pain or grief. She's not crying, Bill, she's making demands. They're both acting, and poorly, I might add."

"Grief does weird things."

"I know. I've seen the gamut."

Bill nodded his head in a wide arc. "So, psychologically speaking, she's not reacting well."

"Psychologically speaking, she's been acting like a grieving mother this entire time. Her every move is calculated and planned, and you know what that makes me think?"

"Huh?"

"It makes me think she's had plenty of time to imagine, to think, to run countless scenarios through her head."

Bill ran his hand through his hair. "So, what do we do about it? If they know something, they're not saying it. And we can't hold them here."

Seth walked over and peered out the blinds into the bullpen, at the closed doors to Interview Rooms 1 and 2. He caught Joe casting quick glances in on them as he typed into his computer. Seth turned back to Bill. "We've got to get over to their house. And I mean directly from here. We can't allow them to get home before we arrive. The most likely place Sarah had been staying was with her parents."

"There was no sign of a baby when I was over there yesterday."

"Did you look? Did it even cross your mind at the time that there could be a baby?"

Bill shook his head. "No. And you're right. That baby, if it's still alive, is our top priority. But if it's not there, though, where else could it be?"

"I don't know, but it has to be here in town."

Bill narrowed his eyes. "Why does it have to be here when we know she was going to school in Texas?"

Seth pointed to the crime scene photo of Sarah Elizabeth's body on the beach. "Because this is where we found the body. If she wasn't in Lost Grove, that would mean someone specifically drove her body into town and placed her on our beach. You know who disposes of bodies like that?"

Bill shrugged. "The mob?"

Seth let a tempered laugh escape his lips. "No, Bill, not the mob. Serial killers."

"I just can't…I can't believe this is a serial killer."

"Nor can I. Joe's already been looking into the possibility of this being similar to other recent crimes and found nothing. And I can't recall a serial killer in history who helped deliver a baby or had knowledge of a medieval procedure like Wes explained. More importantly, it's roughly a thirty-hour drive from here to Texas. The most dedicated serial killer on the planet wouldn't even consider that drive. Much less from San Francisco. She was here."

Bill nodded. "Okay, so it's got to be someone in town then."

"And this is where we focus our search until intel or evidence tells us otherwise."

Bill started pacing again. "So that brings me back to my earlier question. Who?"

Seth held his hands up in the air. "At this point, your guess is as good as mine. We're going to have to reinterview everyone in town that was close to her, with a new tactic."

"And with a lot more urgency. Sure would be easier if she had a boyfriend that we knew of," Bill added.

"Well, there's an awfully long gap of time for her to have found one at Baylor and gotten pregnant."

Bill crossed his arms. "If it was a boyfriend from college, why would she be back here?"

"Boyfriend could have bailed. It happens all the time." Seth walked up to the board of evidence and let his eyes cross past every photo. "Could have been raped."

Bill winced. "Mother of God."

"Could certainly explain why she came home, maybe wanting to keep it a secret."

Bill stepped up next to Seth and sighed. "I hate to think that was the case, but could also explain why Richard and Bess wouldn't want to admit to knowing. Not wanting to bring shame upon her."

"Could." Seth looked at Bill. "There's also the option, and maybe more likely, that she had a local boyfriend. It could be where she was staying. Could be where the baby is."

"But everyone swears she didn't have a boyfriend, much less even dated anyone from here."

"Story Palmer believes she did."

"I know, I know, you don't need to remind me."

"I'm going to pursue it either way. We're grasping at straws at this point."

"No question." Bill walked over to his desk, started flipping through notes, and then halted and looked up. "Still, what about Jeremy?"

Seth turned around. "As the boyfriend?"

Bill shrugged. "I don't know; maybe he's bisexual, or they had some experimental friendship thing."

Seth grimaced. "I don't see it."

"He's local. He could have supported her if she came home in a time of need. Something went wrong…"

Seth nodded. "Okay. I'll go see him again after we're done at the Grahams."

"And what's the plan with that?"

"Let's lay it all out on the table and see how they react to the specifics."

"How Sarah died?" Bill asked. "I thought you wanted Wes to sit on that."

"I did. Until I was sure we got everything we were going to get from them. They're not going to break at this point, so let's see if this news does."

Bill slowly nodded. "Right. That's assuming they know something. If they don't, hearing what happened to their daughter is going to devastate them."

Seth stopped pacing and looked at Bill. "It is what it is. If they don't know what happened to her, they deserve to know. This is the worst part of the job."

Bill looked down at the ground. "I know it. I only had to go through it once, with the Fulsons, and it still hits me every time I think of it."

"If they stick to their story, whether or not we believe them, we need to get constant surveillance on them after we go to their house."

"For what?"

"Once they find out how much we know, if they had anything to do with it, they're a flight risk."

Bill raised his eyebrows. "So, you think they could run?"

"If they're lying about any of this, holding back any information at all, I'm not putting anything past them," Seth explained. "People do strange things in scenarios like this. Some run because they don't want to face the consequences of their actions. Others run because they can't deal with the pain and don't know what else to do. And some take their own lives, whether out of guilt for having something to do with it or out of sheer heartbreak they can't get past. I've seen innocent people in such fear from being questioned that they admit to something that they didn't even do. For our sake and their own, we need to keep a close eye on them."

Bill shook his head. "I still just can't imagine that… Then again, I haven't seen the type of shit you have. I'll follow your lead."

Seth nodded at Bill and stepped toward the door. "Let's go."

"Hold on." Bill walked to his desk and picked up the receiver of his desk phone. "I better put a BOLO out on the baby."

Seth dashed over and covered the desk phone with his hand. "A BOLO on the baby?"

"Every minute that goes by could be critical."

"What are you going to broadcast? 'If you happen to see an infant that may or may not be alive in a vehicle, or on the street in a stroller, or'—"

"Okay! Then what do we do? How will it look if something happens and we didn't put an alert out?"

"The same way it might look if we jump the gun, tell the whole town about it, and cause whoever is responsible to run. I know everyone's going to know about Sarah Elizabeth if they don't already, but they won't know there was a baby or that we're looking for suspects. And if the Grahams really have nothing to do with this, we can't afford that risk. Right now, everyone in this town is a suspect."

Bill sighed. "Okay, then. Let's go."

"About time you let me see my wife." Richard was trailing behind Bill, Seth behind him, as they made their way to Interview Room 2.

"We're done taking your individual statements," Seth offered.

Richard looked over his shoulder and sneered at his old classmate.

Bill stopped and gave a gentle knock before opening the door. Richard blew past Bill and embraced his wife.

Seth walked in and noted the couple exchanging muted words as Bill shut the door behind them. Richard gave Bess a perplexing look. "Have a seat, please."

Bess twisted toward Seth. "Are you going to explain just what in the world—"

Bill held up his hands as he slid into a chair opposite them. "Yes, we'll explain everything we know. Just please have a seat, and we'll wrap this up."

Bess huffed and took her seat as she locked eyes with Richard, who was pulling a chair over to join her.

Seth sat next to Bill. "If there's anything else you'd like to tell us now that—"

"I think you have that backward, Sergeant. You both have a lot of explaining to do. How dare you…" Bess looked at her husband. "Did they mention anything to you about a baby?"

Richard nodded. "Just asked me where it was. I have no idea."

Bess twisted back toward Bill and Seth. "You both mention a baby and just leave? What sort of game are you playing at?"

Bill shook his head. "Not playing at anything. We—"

"Then tell me…tell us just what on earth you're talking about."

Bill leaned in. "Your daughter was pregnant."

"What?" Richard yelped, tears almost appearing out of nowhere.

Bess's eyes opened wide, her jaw clenching.

Seth looked back and forth between the parents, closely gauging their reactions. If he wasn't certain before about their reactions being a performance, he was now.

Bill continued, "We're still awaiting the full results of the toxicology report, but what we do know is that Sarah Elizabeth died during childbirth."

Richard looked frantically at both men. "What? Where?"

Bill shook his head. "We have no idea where she was before we found her on the beach."

Bess swallowed heavily. "How…" Her bottom lip trembled as she struggled to get it out. "How did it happen?"

Bill turned his head and looked at Seth.

Bess followed Bill's eyes. "What?"

Seth put his forearms on the table and looked at Richard, who appeared like he might pass out, and then at Bess, who had fresh tears percolating in her eyes. "It appears there were complications with the birth. From what our medical examiner can surmise, and he'll be reaching out to you shortly, there was an obstruction that put the child in grave danger. And whoever was delivering this child resorted to some rather outdated surgical methods to get the child out safely."

"Oh my God," Richard cried, dropping his head into his hands.

Bess's trembling hand was over her mouth, staring right through Seth as tears rolled down her cheeks. The reactions from both her and Richard to this news felt genuine. He made a mental note to make a list of which reactions seemed rehearsed and which didn't to see if he could find a throughline.

"Your daughter either died from excessive blood loss and/or a heart attack brought about by the pain. I am truly sorry."

Bill had his chin in his hands, trying desperately not to cry. Wes's descriptions of the barbaric surgeries flooding back into his mind. Richard's head was still buried in his arm on the table, weeping, and Bess appeared to be in shock.

Seth, gauging that neither parent was going to speak, continued, "There's no indication the child suffered or died in the process. And there's no reason to believe that the child isn't alive, and we—"

"Then what was Sarah doing on a beach and not in a hospital?" Bess burst out of her temporary shock. "And who was the doctor, or person, that…"

Bill held up his hand. "Bess, I'm so sorry. And I understand that—"

"And what are you both doing sitting here talking to us?"

"We're trying to get as much information as we can so that—"

"Look, Bill, I don't know what Sarah got herself into, but if you're telling me that I might have a grandchild out there alive, then you better find her."

"That is our primary—"

"Why are you wasting time asking us a bunch of mundane questions?

Shouldn't you be out with a search party looking for an infant in danger?"

Seth leaned in and grabbed Bess's attention. "A search party? Mrs. Grahams, if your grandchild is alive, it's not out wandering the streets or in the forest; it's with someone."

Bess met Seth's gaze. "Then you better find out who."

"We plan on it. In the meantime, we're going to need to search your house—"

Richard looked up, his eyes wet. "For what? We don't know any—"

Bess firmly grabbed onto her husband's bicep. "I don't appreciate what you're insinuating, Sergeant, but we've got nothing to hide."

Seth nodded, his eyes never once glancing at the claw Bess had wrapped around her husband's arm but seeing the pale fingers glow white where she had him in a death grip. "Good. Then you've got nothing to worry about."

Bess pushed back from the desk and stood up. "Let's go, Richard."

"On the other hand," Seth said, raising his voice while standing, "if we find out that you do have something to hide, I'll have you both arrested for obstruction of justice. At a minimum."

"How could you even…" Bess sneered.

Bill rose and walked toward the door. "I'm sorry, Bess, but this is serious business. And—"

Bess grabbed the handle before Bill. "Just do your job, Bill. I would have expected more out of you," she said as she pulled Richard out behind her.

Chapter 17

Patriarchal Mistrust

The subtle sounds of his mother putting dishes in the washer guided Noble through the dark house to the warmly lit kitchen. The house still smelled of the cozy, buttery crust from the pot pies she had made for dinner. His mother hummed to herself, drinking a glass of wine.

"Hey, Mom," Noble said, entering the kitchen.

"Hey," she replied. "What are your plans for the weekend?"

Noble shrugged. "Not sure. Why?"

"No reason. We could use some help cleaning out the old paddock for the new horses we're getting in a few weeks. Nothing major."

Noble nodded, not committing but considering it. He slid onto the barstool at the island counter.

"So, I ran into Mrs. Fulson last night. At the store."

Jolie pushed the dishwasher door closed, pushing up the sleeves of her thermal shirt, and turned around, snatching her wineglass. Her long brown hair was just starting to show signs of greying, little wisps of silver fanning through her thick locks like starlight. Her high-set cheekbones and sun-kissed skin gave her a youthful glow.

She glanced across the room at her son, trying to gauge where this was going. "Mm-hmm," she finally verbalized, taking a sip of her wine.

"She looked at me weird."

Jolie set the glass down, crossed her arms, and leaned back on the counter. "Did she say something to you?"

"No. Just looked at me weirdly."

Jolie nodded once.

"But," Noble started, "it wasn't the first time she's looked at us like that."

"Us?"

"I didn't remember this until after I ran into her last night. But something about her look brought this memory back up. When I was a kid, I was up there with Dad, at the store, and she glared at him like she did me, last night. And she said something like, 'You shouldn't feel right showing your face around town.' And then something about him knowing something about what happened to her daughter." Noble felt the words poorly tumbling from his mouth, but once they started, he just had to get them out.

Jolie often wondered if a time would come when the people in town stopped caring whether the children of Peter Andalusian overheard what they said about him. Perhaps the time was up.

"I looked it up—"

"Noble," Jolie interrupted her son. "The Fulsons lost their daughter in a way no parent should have to live through."

"Why would she say that, though? Why would she say that to Dad?"

Jolie nervously shuffled to the kitchen island, her heart pounding in her chest. She paused for a moment and let out a heavy sigh before resting her elbows on the cool marble countertop. She could see the apprehension and uncertainty in her son's eyes, and she knew that this conversation would be difficult. Taking a deep breath, she braced herself for what was to come.

"The police questioned your father."

"What? Why?" His voice nearly broke on the words, something he hadn't had to deal with for years now.

"Kelly was the receptionist at Ross Ranch. More often than not, her car wouldn't start or was already at the mechanics. She was saving to buy a new one, but your dad would give her rides home."

"Who gives a fuck!"

Jolie offered her son a half-hearted mother's glare for his language.

"Sorry," he said, lowering his voice. He knew the volume more than the language was what she was mad about. "But seriously. Is it a crime to drive someone home? Someone you work with?"

"There was more." Jolie tried to keep her tone even. She wouldn't influence her son's opinion. He was old enough to make what he wanted of the story.

Noble's heart dropped to his stomach, then his stomach flipped down to his feet. "Okay…"

"A few times, people saw them sitting together at Reggie's, talking. He drove her home when she was a little inebriated."

Noble gulped. "And?"

Jolie studied her son's waiting eyes. *God*, she wondered, *when did he grow up?* "Whatever you're thinking, that was never the case. She was a young woman who he tried to help. If she had a crush on him, your father didn't reciprocate."

"Did she have a crush on him?"

Jolie shrugged. "Only she knew that. People, eyewitnesses, said it looked like she was very flirtatious. She looked at him a certain way."

Noble felt the hairs on his back rise. "And you're sure—"

"Noble," Jolie cut him off. "Your father may be a handful of things people can't explain or understand. He's got secrets he'll never divulge to me. But I trust his word. He never did anything with that girl."

"Are you talking about his time in special ops? His secrets?"

Jolie nodded. "His time in the service was difficult. I mean, you know how we met. He was working at the ranch and the state park—"

"Yeah, you guys have told us like a hundred times."

Jolie held her hand up. "Well, something we didn't tell you is that once things got serious, and we both knew where the relationship was heading, there was a conversation."

"A conversation about what? What he did in…"

"No, not the specifics of what he did. He sat me down…" She gave a short laugh, thinking back on it. "It wasn't very romantic, but it hit a chord for me. He sat me down to tell me what would make or break this relationship. I found it refreshing. Some wouldn't. What I'm getting at… Your dad took me out for dinner and laid out his limits."

Noble furrowed his brow. "Limits, like what?"

Jolie paused, trying to ensure she recalled them all as he had said them to her that night. "He told me he needed time to himself. For jobs he'd take like he does now. Not out gambling or seeing other women. He'd work, but it wouldn't be local. If I had a problem with him taking on jobs away from home, this would never work out. He also told me he was a one-woman type of man. If he was gonna be with me, and I could take him for what he was, then he'd be with me and me alone. He said he wanted kids, at least two." She paused, smiling at her son.

Noble smiled back.

"He said he had secrets. Some of them, he told me. The rest? He just didn't want to. But he said he'd tell me this once, right then at dinner, and not again. They ordered him to do some dark things. He said it was…a certain type of killing that normal people can't do, won't do. He said they weren't his proudest moments, but he also didn't regret them. So, if I could live with that knowledge, and he really hoped I would because he was very much in love with me and wasn't sure how he'd get past losing me, then from that moment on, we'd be together for the rest of our lives."

"And you were okay with those things?" Noble asked.

"We wouldn't be sitting here having this conversation if I wasn't."

Noble wasn't sure anybody could really be okay with knowing that sort of thing. Then again, his mother was kind of different as well. Maybe that was why they were so drawn to one another. After a moment, Noble asked, "Okay, so, you're telling me he was a suspect because he drove home a coworker a couple of times?"

Jolie opened her mouth and shut it again. The shift from storytelling, recalling old, happy memories, was gone in a snap. Noble's mind was still on the crux of the conversation, which didn't surprise her. Her son was smart and focused. When he wanted something, he was pretty damn good at getting it. She turned, grabbed her glass of wine off the other counter, then returned to stand opposite her son, taking down a healthy series of gulps.

"Jesus, what?"

"He rented a boat," Jolie finally responded.

Noble's brow scrunched. "What the hell does that mean?"

"You were ten. Do you remember when we took a boat up the coast four days in a row? It was for all those concerts in the park? You got sick because you ate too much cotton candy."

His brow was still tight in a knot. "Yeah, I mean, yes, sure. But…"

"They found Kelly washed ashore. She'd been out in the water for a while. The coroner guessed approximately four days. Well, everyone in town was so eager to tell the cops about how your dad and Kelly were sleeping around and that they'd seen him on the boat. Turns out, the timing of the boat rental and when she most likely went into the water lined up." Jolie finished her glass of wine.

"But…" Noble started.

"But he was with us the whole time? Yes. Aside from dropping the boat back at the rental place. He requested a late drop-off time to take you out fishing one last morning before heading to work. He had a full day of work, so he'd asked to bring the boat in late. The rental place had no issue with it."

Noble waited for his mom to continue, but she just crossed her arms like the story was over. "But?"

"What?" Jolie asked.

"You have the tone like you're about to put in a 'but' somewhere."

"Do I?" Jolie sighed ever so slightly. "I suppose there is a tiny 'but.'"

"Doesn't seem so tiny."

Jolie sat down on the stool next to him. "There was an unaccounted for time when your father wasn't at work or home. He was taking the boat back, but slightly earlier than expected."

Noble glanced down at the table, trying to process what he was hearing, and then looked back up at his mom. "Did he get the boat back in the time it would take him to drive it—"

"He didn't drive it with his truck. We didn't have a trailer. He drove the boat back up the coast to return it." Jolie watched, waiting to see her son process the meaning behind all that.

Noble gulped. "He was out on the water."

"He was out on the water. No traffic cameras to catch him, no time stamps. Unaccounted-for time."

"Then how'd he get home?"

"Paddy picked him up."

"Jesus." Noble ran his hands through his hair.

Jolie noticed how his long hair stressed the Romani heritage her son had inherited from Peter. When she'd met Peter, he'd still been rocking the nineties grunge hair he'd grown just out of the service.

Noble placed his head in his hands. His eyes darted across the countertop, searching for hidden clues or epiphanies in the marble veins.

Jolie leaned down to grab her son's attention. "It was all circumstantial. They didn't arrest your father for anything, and there was no evidence. Just a bunch of coincidences and a lot of rumors fueled by the people in town."

"But why would they?" Noble asked. "Why would they spread all these rumors about him?"

Jolie shrugged. "He's an odd one."

Noble's nose and forehead scrunched. "He's not the weirdest in this town."

Jolie tipped her head at his response. "There is Paddy."

Noble rubbed his nose, searching for his next words. "The whole town's weird. I mean, Clemency Pruitt puts up signs there's a ghost haunting their coffee shop. So there must have been something Dad did."

"Not that I can think of," Jolie answered. "Aside from stepping in to end a few bar fights. I think it's just the way he lives his life."

"There are other people who live lives like that. I mean truckers? Oil rig workers? It's not all that odd."

"I don't know, Noble." Jolie sighed. "Sometimes there is no explanation."

Noble shook his head. "Nah. That shit doesn't stem from nothing. How Mrs. Fulson looked at me wasn't like I'd just rudely bumped into her. It was like I'd killed her daughter."

Jolie snapped her fingers and pointed at him like when he was a misbehaving child. "Don't you ever say that. Ever. It's not a joke; it's not something to be flippant about. Her daughter was murdered."

"But you didn't see it, Mom. That is exactly how she looked at me," Noble argued back. He felt tears threatening, stinging the bottoms of his eyes. "Like I had done it, not Dad. Me. Like I had the freaking plague, or that I was evil, or I don't know, fucked up somehow."

Jolie pulled her son into a hug. He was much too big now, but he let her do it. "Your father did not kill that girl," she whispered. "I'm sorry you have to deal with this."

Noble pulled away. "It's because of the new body, isn't it?"

Jolie briefly shut her eyes. When she'd heard there was the body of a young woman found on the beach, anxiety clutched at her insides. Peter had left the same morning they'd found Kelly. The same had happened yesterday morning.

"The whole town's going to be thinking back to Kelly Fulson and how Dad was involved with her and—"

"Your dad didn't even know Sarah Elizabeth," Jolie interrupted, trying to calm her son.

Noble leaned back from his mother. "Sarah Elizabeth? Sarah Grahams? Are you saying…?"

"Oh. Shit," Jolie said, walking across the kitchen to grab her phone. "I got an alert about it. Here." She slid her phone over to Noble. "Sarah Elizabeth Grahams," she explained as he read the article posted on the online *Gazette*.

There was a photo of the young woman, gorgeous auburn hair and a sweet smile. He'd seen her around town, mingling amongst the kids during lunches. She wasn't more than a few years older than him. He'd been a freshman, her a senior.

"Fuck," he said under his breath.

Jolie felt the air change. "You knew her," she commented.

"She went to school with…" Noble placed his hand over his mouth, resting his elbow on the counter, and scrolled pointlessly through the brief article about the young woman found on Mourner's Beach.

"Noble, I'm sorry."

His eyes paused on a string of words, remaining there for a while. Eventually, he said, "She worked at Devil's Cradle."

Jolie had moved to top off her wineglass, a small bit extra for the night. She spun around, glass in hand. "What?"

"'She is remembered by her parents, her brothers and sisters of the First Lutheran Church on Beaumont, and all the children's lives she touched while working as a summer camp volunteer at Devil's Cradle State Park.'"

Jolie blinked at her son. She wasn't sure where this was going.

Noble slid the phone to the counter, pushing it back toward his mother with his fingers. "Dad knew her."

"I don't think—"

"He knew her," Noble said. "If she volunteered at the park during the summer…"

Jolie stepped forward, almost reaching out as if to say, 'Stop, Noble, don't go down this rabbit hole.' Because she knew where it would lead, the truths he might uncover. "That means nothing."

"The hell it doesn't. To everyone in this town, when they put two and two together. I mean, fuck."

"Keep your voice down," Jolie instructed. "Noble, look at me. Listen to me. People will say things. I agree. I didn't process that. I haven't processed…shit. Do you trust me?"

"Of course. What kind of—"

"Do you trust your father?"

Noble paused and swallowed the lump in his throat. "I don't know."

Jolie's heart shattered. She bit down hard on her lower lip. "Okay. I understand you need time to process everything. And maybe when Dad gets back, you can talk to him about it. For now, you know people are going to talk. They might even cast you looks like Mrs. Fulson did. I know you can handle it. You may not like it, but you're old enough to deal with it. But by God, Noble, you keep your sister away from all that. You hide it. You don't react."

Noble physically flinched. "I wouldn't let anyone say anything. I wouldn't let them look at her funny."

"Yes, but you have to stay in control. You're gonna get angry, 'cause Lord knows I did. But you can't react. Not with Zoe around."

Noble began nodding. "Yeah, of course."

Jolie nodded as well. "Okay."

She reached across the island counter, taking hold of her son's hand and giving it a squeeze. He squeezed back.

Her mind was running through scenarios, getting a hold of Peter, handling the recollection of the past, wondering if the long-held trust between her and her husband had just been completely obliterated. She'd abided by his wishes for their entire relationship. She had asked few questions, and when his responses were cryptic and short, just enough to gather the meaning of, she'd lived with that.

But this wasn't just an old wound reopened. It was a completely new one. It was a wound she'd have to wait to address until she could look her husband in the face.

Chapter 18

Alstroemerias in the Tea Leaves

Seth parked his police-issued Bronco on the right side of Main Street, lowered his passenger-side tinted window, and peered out. "Shit."

The lights inside the Lost Grove Public Library were off. He knew it had closed fifteen minutes prior, but hoped that Story Palmer might still be wrapping up for the night. Not having her cell number, Seth pondered if he should go see Jeremy Stapleton first; he might have her number if they were as friendly as Story said they were. There was also the option of calling Joe to get her home address, something Seth was hoping to avoid. As professional and important as the visit was, there was something cryptic between him and Story. He didn't want to send the wrong message by turning up at her doorstep on a Friday night, even if he was still in uniform.

Seth leaned back and let out a sigh, his breath hanging like a cloud in front of his face. The visit to the Grahams residence revealed nothing of relevance to the case, aside from getting a further idea of what Sarah Elizabeth's teenage years were like. Her bedroom was spotless and eerily maintained. Someone had symmetrically aligned the knickknacks on her dresser with military precision. The room had been recently dusted and vacuumed, the lines on the carpet still visible. There were no posters or cutouts of bands or movie stars on the walls, nothing to gauge her personal interests, only an ornate wooden cross and a framed photo collage of her and Brigette from childhood to graduation.

That there was no sign of a baby in the Grahams house wasn't a surprise. The couple offered no resistance when Bill told them he and

Seth wanted to follow them home to search for any clues that may help them with the case. However, something Seth found suspicious and a little unsettling was an empty bedroom with nothing but a rocking chair in it. Bess claimed that they never had use for it, but he sensed a story underneath her words.

Seth pulled his cell phone from his pocket, deciding he had no more time to waste. Just as he unlocked his phone and went to tap on Joe's name, the sound of a door opening grabbed his attention. He looked out the window to see Story Palmer hoisting a large bag over her shoulder as she closed the door to the library. "Great."

Seth exited the Bronco and trotted toward the steps to meet her. "Evening," he said on the way up, not wanting to startle her.

Story looked over her shoulder with a smile as she finished locking the front doors. "I was wondering," she mused.

Seth stopped a step below her, eyebrow cocked. "Wondering what?"

Story turned fully around and met his eyes. "When you might follow up."

"Right." Seth shoved his hands in his pockets, his fingertips brushing the acorn he kept forgetting he had with him.

"Unless, of course, you're here for a book, Sheriff," she joked, pulling her scarf up around her exposed neck to shield it from the frigid October air.

Seth laughed. "No, no."

"And I assume this isn't a social call?" she asked more than stated.

Seth felt a lump in his throat. "Uh, I was hoping—"

"Sarah Elizabeth?"

"Yeah, I was hoping to catch you in time to ask just a few more questions. It—"

Story took a step down, closing the gap between them. "I'm heading over to the Inn for a glass or two of wine. Would you care to speak there? They have tea and such, as I assume you're still on duty." Story grinned, nodding to the badge on his jacket.

Seth slowly nodded, considering. "Sure, that would be fine."

"Walk or drive? Even in this unseasonable cold, I like to walk, but if you'd prefer to drive, it'll have to be in your fancy police vehicle."

Seth glanced over his shoulder and chuckled. "Just a Bronco, not much fancy about it."

"The decal makes it fancy," Story said.

Seth laughed and started making his way down the steps. "We can walk."

"Before we head off"—Story grabbed Seth's attention—"are you able to confirm that it was, in fact, Sarah's body found on the beach? If we're going to have an open conversation…"

Seth stepped back up to meet her. "Yes, I'm afraid it was. Her parents identified her body yesterday. A press release is set to go out tonight in the *Lost Grove Gazette*. Might already be released, come to think of it."

Story swallowed, her heart instantly heavy. She already knew, but hearing it didn't take the sting away. "That's heartbreaking," she said, adjusting her bag higher onto her shoulder.

"Indeed," Seth agreed, happy she didn't know the extent of how heartbreaking.

Story mustered a smile. "Shall we?"

"Here you are, Story," Jeremey said, setting down a glass of red wine in front of her. Seth had asked Jeremy when they arrived if he had spoken to Brigette. A somber nod showed he had. But by the time he approached the table for the first time, Jeremy had adopted his professional game face. "This is from a winery in Oregon called Valley View Wines. It's something from a fun, retro collection called Crystal Lake Wine. Does that ring a bell?"

Story looked up from sniffing the wine. "Sorry, no. But it smells lovely."

"How about you?" Jeremy asked, turning to Seth. "Crystal Lake…"

Seth squinted at him. "Only Crystal Lake I know is from *Friday the 13th*."

"That's it!" Jeremy thrust a finger in the air and turned back to Story. "From the eighties' horror film," he explained.

Story grimaced slightly. "I don't really like horror movies."

"Well, that's a bit surprising." He laughed and looked over at Seth, raising his eyebrows.

Seth didn't quite grasp what the inside joke was, but smiled.

"Fun fact: the lead actress in the film actually produces the wine there."

Seth raised his eyebrows. "Wouldn't have guessed that."

Jeremy turned back to Story. "It's called Cabin A Sauvignon. It's got notes of…"

Story continued sniffing the wine. "More on the fruity side. Cherry maybe…and black currant?"

Jeremy shook his head and looked at Seth. "Every time with her."

"That's what's in there?" Seth asked.

"That and red plums, and a host of herbs, I'm sure. Tastes very herbal to me."

Seth watched Story sip the wine, noting her dark violet lipstick.

"Mm." Story smiled. "I love it!"

"Excellent! Your tea will be ready in just a few minutes." Jeremy nodded at Seth and retreated behind the bar.

Seth and Story sat at a small table for two near the window of the quaint dining-bar area of the Victorian Inn. There were five other tables, all but one with guests or customers, and stools for up to eight patrons at the bar, half of them occupied. The walls were a rich burgundy with off-white trim, the bar a dark, polished oak, and the lighting soft and warm.

"He's trying so hard to be professional and smile, but I can sense the pain behind his eyes," Story said.

Seth nodded in agreement. "Yes, it looks like his bottom eyelids are struggling to hold tears back."

Story locked eyes with Seth. "Very intuitive."

"I can intuit as well."

Story smiled and casually leaned in closer to the table. "So, what is it you'd most like to know about our mutual friend?" Story was keenly aware of the sensitivity of the situation and wouldn't be the one to bring up Sarah's name in the public setting. Even if they were speaking in a lower register for privacy.

Seth let his eyes run across the other people in the bar, wondering how many of them already knew. The locals had gazed with intrigue the moment he and Story walked in together. They wouldn't have received a look of acknowledgment from a single person in San Francisco. But in Lost Grove, this, along with the mourning of Sarah Elizabeth, was sure to be hot gossip tomorrow morning at the coffee shop. He pulled out his notepad and pen. "Well, the one thing—"

"Do you realize how uncomfortable you look?"

Seth chuckled. "Yes, I believe I'm quite aware of it."

"First time out with a woman since you came back."

Seth nodded. "Aside from my mother, yes, that would be accurate."

"It wasn't a question." Story grinned.

Seth drummed his fingers on the table. "Yeah, that's sort of the issue then, isn't it? The privacy factor in Lost Grove. I'll tell ya, in high school, this town didn't feel near as small as it does now."

"What an interesting thought," Story said, resting an elbow on the table.

"What's that?"

"The mind of a young, teenage Seth Wolfe versus the mind of the man in front of me. Back in his hometown. The same person, yet different in many ways."

Seth nodded, the moment in the cave creeping back into his head. "Still adapting."

"You miss it, don't you? The big city."

Seth looked directly into Story's eyes. "I do. Most parts of it anyhow."

"What parts don't you miss?"

The haunting scene at Golden Gate Park flashed through his mind again. He considered his answer. "The despair. Seeing so many helpless, hurting…the constant feeling of not being able to help everyone. The guilt of not always wanting to."

Story wanted to slide her chair over and wrap her arms around him. She could sense the considerable toll his role as an officer of the law had taken. To her, it felt like heavy, starched cotton uncoiling in long sheaths onto her shoulders. She drew a sigil into the tabletop with her right index finger to release him from some of that pain and to keep it from bogging her down. "But you want to help her, our mutual friend."

Seth nodded, noticing her tracing her finger around the tabletop. "I do." Jeremy approached, catching Seth's eye.

"Sergeant, here you are." Jeremy set down a cup of tea on a saucer, along with a ramekin with lemon wedges and a small dish with packets of sugar and honey.

"Thank you." Seth noticed a momentary lapse in Jeremy's professional face, sadness creeping into his eyes. "Would it be alright if I swing back here after you close up to speak with you again for a few minutes?"

Jeremy forced a smile. "Of course. We close at ten."

"I appreciate it."

Jeremy nodded at Seth and then smiled at Story. She reached out and gave his hand a squeeze before Jeremy headed back behind the bar.

"So"—Story straightened her back and took a sip of her wine—"let me help you."

Seth chuckled and looped his finger through the handle of the teacup. "I appreciate your enthusiasm."

Story felt tingling on her forearms. She liked when he smiled.

"I think you have the unique ability to help in a way no one else can."

Story's eyes narrowed. "How's that?"

Seth took a sip of his tea and leaned in. "You are the only person who seems to think it's even a possibility that Sarah had a lover. Her parents, teachers, her best friends Brigette and Jeremey," Seth said, nodding over his shoulder, "all say there was no way she had a boyfriend or girlfriend when she lived here. You said you were sure she did, that you could tell. But you had no idea who it might be."

Story rolled up her left sleeve, keeping her hand on her forearm. "There were occasions when it was getting late. Late at the library means nine p.m., when we close. And I would sense a distraction, a preoccupation outside of her studies. It was easy to spot because she was glued to a book most nights, to the point I had to alert her we were closing up. The times I mentioned, her eyes were up and wandering, almost in anticipation."

Seth finished writing in his notepad. "I'm not sure I see how that translates to a lover," Seth said, and grabbed his teacup.

Story smiled. "That's because you didn't see it. If she were pondering about what she was reading, I would have known. This was something else, something that made her happy."

Seth set his tea down and swallowed. "Okay. I get the differentiation, but there must be something else."

Story sipped her wine, set her glass down, and pointed to her lips. "Makeup. Sarah didn't wear much of any makeup. But there were times on those distracted nights that, before she left, she would use the restroom and come out with more makeup on."

Seth shrugged. "Couldn't she have just been going out to meet friends? A party?"

"I have two sisters, Maevel and Asterin. We're extremely close. We don't keep much from one another, never have. But when it came to dating, sometimes, if one of us wasn't quite sure about the person we'd become interested in, we would try to keep it quiet for a time until we were sure it was something worth pursuing, worth talking about. Never worked, though. You pick up on things, a different shade of eyeshadow, an extra half spray of perfume, a dress or blouse that hadn't been worn in a long time. Sarah was definitely seeing someone." Story smiled and took another sip of wine.

Seth offered her a lopsided smile. "I'd love to have more to go on."

"You know"—Story leaned her elbow on the table, continuing—"since yesterday, it's been bothering me. I called my sisters to ask about it."

"You called your sisters to ask about a girl they've never met? Or had they met?"

Story smirked. "No, they've never met her."

"Okay…"

"My younger, well, they're both younger, but the youngest, Asterin, she has…" Story paused, her left hand tipped one way and then the other. "A way with…let me put it this way, she's an excellent matchmaker. Based on how I described things about our mutual friend, she is certain it was a man she was seeing."

"A man? And your sister Asterin, she lives…?"

"Back home, on Prince Edward Island," Story said.

"That's in Nova Scotia? When did you move here again?"

"Three years ago."

Seth nodded, watching her take a sip of wine. "What brought you to Lost Grove?"

A grin blossomed across Story's face. "I had some signs pointing me in this direction."

"Like the signs telling you that Sar…our mutual friend had a boyfriend?" Seth asked in a humorous tone.

Story understood his hesitancy toward believing her, though there was clearly something inside him saying he should believe her. Otherwise, he wouldn't have come to see her again, as she expected. "Do you recall the time I came into the station and told Bill about Mitch Roberts?"

Taking a sip of his tea, Seth nodded. "I do."

Story kept her eyes locked on his.

Seth noticed the small candle on the table flickering in her pupils, dancing in a mesmerizing fashion. Seth looked down at the candle, noticing the flame was still. He promptly met Story's eyes again, but she broke the gaze, reaching for her glass of wine.

Was he only entertaining this idea of hers from the start because of the peculiar draw she had on him? Or was it more? He'd endured his fair share of soothsayers in San Francisco. People who came forward spouting about how they'd dreamed of where that little missing boy or girl was. Or those who would come in and confess to being a serial killer when they hadn't hurt a fly. His time in the city had hardened him against any belief in the strange and unusual. But that disbelief hadn't just been suspended; it had been eviscerated yesterday morning when he crested over the sand dunes and saw Sarah Elizabeth's body.

Knowing his own experience, was it so far-fetched to think Story Palmer's sister, halfway across the planet, could discern that a young woman she'd never met was seeing a man? Not to mention the small oddities that

Story managed to suss out of him and everyone else in this town.

"…I suppose I should have mentioned it, though I don't see any relevance to this current case," Story said, drawing Seth out of his thoughts.

He cringed inside, having missed the start of her sentence. "What's that?"

"She asked me to read her palm once. It was…well, it was strange for a few reasons." Story laughed. "For one thing, I wouldn't have suspected she'd put much weight in something like palm reading. For another, it was the most abrupt and out-of-nowhere question from her."

"She asked you to read her palm? Like, fortune-telling?"

Story nodded.

"And when was this?"

"It was the summer before she left for college. I believe it was the last time she was in the library, come to think of it. I wondered where it came from, why she was asking me, but I didn't press her on the motivation. It was only the two of us in the library. We sat in the back corner, away from any windows, while I did the reading. She had a very unusual fate line."

Seth looked at his palm. "Which one is the fate line?"

Reaching across the table, Story took his hand in hers, then traced her finger from the base of the palm up to the middle finger. "This is your fate line."

A tingling sensation traveled from the top of Seth's head down his shoulders as her warm finger slipped across his palm. "Why was hers strange?" he asked, still looking at his hand settled in her smaller one.

"Hers was strong until it came to a very abrupt end. Then it continued again," she said, while tracing the path of Sarah's fate line across Seth's palm. "Only as it continued up to her middle finger, it spread into tiny lines, so many minuscule lines. Not like yours. It was the break, though, that really felt off." Story finally released Seth's hand.

"And you took this to mean…what?"

Story bit the inside of her lip before responding, "I took it to mean her fate ends rather abruptly, with either no future paths, or…she hands her fate off to someone else."

Seth took a sip of his tea. "So, would you say that you weren't surprised by…by what happened?"

"I would say." She paused and sighed. "No. No, I wasn't surprised in the sense that I didn't have reason to look back and say, 'Ah, that makes sense.' I was surprised to see it come in the form of death. It didn't necessarily have to mean she died young. Just that, well, that her fate had run its course at a very early age."

Seth swallowed hard as a chill passed through his body. How had he become part of Sarah's fate, being there, traveling there through time, years, decades, before that fate occurred? It was the base of this question that had him accepting everything Story was telling him, believing that she somehow knew more about this case than anyone else. Or at least anyone else willing to talk.

"Are you okay?"

Seth looked up and cleared his throat. "Yes. Sorry. Just taking this all in, thinking it through. Um…"

"Take your time," Story said, and took another sip of wine.

Seth looked down at his notepad, quickly reading what he had written thus far. "Right," he spouted and looked back up at her, "your sister…Maevel or Asterin, you never got to explaining how she knew, or figured out, that our mutual friend was seeing a man."

Story smirked. "It's a tad complicated to explain. Suffice to say, if you believe any of what I just said, what Asterin deduced was along the same lines."

Seth once again met her eyes. "You are a fascinating person, Ms. Palmer."

Story glared at Seth, lip curled.

"Story," Seth said with a laugh. "Okay, I believe in your assessment. But why would this be someone she wouldn't have wanted her best friends to know about? I get the parents, but"— Seth glanced over the bar to see Jeremy talking with a customer—"she seemed to be very close with both Jeremy and Brigette."

"I hadn't thought much about it until you came to see me yesterday. But after some…searching, I decided it must have been someone that she was embarrassed about, either because of that person's status, whatever that means in a teenager's head, or because she knew it was…'wrong,'" Story finished, using air quotes.

Seth's eyes narrowed as he leaned in further over the table. "Can you elaborate on that?"

Story mimicked him, leaning closer too. "Oh, you know, a married man, a teacher…"

Seth wanted to laugh at the thought, but it rang as possible in his gut. He glanced down at the table, thinking of where she would have met someone outside of school. He looked back up and met Story's eyes.

"Youth group."

"Go on."

"A teacher seems…I don't know, a little too risky. Not that I'd rule it out. But I was trying to imagine where else she could have met someone, considering she seemed to be studying all the time. Her parents said she went to a youth group at their church. Even mentioned that they spoke about sexual education there."

Story raised an eyebrow. "Oh? How risqué,"

Seth chuckled. "Well, I doubt they actually covered all-encompassing topics, but her mother said they preached abstinence as a means of protection. And that they handed out chastity rings."

Story closed her eyes and took in a meditative breath. She casually looked around to make sure no one was within earshot. "So, maybe a married man from her church? A pastor?"

Seth jotted down what she said, which is precisely what he was thinking. His mind was already running through various members of the community, searching for anyone that popped out as a potential lover. He would have a lot to think about when he left. "Any other thoughts?"

"Hm." Story ran her finger around the edge of her wineglass before taking a sip. "I think that there aren't too many places to hide around here without someone seeing and talking."

Seth glanced around the bar. "Indeed."

"Did you go anywhere secret when you were in high school? With your friends? Or a girlfriend?"

Again, Seth's mind drifted to the caves. "I can think of a few places, yeah."

Story smiled. "What's your gut tell you?"

Seth took a sip of his tea and then let out a sigh. "I think she had a lot of secrets. And that she was a lot more complicated than anyone seems to think."

"I think you're right."

Seth closed his notebook, set his pen down, and then brought his hand to his chin, elbow on the table, eyes on Story, debating how much to tell her. He felt safe with her. Like he could tell her anything without her talking or judging.

"You can tell me."

Seth laughed. "Well, there are certain things regarding the case that I—"

"I know. I wasn't talking about those things."

At the moment, Seth desperately wanted to tell her about the cave, the beach, the unbelievable experience of time travel, or whatever happened to him. He had a feeling she might even believe him.

Story dropped her chin into her propped-up hand. "I am so very intrigued."

Seth opted to tell her about the other unbelievable story floating in the back of his mind, saving his own story for another time, when he was ready to talk about it. He leaned in. "Her best friend, Brigette, told me that she believes she saw a divine being once."

"When? Where?"

Seth marveled at Story's unchanged expression. "As you're keenly aware, Sarah had sleep issues, bad insomnia. It's my understanding that the insomnia was a symptom of…well, she had visions."

Goosebumps sprouted from Story's arms and the back of her neck. "Sar—our mutual friend had visions?"

Seth raised his eyebrows and nodded. "Her friend Brigitte told me she spoke to her about them a few times. I'm inclined to put two and two together and say she had them many times and often. Several people I've spoken with comment on her sleep issues."

Story blinked, considering this new information. "So she can't sleep because of visions and everyone is basically telling you she had sleep issues. I would have approached it all differently," she commented offhand.

Seth scrunched his eyebrows together at her comment, but Story continued before he could ask what she meant by that.

"What did this divine being do?"

"Do?"

"Did it say something to her or…?"

"I don't know. I don't think the conversation got that far."

"Why?"

"Brigette said she poked fun when our mutual friend told her about it; something she horribly regrets."

"Poor girls." Story sat up straight and grabbed her wine. "I wish she would have talked to me about it."

Seth's head jutted back. "Why would she have come to talk to you?"

Story shrugged. "She came to me about the palm reading, didn't she? And the potion to help her sleep. Also, I can let people know, in a way, that they can speak to me about anything. That it's safe. I know she was aware of this."

Seth furrowed his brow.

"Didn't you just feel it a couple of minutes ago?"

Seth swallowed and held her eyes. "I supposed I did."

"Well, there we go."

Seth smiled and lightly shook his head. He was curious what she meant by those words. That she was open, and people somehow felt that energy? Or did Story mean she literally let them know, through some, well, witchcraft?

"Did Brigette mention what the visions were about?"

Seth rolled his shoulders. "She said our mutual friend described them as being intense. They often left her feeling emotions long after they'd passed. Typically, they were about someone that she felt she knew, but couldn't place, that needed help."

Story sighed, closing her eyes and shaking her head. "This sounds like a terrible burden."

"That is does."

"And the divine being vision?"

Seth took a sip of his tea and set it down. "Yeah, Brigette felt like that one really traumatized her. There was pain and fear and then this being came into it and everything was calm, and the pain was gone. She said the being shimmered and that there were feathers or snow."

"Visions can sometimes be like making sense of surrealist art," Story commented and sipped her wine, letting it marinate in her mouth a moment before swallowing. "She must have felt so alone. Like there was no one she could talk to who would believe her."

"Yes, I've got that impression myself." Seth looked down at the table. He wished his vision had been surreal, something he could pawn off as a really wild and lucid dream, only it hadn't. Instead, he'd felt, heard, smelled, tasted everything: the frigid wind, sand grit in his eyes, salty spray from the crashing waves on his lips, the pounding of his heart, the taste of toothpaste, the young woman's body, her pale auburn hair brilliant in the rising sun, her skin bleached and alabaster, the hypnotic blue of her speechless lips. It sat with him, a reminder that this case was far from normal, that it was complicated in ways beyond his call of duty to solve it. He felt closer than ever to Sarah Elizabeth, fully understanding how her visions would have tormented her daily.

"What?"

Seth looked back up and smiled. "Nothing."

Story squinted at him. The words were on the tip of his tongue, begging to come spilling out. She felt them as one feels the tug of the waves washing back out to sea, and they tasted as salty as seawater on your skin. But there was more inside his unspoken words. They were a secret he'd held on to for a very long time, since childhood.

The evening had been strange in not only how much she felt Seth wanting to divulge himself to her, but how hard she had to struggle to keep herself from revealing her true nature as well. Story liked to say she was an open book, and frequently she was. But matters of the heart were different. Seth captivated her. With his mischievous yet sincere grin, honest eyes, and manners, she found herself in trouble of falling for him. Her sister Asterin would suggest that be exactly what she does. Story preferred to be certain he'd accept what she was, lest she end up with a broken heart as had happened in the past.

She pivoted on her approach. "Do you want me to read your tea leaves?" she asked.

"What?"

"It's like palm reading, but different."

Seth grinned. "I, um…I guess."

Story glanced at his teacup. "Finish your tea and then set it down. Over here by me."

Seth shook his head, finished his tea, and then set it down in front of Story. "Should I be nervous?"

Story shrugged. She took the cup and flipped it onto the saucer. "Put your hands, or two fingers, on the cup please," she instructed.

Seth licked his lips as they spread into a grin. He lifted his right hand and placed it over the cup, watching her eyes.

"Okay, that should do it," she said. Seth hesitantly lifted his hand from the cup and she then turned the cup three times in the saucer before picking it up.

Seth scratched his jaw as he looked around the bar to see if anyone was still peering over at them. He and Jeremy met eyes. Seth gave him a nervous nod.

Jeremy shifted his head to see what Story was doing. He grinned widely and gave Seth an enthusiastic thumbs-up.

"Let's see," Story said, turning the cup over and peering inside. "Your mother is your anchor."

Seth looked back at Story, still focusing on the teacup.

"Bring her flowers when you see her next. Alstroemerias."

Seth's brow furrowed. "Okay…"

"There's a struggle…" she explained, tipping the cup into the candlelight. "A deep one. With morals or values, perhaps, in your near future."

"Near future?"

"We split the cup into sections. This top part, that's something in the present. The very bottom of the cup is something in the past. Think of it as splitting a lifetime into thirds. Then think of it again as quartering the uppermost parts of the cup. From the moment of this reading to nine to twelve months later. So this section here." She pointed to the upper right of the cup. "This is one to three months, and so on."

"I see," he said, not fully comprehending but capable of grasping thirds and quarters.

Story glanced at him from under her lashes, offering him a reassuring smile.

Story ran her fingers around the outside of the cup. "Hm," she said, tilting the cup. "Your youth is revisiting you. Or will be soon."

Seth swallowed hard as his breath caught in his chest.

Story looked up and caught the look in his eyes. "Ah."

Seth forced a smile.

"You just let me know when you want to talk about that. I promise I'm a good listener."

Retrospective No. 5: The Graff Twins

Ember Graff possessed the same tightly curled hair as her mother. Her skin tone was the same maple tone as her twin brother. Both of them had their father's pale green eyes, but Emory also inherited his dark brown, glossy, straight, thick hair. He fit in better among their peers at the prep school because of this. Unfortunately, racial characteristics were still a basis for bullying, a fact that disturbed her greatly. Her reclusive study habits, passion for manga comics, and, more recently, her sexual preference didn't help her blend in.

Cassidy Zimmer was one of the "popular" kids, but not in the classic high-maintenance blonde kind of way. She didn't fit any of the tropes set up in movies from the eighties and nineties. In fact, she was big-boned, with brown wavy hair, and was constantly chewing her nails. On the first day of school at Kittridge Junior High, Ember met Cassidy Zimmer by tripping over someone's backpack and spilling her plate of cafeteria food all over her. It didn't help that Ember was the dorky new girl recently transferred from public schools into the high-cost private junior high. The cafeteria incident wasn't the last of the mistakes she made against Cassidy. The girl had invited the whole school to her birthday pool party, and Ember had ruined it by getting her period in the pool. It was the penultimate level of embarrassment for Ember. Cassidy claimed it was worse for her, and most of the school agreed.

By the eighth grade, Cassidy had developed a crush on Ember's twin brother, Emory. Try as she might, Emory wasn't interested, which had nothing to do with how Cassidy treated Ember. It didn't matter that

Ember repeatedly explained she had never talked to Emory about her. There was no other explanation for Emory's lack of interest in her.

Going into freshman year, Ember was hopeful Cassidy's parents would enroll her in Sacred Heart Prep. It would mean Ember could have a little peace going into the high school years. Unfortunately, that move didn't happen. Cassidy told everyone that her parents believed their current school, Convent and Stuart Preparatory, was the better school, but the truth was Cassidy didn't have the grades to be accepted to Sacred Heart.

The torment continued. Though it wasn't exactly day to day, the hate was always there. And it rubbed off on Cassidy's large circle of friends. Ember was a leper. She wasn't to be touched, not even outwardly bullied. It was simpler than that. They ignored her. Unless, of course, she drew attention to herself. It seemed to Ember that her every misstep was on Cassidy's radar. Any and every moment Ember made a fool of herself, Cassidy exploited it.

Like today, when Ember had fumbled a word in response to their chemistry teacher.

"…why you don't want to use dicstrose, um, dextrose?"

The class giggled at her minor slip of the tongue, especially Cassidy Zimmer.

"Like you know anything about *dicks*-trose," Cassidy taunted, giggling.

Ember turned in her seat to respond. "You're right, because you're too busy gobbling every dick in this school."

"You bitch," Cassidy snarled.

"Alright, enough." Mr. Lammle attempted to quiet the room.

"She can't say shit like that. This is a no-tolerance school on—"

"I know the rules, Ms. Zimmer, and the same would apply to you. Now, can we get back to discussing the reduction of methylene using alkaline glucose?" Mr. Lammle walked through the tables, making sure all the students' attention turned back to class. "You'll both see me after class," he finished before heading back to the front of the room.

Now they were stuck in a quiet room, alone, together, cleaning the chemistry equipment and putting everything away. The minute Mr. Lammle stepped out, Cassidy continued her taunting.

"You know this isn't gonna go away," Cassidy warned.

Ember ignored her, keeping her attention on her breath. She didn't want to lose her cool as she had earlier. She shouldn't have talked back to Cassidy. It just made things worse.

"I can't believe the balls you have. You should thank me—"

Ember coughed a bitter laugh. "Thank you?"

Cassidy smiled her pretty, fake smile. "The only reason my dad isn't taking you to court for hitting his antique Mercedes is because I told him we went to school together and you were kind of a retard. He feels sorry for you."

"I didn't ask you to do that." Ember carefully set the glass beakers on the metal shelves.

"I didn't do it for you. Imagine the shit your brother would have to deal with. Just another thing he has to cover for his awkward sister. I couldn't imagine having you as a sibling. Like, can't you do anything normal?" Cassidy asked with a pitiful laugh.

"You know what, just tell your dad to take me to court so I don't have to listen to you whining about this bullshit anymore." Ember shut the metal doors, twisting the handle so it locked.

Cassidy leaned her hands onto the table, staring Ember down. "Trust me, you don't want my father to come for the repair costs."

Ember began picking up the workbooks, stacking them one atop the other, trying to ignore the prickling feeling inside her skull, hinting that her brother was searching for her. He wanted to talk, but she didn't want to let him in so he could see her thoughts right now. The prickling increased.

"Your mother isn't good enough at sucking dick to go against my dad's legal team," Cassidy finished with an expression of relish on her face.

Ember paused her task of stacking the workbooks. "What?"

"You think your mom got to be a partner at Dollen, Hardy, & Geller because she was an excellent lawyer?" Cassidy sniveled.

Ember slammed the workbooks down on the table with as much force as she could muster. The sensation in her brain prickled out across her skull, along her skin like vicious goosebumps. "Why the fuck can't you just be nice for a change?"

Cassidy pulled her head back, blinking wildly. "Excuse me? Why the fuck can't you be normal for a change? I mean, you have to realize how much your brother deflects the rumors and bullshit people say about you, right?"

"What are you talking about?" Ember asked, but she was thinking how much she wished Cassidy wasn't in her life.

    Cassidy snorted. "Your brother is constantly defending you. Or telling people to keep their mouths shut. I mean, you coming on to Elsa Ravecchio… like, read the room. She's not a lesbian. She's, like, dating Drew—"

    "They aren't dating." Ember wanted Cassidy to leave. No, she wanted her more than out of the room. She wanted her out of her life. Couldn't she move? Or transfer to a different school?

    "She's into him."

    "She's also, confoundingly, into me. She kissed me at the—"

    "Oh my god, you are delusional. She kissed you? She's telling everyone you forced a kiss on her. You know that, right?" Cassidy glared across the table at Ember, mouth agape in disgust.

    Ember's thoughts grew dark. "You're lying," Ember said. She wanted so badly to hurt all the people who hurt her. She was angry at Elsa for telling that lie. Elsa had kissed her outside in the gazebo of Dillon Franklin's house during the homecoming party.

    "This is what I'm talking about. Your brother keeps people from saying this shit to your face. You know everyone thinks…"

    Ember's heartbreak muddled the following words. She saw Cassidy's lips moving but couldn't hear the words coming out of them. Elsa had been the one texting her ever since. Elsa had been the one who asked her to meet at the mall.

    "Wait, was this a setup?" Ember asked.

    "What?" Cassidy snarled.

    Ember leaned into the table for support. "Did you plan all this? Tell Elsa to lead me on and set me up for the humiliating scene at the mall?"

    "Oh my god, are you not hearing me? Elsa didn't—"

    "She did!" Ember growled. "She did, which means you set this all up like some sick joke." In that dark moment, in those dark thoughts, Ember wished Cassidy would just die. That would get her out of Ember's life for good. It's not like she was the first teenager who wanted her bully dead. The ferocity of the thoughts sprung from a place of deep-seated pain and hurt.

    Cassidy laughed. "I kind of wish I'd been that creative."

    Ember felt a tear slip out from her left eye.

    "Oh Jesus, are you crying?" Cassidy asked, looking appalled.

    "You'd be that cruel? You'd actually be that fucking cruel and set me up like this?" Ember whispered. She noticed the pair of scissors on the table. It sat between them, closer to Cassidy. She felt her thoughts slip away, down the dark rabbit hole that was fear and torment and heartache.

"I didn't do anything. I wish I had, but you did this to yourself," Cassidy remarked, sliding a chair under the table and using a rag she'd been carrying to wipe down the top. She glanced at Ember with a sly cocksure smirk, all but admitting she had set her up.

The look incited Ember, which triggered a familiar sensation of pressure and tingling that crept along her skull. In a moment of sheer mania, she imagined Cassidy offing herself. She could pick up those scissors right now and take herself out of the equation. No doubt it would keep other people from being hurt and berated by Cassidy Zimmer in the future, if she'd just die now.

"You are a waste of space and oxygen, Cassidy," Ember said. "You're the most ignorant, stupid person I have ever met. You are the cruelest… you're a monster. The things you say about me, the things you've done to me."

She imagined the girl across from her taking the scissors and plunging them into her stomach. Ember wanted it to happen. She wanted Cassidy to feel physical pain the way Ember had felt each emotional blow that had come with being bullied all these years by Cassidy.

Cassidy stopped wiping down the table and lifted her gaze. Her face was slack and relaxed. None of the snarky repartees she'd just been delivering were there anymore. Cassidy dropped the cloth, her hand sliding toward the center of the table.

"You're selfish and evil. I really wish you would just die!"

The tingling pressure Ember felt dissipated with a shiver of exhaustion and relief. She recognized that sensation from the past when she and her brother would manipulate their parents into thinking they got home before curfew. The relief swiftly moved into horror.

Cassidy's fingers wrapped around the scissors just above the handle. Ember's thoughts scrambled inside her head. She felt her brother break through into her mind.

Where are you? Why were you keeping me out of your thoughts? I thought we agreed you'd just stay out of Cassidy's crosshairs for a….

His voice inside her head droned on, though she couldn't comprehend the words. The world moved as if time had slipped into different increments. Cassidy's arm swung in a wide arc, the scissors clutched in her fist like a toddler.

Ember focused on her thoughts. *Stop! Don't, Cassidy. Stop!*

Her body leaned forward across the table, her hand lifting to reach out and grab a hold of Cassidy's arm. But Ember knew it wouldn't do any good. The violence, the conviction behind her previous imaginings, would make changing the influence she'd created over Cassidy nearly impossible to reverse in such a short time frame. And she was exhausted. The effort it took in wishing Cassidy dead had drained the energy it took to implement such an act in the first place.

Momentum brought the scissors up toward Cassidy's face, and Ember was too slow to reach out and stop her from bringing the pointed end up into her own cheek.

Outside the classroom, down the hall, Emory felt, heard, and saw all the thoughts and emotions his sister had just felt. They washed over him like they were washing over her, and the scent and taste of regret, heavy like a spoiled onion, almost overwhelmed him. He broke into a sprint, shuffling through the few straggling students filing into their next class.

Back in the classroom, Ember made a strangled sound as the sharp scissors decimated the flesh on Cassidy's face. The metal sound clacking and clinking against the porcelain of Cassidy's teeth made her wince.

Cassidy pulled the scissors out, fist still clutched onto them like a kid who didn't know how to hold things properly. Blood pooled across her lips. Her mouth fell open in pain and shock, teeth clattering to the tabletop and floor. Then Cassidy brought the scissors up again, pushing them into her eye socket. Ember jumped back, hands flying to her mouth to stop the strangled scream escaping her throat. Cassidy repeated the sweeping arc, up, down, up, down, slashing at her own face.

Ember's feet and legs felt heavy, unstable. She stared in awe, eyes widening, adrenaline kicking her system into overload. A tidal wave of regret, anger, and fear rolled through her frozen body, unable to do anything to stop the atrocity she had started. Cassidy moved from her face to her throat, stabbing herself over and over, seemingly unable to stop even as she cried out.

Ember maintained stillness as the girl careened toward her. Cassidy reached out and feebly grabbed a hold of Ember's shirt, her arm. The scissors came out of her neck, and a spurt of warm blood sprayed across Ember's neck and shoulder.

Emory rushed into the room. He felt the tingling pressure building up as he gathered his thoughts into a condensed and powerful singular action. He rushed up to Cassidy, grabbing a hold of her wrist.

"Stop! Stop!" he said and thought at the same time.

The force of it made Ember cringe and grasp at her head. An immediate surge of pain came on, like a migraine taking hold.

Emory tried to wrestle the scissors from Cassidy's hand, but the grip was shocking in its intensity. He watched her eyes come back to life. The dullness dissipated, and the pain struck her. Her eyes watered with tears. They grew wide and wild. Her hand came to her neck, felt the blood pulsing out of it.

"Wait, Cassidy, wait," Emory begged as her legs gave out. Blood soaked the front of her shirt as it streamed out of the artery in her neck. He followed her to the floor, wishing he could do more than manipulate thoughts and objects with his mind. He desperately wished he could stop the flow of blood, pressing his hand to the wound, but the frantic fear in her eyes was already draining to lifelessness.

She lay back, her hands falling slack, her heart slowing. He watched as the pulse in her neck spewed less and less blood.

It was at that point that Ember screamed.

Emory stood, turning to his sister and grabbing a hold of her shoulders. "Ember, what did you do? What did you do? Why the fuck would you do that, Em?"

A scream from behind Ember shocked them both. Emory saw Mrs. Gilroy, pale and stunned, staring in horror at the body.

Mr. Lammle came storming in. His breath caught, and his legs fumbled, but he made it to Cassidy, bent over her, and checked for a pulse. He pulled his cell from his pocket and dialed 911; bloodstained fingers smeared the phone.

The world would say they got off lightly because their mother was a top defense attorney. But there was no evidence that Ember had ever held the scissors. No fingerprints, no residual DNA, no blood on her hands, or cast-off patterns on her clothes. Even her footprints showed that she'd moved away from the girl, not toward her. The blood patterns didn't suggest a struggle. Still, she had been in the room. Even her testimony, which was given twice before Ember refused to speak, was that she was helping put away the workbooks when Cassidy picked up the scissors and started stabbing herself. Emory figured that Ember's traumatic reaction, her refusal to talk, helped her case.

Emory was a suspect. For what reason, he didn't know. Because he was there? Because he had more blood on his body than Ember, and someone had to have done this? No one could believe a teenage girl would have the force or the wherewithal to commit such acts on her own body. Stabbing herself so hard she knocked her teeth out. Stabbing herself multiple times in the face, eye, and neck.

Mrs. Gilroy made an impressive witness for the prosecution, reiterating how she heard Emory ask why Ember would do what she did. There was also testimony from the school counselor who went over the occasions when the school got involved in the bullying aspects. Oddly, the counselor was of the mind that she'd been mistaken over who was bullying who. Cassidy, in her opinion, had always come across as quiet and respectful.

Plenty of students came out to tell how Emory went running down the hallway before they heard the scream, which had been from Ember. They were also happy to mention the recent events in which Ember had forced herself on Elsa Ravecchio at a party and that Cassidy had been the one to stand up for Elsa when again, Ember was overly aggressive at the mall, cornering Elsa in the bathroom hallway off the food court and trying to get her to agree to go on a date with her.

The defense was just as tough, pointing out the physical evidence. Blood spatter analysts all suggested that neither of the twins could have been the one stabbing Miss Zimmer. They cited the lack of fingerprints and the movement of the shoe patterns in the blood. To match the defamation side of things, the defense cited things like hysteria and Cassidy's history of self-harm.

With Ember refusing to speak and the delicate nature of the incident, the judge ordered a psych evaluation of both the Graff children. They found both Ember and Emory to be mentally incompetent, with such diagnoses as post-traumatic stress disorder, mild dissociative disorders, and, with Ember, depression. The judge suspended the proceedings and ordered both defendants to seek care at a mental facility. He recommended one of the best, the Orbriallis Institute in Lost Grove.

So, they packed up their things and moved to a rental outside the city. Part of their sentence, because it was a sentence, even though no one would call it that to their face, was therapy sessions at the Orbriallis Institute three times a week. Their mother stayed in town while their father, who was a stay-at-home dad anyway, chauffeured them off to the boonies.

Throughout the proceedings, the move, and even now, only Ember and Emory knew the truth. Ember wanted Cassidy to stab herself, and she'd gotten her wish.

Chapter 19

Pod People

Emory lay on the silken sheets of his hospital bed, eyes glued to the rotating blades of the ceiling fan. How many hours had he been counting those revolutions? Two? Three? Four? He longed for the trancelike sleep its regular rhythm usually brought him, but this was no ordinary weekend. Not like the others. This was the second Saturday in a row that his father dutifully dropped them off at Orbriallis Institute for the "requested"—a word the lead doctor used when she meant it more like a demand, imperative to their care—twenty-four-hour admission.

Emory let out a sarcastic, dry huff, flipping the thousand-thread-count sheets off his body. He swung his legs over the edge of the twin bed, settling his toes into the plush carpet, then yanked the little electrodes from his temples, the back of his neck, and from the pulse points on his wrists. The readouts be damned, he would deal with the consequences when the doctors reviewed the reports the following morning and saw a massive blank.

"'Imperative,'" he said aloud. "Yeah, sure."

Pushing up from the bed, he grabbed his hoodie, slipped into his Converse, and pulled open the door to his private room with such force he had to stop it from slamming against the wall. He made his way down the hall, following the thoughts of the nurse he'd intruded on earlier, thinking how ludicrous it was that they collected their phones and locked them away in small cubby lockers. This recent activity, locking away phones, keeping them overnight for twenty-four-hour holds, along with asking them to complete weird sensory tasks, all came after a very distinct interview with the head of the psychology department, Dr. Jane Bajorek.

A little over four weeks ago, he and his sister walked into the Orbriallis to be greeted in person by their new doctor. Emory recalled the way Ember reacted. He didn't even need his special gifts to pick up how she stiffened, how she swallowed heavier, how her eyes darted around the hospital, looking for a way out.

Dr. Bajorek called them into her office one at a time. Emory remembered the way his heart kicked up when he noticed an older woman sitting in the darkest corner of the office. She didn't say a word during the entire session, which was more unsettling than if she'd hissed witchcraft spells in a foreign language at him. Why would this woman be sitting in a cloak of darkness if everything was on the up and up?

Dr. Bajorek asked him a series of questions he couldn't even recall because the older woman, introduced as a colleague who was just there to supervise, had such a penetrating, intoxicating stare. He would use those words to describe it later to Ember, but what he really felt was like she was a predator. Emory could have sworn he sensed something, someone feeling around inside his skull, similar to how he and his sister connected, but this felt alien and dark. He'd done nothing to prevent it, instead growing queasy as a surreal atmosphere clouded the entire session.

He left feeling like they'd drugged him. Rather, like he'd taken a peculiar concoction of recreational drugs and found a tonic that didn't all mesh well together. On their ride home, he demanded answers from Ember, because it was clear she had her own thoughts on the situation.

He asked, *In the interview, what did you do?* Already feeling like he knew the answer.

She'd replied, *I didn't do anything... I mean, I tried to find out what it was, but—*
Jesus! Why the hell would you do that?
I think the other woman in the room is like us.
No. She's not like us. She might sense us, but she's not like us. And what the fuck? Why are they even... Why would they know about this kind of shit?

Ember went silent. Emory felt her try to close her thoughts, but he was the stronger one. He was the one who had the most control. He practiced, always in increments, building nuance and strength to their talents, where Ember haphazardly charged forward, not knowing what she was capable of. Before she could even begin locking him out, he'd gathered enough detail to see what had happened. He grabbed his sister's wrist as their father pulled into the driveway and turned off the car.

"Guys okay?" his dad asked from the front seat.

"Yeah, fine. We just need a minute," Emory replied.

His dad nodded, slid from the car, and headed into their new home.

Emory spun in the seat toward his sister. *Ember, you need to communicate with me. What the hell is going on?* he demanded.

His twin sister confessed how she may have mis-stepped, which might have led them to be in the care of Dr. Bajorek. The first time, she believed, was in a session with one of their original therapists. Ember preemptively began writing her answers before the doctor finished asking questions about the bullying.

The second time could have been when they'd asked her to go back to that day to recount the details. Some low form of hypnotism was involved. She'd lashed out and caused the therapist to have a bloody nose.

The third time was during a session with her counselor, who kept asking her over and over about how she felt. Asking her to point to a series of cartoon faces with each question.

"How did you feel when the police first questioned you? How did you feel when the lawyers asked you to testify in court? Were you scared of what people would think? Were you scared you'd done something wrong? Do you feel you have done something wrong?"

I just wanted the questions to stop. I hated the way they presented the sad to happy faces, as if I was incapable of grasping what they were doing. Didn't they get this was a choice of mine, not to talk? So I planted a thought in the counselor's mind that their time was up and that I had already left. The counselor got up and walked out of the room.

"Ember, what the fuck?" Emory asked, jumping out of the car.

She followed, trying to explain. *What did you want me to do? They keep asking the same—*

"There are cameras all over the place. In every room, every hall…I mean, Jesus. She walks out early, then comes out of the fog you created and wonders where all the time went. She watches the video, brings it to her superior, Dr. Bajorek, and here we are. Fuck's sake," Emory had said before storming into the house and slamming the door.

They don't know anything. You're being paranoid. We haven't met anyone like us in the city. Why the hell do you think we'd meet one in this small town? Ember had argued once she caught up with him and followed him through the house.

Emory glared at her before pushing his bedroom door shut.

The problem was, after what their new classmates had said, he had the distinct feeling that the Orbriallis Institute knew exactly what talents he and his sister had. Not only that, they were interested. And he wanted to know why.

Using the code he'd pulled from the memory of the nurse, he opened the small cubby, grabbed his phone, and pressed it shut again. He was careful as he shuffled down the hall. Not that he had to hide. The staff had said the floor was theirs to roam and explore. If confronted about his wanderings, which he planned to do a lot of tonight, he'd just manipulate their memories to recall something different. Another part of him didn't give a shit. He almost welcomed the questions, asking why he couldn't sleep, how he got his phone, what he was looking for.

Emory wished he could say that was his personality, but deep down, he was afraid. The doctors and nurses made him cringe. There was something off in their demeanor, their pattern of speech. Another thing that made the place unsettling was the peculiar and disturbing sound that emanated throughout the walls. He hadn't been able to place it during their first visit, or the first few visits, but it was always there, a constant surge of noise and electricity that ran up and down the sky-scraping institute, like an ice maker recycling repeatedly.

Fear was a driving force. It was making him do reckless things, but at the moment, he couldn't care less. The doctors had shifted away from focusing on the actual issue of PTSD his sister was suffering with, of remorse, guilt, thoughts of suicide, dark dives into despair. They didn't give a shit about that anymore. But Emory did. So, yes, he was afraid. Of the Orbriallis Institute, for his sister… Part of it was simply the fact that he was afraid of himself.

No, he knew that was a major part of it. His sister had killed someone, and he had the same abilities as his sister. The way she'd made someone do something so violent against their will was a new discovery in their abilities. A few times, they'd worked pretty hard to influence an answer from their parents. Emory had even made a gentle push on one of his teachers to up the grade on his final paper, though he had a pretty solid argument about why it deserved a better grade.

After Cassidy Zimmer had stabbed herself to death because Ember had hacked her brain, Emory wondered if he could do something so severe. He wondered if he could make someone do something completely opposite to their personality. No, more than that, he wondered if he could make them do something their base survival instincts should protect them against.

It terrified him that the same thing his sister had done, he could do. He met a homeless teenager and struck up a quick relationship with a bag of chips and a half pint of whiskey that led them to an underpass. One moment he was sitting there with the kid, talking about random crap that seemed to plague every teenager, whether homeless or from a prominent family. The next moment, the kid was up and walking into the speeding traffic. Emory jumped up and pulled the kid away from the roadside before he got clocked by a truck. Removing the thought was almost harder than putting it in the mind of the stranger, but he got it done. The weight of exhaustion that came after the mental exercise, along with the wave of guilt, hit Emory like a four-ton truck barreling down the highway. It was a miracle he'd even made it home.

He was constantly afraid now. Afraid of what his thoughts could do without too much effort, what they could do if he put his mind to it. He was also afraid these studies would show the scientists what they were capable of. Pausing in the large gathering area, Emory looked around, glancing out the tall windows at the gorgeous trees, the mist, and clouds. He plopped down on a sofa, brushing aside the reading material on the massive concrete-and-glass coffee table. Comic books, spine-worn books by Roald Dahl, fashion magazines.

Emory slouched back and pulled out his phone. The blue light lit up his skin, his thumb skimming over the social media feed. He started checking comments, text messages, liking photos, when the strange sound whirred back up the building past him. He listened to it slowly descend, then fall below him. Emory stood, pocketing his phone, and moved to the windows to see if there was literally some strange electrical current floating up and down the tower. There wasn't.

He turned at the waist, looking back toward the elevators. Emory walked over and pressed the button. A part of him didn't expect the elevator to respond, but it did. The doors opened to a warmly lit cabin. He got in, looked at the numbers, and pressed a button for B3. Seconds clicked by. He was certain the elevator wouldn't move, that pressing that number would mean he'd have to swipe some security card on the reader above the buttons. Just when he was reaching to press another button, the doors slid closed, and the elevator picked up speed, shooting downward.

Riding the elevator, it was easy to feel the way it slowed. Coming to a stop put pressure on his whole body. Emory swore it hadn't felt that way earlier. The doors opened on B3 to a faintly lit and quiet floor. The lights weren't blinking like some run-down facility or in a horror movie. It was more like warm holiday lights, bringing cheer and merriment to the season. The fluorescents above were off completely, but bright running lights lit up the floor and hallway. The most surprising thing was their warmth. Emory would have thought a cool, blue light would be the norm in such facilities, but these were the cozy color of a grandmother's lamp.

Emory leaned out of the elevator, peering down one part of the hall, then the other. The elevator chimed at him, doors threatening to close. Instinct made him jump out. The doors closed, and the elevator was off to another floor in the building. He shoved his hands into his front pockets and moved down the hall to the right. The sound whooshing past him this time felt louder. He felt it more, his hair standing on end as it passed him by. He shrugged his shoulders up to his ears, held them there for a concentrated moment, then let them drop before moving down the hall.

Emory rounded the corner and was startled as the lights along the baseboards lit up at his movement. He paused, wondering if he should continue. Recalling the urban legends his new friends had divulged about the Orbriallis Institute had put plenty of ideas in his head. He pressed on; the lights illuminating and then darkening behind him. The hallways seemed to twist back on themselves so that he wondered if he shouldn't be marking his path, lest he stumble into an old wicked woman's oven.

A door suddenly opened ahead of him, causing Emory to stumble backward before he stilled. A person in scrubs exited with a tablet screen coloring his chubby face, and proceeded away from him down the hall. Emory followed the man with caution, keeping his footsteps as quiet as possible. When he rounded another corner, he inhaled and catapulted himself back against the wall. The hall he had almost charged down had a line of people in hospital pajamas.

Emory held his breath and leaned around the corner and watched the people slowly file into a room. The last person entered, followed by a woman in a grey lab coat. The door hissed closed and clicked shut. After a moment's debate, Emory crouched and scurried across the floor to the door. He slowly stood to peer through the oblong windows.

Several young adults, some looking a little younger than himself, others maybe ten years older, were climbing into pods. Emory scanned the room, taking in the tubes, the mist rising from the open pods, the ostentatious amount of cables running across the floor, connecting each pod to a massive console at the back of the room. He shifted so he could get a better look. Two other doctors in lab coats were working at it, turning levers, and gauging readouts on screens obscured from his vision.

He turned his attention back to the people in the hospital-issued pajamas. They were removing their clothes so that they now stood in their underwear. A few of them were already climbing into the pods. When he stood on his tiptoes, he got the impression they were stepping into water, but he didn't take the time to get a good look. It put him at too much risk of being seen. It came to Emory suddenly that the pods must be sensory deprivation tanks. For a moment, he let his breath out in a not-too-silent gush of air.

Enthralled by this sci-fi movie inspired scene that reminded him of one of his favorite artists and designers, Arthur Max, Emory leaned further still to gape through the windows. What kind of study had a room full of people entering sensory deprivation tanks? His mind flickered through various accounts of weird experiments, urban legends, and his favorite films. He'd heard about synergistic experiences, like the town that all saw and experienced a visit from an alien spacecraft, but making sense of what he was witnessing just wasn't logical. All he could think of were the precogs from *Minority Report*.

Emory's gaze bounced around the room until his eyes locked with those of a teenager who appeared to be twelve or thirteen. Emory ducked down, his breath caught in his throat. Had anyone else seen him? Should he run? Use his powers? Before deciding on a course of action, he peeked back up through the window to see the kid hadn't budged. His eyes seemed vacant, and as Emory stared back at him, the teenager's eyes slowly came to life. His lips twitched and parted, brows pinching together. On instinct, Emory lifted his finger to his mouth, urging the kid to stay quiet. The kid's eyes moved to the nurse or doctor attending to him.

"Oh, shit. Hey, it's okay, G." The male nurse tried to calm him.

Emory relaxed his senses so he could clearly make out what was being said, the nurse's words just barely clear enough.

"Brant!" the nurse shouted to a coworker. "I need another dose of M13. G is showing signs of cognition. Wait here," the nurse guy said to the kid known as G.

Emory felt pain prick his throat as he tried to swallow. "What the hell kind of shit is this?" he whispered to himself as he let go of all nonauditory senses.

With the nurse's back turned, the kid waved Emory away, his head shaking back and forth in more violent and extreme ways. His hands came up to his head, gripping at the short hairs on his head.

"No, G, don't do that," the nurse instructed, grabbing G's wrists.

A dull, deep moan crawled out of G, growing in volume. The other candidates in the room shuffled, turning their attention to the commotion.

Emory reached into his hoodie, pulling the phone from his pocket. Half looking at the scene unfurling behind the doors, half at his phone, he opened the camera app.

"Shit! Brant, the dose. Now!"

"I got it, don't shit the bed." Brant stepped casually over the cables and expertly shoved a needle into the neck of G.

"I told them to cut their hair. He's latched on and won't let go," the nurse said.

It clocked in Emory's brain how all the kids in the room had extremely short hair. The girls and the boys all had buzz cuts. He fumbled with his phone, bringing it up to the window as he pressed the record button.

Brant swiftly pulled G's arms, and with them came chunks of hair. "There. Hair problem solved."

"Jesus, Brant."

"Don't be so sensitive, Kev. We can't have mistakes with these kids," he said, returning to his post.

Emory glanced down to see the phone was recording the pale cream of the door. He moved it upward, a blur of motion across a window interlaced with crisscrossing lines. The camera focused on the floor, all the numerous cables and tubes. Emory tilted it further upward, following the cables toward a dashboard where two people in scrubs and lab coats worked with their heads down.

He panned over quickly, making the screen a blur before slowing just enough to catch sight of a person between the age of seventeen and twenty-five, head shaved, looking like skin and bone with dark circles under their eyes and a vacant stare. Someone in scrubs was inserting what looked like an IV into their arm, though it was hard to judge from the distance. A brief glance at the number of pods and people who all looked the same, unhealthy, vacant, readying themselves to climb into the pods before settling on the face of the kid known as G. He stared directly at the camera, eyes wide, mouth aghast.

Emory lifted his eyes, trying to find the face through the window instead of through the view of his camera. As he did, a man stepped in to block the window.

"What the fuck?" the man said. He pushed the door open, sending Emory stumbling backward as it caught his forehead.

He briefly caught sight of the young female doctor staring out the door in surprise before Brant and Kev joined their coworker out in the hall.

"Who are you?" the man without a name asked Emory.

"What the fuck are you doing down here?" Brant asked in a far more threatening tone.

Kev and the other guy, both fit, circled Emory, locking him between themselves and the wall.

"You're not supposed to be down here," Kev said. "How did he get down here?" he asked Brant.

"Hey, you need to answer us now. Who are you?" the unknown guy asked.

Emory caught a flick of movement in Brant's hand. He clutched a syringe that seemed to glisten with a deadly concoction.

Emory looked up, met each of their eyes, and concentrated. The tingling pressure built along his neck, crawled up the back of his head, and spread across his skull, deep inside his head.

"I'm not here," he said. His voice was firm but not raised. The last thing he needed was to draw more attention. "I was never here. You never saw me. You'll turn around and go back to what you were doing."

Emory heard something chiming further down the hall, like a passive alarm. He tried not to let it distract his focus. A second passed, and then all three of the doctors casually turned and moved back into the room as if going about their business. Emory wanted to collapse onto the floor. His legs were like jelly, his brain pulsed with pain, his mouth dry, his eyes burning, and his skin coated in a film of sweat. But that alarm in the background kept him from collapsing.

Emory used the wall to head back the way he'd come. Looking back once, he saw the woman standing at the door, watching him. She didn't make a move to follow. Emory rushed as quickly as he could down the halls, confused by the twists and turns. Footsteps drew a fresh surge of adrenaline into his system.

Emory ducked into a dark room, waiting for the security guards to pass. Then he rushed onward in search of an elevator. Finally, he found a set, uncertain if they were the ones he'd come down in. His finger pressed the button over and over, as if that would make it arrive sooner. He kept pacing, his head on a swivel as voices carried down the halls, all in search of him. The elevator door whispered open. Emory fell in, pressed the button to his floor, and sighed with relief when the elevator rose quickly up to the twenty-third floor. He only just made it back to his room before collapsing on the bed without a moment to contemplate the video cameras that recorded his every move.

Chapter 20

Quiet Conversations

There was no sign denoting a haunting at Main Street Cafe by Saturday morning. Seth pulled open the door, the bell ringing, the warmth and scent of pastries and coffee sweeping over him, and stepped into a very crowded cafe. The usual hum of weekend energy was gone. In its place, a thick palpable atmosphere hung over the bowed and hushed heads. It reminded him of the mood in the San Francisco Police Department after they had lost fellow officer Macon Blaire during a domestic dispute call in 2019 when a gun was in play.

As soon as the patrons of the cafe registered who had walked in, the conversations ground to a halt. Seth nodded to the few individuals with whom he made eye contact, all of whom gave him a second look, eyes inquisitive and eager. He hoped no one would have the audacity to shout a question across the room to open a town hall meeting. Seth instantly regretted offering to bring his mother and father coffee and pastries. He fought the urge to leave as quickly as he had entered and made his way to the counter.

"Well, hello, Seth," Clemency greeted him with a big smile. She swirled a washcloth over the counter.

"Morning, Clemency. Pretty quiet in here this morning."

"Well, stands to reason. Usual?"

"Uh, yeah." Seth knew it was a stupid observation but wasn't sure what else to say. "Oh, I need a pumpkin spice latte for my mom. And—"

"Oatmilk?"

"Yep. And um, what's my dad's favorite, the bear claw or the apple fritter?"

"Bear claw," Clemency answered without a beat. "Speech therapy today?"

Seth nodded. "Yep."

The aftermath of his father's stroke resulted in an almost total lack of the ability to speak, along with nerve issues on the left side of his body. His mother was not in an ideal position to take proper care of him, despite her protestation to the contrary. When Seth realized his father's road to recovery would be lengthy and his return to running their pharmacy seemed unlikely, Seth knew he'd be home in Lost Grove for longer than a family leave of absence covered. It was the reason he turned in his detective badge and took up Bill's offer to become sergeant of Lost Grove Police.

"Think the pastry will cheer him up?" Clemency waited for the milk to steam, pulling a bear claw from the glass display. Before Seth could answer, Clemency started back into a conversation with the woman who owned the quasi-art gallery and showroom down the street, Lynne Everett. "No one I've talked to this morning says they've heard from them."

"Didn't figure as much. I can't even imagine the devastation. Evan's at Cal Long Beach—"

"I recall."

"And I worry about him every day. Especially on the weekends when lord knows what he's getting into. I just hope Bess and Richard are holding it together," Lynne said, and then looked over at Seth.

Already having diverted his eyes, Seth took a step away and put his hands in his jacket pockets, his right fingertips brushing the acorn. He wasn't about to fall into a conversation about the Grahamses.

Lynne looked back at Clemency. "I swear it doesn't feel like that long ago I saw her in here, studying away."

Clemency poured steamed milk into a to-go cup, set the frothing pitcher down, and pointed to a small two-person tall table in the front corner up against a window. "Sat at that same table right there every time. Must have studied more than any kid I've ever seen, a damn shame it is."

Seth glanced over to where Clemency was pointing, and his eyes widened. Sitting at the table with a woman he didn't recognize was Jaime Miller, formerly Jaime Goodacre, Seth's high school girlfriend. Likely drawn by Clemency's blatant pointing, Jamie looked in their direction. Another double take.

"Seth?" Jaime bounced up from her chair and glided across the cafe floor. She wrapped her arms around him. "So good to see you!"

"You too, Jamie." Seth patted her back, hoping she would let go of him. He had fond enough memories of their friendship throughout school, which turned into a relationship during their junior and senior years. But ever since he came back, every time they crossed paths, her reaction was overwhelming.

"I've been thinking of you ever since I heard the news. This must be so hard on you."

Seth grimaced. "I'm sure it's harder on everyone else. Part of my job and all."

Finally releasing her embrace, Jaime pulled back and squeezed Seth's arm, giving him an empathetic smile. "You were always so strong. The way you bounced back from being stuck in that cave. My goodness, I would have been a wreck to this day."

A chill traveled down Seth's spine. "I think I was actually pretty messed—"

Jamie looked over at Clemency and Lynn and loudly whispered, "Seth and I dated in high school."

"We know," they said in unison.

Jamie flung her hand dismissively in their direction and pulled Seth aside. "Between you and me—"

"I can't discuss the case with you, Jamie," Seth cut her off.

"I know that," she said with a laugh. "I just want to know if I should be worried. You know, as a woman. I mean, should I be carrying mace or—"

"You should always carry mace. Clemency? Are those…" Seth pointed to the coffees sitting on the counter, desperate to leave.

"Oh," Jamie said, bringing a hand to her chest.

"What now? Oh, yes, these are for you." Clemency put the double cappuccino in a to-go tray, and as she grabbed the bag with the bear claw, a chair at the back of the cafe wobbled, then tipped over, cracking to the floor. Clemency let out a small yelp as her wide eyes darted from the chair to Seth. "Have you seen Story?"

Seth stared at the turned-over chair at the back of the cafe, not seeing who could have tipped it over.

"Seth?"

He turned back to Clemency. "Me? Have I seen Story? No, not today."

Jamie narrowed her eyes at Seth. "Oh, I see."

Seth shook his head. "No. Nothing there," he lied and headed back toward the counter.

"I need her to help me get rid of these damn ghosts," Clemency spouted as she put a dollop of whipped cream to the top of the pumpkin latte, followed by pumpkin spice sugar. She added it to the tray and handed everything over to Seth. "You see her, tell her to head on my way."

"If I happen to come across her." Seth grabbed the bag and tray, but before he could retreat, Jamie grabbed his forearm.

"If you ever want to get together, maybe grab a drink or something," she said, her voice lowered.

"That's probably not a good idea."

"David wouldn't mind, you know."

Seth cocked his head to the side. "I'm not sure what that means, but I've got to get over to my parents' house."

"And Seth," Clemency called after him as he was making his way to the door, "let Amaranth know that I'm still seeing those damn lights."

Seth's face scrunched up. "Um, sure. Will do."

There was no point in calling out that he'd arrived. As a child, Seth's mother, Amaranth, had been the only survivor of a school bus accident, having careened over a bridge into a raging winter river. She had survived but lost her hearing. Seth found her in the kitchen, reading a book at the table. He had already passed through the living room and handed off the bear claw to his father, who was watching TV.

Seth set the tray of coffees on the kitchen counter and presented his mother with a small bouquet of alstroemerias.

Amaranth leaned in to smell them, looked up, and smiled widely at her son. Then she signed, "Alstroemerias have always been my favorite. Thank you, darling."

Seth smiled and contained a laugh. Of course Story would have known this. He grabbed a vase from the cupboard, placing the flowers in them, and filled it up with water. Returning to the table, Seth pulled his mother's coffee from the tray and handed it to her as he sat down.

"Thank you," Amaranth signed, "what did you get me?"

"Pumpkin spiced latte," he signed. Seth was as fluent in ASL as he was in the English language, having grown up learning both simultaneously.

Amaranth took a sip and licked her lips. "Mm."

Seth nodded to the book and signed, "What are you reading?"

She held the book up so he could see the cover, *Skin* by Mo Hayder, and signed, "Don't you think it's funny that I've become an addict of detective stories?"

Seth laughed and signed back, "Is that part of the same series you've been reading?"

Amaranth nodded and wiggled her eyebrows in delight.

Seth signed, "Well, maybe you can put all your reading to some use. I wanted to ask you some questions before I take Dad to therapy."

Amaranth set her book down, her smile fading. "About the Grahams girl?" she signed.

Seth nodded and signed, "You said you knew her. What can you tell me about her?"

"I wouldn't say I knew her," she signed, tilting her head to the side. "But I saw her many times as she grew up. Always the sweetest girl."

"Did you have any interactions with her?"

Amaranth nodded. "She was at almost every town event until she left for college. Sarah was always very kind to me. She even taught herself some sign language to say 'hello,' 'thank you,' and 'how are you?'"

Seth smiled. Many of the adults in town had learned some basic ASL in order to communicate with his mother. She had been doing volunteer work ever since he was a kid, becoming a prominent member of the community. Everyone loved Amaranth, and for good reason. "And her parents?" he signed.

"Richard is always quite friendly with me. Bess is nice enough," she signed and shrugged.

Seth pointed at her and signed, "Which, for you, translates into 'she's an asshole.'"

Amaranth ignored her son and continued. "They're friendly at the church events I volunteer for. Other than that, I don't cross paths with them all that much."

"Is there anywhere else you regularly see them outside of church events?" Seth signed.

Amaranth took a sip of her coffee and thought about that for a moment. "At the yearly fundraiser for the Orbriallis Institute. I think they're big donors."

"Why do you think that?" Seth signed.

"They sit at the table with the head of the Institute," she signed. "They shake hands with all the bigwig doctors."

Seth puckered his lips and pondered a moment before signing, "Why would they be such big donors for Orbriallis?"

Amaranth narrowed her eyes at her son. "Why not? We give money.

Does someone need a reason to donate money?"

Seth leaned back in his chair and signed, "Do you have a reason?"

Amaranth smiled, signing, "Well, they've started doing some new biomedical research for the hearing impaired. But we gave money before that. We support every business in our community. Especially one that employs so many."

"You and Dad are good people. Maybe the most decent in town," Seth signed.

Amaranth swatted her hand at him.

Seth laughed and finished the rest of his cappuccino before signing, "I should probably get Dad off the couch and ready."

"You know," Amaranth started signing, looking up and to the right, "ever since you told me about finding Sarah's body on the beach, I can't stop thinking about Kelly Fulson. Did Bill tell you about that case?"

Seth sat back down in his chair and signed, "Yeah, we've actually been looking back into it."

"She was pregnant, you know."

"I know."

"She had been missing for a long time before they found her on Jonathan Baume's property," Amaranth signed. "Seven months pregnant. Just terrible. It devastated her parents, Henry and Molly. They're beloved by the whole town."

Seth leaned on the table, squinting, and signed, "I don't think I remember them."

"You were over at their house at least once."

"What?" Seth verbalized, brows knit.

"I'm not surprised you wouldn't remember," she signed. "Do you remember how we had the Fourth of July parades down Main Street?"

Seth nodded and signed, "Yeah."

Amaranth squinted her eyes. "I think it was around the mid-nineties when the Fulsons decided to open up their farmland to the whole town for an after-parade party. I know you came with us at least once."

Seth's eyes darted back and forth as he thought back to his youth. Then, suddenly, his head jolted up, looking at his mom. "Holy shit," he signed enthusiastically. "I remember. Darren and I were wrestling in this big stack of hay in the barn."

"Sounds about right," Amaranth signed with a wide smile.

Seth had flashes coming to him from that night. He signed, "I remember a young girl, maybe around six or seven. She found us goofing around and told us we weren't supposed to be in there. Would that have been her?"

Amaranth considered a moment before signing, "The age difference would make sense. Did she have bright blonde hair?"

Seth nodded. "It had to have been her. Bizarre," he signed offhand.

"I'm sure it seems that way now, but I think it would have been more bizarre if you had never come into contact with her or her parents."

Seth had an uneasy feeling in his chest, his palms becoming sweaty. He worried he might have another vision. He'd been in contact with Kelly Fulson, even if it was distant, like a meteor passing through his orbit. Seth wondered if he'd ever seen Sarah on any of his few trips home for the holidays. Could she have brushed past him in the aisles of the grocery store? Or skipped across the street in front of him, her bold auburn hair blinking a warning like the glow from a lighthouse warned sailors of shallow shores?

His mother's moving fingers drew his attention back to the present.

"The whole town turned out for the funeral," Amaranth signed, her eyes drifting off to the past. "I'll never forget the feeling of seeing that tiny casket next to Kelly's."

It took Seth a moment to put the pieces together. "For her unborn child," he signed.

Amaranth nodded and signed, "The saddest part was seeing her younger brother in tears. He was weeping."

"How much younger was he?"

"Four years, I believe."

Seth tapped his fingertips on the table a half dozen times before signing, "Mom, do you recall if it surprised her parents that she was pregnant? I know she had been missing, but was there a boyfriend in the picture beforehand?"

"They were shocked she was pregnant," Amaranth signed. "She had a long-term relationship with a boy in town named Luke Riddick, but they had been broken up for a while before she disappeared. Why do you ask?"

Seth kept his eyes level on his mom, debating whether to tell her. Apparently, his gaze wasn't as neutral as he had thought.

"No!" Amaranth signed aggressively. "Sarah was pregnant?"

"We're not releasing that information to the public yet," Seth signed, his eyes stern.

"I just can't believe that. Of all the young women in this town, that doesn't make sense." Amaranth looked down, bewildered.

Seth narrowed his eyes and knocked on the table to grab his mom's attention. "Why would you say that about her?" he signed.

"Well," Amaranth signed and thought for a moment, "I just didn't get the impression that she would put herself in a position to get herself pregnant. She was so determined to go to college. She told me she was going to be a doctor and that's all that mattered to her. And…just who she was. I know how in-tune you are with people, dear. And I think if you had known her, you would feel the same way."

Seth nodded. If there was anyone on the planet whose intuition Seth would implicitly trust, it was his mother. He knew he wouldn't be the person or detective he was today without her openness, honesty, and intelligence guiding him as he grew up. A gentle rap on the table by his mother brought his attention back to her.

"You'll find out what happened to her," she signed.

A faint smile rose on Seth's face. "Is that a question or a statement?"

Amaranth grinned and signed, "A statement."

Chapter 21

Blood in My Ice Cream

The creaky sign outside the Moonlight Creamery & Bistro flapped wildly in the cold autumn breeze. Inside, the restaurant was filled with scents of freshly made waffle cones and simmering hot fudge. A glass case displayed the many flavors on offer, everything from classic vanilla and strawberry to more daring choices like blueberry basil or pumpkin chai. Warm light spilled out onto the courtyard and picnic table seating. String lights danced in the wind. If you walked down the tight alleyway to the back of the shop, the subtle hum of ice cream churns could be heard coming from the basement, and two small windows offered a glimpse into the ice cream and cheese-making process.

Even though it was the start of October and cold by sundown, Zoe Andalusian was a fan of ice cream, no matter the season. She and her brother sat outside at a table with the patio heaters cranked up to warm them, they being the only ones foolish enough to sit outside. But the conversation he was about to have with Anya when she showed up wasn't one he wanted a bunch of people overhearing.

Anya rode up on her bike, nose red from the cold. "Hey," she greeted them. Some of the fresh cream that made this bistro's famous ice cream and cheese came from her family farm.

"Hey," Noble said, shifting down the bench to make room for Anya to sit next to him, across from Zoe. "Thanks for meeting us up here."

"Course," she said, returning Zoe's smile. "You got that whole thing for yourself?"

Zoe, mouth full, nodded enthusiastically, which made the pompom on her wool stocking cap dance. Her sundae was one scoop of caramel ribbon crunch, one scoop of chocolate brownie fudge, topped with butterscotch syrup, whipped cream, and sprinkles. Zoe's attention returned to her book, which turned out to be *Practical Magic*. She'd found the book while biking to her friend Caitlin's house that afternoon, which always took her past the historic Altham House, or rather, Story Palmer's house. The book had been poking out of the brambles of the blackberry hedge that bordered Story's property. Its spine cracked, pages open and fluttering in the gentle wind. Zoe applied the brakes so hard the tires actually squealed a little. She dumped the bike, glanced around, and looked through the hedge toward the witch's house. With no one in sight, she quickly removed the book, tucked it in her bag, and hopped back on the bike. The moment she got back home from Caitlin's house, she'd opened the cover, engrossed ever since.

Anya looked from the book to Noble, pressing her lips into a smirk. He raised his brows and smiled.

"So, ice cream in October," Anya said, removing her knit cap.

"If it's cold, Zoe likes it. The weather, food, water, you name it."

"Ah." Anya leaned onto the table. Her ginger-to-white locks fell out from where she'd tucked them into the back of her coat.

Noble admired the depth of the copper roots, the way it sparkled in the flames from the space heater above their heads. He picked his spoon back up and took a bite from his own smaller sundae, a simple strawberry and vanilla ice cream with hot fudge syrup. "You want me to get you one?" he asked Anya.

"No thanks," she replied. "My dad made his apple streusel, and I had far too much of it earlier. My dinner, actually."

"I wish our mom would let us have streusel for dinner," Zoe contributed, flipping a page.

Anya smiled, returning her attention to Noble. She leaned in and whispered, "So?"

Noble discarded the spoon in his sundae and wiped his fingers on a napkin. He dropped his head down and spoke like he was an informant, giving information to a reporter. "So, I'm pretty sure what Nettie's brother said was Papa LaRange."

"Papa LaRange?" Anya's brows pulled together. "Papa LaRange," she muttered again to herself. "Makes sense with the words. It's actually the only thing that has made sense. I've just come up with gibberish. Still, not sure what Papa LaRange is or why he'd say it."

"You said it was a puppet, right? I thought maybe it was the name of the puppet he was remembering, or a character from a cartoon?"

"And?"

"Nothing."

"Oh," Anya sighed.

"At least nothing regarding a cartoon. But"—Noble pushed the sundae away and swung his leg over the bench so he was facing Anya—"I'm on page three of a Google search when I find something that looks interesting. Turns out to be a weird tweet that links back to a creepy sub-Reddit, but the phrase Papa LaRange has something to do with a court case."

"Really?"

Anya looked up into Noble's eyes. He became lost in her eyes before he forced himself to look away.

"Yeah," Noble said. "I'm invested, right? I'm scavenging for this information. I want to know where it leads. So I plug in searches for Papa LaRange court case, and finally, the Papa LaRange trial gets a hit."

"You're kidding!" Anya leaned closer as Noble pulled his phone from his pocket.

"I found out the county of the trial, and I plugged that into my search, and bam," he exclaimed, turning his phone toward her. "Seven articles about a trial on this guy named Raymond LaRange."

"What?" Anya asked, scouring the search listings for words that stood out or made sense of this connection.

Down the street, the music from Reggie's Pub spilled out toward them, along with the clinking of glasses and the laughter of two inebriated men. Noble glanced across the table at his sister, who was giving him a look from under her long lashes, one eyebrow infinitely raised. Zoe had always seemed to have a soft spot for Anya, even before Noble realized how breathtakingly gorgeous she was. He wondered if his sister knew something he didn't.

"Can I hold this?" Anya asked, pointing to Noble's phone.

"Sure." He handed it over and looked back at his sister, whose eyes went from his phone back to him.

"Who's Papa LaRange, Noble?"

Noble sighed. He was banking on Zoe being wrapped up in her new book. He opened his mouth to respond, but Zoe's eyes looked over his shoulders. Noble turned around, hearing the approaching footsteps.

One of the two drunk men paused, his eyes looking at each member at the table. At the same moment, Seth Wolfe exited Uncle Joe's Grille across the street, his mother ahead of him.

"You should mind who you sit with, young lady," one of the drunk men said, looking at Anya.

Anya whipped her head around, too enthralled by what she was reading to have heard the approach. "Huh?"

Noble straightened his back. "What are you talking about?"

"The likes of the Andalusian men? He's liable to get you in trouble. Or killed." The man, Jeffrey Tacet, worked on one of the nearby ranches and was not a man with soft edges. He had a chin like a snowplow and strong brows. His friend, Angus Weatherspoon, had the pinched face of a weasel and the body of a giant hedgehog. He snorted with drunken laughter.

"What did you just say?" Noble fully turned now.

Anya spoke up. "I think I have more to worry about with men like you in the world than men like him."

Jeffrey grinned. "Oh, darlin', you don't know nothin' about a man like me. Shit, him?" Jeffrey sneered, nodding at Noble.

Noble stood up. "You better watch it there, guy."

Jeffrey huffed, keeping his leer trained on Anya. "I bet you don't even know who you're sitting with. That boy could be just like his father. Do you know who his father is?"

"Of course I know his father," Anya responded, too busy feeling annoyed by the outrageous, inappropriate comment from the older man to care about the subtext of the conversation.

Noble took a step forward. "I'd be careful what you say next."

Seth helped his mother into the car, watching the scene play out. There was no reason a man like Jeffrey Tacet was talking to a group of teenagers, much less with a child at the table. He didn't know the other man but didn't like the look of the situation. Seeing the teenage boy stand, Seth casually made his way over, signing to his mother he'd be right back.

"Oh, the young man's as cocky as his father." Jeffrey sauntered closer, his arms hanging loose by his side. He tossed a look over his shoulder at his companion, Angus, who laughed merrily at the taunts as if they were an inside joke. "He ran off just in time again, didn't he? Gone before the body of another young woman washed ashore."

"I heard about that," Angus chimed in, his testosterone sparked into action. Zoe looked from the men to the back of her brother's head to Anya.

Anya jumped up and moved to the other side of the picnic table, grabbing a hold of Zoe's hand, helping her unravel herself from the bench seat. "You might have the common decency not to be a chauvinist idiot and consider there is a child here."

Jeffrey snorted. "She may be just like her pa as well. A killer."

Noble lunged, connecting a powerful right hook on Jeffrey's solid jaw. The pain shot up his forearm in a way he wasn't expecting, but bone connecting with bone was never as delicate as one expected, and Noble had never thrown a punch in his life.

The blow caught Jeffrey off guard. But he'd been in a handful of fights, one or two with Noble's father, Peter. He gathered his bearings, reeled back, almost catching Angus on the backswing, and swung, catching Noble on his cheekbone with a hook.

The force of it stung, then ached with a deep pain that drove into Noble's skull and through his brain. By some miracle, Noble saw the next swing coming and awkwardly diverted it just in time.

Anya pulled Zoe closer to her body, instinctively sheltering her. "Are you insane?" she screamed at the man.

Angus looked as if he was about to make a move into the mix when Seth grabbed hold of Jeffrey under his arms, hands up behind his neck, and swung him off the teenage boy. In a singular move, Seth walked Jeffrey to the wall of the creamery, pressing him hard up against the brick, monitoring his friend the whole time. Jeffrey struggled against his new assailant.

"Now, Jeffrey Tacet, I don't think you want to try a swing at me," Seth warned. "I'm a sergeant with the Lost Grove Police Department. I'm sure you recall."

Jeffrey let out a grumble. "I recall."

Seth glanced back at Angus as he spoke to Jeffrey. "You know the penalty for attempted assault on an officer of the law?"

"Probably not too good," Jeffrey slurred.

Angus held his hands up in peace and took a step back.

"Who are you?" Seth asked.

"Angus. Angus Weatherspoon."

Seth scowled. "Angus Weatherspoon?"

"It's Scottish."

Seth shook his head and leaned into Jeffrey and spoke with a deep gravel into his ear. "Are you calm?"

"Very calm," Jeffrey replied, trying to nod despite his head being pressed against the hard brick.

"I'm gonna let you go, but if you move from that wall, I'll place you in handcuffs, and not comfortably." Seth eased his grip and stepped away.

"But you're not on duty," Angus protested.

"And you clearly know nothing about the law," Seth warned with a withering look.

"I was just…sorry," Angus said, taking another step back.

"You want to tell me what the hell is going on here?" Seth asked, turning in the direction of the teens.

Noble was pressing his palm to his cheek. Anya was holding the shivering, crying younger child and stroking her hair. The ferocity in her teenage eyes almost gave Seth pause.

Jeffrey piped up first. "It was just a misunder—"

"I'm asking the minors you just assaulted," Seth roared with a force that seemed to shake the ground Jeffrey was standing on. "When I want your side, I'll ask. Okay, what are your names?" Seth asked, looking back at the youths.

"Noble Andalusian," Noble finally said. "That's my little sister, Zoe."

"Anya Bury," Anya answered.

Seth nodded, registering the name Andalusian from the Kelly Fulson file. They questioned a man named Peter in conjunction with her death. There had to be a relation here. "How old are each of you?"

"Seventeen," Anya replied.

"Eighteen and eleven," Noble said.

Seth turned back and glared at Jeffrey. "You have some sort of luck on your side."

Jeffrey shrugged.

Seth turned back, his demeanor flipping, and finally made eye contact with the little girl, cheeks wet with tears, and offered her a reassuring smile before turning his attention back to the only kid that wasn't, technically, a minor. "Okay, Mr. Andalusian. Can you explain what happened?"

"We…we were sitting here, talking, having ice cream. And they, they…came out of Reggie's, and he said something about my dad."

"What's your dad's name?"

Noble paused for a moment before answering, "Peter."

Seth noted the hesitation, keeping his face motionless, registering that it was in fact Noble's father questioned in the Fulson case. "Can you be more specific about what they said about Peter?"

"That their father is no good. When he turns up, young women end up dead." Jeffrey spat blood from his mouth to the pavement. That punch from the young Andalusian had twisted his jaw pretty good, cut the inside of his cheek.

Seth half turned, a fierce glance that left no room for interpretation.

"Sorry. I'm done." Jeffrey's head drooped.

Seth looked back at the boy. "Mr. Andalusian, can you give me specifics about what was said to cause this disruption?"

Anya let go of Zoe, who scurried over into her brother's arms. The young man ignored the question and focused his attention on trying to calm her. Seth was dubious about why he went silent but wasn't in a hurry to stop him. The child was shaking so visibly he wanted to grab a blanket and wrap her in a hug himself.

Anya took in a deep breath to help keep her voice steady. "He said someone like Noble might get me in trouble or killed." Anya's eyes bounced over to Jeffrey, then back to the sergeant.

Seth furrowed his brow.

"Then I said I probably had more to worry about with men like them in the world," she said, pointing casually at Jeffrey and Angus. "He claimed I didn't know the truth about the Andalusians, and Noble asked him to be careful with what he said next. I had to agree, since Zoe is only eleven. You shouldn't say things like that about a child's father, whatever you may think of him," she said, directing it at the drunk man who was still standing by the wall.

"Why don't you ask who started the fight?" Jeffrey urged, taking a step forward.

Seth turned, eyeing Jeffrey's feet. "Did I tell you to move away from the wall? There are two female minors present. Move again, and I swear it will be the last move you make tonight."

Jeffrey nodded and made to step back against the wall. "Should I go back to the wall?"

"Yes, and stay quiet." Seth turned to Angus. "Did you approach this group of teenagers and incite an argument?"

"He was just making her aware—"

"That is not what I asked. Did you approach these teenagers, who were having ice cream sundaes, and incite an argument?"

"Yes, sir." Angus nodded.

"Right," Seth grumbled, and looked back at Anya. "Anything else?"

Anya looked over at Jeffrey, narrowing her eyes. "Yes, in fact." She looked back at Seth. "He made a very suggestive comment about how I wouldn't know anything about a man like him."

Seth's heart rate kicked up a notch. "So he made an aggressive sexual pass at you?"

"Like hell!" Jeffrey protested.

"It was in your tone, asshole!" Noble yelled.

"Okay, just calm down," Seth said, holding his hands up toward the boy. "You believe his intention behind that comment was sexual?"

"It sure as shit sounded like it."

Seth sighed and looked back at Anya. "Ms. Bury, did you feel uncomfortable because of Mr. Tacet's comments?"

"Yes. All his comments," Anya answered.

"Okay, then." Seth turned around, noticing that his mother had stepped away from the Bronco and closer to them. "I'm issuing you both a ticket for disturbing the peace and indecent conduct in public. And Jeffrey, I haven't fully decided what to do with you yet."

Jeffrey scowled and exhaled loudly from his nostrils.

"Now, get the hell out of my sight. Both of you."

"What about the tickets?" Angus asked.

Jeffrey gave his friend an incredulous glare.

Seth smiled. "I'll have them delivered to both of your homes tomorrow afternoon."

"Fuck," Angus grumbled and walked away.

Jeffrey started to leave.

Seth stepped up and grabbed his arm. "Don't let me see you anywhere near this boy and his sister again. You got it?"

"Got it."

Seth strengthened his grip, pressing his thumb into the artery in Jeffrey's bicep. "And I swear, if I see you within a block of this young woman ever again, I'll make you wish you were born a cripple."

Jeffrey tried to struggle free. "Goddamn, man. Yeah, I'll run the other way. Fuck."

Seth released him, watched him catch up with Angus, and then turned back around to the kids. He noticed the bike leaning up against the wall. "This one of your bikes?"

Anya nodded. "Yeah, that's mine," she said, body shaking from the comedown of adrenaline.

"And how did you both get here?" Seth asked Noble.

"We walked," Noble said, still crouched down, holding his sister.

"Come on, I'll give you all a ride home," Seth ushered them toward his mother.

Noble looked at Zoe. "Do you want to walk or ride with the officer?"

Zoe pointed at Seth.

Noble nodded. "Thanks."

Amaranth stepped forward and urged Anya toward the car, wrapping her in a motherly hug. Seth loaded the bicycle into the back of his Bronco, while the kids all filed into the back seat. His mind played over the accusations the men made of Noble's father. He would most assuredly be going back over the Kelly Fulson case when he got home. If it weren't for the crying child in his vehicle, he'd push Noble for more information about his dad. Seth decided he would talk to Bill before making any further moves on the Andalusians.

Seth got into the driver's seat and looked back at Anya. "Your dad is Ethan Bury, right?"

Anya nodded with a quizzical look. "Yeah. You know him?"

"He was two years ahead of me in high school, but yeah, I know him." Seth smiled and turned back to start up the Bronco.

Noble looked at Seth in the rearview mirror. "Wait, I thought you were new in town."

Seth met his eyes in the mirror and simultaneously spoke as he signed for his mother, "Just newly back in town. I grew up here. This is my mother, Amaranth."

Seth's mother turned around and waved at Noble and signed a message to him.

Noble looked at Anya, who shrugged, and then back at Seth.

"She says it's good to meet you, she doesn't know your dad well, but says your mother is a lovely woman."

Noble looked at Amaranth and smiled. He held up his hand and nodded, not knowing exactly how to communicate with her. "Um, thanks."

Amaranth nodded and looked back ahead.

Seth looked back at Noble in the mirror. "Are your parents home,

Mr. Andalusian?"

Noble looked out the side window. "Our mom is."

"When do you expect your father home?"

Noble swallowed. "I don't know."

"Tonight?"

"He's in Alaska," Zoe answered.

Seth turned around to look at the young girl, whose tears had dried. "Alaska? Does he live there?"

Zoe shook her head.

"He's there for work," Noble said.

"He's on a boat," Zoe added.

"How long has he been there for?" Seth asked.

"Two days," Zoe said with a frown.

Seth nodded, his brain racing. Two days ago? He didn't like the timing. "Okay, well, I'll just have a quick chat with your mom then. Let her know what happened and that you're both okay."

Zoe looked up at Seth and forced a smile.

Seth glanced over at Noble, who was still looking out the window with what appeared to be a scowl on his face. Seth turned his attention to Anya. "How about you? Your parents home, Ms. Bury?"

Anya nodded. "Yeah…I didn't do anything wrong," she said, worried eyes meeting Seth's.

Seth let out a light laugh. "No, none of you did," he said, looking from Anya, to Zoe, and over to Noble.

"I punched that guy," Noble said flatly.

"You were protecting your sister and your friend from a couple of drunk idiots."

Anya leaned forward and looked over at Noble. "You were brave."

Noble finally unglued his eyes from the window and looked over at Anya, his heart skipping a beat at seeing her warm smile and aquamarine eyes. He glanced over at Seth, who nodded at him. "Thanks," Noble said and put his arm back around his sister.

"You still on the Bury farm?" Seth asked Anya.

Anya smiled. "Yeah."

"You mind if I drop these two off first so we can get the young one home?"

"No, of course not."

Seth nodded, turned back around and shifted his Bronco into Drive. "Okay then. Off we go."

Noble opened his front door, holding Zoe's hand as they walked in. Seth, Anya, and Amaranth trailed behind.

"Hey, honey," Jolie called from the kitchen as she made her way out to greet them. "What flavors did you guys—oh my god, what happened?" Jolie rushed to her son, seeing his bruise and blackening eye.

Noble pushed her hand away as she tried to reach for it. "Don't! It hurts."

Jolie looked down at Zoe and then up past Noble to see a rather handsome man who looked familiar, a young girl with fascinating hair, and… "Mrs. Wolfe? What's going on?" she asked, looking back at her son.

"We were just having ice cream, talking, and then this…" Noble shook his head, trailing off, clearly flustered.

Seth stepped forward. "Hello, Mrs. Andalusian. My name is Seth Wolfe. I'm a sergeant with the Lost Grove Police Department, and as you might have guessed, that's my mom," he said, motioning back to Amaranth.

"Hi," Jolie stuttered as she shook Seth's hand. "What…"

"I was witness to an incident just a short while ago while my mom and I were picking up food. Your children and Ms. Bury here," Seth motioned back to Anya.

Anya lifted her hand up in greeting. "Hi, Mrs. Andalusian. I'm Anya, a friend of Noble's."

Jolie smiled and nodded. "Hello. Please call me Jolie, both of you," she said, looking from Anya to Seth and then back to Anya. "Nice to meet you. I've heard your name several times over the years."

"Anyhow," Seth started back up, "your children and Ms. Bury—"

"You can call me Anya. I'm, like, still a teenager," she interrupted, latching on to Noble's mom.

Seth glanced back and nodded before looking back at Jolie. "So, your children and Anya were minding their own business, having some ice cream, when they were approached by a rather drunk Jeffrey Tacet and—"

"I know that loudmouth son of a bitch," Jolie spat.

Seth raised his eyebrows and continued, "And a friend of his named Angus Weatherspoon."

"Sure, his fat little crony."

Anya let a laugh slip out. "Sorry."

Noble looked back at Anya, smiled, and shrugged.

Seth went on. "Apparently Mr. Tacet had some unflattering things to say about your husband, in addition to some suggestive comments directed toward Anya, and—"

"That piece of shit!"

"Mom!" Noble said, nodding down at Zoe.

Jolie brought a hand to her chest. "I'm sorry, sweetie. I just—"

"I know the word *shit*," Zoe said. "You guys both say it all the time. And I'm in sixth grade now, everyone swears."

Jolie furrowed her brow. "Oh."

"Anyhow," Seth said, trying to get everyone back on track, "your son, taking exception to things said about his father and his friend, stood up to defend them. Jeffrey kept his mouth running and got closer to the group of kids, and Noble protected them."

Jolie looked over at Noble. "You punched him?"

Noble rolled his eyes. "I mean, yeah, you should have heard—"

"Good!" Jolie said, and looked back at Seth. "And apparently that asshole punched my son back?"

Seth nodded. "Yes, just before I could step in to intervene. I controlled the situation from there and made sure to bring everyone back home safe and sound."

Jolie ran her hand through her hair. "Well, thank you."

"Your son is, of course, free to press charges against Mr. Tacet if—"

"You should," Jolie stated, looking at her son.

Noble sneered. "Mom, it was just a stupid fight."

"It could have been much worse if the sergeant here didn't happen to be there. He had his friend with him and you have no idea how horrible these men can be—"

"I think I've got an idea."

"Especially when they're drunk," Jolie finished.

"I can let you two hash that out," Seth said. "You can reach me through the station, day or night. And for what it's worth, I made it very clear to Mr. Tacet that if I ever saw him around any of these children ever again, and he wasn't running the other way, there'd be hell to pay."

Jolie smiled. "Well, good."

"I understand your husband, Peter, is away working in Alaska?"

"That's right. He works on a fishing boat a couple times every year."

Seth nodded. "Well, when you speak with him, let him know if he has questions about what happened tonight, he can reach out to me at any time. In fact"—Seth reached inside his inner jacket pocket and pulled out a card—"this has my cell on it. Call me whenever."

Jolie grabbed his card. "Thanks again." She signed to Amaranth, "So good to see you. Sorry about all of this."

Amaranth signed back, "No problem at all. I'm glad my son was there. Always lovely to see you."

"You as well," Jolie signed.

"What the fuck?" Noble exclaimed.

"Noble!" Jolie said.

"Since when do you know how to use sign language?"

"Mrs. Wolfe is a pillar in this community, Noble. It's only right that we all learn as much as we can."

Seth turned around to leave and looked at Noble. "My mother can be quite persuasive in teaching ASL to everyone she runs into."

Noble looked at Amaranth and then back to Seth. "How do you say 'thank you'?"

Seth brought his hand to his chin and moved it down and toward Noble.

Noble repeated the gesture.

Amaranth gave the boy a hug and then walked up and kneeled down next to Zoe. She signed, "You're a strong, brave girl. I can sense it." She hugged her and got up to leave.

Zoe looked at her mom. "What did she say?"

"Um." Jolie looked at Seth. "I couldn't quite get all of that. Something about 'strong'?"

Seth smiled and looked at Zoe. "She said you're a strong, brave girl. That she can sense it. And my mother is very smart about people, so I know she's right." Seth walked toward his mother and Anya, both by the front door. "Okay, let's get you home, Ms. Bury."

"Anya," she said.

"Anya."

Chapter 22

Black Salt

The summer Story had moved to Lost Grove, Lucas Rotunda, a local child, had gone missing. After practicing as many castings, divinations, and tarot readings as she could, none of it mattered. The child was stolen in the night, with no clues or reasoning. It was like the Lindbergh child, only, as yet, they'd found no trace of the child. No trail uncovered. No ransom. It was a troubling event that always bothered Story. That was until she met Mary Germaine.

It wasn't happenstance that drove Story to leave her house and walk into town. She felt a prickling on her feet and knew she had to go. Where? Story wasn't sure. So she laced up her boots, shrugged on a heavy sweater, and walked out her front door. Her feet, or her gut, took her into town. The grocery was the last remaining storefront that was open, warm light welcoming in an otherwise dark main street. Story went inside. Up and down the aisles, she looked at items, wondering if there was some ingredient that would pop out, tell her what sort of casting she should perform. Instead, her feet took her back to the meat section.

A tall, fit woman leaned over the meats, perusing the assortment with defined concentration. Story moved closer because the woman gave off a most unusual aura. Closing in on her, Story recognized the woman as the one who always ran, day and night, rain or shine. This woman was constantly running and always at the rarest hours. The most interesting factor of the woman was that as she ran, she left behind her aura, a streamer trailing after her like a visible scent. There were certain people—which wasn't the word people like Story called them—that always left a trailing aura. The young woman with the ginger-and-white hair left one. Anya Bury left an iridescent trail of soft Caribbean blue with specks of gold. This woman's aura was violet and green, like a bruise, with veins or pulses of red.

Approaching, the aura's red veins pulsed with one brilliant shock and then dimmed. Story's attention moved from the aura to the woman to see she was staring right at her, eyes wide with fear. There was no time for Story to reassure her. The woman set her basket down and darted out of the store. When Story approached the basket, she saw it was full of meat, all raw, all red. She lifted the basket, examining the contents, finding one had puncture wounds in it.

Story felt out of her element. What kind of Fae was this woman?

The following day was Sunday. The library was closed. She went into the town's butcher shop and asked for the freshest cow liver, a quart of cow's blood, and three healthy portions of pig skin. This purchase sparked further rumors about what kind of person Story Palmer was, which made her smirk inside. She always thought it was funny to see how people reacted, the way they instinctively knew she was different. Like all people, women, that were different, there was one word used from the Dark Ages to present day: witch.

Walking through the streets, it wasn't hard for Story to work a little touch of her gifts to see the long, residual path marked by the woman's bruise-colored aura. She traced it back to a modest home with a white picket fence. The small front yard was overflowing with native wildflowers, but the house looked kept in order, though the porch may have sagged a little in the front left corner.

Story opened the gate, walked up the steps, and knocked on the door. When the woman answered, there was an immediate dilation of pupils, a quickening of the pulse.

Story lifted the bag of goods. "I'm Story Palmer. We should talk. I think you and I could be friends," she said in a reassuring voice. More than that, she'd gifted her voice with a lozenge made to calm, almost hypnotize, as she made her way over to the woman's house.

They'd done just that, become friends. And it was with time that Story learned from Mary Germaine what she believed had happened to young Lucas Rotunda, that he was taken from his bedroom window.

"A Green Man?" Story asked that night as they shared a bottle of merlot.

Mary nodded. "I don't know why he's green."

Story's forehead creased with questions. "What are the children that you say follow him, if not children?"

"I don't know. They're synthetic."

"Not machines?"

"No," Mary said, pouring more wine into her glass. "They're human. They smell of blood and flesh, but there's…I don't know, a plasticky odor overriding it all."

"I've never seen this man, or these children."

"You won't. He's very careful. He…" Mary trailed off. She took a sip of wine, then a deep breath. "I think he can manipulate the mind or something."

"Has he done this to—"

"No, he doesn't come near me," Mary explained.

"So what makes you think he's responsible for taking Lucas?" Story asked.

Mary stood and moved to the front window. She pointed out, tapping her nail against the glass. "That classic Victorian, the one that's blue and white?"

Story set her glass down, unraveled herself from the couch, and joined Mary at the window. "I see it."

"One of the not-children lives there."

Story's head snapped around to look at her friend. "What?"

"There used to be a little boy living there. His name is—was—George Horne. Now that boy is gone, and one of the fake ones is in his place. I don't know how he looks so identical. And I don't know where the real little boy named George is. I just know there once was a human child in that home, and now there isn't. Well, the older sister, Antoinette, her friends call her Nettie. She's human. But her little brother…"

A year later, Story had fallen asleep on her lawn while meditating and enjoying a moon bath. She woke to the crawling feeling of someone watching her. Eyes open, she gazed into the stars, listening, feeling the vibrations of the earth humming around her. The sound of footfalls suddenly darted past her and she bolted upright. She stared into the darkness of the trees to her right, then to her left, into the bramble of blackberry bushes that lined the corner of her lot. Was it the limbs of the vine moving, or something else? Someone else?

Story pulled her legs under her and carefully stood, unconscious of her nakedness. From the trees, now behind her, she heard a snapping branch, the careful giggle of a kid. Several feet now rushed along the tree line, toward the blackberry bushes. She followed the sounds of the feet, trying to see what was inside. As they darted from the tree line to the bushes, she caught glimpses of wild little children. Unkempt, knotted hair, skin smeared with dirt and moss. A few of them dared to look her way as they moved, fleeing like wild animals scared from their grazing.

Story felt her heart beat in her throat as the last of them paused, stared at her with the most inhuman blankness she'd ever seen. Then a whistle pulled its attention away. A whistle like the call of a bird, and the last of the wild not-children turned and fled through the bushes. She heard the pitter-patter of bare feet on the street as they flocked down the road.

Deep in the shadows, she saw a figure unfurl itself from the brambles. This was no child, but a man. As he uncloaked himself from the twisting vines, the full, brilliant moon caught his skin, and she saw the patina his skin had taken on. He stepped out from the bush toward the larger gap, making his way to follow his child-things. To this day what haunted Story most, what turned her stomach, was the moment the man with the green skin's face caught the moonlight and she saw his twisted smile.

Since that night, she had added protection to all the homes with young children in them. It wasn't foolproof; she knew that, but more than anything, she wanted the man with green skin to know she was a force to be reckoned with.

The new moon was three days away, and Story had four homes to cast protection over tonight. She knew it was the coldest day since she'd moved to Lost Grove, because it was the first time her body told her she needed her thick wool quilt coat last worn in a Nova Scotia winter.

She sprinkled the black salt, a strong protective agent which was a mixture of charcoal, sea salt, white sage, galangal root, bearberries and peppercorns, along the perimeter of the lawn, chanting:

"*Protect this home,*
High to low
Fence to fence,
Door to door,
Light to dense,
Roof to floor."

The condensation trail of her hot breath wrapped around her head as she spoke. If you were a passerby, and looking closely, you'd be able to see a white light spread along the perimeter, meeting each little pile of black salt she'd placed. For added protection, Story had sprinkled seeds of wild mint and wild mountain thyme. Now, all around the downtown proper, the homes had mint and thyme sprawling along like a protective border.

It supposedly brought luck, too. Mary wished for a spot of luck right now. She was waiting a few houses back, watching Story go through her routine, wondering if it helped, if it could really stop someone as evil as the Green Man from taking another child from their homes. It wasn't for lack of belief. Mary had seen what Story was capable of in other aspects of her witch's abilities. Story had deduced not only what both Mary's parent had died from but when they had died almost down to the exact day. She'd somehow divined that Mary had become what she was as a child, but she had not been born that way. She even knew it was an animal bite that gave Mary the condition.

But could salt, thyme, and mint really stop someone from walking onto the property and doing one harm? Mary wanted to believe it would work. She truly did, because then it would mean Story could find a cure, or at least a tonic, to keep Mary's growing hunger at bay. The cravings had been increasing since she'd given in to consuming the not-child that had been mauled and left for dead. The incident was not something she'd broached with Story yet, afraid the one person in this town she could actually call a friend would admonish her, or worse, find her disgusting.

"Come out of the dark, you gooseling," Story chided with a smile.

Mary moved away from the home, crossing the street to her friend's side. Mary didn't feel the cold like the rest of the townspeople in Lost Grove, but tonight the chill was so potent she'd plucked a heavy, midnight-blue turtleneck sweater from her dresser drawer to wear before leaving her house.

Story stood from her spell casting and plucked a bottle from her vegan leather satchel. "Ta-dah!" Story exclaimed in a hush.

Mary laughed, equally quiet, and took the bottle. "A sauvignon. I need it." Mary pulled off the wrapped top and dug the thumb of her fingernail into the cork.

Story watched how eager her friend was to get in the bottle. "I brought a corkscrew. And this," Story said, pulling a small sachet from her bag of tricks.

Mary pulled out the cork, looking over at the sachet. She could smell the anise, the metallic pang of blood and liver, a touch of rose. Her hand shook as she reached out for it.

Story handed it over. "I made it just the size to hold in your mouth.

Dried duck liver, baby rosebuds, star anise. I can make you more. You can store them in a cool dry place for a bit. Carry one around with you."

Mary took the tiny sachet and placed it on her tongue like a reverential wafer. She pressed her tongue to the roof of her mouth, feeling the crinkle of the rosebuds, the hard star of the anise, the earthy blood of the liver.

"I'm still working out the blood lozenges, which I know you'd prefer. Especially if I can infuse them with the right assortment of vitamins to help you. The size and feel would be more your thing."

Mary jumped at the sound of a screen door slamming down the road. Story scowled.

Mary pulled the sachet from her mouth. "You're going through a lot of trouble for me."

"It's not that much trouble." Story smiled as they started walking toward Mary's home to share some wine and relax.

"I know, but…" Mary paused and reached for Story's hand, giving it a squeeze. "It means a lot to me. That you're trying to help."

Story squeezed the icy hand of her friend in return. "We will find something that helps. I promise. My mother's been trying to get a hold of her high priestess, oh from years ago now. She was old then, so my mother says. But she has a wealth of knowledge, and…well, she knows about things, species, like what may have bitten you. She's from Turkey. Doga, that's her name. She lives way out in some place without electricity. Hopefully, we'll hear from her soon."

"I didn't know you'd asked your mother to help."

Story looked at her friend's surprised face. "Why wouldn't I? Witches are only as strong as the knowledge we all hold. We must rely on the elders of our kind to pass on their knowledge."

"And if she is dead? The knowledge is as well," Mary said.

Story gave Mary a sidelong glare. "You're not being very positive."

"How did you explain it? Me, I mean. How did you explain me to your mother?" Mary ignored the comment about her depressed mood.

Story smiled. "The easiest way, I suppose. I called you a vampire."

"Vampire!"

Story laughed, taking the bottle of wine and drinking a small gulp. "Would you prefer to be called a ghoul? Or maybe you'd like wendigo?"

"I'd prefer none of those options," Mary stated.

Story stopped on the sidewalk. "You usually like morbid humor.

What is the matter with you?"

"What? Nothing."

"Something is wrong. Are your cravings acting up? Is it the stomach cramps again? Are you in pain?"

"No," Mary huffed and continued on. She stopped and turned back to address Story. "I am having *powerful* urges. I'll admit that."

"Okay, well. We don't need to talk. You can use the sachet—"

"The sachet isn't going to work! I…shit," Mary hissed and sat on the curb. She put her face into her hands, pressing the palms into her eyes.

Story's brow creased with concern, approaching Mary and sitting next to her on the curb. She set the bottle of wine between her feet and waited.

"You know," Mary started, her voice muffled by her arms, "I found Sarah Elizabeth on the beach that morning."

Story's eyes opened wide, and then her mouth parted, contemplating. "Mary? Did you—"

"No!" Mary swung her face to look Story in the eye. "No. I didn't do anything to her or her body. I was tempted."

"You called the police?"

Mary shook her head. "I couldn't. I-I just couldn't. So I left a note on Bill's door. I knocked really loud, and I left."

"So they don't know what you saw? They don't know you were a witness to the body?"

"No," Mary said, shaking her head and wiping her nose.

"But you could have seen clues that got washed away by the time they got out there. Mary, you need to say something. They're having a hard time finding answers to this—"

"Why do you care so much?" Mary interrupted.

Story swiveled her knees to better face her companion. "A young woman is dead."

"Yes, but why do *you* care so much?"

Story leaned back, sat a little straighter. "Because something evil is in this town and the night before you found Sarah Elizabeth on that beach, I could feel it spreading, trying to work its way into my home. That young woman died in a way— How do I explain?"

"To me? You know you don't have to. There's something about it you can feel?" Mary asked.

"That," Story said. She pulled her lips inward, pressed them between her teeth. "Sarah used to come into the library all the time. She'd study there. She once asked me to read her palm."

"Really? I thought the family was super religious. Probably burn me alive in my home if they knew—"

"Stop." Story nudged her. "She is, was. But this one time she asked me to read her palm."

"What did you see?" Mary asked.

Story tilted her head as she explained. "Her fate line was strange. She had a break in it, then it split, continuing on. It was the same on both hands, her dominant and her nondominant. Usually there is a difference, even slight. But Sarah's were exactly the same. Did you know she had visions? Seth told me she had visions recently. On top of everything, the trouble sleeping—"

"Seth? As in Seth Wolfe?"

"Yeah."

"He asked you about Sarah?"

"Yeah." Story stared off into space, eyes focused on the pavement for a minute before she blinked her thoughts away. "Did I tell you she came to me, that first winter break?"

"No. For what? Not witch stuff?" Mary asked.

Story smirked. "Yes. For witch stuff. She wanted a potion to make her sleep. To think she was that desperate. It must have taken a lot for her to work up the courage to come to me." Again, Story's mind unraveled, her eyes glancing over the pavement. "It surprised all of us to hear it was her, you know. We all thought she was miles away, at school."

"Yeah. It's definitely bizarre."

"Mary?" Story drew her friend's attention.

"What?"

"Mary…"

Mary looked at her friend's gentle, smiling face. "I don't want to talk to anyone about this. Can't you just tell them?"

"No, Mary. You have to go to the police. You could have loads of information up there about the scene. Come on, you know you have to do this," Story cajoled. "Seth is very nice."

"I know he is," Mary said. "I went to school with him."

"Ah, right. Well then, what's the issue?"

"I just don't want to put myself in the spot to be questioned. Like, what if…"

"What if, what?" Story asked after a moment. "What aren't you saying? If you didn't do anything to Sarah, then you have nothing to—"

"It wasn't Sarah I did something to," Mary blurted.

It took Story a moment to puzzle those words together into something cohesive. "If it wasn't Sarah, who was it?"

"What was it? You mean to say, what was it?"

"An animal?" Story almost laughed. "So you ate an animal—"

"No, not an animal. What is something not human but not an animal," Mary hinted, looking at her friend from the corner of her eye.

"The…the Green…a not-child?"

"One of the not-children, yes," Mary exclaimed as her friend finally came out with the words.

"You killed one of them?"

"No!" Mary looked around at the houses, afraid she'd been too loud. "No. It was already injured."

"By what?"

"I don't know. Something with massive claws. Tore it to shreds. I just…the smell of the blood. I gave in."

Story took a moment to digest this information. "It was still alive?"

Mary cringed. "Yes, but it was dying."

"And you, you drank the blood or…?"

"I sipped the blood and, yeah, I ate some of the flesh."

"Mother and Crone," Story said instead of the biblical taking in vain. Mary stood, then sat again. "It's not like I wanted it to happen."

"Okay, but no one found that child, or what was left of it. So…?"

"Someone saw me."

Story blinked, mouth open as she jutted her chin forward. "Someone saw?"

"Noble Andalusian."

Clenching and unclenching her hands, Story considered these events. "What, exactly, did he see you doing?"

"He saw me covered in blood," Mary explained while waving her hand around her face.

"But he didn't see you eating, like really eating the thing?"

"He was too far away. I told him I was trying to give it mouth to mouth."

"You've talked to him?" Story asked, incredulous.

"I had to explain!"

"You did not have to explain," Story reacted. "Okay, I take that back. When did this happen?"

"Last Saturday morning."

"When did you talk to him? When did you explain it away as nothing? No, wait, how did you explain it away as nothing?"

Mary gathered her nerves to look Story in the eye. She turned her head and held her gaze. "Thursday night. I ran into him on the street and I knew I had to say something. But how would I explain I left a little kid on the roadside to die?"

"Yeah?"

"He knows what they are, Story. He knows what they are because he goes to school with the sister of the boy I told you about. The one that lived in the house down the street from mine? Antoinetta Horne knows the Green Man because the Green Man took her brother. Remember? Noble knew what I said—when I told him they weren't really children—deep down, he knew I was right."

A chill passed over Story. "Does Zoe know about the Green Man?"

Mary shook her head. "I don't know. I hope to God not."

A sudden gust of wind came rushing up the street, whipping their hair around their faces, and with it came the scent of carrion, moldy leaves, and a woman's perfume. Mary felt the predator in her rise, her gums aching with the pain of her eyeteeth pressing outward. Both women turned their attention to the direction the wind had come from. Church bells rang in the distance, causing both women to frown. The only church with bells was First Lutheran on Beaumont, and those only rang for a wedding. When the bells stopped, a new sound met their ears. It was the sound of metal rolling along the pavement. A tiny object wheeled to a stop, bumping against Story's shoe. It spun and spun, finally landing heads up. An old copper penny, its brilliant metal turned a patina green.

Story reached down and picked it up.

"What was that smell? Not a farm," Mary voiced her thoughts.

Holding the penny up between them both, Story said, "Not a farm. This is an omen. The universe is trying to tell me something. Mary?"

"Yeah?"

"Would the Green Man kill a woman, a young woman?"

Mary hesitated but shook her head. "No. No, he goes after children."

"Then I need to figure out how else he could be connected," Story said, standing and wiping the dirt off her clothes. "Mary, I need you to show me exactly where you found Sarah's body."

Chapter 23

Sleep Deprivation

Seth forced his fluttering eyes open wide, the darkness of the obscenely early morning not doing him any favors. The rhythmic, vibrating sounds of the tires were like a lullaby, and with the dearth of sleep he had gotten over the last few days, he knew he shouldn't be driving up the coastal highway. Seth squinted and looked to his left. The ocean reflected the light from the moon, the waves cresting unusually high. Why was he driving down to Lost Grove? Seth couldn't even remember what had sent him venturing north in the first place. He looked to the passenger seat, then to the floor. An open cardboard box. Plastic bags securing…

"Evidence," Seth mumbled. The crime lab was forty minutes north of Lost Grove, though he couldn't recall why or what he was bringing back to the station.

Seth shook his head like a dog shedding water. He needed to stay awake, focus on the road. He took a deep breath, and as he was slowly blowing it out, he spotted a tunnel ahead, burrowed into the side of a mountain.

"What the hell?" Seth was positive he hadn't gone through a tunnel on the way up.

Seth turned on his high beams as he approached, his foot easing off the gas pedal. Just before passing through the entrance, he noticed it was only the one southbound lane going under. Had he split off from the northbound lane? Were there two separate tunnels? It was too late to check; the stone arch of the mountainside enveloped the Bronco like a school of fish into a whale's mouth.

Seth inched his body closer to the wheel, more alert now. Being in an enclosed space for too long was not something his body and mind reacted well to since the incident in the cave. The tunnel was long, and the absence of sound was unnerving. He rounded a long, slight bend, and finally, the exit came into view. Seth loosened his grip on the wheel, but just as his nerves were abating, his breath caught in his chest. The dim light forming the archway started to shrink.

"The fuck?" Seth's eyes grew large as the cave walls began closing in around him, and the outlet continued to compress. He pressed his foot on the brake, steadily at first, then slamming down as he found himself inches from a slim crevice that was once a wide exit. His heart pounded against his rib cage like a sledgehammer. He looked left, then right. The walls were so close that he could never open his door far enough to get out.

Seth shifted gears to reverse and looked over his shoulder. The eradication of reality sent a wave of horror through his soul; the cave was flush up against the back window. A feeble moan seeped past his lips. He turned toward the front, and the whimper turned into a shriek as Seth jumped back against his driver's side door. Sarah Elizabeth was in the passenger seat, staring directly at him with dead, grey eyes and sallow skin. It froze Seth stiff, unable to breathe, unable to close his eyes. Sarah's head dropped forward, causing her body to collapse toward him. He pushed himself further back, trying but unable to scream. Then came a loud hammering and shaking of the glass behind his head.

Seth jolted awake, slouched down in the driver's seat of his Bronco.

"Morning, Seth!"

He looked to his left to see Clemency Pruitt standing outside his window. Seth took in a massive breath of relief and rolled down the window. "Hey, Clemency."

"How long you been sitting here?"

Seth looked to the dashboard, but the ignition wasn't on. He checked his watch, genuinely not having any clue what time it was: 5:30 a.m. "I guess about…hour and a half."

"Couldn't sleep or still working?"

Seth's brow furrowed as he pondered. "Guess a bit of both?"

Clemency slapped the windowsill. "Well, come on in, I'll get it going, extra shot?"

Seth smiled. "Yes, please. Thanks, Clemency."

"Mm-hmm," she murmured and headed toward the cafe.

Seth let out another long sigh and cautiously glanced over at the passenger seat, still feeling Sarah's presence, her eyes burrowing into him, the imprint of the dream still heavy in his mind.

"Can you see me?" Seth shook his head. "What are you thinking?" he mumbled to himself before getting out of the car.

After downing his cappuccino and a hyper-alert drive to work, Seth entered the station's front door with purpose, having spent most of Sunday going through the Fulson files, reading transcripts, and listening to the audio recording of the interview with Peter Andalusian back in 2015. Joe was working the phones, and Sasha was pinning a sheet of paper up next to a sea of others on the bulletin board by their desks.

"Morning, Sasha," Seth announced as he approached them, Fulson's case file under his arm, returning the wave from Joe.

"You almost took the door off there, Sarge," Sasha commented, glancing over at him.

"Sorry about that. What's going on?"

Sasha smiled and looked back at the board. "Bill's got me on handwriting duty. Trying to figure out who left that note on his door."

"Great. Those DMV forms?" Seth asked, leaning in.

"Yep. Not sure how much luck we're going to have here, but I can't say I've got any better ideas at the moment." Sasha turned and grinned at Seth. "I heard you were out with Story Palmer this weekend."

Seth sighed and made a beeline toward Bill's office, shouting over his shoulder, "Good work, Officer."

"With the forms or uncovering the local gossip?" Sasha called out.

Seth shook his head and stepped into Bill's office to see a similar setup. Bill had a new board next to his desk with DMV forms pinned up. "Hey, Bill. How'd you get your hands on these forms?"

Bill looked up from his desk and took off his glasses. He grimaced as he took in Seth's appearance. "You're not looking so hot."

Seth stood in front of Bill's desk, choosing not to sit and allow himself to lose momentum. "Thanks. I'm fine. Just been up all night thinking about the case."

"You gotta know when to turn it off and take care of yourself. You'll burn yourself out in no time."

Seth grinned at his boss. "I do my best work when I'm burned out. Now, about the forms?"

Bill laughed. "Have it your way. I went to see an old friend of mine Friday, Shawn Malone, administrator at the DMV."

"Ah, I see."

"Asked him to make me copies of all driver's license, ID applications, and renewals over the past ten years. He worked over the weekend and dropped them off this morning."

Seth nodded as he made his way over to the board to see if he recognized any of the names on the pinned-up forms. "Good idea. Thankfully, this isn't San Francisco."

"Wish it was a better idea. Too many people filled out their forms online, so all we have are their signatures. Sasha's confident it's a female who wrote the note."

"That was my first impression as well."

"Still looking at everyone, though."

"Good. What other avenues have you been pursuing?" Seth wanted to push Bill on the subject, the significance of identifying the person unmistakable.

Bill stood up, hung his reading glasses from his collar, and walked around to sit on the front of his desk. "Eddie and I are making stops at the elementary school and high school today to talk to the kids, make sure they know they're not in danger."

"We don't know that."

"Well, they need to hear it. I'll get the point across that they should all keep their eyes peeled if they see anything or anyone suspicious."

"Fair enough."

"We'll see if they have any questions. Hopefully no morbid ones, or kids not taking it seriously. My plan is to let them know there was an anonymous message that led me to the body on the beach and, if they know anything at all about it, to call the number on the pamphlets we'll be handing out."

"Smart. You having second thoughts that it might have been a kid?"

"Nope. Can't hurt, though."

"Could be one of the kids' parents. Maybe get lucky if they overheard them talking. Kids hear everything."

Bill smiled. "Don't they always?"

Seth shrugged and pulled the Fulson case file from under his arm and set it on Bill's desk. "Look, we need to talk about this Kelly Fulson case and Peter Andalusian."

Bill stood from his desk. "I know. And sorry about yesterday. I know this case is of the highest priority, but—"

"It's fine, Bill. You had family plans. I had them on Saturday. How were Stacey and Julie?"

"Good, good. They just had their one-year wedding anniversary. Their restaurant in Seattle is doing great. You know, if they were in town for any longer than the weekend—"

Seth patted Bill on the back. "Bill, forget it. Let's just focus now."

Bill nodded. "Okay, so what are you thinking?"

Seth began to pace. "I think it's an odd fucking coincidence that he just happened to leave town the day we discovered Sarah's body."

"It wouldn't be that odd if he wasn't brought in for questioning on the Kelly Fulson case, though."

"Right, but he was. And a coincidence is as good as a fingerprint."

"Huh?" Bill asked, perplexed.

Seth grinned. "Just something we used to say in homicide. I can safely say that a coincidence, or series of coincidences, led us to solve more cases than a fingerprint."

Bill raised his eyebrows. "Never thought of it like that."

"And, Bill, that interview with Peter Andalusian was no straightforward interview."

"I know it. I was there."

Seth turned around to face Bill. "He played that old sergeant of yours like a fiddle."

Bill shook his head. "Dale rarely got intimidated like that, but—"

"He ran the room, Bill. Even when you entered to question him."

Bill held up his hands. "What's that got to do with Sarah Elizabeth?"

"It could have everything to do with her. Reading the transcript of that interview about Kelly Fulson was one thing, but listening to the tape? That was not just some misunderstood Lost Grove father. Assuming he wasn't a lawyer or a detective before retiring to go work on fishing vessels in Alaska, I'd have to assume he was military. Likely special ops."

Bill raised his eyebrows. "Was that in the report?"

"There was nothing about his past in any of those files."

"Jesus. That's exactly what he was."

"Great." Seth returned to pacing. "So, Kelly Fulson disappears on a night where she was supposed to meet up with her best friends to celebrate her birthday. By the time her parents are allowed to file a missing persons report, they find her car missing, her purse missing, and some personal belongings. You find searches on her computer for bus rides to Seattle and ferry rides out of Anacortes to Vancouver. She's clearly making her way up the coast of North America. This leads you to find security camera footage of her getting on a bus to Seattle. No one speaks to her or sees her again until she's found dead on the edge of Jonathan Baume's farm sixteen months later, seven months pregnant."

"That's the long and short of it," Bill said.

"And you find out that not only was Peter Andalusian in Alaska at the same time Kelly Fulson was making her way up that direction, but that he left Lost Grove the day after you found her body."

Bill stood from his desk and joined Seth, who had stopped to stare at the Sarah Elizebeth board. "Look, I know how it sounds, and how it looks, but I really don't think Peter had anything to do with Kelly's death."

"If it looks like a chicken and sounds like a chicken…"

Bill sighed. "I know it, but I've known that family for almost twenty years now. As long as you've been gone. All I can say is that I believed Peter when he said he didn't have an affair with her. He's a bit strange compared to most folks around here, but he loves Jolie and those kids."

"And maybe he didn't have an affair with her. That doesn't mean he had nothing to do with her body turning up."

Bill scratched his head, overwhelmed and embarrassed.

Seth turned to look at Bill. "What does Jolie have to say about all the accusations, and that he leaves town to go work in Alaska twice a year?"

"For starters, she's not stupid."

"I didn't get that impression."

Bill lifted an eyebrow. "When did you—"

"When I dropped Noble and Zoe off at their home. I had to go in and let her know what happened. There was a child present and both Noble and Anya Bury could press charges if they so desire."

"Right. Well, Jolie knows Peter grew up an Army brat and moved around a lot. She says that it's in his DNA not to stay in one place for too long, and she genuinely doesn't seem to have an issue with it. He's taken other jobs across the country, not just fishing up in Alaska. Jolie knows people talk, that they think he's odd and that he's out having affairs and what-not. But she's unfazed by it. She says none of these people know who Peter is. She does. And she trusts him."

Seth twirled the acorn in his pocket around with his fingers. "I don't know, Bill. I trust what you're saying, but there's also this." Seth walked back to Bill's desk and opened the case file. He pulled a page from the report and a newspaper clipping from the top. He walked back to Bill, lifting the report. "On page three of the transcript, you ask Peter this: 'You were working at Devil's Cradle the year Daisy Sutherland fell off the High Trail, correct?'"

Bill stroked his beard. "Right…"

"Later on, you mention this incident was in 2005. Tell me about Daisy Sutherland."

Bill let out a long exhale. "Well, the search party found Daisy's body at the bottom of a cliff underneath one of the hiking trails. From what I recall, she was an active hiker, and it wouldn't have been uncommon for her to go hiking by herself. And—"

"Yet she somehow fell off a cliff?" Seth asked, somewhat rhetorically. "Was she injured or—"

"Found dead. Neck broken, a few other bones too, I believe."

"Great. So, here's the body of another dead girl linked to Peter."

Bill cocked his head to the side. "That one's a stretch. Just because he worked there during—"

"Yet you brought it up to him during your interview about Kelly Fulson."

Bill nodded. "We were just trying to make connections."

"And you did, which has now run through Kelly Fulson to Sarah Elizabeth."

"Yeah, but how do those—"

Seth held his finger up. "Did you read the obituary that was printed in the *Gazette* on Saturday?"

Bill narrowed his brow. "Yeah."

Seth grabbed a pin off the board and pinned the newspaper clipping under a photo of Sarah Elizabeth's body from the beach. "Well, read it again. The highlighted part there," Seth said, pointing.

Bill put back on his reading glasses and leaned in. "'She is remembered by her parents, her brothers and sisters of the First Lutheran Church on Beaumont, and all the children's lives she touched while working as a summer camp volunteer at Devil's Cradle State—' Shit."

"We need to get in contact with Peter. Like, yesterday."

Bill nodded. "I'm on it. I'll track down Jolie and make it happen."

Seth spun away from the board, pacing once more. "There's one other thing. Not about Peter, but about the Kelly Fulson case. The baby.

Do you remember much about Wes's findings in the examination of the unborn child?"

Bill frowned, thinking back. "I don't recall anything too specific, no."

Seth shook his head. "There were some really bizarre findings. The report said the infant, a boy, had a malformed spleen and intestines. The lungs were poorly developed. And the head plates weren't fully together; that the brain was exposed and overgrown."

"Christ, I don't remember any of that at all."

"I'm sure you were focused on Kelly. Just like we've been focused on Sarah Elizabeth. Rightly so. But there's something really…puzzling about these abnormalities of Kelly's unborn child and how the birth of Sarah Elizabeth's child went down. I don't know if it will amount to much, but I think it's something we need to look into. Talk to Wes again."

"Sure thing," Bill said. "It's definitely—"

The door to Bill's office flew open, startling both men.

Joe leaned in, his eyes wide, like he had seen Clemency's store-haunting ghost. "Sorry to bust in, but you guys are going to want to hear this."

"What is it?" Seth asked.

Joe stepped into the office. "I just got off the phone with Sarah Elizabeth's counselor at Baylor…"

"And?" Bill motioned with his hand for him to get on with it.

"She never came back to school after her first semester."

The muscles in Seth's face fell slack as goosebumps covered his forearms.

"The last time they saw her on campus was before she came home for that winter break. Her roommate reported it, but nothing ever came of it."

Bill's hand fell to his lap. "Mother of God," he said through gritted teeth.

Chapter 24

Morning School Announcements

The rest of the weekend had been a mental and emotional disaster for Noble Andalusian. The conversation with his mother Friday night, segueing into the confrontation Saturday night, had put Noble in a worse funk than he was in after he saw Mary Germaine coddling a bloody not-child. And it stood to reason, this was personal, possibly catastrophic for his family. Could his father really have known Sarah Elizabeth? Could he have done something terrible to her? Even Kelly Fulson? It was difficult to pinpoint what about this scenario, the people around town talking, the events of boat rentals and returns matching up, his father skipping town once again the same morning police discover a young woman's body, got under his skin, burrowing deep into his soul the most.

Pulling onto the street that took them up to the school parking lot, Noble heard a tap on his driver's side window. He looked out to see Anya on her bike, waving at them. He grinned, waving along with Zoe, a momentary surge of hormones lifting his mood. Anya slowed and turned behind the vehicle, heading for the bike rack near the school's entrance.

"You look stupid," Zoe said, smiling at her brother from the passenger seat as they pulled into the parking lot.

"What?" Noble looked from her to the parking lot of Lost Grove High School.

Zoe laughed. "You're smiling all over! You like her."

Noble scowled at his little sister, but still grinning.

"You are so obvious." Zoe giggled.

"Don't start," Noble playfully admonished.

"Well, she's way cooler than Ashley."

Noble set the car in park and turned it off. "Way cooler than Ashley?" he asked, though he immediately agreed with his sister's assessment; Anya was in a completely different league than his ex-girlfriend.

"Way," Zoe clarified. She grabbed her bag from the floor in front of her and opened the door.

"Hi, Zoe!" Anya greeted them.

"Hi!" Zoe said back.

"You left your book in the car on Saturday. I took it when the officer—sergeant—dropped me off."

"Thank you! Thank you!" Zoe jumped up and down, taking the book from Anya.

"Hi," Anya said, waving over the top of the Crosstrek.

"Hey," Noble said back. He opened the back door and grabbed his backpack, then joined them, heading toward the schools. "Hey, Zo, don't talk back to Mrs. Steiner. Mom told me to remind you."

"I *know*, good grief. She was wrong though," Zoe said in a singsong voice, already heading down the sidewalk to the junior high.

"I hated Mrs. Steiner," Anya said.

Noble smirked. "Me too."

"So, did you get into any trouble after we left?"

"No. You?"

Anya let out a laugh. "Not really. My parents were cool. But I don't know. I think my dad was pissed."

"At you? Oh, you mean the asshole coming on to you?"

"Yeah." Anya felt his hand brush against hers and looked down. Instinct had her reach out and take it, giving it a squeeze. "I know you mostly hit the guy because of what he said about your dad and sister, but thanks for standing up for me, too."

Noble held on to her hand, in a momentary state of disbelief mixed with elation that Anya had grabbed his; her cool fingers intertwined with his felt like heaven. "It was so out of line."

Anya's nose wrinkled. "It was pretty gross."

"And those assholes interrupted our conversation before we really got into it," Noble said. "We both have a free study at the same time I think. Should we meet—"

"What the shit happened to you?" Nate interrupted. He noticed the intertwined hands that quickly parted, causing his brow to rise even higher. If he wasn't so shocked seeing Noble's busted face, he surely would have called attention to the public display of affection.

"I got beat up," Noble answered, feeling the slip of Anya's fingers like a ghost lingering in his hand.

"By who? When?" Nate looked from Noble to Anya and back again. "What is going on?"

"Okay, Nate. I don't want to hear it this morning," Stan called out, approaching the group. "You can keep all your questions, because I still don't know more than you do—whoa!" Stan exclaimed from over Nate's shoulder. She leaned in close, examining the black eye. "What the balls happened to you?"

"Jesus," Noble sighed. "A slight altercation."

"With who?" Stan demanded. "I'll knock the shit out of 'em."

"A drunk asshole." Noble gave his best friend a funny glare as she poked at his cheek.

"A grown-ass dude?" Nate asked.

"Yeah, a grown-ass dude," Noble replied.

"Who?" Stan asked.

"It doesn't matter," Noble said.

"The fuck it doesn't," Nate protested.

Ryker came jogging up and gave Anya a hug. "How're you holding up?"

"I'm fine," she replied.

"Wait, what happened to you?" Stan asked, looking at Anya.

"She was with me during the fight," Noble answered, casting quick observations at the body language between Ryker and Anya. On the outside, their hug looked similar to ones he and Stan would exchange.

"I need to teach you some self-defense," Ryker added to the group.

Anya grinned. "It wasn't me in the fight."

"Yeah, Noble, I heard you decked him. Way to go, bro," he said, holding his hand up for Noble to slap.

Noble slapped his hand into Ryker's.

"The guy was bleeding pretty bad I heard."

Noble looked at Anya, who shrugged. "Just a busted lip."

"You made him bleed, bro?" Nate said.

"I want to know what the hell is going on. Where were you guys?" Stan asked the group.

"Zoe and I went to get ice cream. Anya met us up there."

"And some guy just came and beat you up?" Stan asked.

They'd all started heading toward the doors.

"Something like that," Noble replied.

"Nah. You're gonna have to tell me the entire story. Anya?" Stan turned her attention to her fellow teen.

"Uh," Anya started, seeing Nettie ride up on her bike. "I'll tell you at lunch. Um, see you during free study?" she asked Noble, already backing away.

"Yeah," Noble said, smiling.

Stan's eyes moved between the two. A smirk revealed itself. "Wait a minute, are you—oof!"

Ember Graff had come from the opposite direction and leapt onto Stan's back. The two had been texting all weekend, at least when the doctors hadn't confiscated her phone from her.

"Hey, wow, what happened there?" Emory asked, pointing at Noble's face as he joined them.

"Oh, you know, the usual weekend bar brawl," Noble joked.

"Okay, enough about Noble and his stupid face," Nate said. "Stan—"

"No," Stan stopped him. "No. I'm not getting into your murder mystery shit this morning, Nate."

"Yeah, but can we all just talk briefly about the fact that we finally know who it was? Sarah Grahams, guys!" Nate said, starting before Stan could even finish her sentence. "I mean..."

"It's pretty bizarre and fucked up. I'm not sure it's fully settled in for me," Ryker said. "We knew her, right? I mean, we all knew her, but we didn't. We saw her in the halls, sure. Around town. But...it's weird, like, I feel like I should have known her."

"But we didn't," Noble agreed. "I can picture her, though."

"Her hair," Stan added. "She had that thick, long—"

"Auburn hair, yeah," Nate added.

"I thought she was in college in, like, Texas," Stan commented, shaking her head, her tone reverential.

Noble also nodded serenely, as if offering penance at a church altar. He would love to avoid this subject for one full day, to not be reminded that his father's actions were suspicious and that many people in town were ready to point their fingers at Peter Andalusian now that another young woman had washed ashore, gone before her time.

"Has your dad mentioned anything about the autopsy?" Nate scrambled to get the question out.

Stan turned to him, taking a deep breath, acting eager. "You know what, last night at dinner, he was mentioning how he was waiting for some information before finalizing his report. I'm trying to recall…"

Nate nearly leapt out of his skin. "Oh my God, for real? Was he waiting for toxicology?"

Stan's face switched from false excitement to a deadpan glare. "No, Nate. My dad doesn't talk about dead people at the table with four-year-olds." She narrowed her eyes at him, making a face that expressed how stupid he was to have fallen for her act and dripping sarcasm.

"Oh, come on," Nate huffed.

Stan sighed and turned back to Noble. "I want to know what happened this weekend between you and Anya," Stan pointedly remarked to Noble.

Noble sputtered. "What?"

"Yeah, bro." Nate was happy to switch topics. "I totally saw you guys holding hands."

"We—"

"What?" Stan shouted and backhanded Noble across the chest.

"Ow! It was just a squeeze. She was thanking me," Noble said.

Nate laughed. "Oh yeah? Was it for—"

Stan jacked Nate in the bicep.

"Ow! Goddamn, woman."

"I know where you were going with that, pervert." Stan turned her attention to Noble. "And you. You and Anya have, like, never hung out. Not like *not* within the whole group."

"That is kind of true," Ryker added, joining Stan's side in the inquisition.

Noble shrugged. "It's this thing."

"What thing?" Stan asked, pulling open the doors.

Nate hugged himself as he started his quippy response. "I think you know the thing between—ow! Stop hitting me."

"Stop being a creep," Stan said.

"Fine." Nate turned to Emory. "What did *you* guys do this weekend?"

Emory took a deep breath. "Actually," he started, pulling his phone from his coat pocket. "I was hoping maybe you guys could—"

"Oh shit," Nate gasped, jolting all of them to look where he was staring. Across the parking lot, two officers were getting out of a police car. The chief of police and an older cop they all called by his first name, Eddie. He was always at the football games, making sure everyone stayed safe. Eddie was the cop who stopped and said hi, not to see if you were doing something wrong but to chat. The kids all liked him because he treated them as equals.

"What are they doing here?" Emory asked. He'd had all weekend to consider that the Institute had caught him on tape. That no one had said anything or asked him anything, all weekend, only creeped him out more.

"I imagine it has something to do with the talk of the town," Noble almost growled. The last thing he wanted to deal with was the constant reminder that more than one person in town thought his father was a suspect in this recent case. He caught sight of the sergeant, Seth Wolfe, locking eyes with him from all the way across the parking lot.

"I bet they've come to talk to us about Sarah," Stan said, walking through the doors.

"Maybe they're looking for leads," Nate enthused, following.

The speakers crackled on as the kids made haste into the halls. "Good morning, students!" The principal came across in his usual cheery tone. "If you want to help prep for the Halloween formal, please sign up on the board outside the office. We still need help planning the hayrides and the corn maze for the city celebrations. We've got rain this afternoon, so gym classes at those times will be indoors. Some very sad news has come to us over the weekend, as most of you have likely heard by now. A former student of ours, Sarah Elizabeth Grahams, is mourned in her passing. The chief of Lost Grove Police is here to talk with us about the events and answer any of our questions and concerns. Everyone, please proceed to the gym, and let's be respectful of the situation."

The speakers crackled off. Noble's sour mood returned.

Chapter 25

A Pastor's Trust

The angel's wings stretched out against the inky night sky like a graceful paintbrush, his feathers rich with a hue of grapefruit and perfectly symmetrical. Rays of golden light seemed to emanate from the figure's head, illuminating the area around them with an otherworldly glow. The angel wore a flowing robe adorned with a teal-and-yellow motif that hugged his frame gracefully. An expression of serenity and compassion was etched on his face as he extended his hand in a reverent manner. Was this the feeling Sarah had when she saw a potential heavenly figure in her vision that Brigette had laughed at? The phrasing of the figure she saw sounded angelic, yet not necessarily an angel like the one commanding his attention now. What did that vision mean to her? Did she need help, or was the vision something more sinister? Seth closed his eyes, a wave of anguish sweeping over him as he remembered seeing her all those years ago. Had he failed her when she needed him most?

"Michael."

Seth jumped, his eyes snapping away from the stained glass to see a stout man approach with short brown hair and a cheery smile. He looked like a little league baseball coach, kind, supportive, someone who taught positivity and teamwork more than winning. Seth let out an embarrassed laugh. "Sorry. Um, what did you say?"

The man pointed up to the stained glass mural. "Michael. The archangel."

Seth shook his head. "Right, sorry. I was kind of zoned out there."

"They have that effect," the man said and extended his hand. "Pastor

Todd Marquette."

Seth met his hand, a firm but friendly shake. The man didn't look like someone who could have kept Sarah prisoner in his basement the past two and half years, but that meant nothing. Someone was the father of the missing child, and everyone was a suspect. "Sergeant Seth Wolfe. Thanks for seeing me."

The pastor's smile dipped. "Of course. This news has shocked our congregation, our town, really. It's a terrible tragedy. I understand you have a few questions for me."

Seth nodded. "I do. Is there somewhere we can talk in private?"

Todd looked around at the empty church. "Mondays are typically pretty quiet. Why don't we just sit over here?" he offered, gesturing to the nearest pew in the back row.

The men sat down next to each other. Todd crossed his legs and angled to face Seth, who pulled out his phone, notepad, and pen. As much as Seth would have loved to have gone directly to the Grahams residence after hearing the bombshell about Sarah Elizabeth never returning to college, both Bess and Richard were already at work. Interrupting them at their places of work would be too much trouble, not to mention the ruckus it would stir up. Seth wanted to catch them somewhere they felt comfortable. He wanted to surprise them at home. The confrontation with the Grahamses would have to wait for early evening. In the meantime, interviewing the man who, according to Richard and Bess, was the family's closest confidant could prove just as valuable, if not more.

Story had said, and Seth agreed, that whoever Sarah may have been in a relationship with was likely someone she was embarrassed about or thought that it was "wrong." She could have met whoever the mystery person was anywhere in Lost Grove, though it would be more likely she'd met them someplace she frequented. Devil's Cradle State Park, where she worked at summer camp with his most likely suspect at the moment, Peter Andalusian. School, where he was headed next to look closer at the teachers or the principal. The library, where he had to believe Story would have plucked out the person with her eyes closed. Or her church, where she went to weekly services and was a part of the youth group. Pastor Todd was a candidate, of course, but if it wasn't him, Seth felt the pastor would be the best potential witness to anyone at church it could be.

The other, much darker scenario was the possibility that the child wasn't conceived out of mutual consent. If Sarah was taken against her will and held prisoner, he would have to believe that Richard and Bess, fully aware now that they absolutely knew she never went back to Baylor, would have lost their minds with worry over her whereabouts and caused an uproar to find her. Unless said abductor was holding something over the Grahamses, threatening them. And then there was the most revolting scenario: that Richard was the father and Bess was implicit, hence their stonewalling. Seth's gut told him this wasn't the case, but that wouldn't stop him from pursuing every option.

Seth met the pastor's eyes. "So, how did you hear about Sarah Elizabeth's passing?"

"Richard called into the office Friday morning. He was hysterical. He just kept saying, 'she's gone,' over and over. At first, I thought Richard was referring to his mother. She's had some recent health issues and has been suffering with dementia for a while. But when he finally managed to get out Sarah's name…I just couldn't believe it. I was shocked, confused… devastated. I christened her at the hospital when she was born. And then, with Richard and Bess estranged from Sarah, that's the first news they'd heard in years?" Todd went silent and collected himself. "I can't even imagine their pain."

Seth caught the stutter in the pastor's voice that belied the strong front he was putting up. "Have you talked to or seen Richard and Bess since?"

Todd nodded. "Yesterday. I talked to them before service to see if they were agreeable to me saying some words to the congregation about Sarah, which they were. I also presented them with the idea that we hold a special gathering with our youth group after Sunday's service. We wanted to give our young congregants a chance to ask questions and recall fond memories in a more personal space. Richard and Bess didn't hesitate. It was emotional, but also beautiful. So many kids shared their thoughts and stories. We sang her favorite song and recited some prayers. I think the children needed it. I think Richard and Bess needed it."

"I imagine it was difficult. Perhaps also cathartic."

"Yes. In a way, it was."

"Was it difficult for them to hear the questions the children were asking?"

"Oh yes. Well"—Todd considered—"Richard stepped out a few times, but Bess…you know I see this from time to time, with those who remain after a loved one has gone. This unbelievable strength arises in them. It's astonishing." Todd smiled and dropped his gaze to his lap. "It's funny. Right now, all I can think about is what Sarah might have said about her mother's stoicism."

"What would she say?"

"She'd call it grace," Todd said.

Seth would have liked to agree, but after hearing the news from Baylor this morning, he was more inclined to call it bullshit. "You spoke to them before the service. Did they fill you in on any particular details regarding her death?"

"No. They told me they had yet to hear details from, well, I guess, your medical team."

Seth tried to keep his eyebrows from darting up into his hairline. "And to be clear, this was just yesterday they told you this?"

Concern etched its way into Todd's brow. "Yes, why?"

Seth tapped his pen on his notepad as he pondered why on earth the Grahamses wouldn't have told their closest confidant, a pastor, that Sarah was pregnant and died during childbirth, why they wouldn't have had their pastor announce the missing child to their service after the fuss Bess had kicked up in the police station. Guilt? Shame? Because they were protecting their pastor? One way to find out.

Seth leaned in closer to Pastor Todd, locking eyes with the man. "Sarah died during childbirth."

The expression on Todd's face left no doubt in Seth's mind that he was not, in fact, the father of the missing child. Faking genuine shock was perhaps the hardest act on the planet to pull off. There was always a giveaway, a flinch, a hitch in the breath, eyes freezing for a fraction of a second before reacting, and the biggest one, overacting. Todd Marquette was genuinely shocked, and the pain that followed was palpable.

The pastor raised his trembling hand to his face. "Heavenly Father," he whispered.

"We informed the Grahams of this on Friday after we concluded the autopsy."

"Why wouldn't they have…"

"Told you?" Seth finished his thought. "I guess I'd like to ask you that question. You've known them for decades. They described you as their closest confidant. Can you think of any reason they wouldn't share that information with you? Especially considering there is a potential infant that they're the grandparents of."

Todd's hand clasped over his mouth and muttered, "The child?"

"We have no reason to believe the baby also died during the birth.

In fact, there is certain medical evidence that leads us to believe quite the opposite."

Todd shifted his glance toward the front of the room, searching for meaning, for answers.

Seth wondered if the statue of Mary in the corner offered him advice, or if the divine Christ fixed to the cross would raise his head and whisper reverent words.

"It doesn't make any sense. Why would they keep something like that from me?"

Seth let that unanswerable question hang in the air.

"And Sarah…I just can't believe…wait," he said, looking back at Seth, his eyes now wet. "Who was, rather, who is the father?"

"That's the number one question we are trying to answer. Because right now, we have no witnesses who have seen or heard from Sarah for over two and a half years. When was the last time you saw her?"

"Um, well, it was her first Christmas home from college. She came to see me the day after she got back to let me know she couldn't do the nativity play."

"And why did she say she couldn't do the play?"

Todd slowly shook his head as his hand rose from his face to run back through his hair. "Well, she said she was exhausted from her first semester. She said she needed to rest, to get her strength and focus back."

"Did you know that she never returned to Baylor?"

Todd's lips parted, but he hesitated to speak. He looked down at the ground, his shoulders slumping.

Seth's eyebrows drew together. Not exactly the response he was expecting. "What is it?"

Todd slowly shook his head and murmured to himself, "I should have checked. I never thought…"

Seth's heart kicked up a notch.

Todd sat back up and took a deep breath. "It must have been even worse than I thought. She was having problems her first semester there. She was having rather severe sleep issues, for one."

Seth clicked his pen off and on. "She spoke to you about this?"

"Yes. During that winter break. She came to see me one more time. It was…maybe the twenty-eighth or twenty-ninth, between Christmas and New Year."

"And was this something she had spoken to you about before?"

Todd wrung his hands. "She…"

"I understand if it's something she confided in you."

"No, no." Todd offered a knowing smile. "I've just never been in this position before, to discuss what someone confided to me. What my parishioners tell me in our private conversations is, well, I treat it like a psychiatrist might. Everything stays between the two of us and the four walls, unless of course what they speak of gives me reason to believe they're a danger to themselves or others." Todd brought his hand to his brow and massaged his forehead.

"Take your time," Seth said.

"Well, Sarah had sleep issues for…well, since she was quite young."

"Did you hear about this from her or her parents?"

"Sarah told me about her sleep issues when she was about twelve. But it had always been something she seemed to manage. I mean, if you had met her while she was in high school, you never would have guessed this was someone with severe insomnia. She was bright, always cheerful. And whatever her insomnia was before, she still managed a GPA over four."

Seth tapped on his notepad. "I've heard. And the description of her is rather unanimous. Which, of course, makes this all the more troubling."

Todd glanced past Seth. "That look. Those bright, gleeful eyes. They had…they were gone the last time I saw her. She said sometimes she would go days without sleeping."

"Did she give you a reason why it had gotten worse?"

"Well, yes, that's part of my remorse, I suppose. I should have checked on her. She said she was stressed. She was finding it hard to focus at college, having difficulty finding a balance between her studies and social life. I believe she, well, she implied she was having trouble connecting, building strong friendships like the ones she'd left behind here in Lost Grove."

"Did she mention any specific event, an altercation, anything along those lines?"

Todd shook his head. "No, nothing like that. Not that there couldn't have been something along those lines, but she didn't say so to me. So… wait, I don't understand. Where has she been then?"

"We don't know. Richard and Bess said that they drove her to the airport to go back to school and never heard from her again."

Todd frowned. "But wouldn't the school have called them? Or sent them emails, or…"

"That would be my assumption, yes. Can you think of anywhere she might have gone?"

"No, not at all. I've just assumed she was at Baylor this whole time, and that…"

"Pastor Marquette, I believe the answer to our most pressing questions goes back to what you asked me earlier. Who is the father? And I'm hoping you might be of some help here. Did Sarah ever speak to you about a relationship?"

Todd swallowed. "Yes. She did."

Seth's brows lifted, unable to suppress his surprise. "She did?"

"On a number of occasions, yes."

Seth resisted the urge to pump his fist.

"When did you first hear of this relationship? And what did that conversation entail?"

Todd shifted on the bench, straightening his posture. "It was during her senior year in high school. I'm afraid I don't recall the exact date, or even the month now that—"

"That's fine. What did she tell you?"

"She confided in me that there was a relationship, someone very special to her. I believe it was a boy, though I can't confirm that. It's just the sense I got. And of course, knowing what happened, it must have been."

"Okay. What else did she say?"

"Well, I know it was something quite serious because she asked about her chastity ring."

Seth's eyes widened.

"Yes, that serious. Sarah asked when the right time was. How one knows. She was very sincere. She took her faith extremely seriously, more so than many her age."

"What do you mean by that?"

Todd smiled. "I'd like to think I've grown and adapted along with the world and those around us. I truly want to connect to the youth that come here, not just preach sermons that maybe aren't so relatable to them while they secretly play games on their phone or nod off in complete boredom."

Seth felt a welcome swell of affection for the pastor.

"I like to ask them questions and listen to what they have to say. They're not just one flock that you approach with a single goal or method. I think most of the kids are curious, if not maybe skeptical."

"Of God?"

Todd shrugged. "God, Jesus, some, but more so the Bible. Where it came from, what stories are true, what stories are too far-fetched for their minds to comprehend. I find that the majority of the youth now connect more with the lessons, what the stories teach us, and how it applies now in the twenty-first century. Like Aesop's Fables, there's a moral in the words more important than the words themselves. Sarah was very much like this. She was devout, no question, but she truly believed that Jesus would want us to apply his teaching to today's world. She loved debating. Most kids her age just sit there and nod their head or mumble a response if I call on them. Sarah was incredibly intelligent. I will say…I think Sarah may have opened up more of the youth to the Bible's teachings than I did during her high school years."

"How so?" Seth asked, genuinely intrigued, thinking back to what Brigette told him about Sarah's faith.

"As I said, most are skeptical. And not necessarily verbally, but with their eyes, their mannerisms. It's my job to gauge that and try to guide them accordingly. Which I do. But when one of their own is so vocal, so passionate, and brings this relatability to the Bible…and with so much faith. She was so special."

Seth grinned. "Back to the relationship."

"Yes. Well, the fact Sarah was even considering giving up her chastity ring speaks to how serious she took this relationship."

"Do you happen to know any information about this other person? You said you believed it to be a boy. Do you mean that in the sense you're referring to a person of the male persuasion or someone within her age group?"

"I mean it in the sense of a person of the male persuasion. Sorry if that was unclear."

"Not at all. Just want to narrow things down. Is there anything else that might help in identifying who this was?"

Todd glanced down, chewing on the corner of his lip. "I'm sorry. I really can't recall anything. It was more about her, not the other person."

"Did Sarah say she was in love?"

Todd nodded.

"Did her parents know?"

Todd shook his head. "No, no. She admitted to me she hadn't told them."

"Did she say why?"

Todd looked up, pondering how to explain. "I guess I would say that she feared their response. That would be the easiest way to put it."

Seth jotted down a note and then looked up. "I'm sorry, but I have to ask. Did you ever say anything to her parents about the—"

"No," Todd replied. "Funny to say that now as I discuss all this with you," he added, realizing the irony of his words.

"It's okay," Seth assured him. "You're not betraying her trust. Sadly, there are no repercussions that can come to her now."

"But what about the boy, or man, she was in love with?"

Seth nodded. "Yes, well, thus far, you haven't told me anything that will help identify that person. You've only confirmed what I already suspected, and that in itself is a tremendous help to me, and ultimately to Sarah."

"I hope so."

"But I do need to ask. Is there anyone you can think of in your congregation that Sarah was close to, or that you saw her speaking with regularly?"

Todd narrowed his eyes. "Do you mean someone from youth group, or are you referring to—"

"Anyone. You're the only person we've found who could even verify she was seeing someone or was in love with someone. Her best friends didn't know. Her teachers, her parents. So we're inclined to believe it might have been someone that—"

"Was married?"

Seth nodded. "Married, much older, someone she might have been ashamed or embarrassed to let anyone know about."

Todd let out a heavy sigh. "Dear oh dear. Well, from her youth group, I would say she seemed close with Nicholas Avery…Chad Vanderbilt…maybe Parker Cho. They're all off at college now though, and none of them went to Baylor. That doesn't necessarily mean anything, given the circumstances."

Seth finished writing the names down. "Thank you. And do you have contact information for—"

"Yes, of course. I can get you that before you leave."

"I appreciate that. And I do hate to put you in this position, but outside of her youth group…"

Todd groaned as he ran his hand through his hair again.

Seth casually leaned back, not wanting the pastor to feel any unnecessary pressure.

"I honestly can't say I've seen anything with any of the married men that would give me any pause. And I feel it would be improper and quite dangerous to suggest someone on the off chance—"

"I understand."

"There aren't too many unmarried men, well, outside of some elderly widowers, in our congregation. The only one I can think of who would make any sense at all would be Will Bernthal, the principal at Lost Grove High, but—"

"Did you see anything—"

"No, I was going to say that I never saw anything that would make me think, even in retrospect, that there was anything there. Certainly nothing salacious."

Seth flipped a page on his notepad. "I really appreciate your candor, Pastor Marquette. I know this is all very sensitive—"

"Honestly, anything I can do to help. I'm still having a hard time dealing with her death. So tragic and…now knowing about the child. I can't believe Sarah was pregnant. It just doesn't fit with…her goals. And her drive. But then again, one's life can take unforeseen detours, especially over a matter of years."

"Indeed. And I am sorry for your loss. You were clearly very close to Sarah."

Todd simply nodded.

"I'd like to ask about Sarah's relationship with each of her parents. Can you tell me how you perceived her unique relationship to each of them? And please, be candid. We need to know everything we can about Sarah and what led to her disappearing for so long."

Todd slowly nodded. "I'll start by saying that I believe Richard and Bess both loved Sarah very much. And not just because they're her parents, or were…they really did beam when they talked about her or were watching her read or sing in church."

"Did it seem excessive?"

"No. No, I don't think so. It never struck me as such."

"Okay," Seth said, letting the word drag out.

"That being said, I would say that perhaps the relationship between Bess and Sarah could be strained."

"How so?"

"Sarah felt she was overbearing, pressured her too much."

"With what?"

"Oh, with how to act, how to speak, what to wear. Sarah once told me she felt like her mother would be happy if she could control her like a marionette."

Seth jotted down the line, wholly believing Sarah felt that way.

"But there was just as much positivity. I think Sarah felt genuine happiness making her mother proud. I saw plenty of exchanges of smiles between them and it's not surprising that the older Sarah got, the friction built. Sarah was quickly becoming her own person. She was very mature for her age. I would almost say she possessed some rare wisdom for someone so young."

"From what I've heard, I can believe that."

"As far as Richard, I guess I would have to say she seemed closer to her father. I never really sensed that icy friction between them. Their relationship seemed…easier, more understanding of each other. I would imagine if Sarah wanted something or was going to ask permission for something, her inclination would be to ask her father."

"Did you notice their relationship change at all at any point in her life?"

Todd narrowed his eyes, giving the question some thought. "No, I really don't believe so. I would only say that Richard displayed much more outward concern for Sarah during her first semester at college. I think he worried about her a great deal. As I mentioned, Bess, in general, is more stoic, keeps her emotions to herself."

"I want to apologize in advance for needing to ask this, but with all the mystery surrounding this case, we need to explore every avenue, no matter how unlikely, or how dark. Did you ever sense that Richard was overly close with Sarah?"

"Absolutely not," Todd said with force.

Seth held up his hand. "I don't mean to offend."

Todd closed his eyes and muttered some soundless words before opening them back up. "I apologize for the outburst. I'm not immune to the contemptible things that happen in our world. It's not that. In fact, before I came to Lost Grove, I was at a church in Spokane, Washington, and there was a situation to which you insinuated—"

"Again, I do apologize."

"No, no. I use that word for its literal definition, not as an accusation. But there was an unfortunate situation, charges were filed, etcetera. I will just say that it did not come as a shock. In fact, it was my worry that prompted me to inquire with the unfortunate child if everything was okay at home. My point is, I can tell you with the utmost certainty, nothing of that nature was transpiring."

Seth nodded. It was good to get confirmation from someone he believed would notice the warning signs. Not to say that it was an impossibility, but it wasn't something Seth would focus all his attention on. "Thank you, Pastor. I appreciate your honesty, and I believe you."

"Again, I apologize. I know you're just doing your job, and you wouldn't be doing it very well if you didn't look at everything."

"Thank you." Seth had one more avenue to pursue before leaving the pastor to his day and heading over to the school to interview the teachers again, especially Principal Bernthal. "I read the obituary in the *Gazette*. Did you help write that?"

Todd smiled. "Yes, Bess and Richard asked me to handle that."

"I thought that might be the case. Can I ask you about Sarah's summer camp volunteer work at Devil's Cradle State Park?"

"Sure. Of course."

"Was that run through the church, or something she did on her own?"

"It was through the church here. It's a camp where parents drop their children off in the morning and they spend the day doing all sorts of activities, archery, horseback riding, learning about different trees and leaves. Things like that."

Seth nodded, jotting down notes. "And how long did Sarah take part in that program?"

Todd looked up. "Oh, let's see here…I would guess it was eighth grade when she started up. She became a camp leader by the time she was in high school."

"That doesn't surprise me."

"And I'm sure you've heard about the summer she found and rescued the young boy who had gotten lost, separated from his parents."

Seth tilted his head to the side. "No, I'm afraid I haven't."

"Oh, well, it was big news in Lost Grove. It was a family from out of state, a mother, father, and their only child. I think he must have been four or five years old. Very young. Apparently, the boy wandered off on a hike, the parents were frantic. They found the park ranger, who called in other rangers and volunteers to search for the boy. But it wasn't any of them who found him. It was Sarah Elizabeth."

"How?" Seth asked.

Todd beamed. "She said she could feel the boy's presence, that it guided her to him."

Seth's intrigued smile dissipated. "I see. Did she…"

"Well, Sarah didn't elaborate any more than that, but it was a big deal for the church. We all rallied around her. It was a front-page story in the *Gazette*." At the mention of the *Gazette*, the pastor's expression fell. "Anyhow…"

"Right." Seth swallowed, deeply intrigued by how Sarah found the boy. "This is off subject, but does the Andalusian family attend service here?"

Todd's brows drew together. "No…"

"Do you know of them?"

Todd nodded. "I do. Not well, but I know of them. Does this have anything—"

"No, no." Seth jumped in and held up his hand. "It's just, Peter and Jolie's two children, Noble and Zoe"—Seth paused, letting Peter's name hang in the air, but caught nothing in the pastor's eyes—"were unfortunately on the receiving end of two belligerently drunk men this past weekend. I was there to intervene, but not before punches were thrown between one of the men and Noble."

"Oh my. No one was seriously hurt, I hope?" Todd brought a hand to his chest.

"No, nothing serious. One of their friends was there as well. Anya Bury."

"Yes, I know the Burys. But they also do not attend service here."

Seth waved it off. "All good. Just thought if they attended, they could use some support. Some comfort. Maybe guidance if they asked."

"Of course. That's terrible to hear. I'm glad you happened to be there."

Seth pocketed his notepad and pen and then handed the pastor one of his cards. "Well, if you recall anything else, no matter how insignificant you think it might be, please call me."

Todd grabbed the card and nodded. "I will."

Seth stood and shook the pastor's hand. "Again, thanks for your time. And please call me day or night if you think of anything at all that may help with our investigation."

Todd nodded. "Absolutely. I pray all goes well with the investigation."

Chapter 26

Intertwined Legs and Careful Flirtations

The door to the school library closed with a hydraulic hiss, bumping into Noble's backpack. Anya stood out like a beacon, her vibrant copper-to-white hair a calling song through the dimness of dusty paper, academic scribblings, and dark leather-bound tomes. He had been looking forward to this moment all day, being near her with no one else around, no Nate making lascivious comments, no Stan making blatant eye gestures. Coming to her like a dog eager to see his master, the anxious flutter of the heart, the wag of the tail, to feel that fire again, the fire that started as a spark, her eyes like gasoline every time he saw her again. Noble's long legs drew him to her in a matter of moments, her face lifting to greet him, her piercing eyes igniting that fire.

"Hey," he said, sliding into a seat next to her, his heart beating as if he had just finished a 400-yard dash, not a leisurely twenty-foot stroll across the library.

"Hey," Anya replied, pulling out her earbuds. She felt her cheeks flush as her stomach did happy somersaults that made her heart join in with a pitter-patter jig. His broad, brilliant smile lit up her insides. Warmth radiated off him as he sat near. Anya felt like he always gave off that gentle warmth, like the sun clung to him as if it too had a crush on him.

Noble thought he heard the faint strains of the powerhouse vocals of Florence Welch. They stopped as Anya tapped on the screen of her phone sitting next to her notebook.

"Sorry I'm late. Stan accosted me for the entire story about why we were having ice cream together and how the fight started."

"When did it become us having ice cream together?" Anya grinned, giddy with the idea that maybe they would have ice cream together and share a kiss that was cold and sticky and sugar sweet. Her eyes darted to his lips, then down to the notebook in front of her. She tapped her pen on the pad of paper.

"Typical Stan, twisting my words. I made sure she knew you had no ice cream."

Anya laughed. "Did you tell her why we actually met?"

Noble shook his head. "Just said it was some school shit."

"And did you tell her what started the stupid fight?"

Noble cleared his throat. "I didn't really, no. I just said it was some drunk assholes, and they were creeping on you—"

"Which is true."

"Exactly. And with my sister there, I had to do something. Easier than saying, 'People think my dad is a killer, and they called us mini-killers.'"

Anya glanced up at Noble, but now he was looking at the table, his hands resting on top as his thumbs beat out a meandering rhythm. She sucked her bottom lip into her mouth and bit down. She didn't know Noble's father like she knew Nettie's father, even though she gave that impression to the men that night. After the sergeant had left, her father came to her room and spoke with her about the incident more, and though he was most upset over the older man's salacious insinuations directed at his seventeen-year-old daughter, he wasn't pleased with the comments they'd made to Noble and his sister.

"It's inappropriate, and it's hearsay nonsense. People in this town," her father had scoffed, running a hand over the quilt on her bed. "And to say that to those kids."

"They were drunk, Dad," Anya had added, cross-legged, sitting beside him.

"I don't give a damn," Ethan had retorted. "You know Jeffrey Tacet isn't any good."

"I know."

"I want you to stay away from him if you ever see him again. Which you likely won't once I've had a few words with him." Ethan shuffled his feet and leaned his elbows on his knees.

Anya smiled. "Sergeant Wolfe already warned him pretty harshly."

Ethan looked back at his daughter, the smirk on her face. "Oh yeah?" He smiled back.

Anya was assured of her father's opinions about people, so she was pretty sure Noble's dad was a good guy. How could he be anything but? Noble was one of the most considerate and kind people she'd ever met. The way he doted on his sister spoke of a loving family.

Anya dropped her head to grab Noble's attention. "I think it was just some drunk asshole who has a chip on his shoulder. Jeffrey Tacet is not a nice person," she said. "And Stan wouldn't care. She'd likely feel that was even more reason to go beat the crap out of him herself."

"Yeah," Noble laughed. Stan had been pretty adamant she was going to exact some sort of revenge on the man. But Anya didn't know about Mrs. Fulson. And did Noble want to go down that road? Did he want to tell her all the nasty things people thought about his dad?

"Noble?" She interrupted his thoughts. "Are you okay? Do you want to talk about what happened that night or…?"

"I don't…I mean, my dad didn't *kill* anyone. I don't know where they…Jesus, I'm trying to say that I hope *you* don't think my dad's some whacko, or that I'm a nutcase or something." Noble felt like shoving his fist in his mouth; he sounded like an idiot. He was trying too hard, desperately afraid that she might think less of him.

Anya reached over, grabbing his fidgeting hands, finally getting him to stop talking. "I don't think you're a nutcase. I think you're amazing."

Noble's eyes swept up to meet hers, which she quickly cast aside. He watched her skin turn rose around the cheeks and down her neck. He felt like his heart had been hooked up to car jumpers and jolted into the stratosphere. A stupid grin broke out across his face, knowing she hadn't meant to admit what she thought of him. Her admission made him dizzy with endorphins.

"And I don't think that about your father," she quickly added. "My dad says he's a good guy."

Noble raised an eyebrow. "Your dad?"

"Yeah. Your dad has helped on the farm a few times during peak season. Like worming and calving and stuff like that." Anya shrugged. She looked down at their hands intertwined.

He ran his thumb across her knuckles, unconscious of the movement or how intimate it was.

"I wasn't brought up to judge or to believe the talk of the town. Hell, if I listened to what people said about…" She trailed off. She'd almost brought up what some people said about her mom. What a weird person she was, or the one incident when Anya had been in utero, and a couple people in the grocery store had seen her mother lick larvae off a bunch of polluted bananas in the grocery store. "The point is, there's talk about everyone. I mean, people think my mom is vain because of my hair. Like she's taken me to get this done since I was a child or something."

Noble gave a shallow nod. "But she, I mean, your hair… Is it just naturally this—"

"Yes, it is natural. It's genetic," Anya said plainly.

"Huh." Noble looked at her hair and nodded. He had never heard of multi-color hair being a genetic trait, but he wasn't about to question her on it. "So, we're good then?"

Anya laughed and gave his hand a squeeze, mostly to stop him from brushing her knuckles and the back of her hand in that gentle way that made her feel woozy and warm. "We're fine, Noble. Unless, of course, you were the one who left the anonymous tip that Sarah Elizabeth was on the beach?" she joked, pulling her hand away.

"Why would you think—?" Noble looked up and caught her grinning. "You're just fucking with me."

"I am," she said, then squinted her eyes. "Although now that I think about it, you and Nate are always training. So you would be up early enough to have found her."

Noble laughed until he thought about what she was saying. Noble dug his palms into his thighs, then put them back on the tabletop. When he'd heard the chief of police mention that, as casually as he could, his whole body went cold. Had his father found the girl on the beach? Was that why he left? Had he called it in and then taken off? The news didn't sit well with Noble, who was trying hard to believe his father wasn't a murderer.

But with the information Anya had pointed out, he couldn't help but think of another person who liked to go out running in the very early hours. Another person who he'd seen covered in the blood of a child-thing like the one Nettie Horne believed had replaced her brother.

"What?" Anya asked.

"Huh?" Noble's head snapped up.

"You look like something's bothering you."

"Oh, um, no. I'm just thinking that over."

"You don't think Nate found her," Anya said lightly. "I mean, he would have been—"

"Bragging all over town about it." Noble scoffed. "No, I don't think Nate found her. I'm trying to, sorry, just trying to think of other runners in town that may have spotted her."

"Oh yeah. I hadn't thought of that."

Anya and Noble fell into a thoughtful silence before she broke it.

"I can't think of anyone that would have left an anonymous note. I think most people would have just called the police."

"Any normal person would have immediately called the police," Noble agreed. His dad was not normal. His dad was ex-military, special forces. A dead body wouldn't scare him.

"Do you think the killer left the note?"

"Killer?" Noble asked.

"Well, like, the person who...I mean, the way the cops were talking about it, seems like something suspicious is going on with her death, right?"

"Yeah. Yeah, I guess that makes sense." Noble felt a different kind of nausea course through him. Not the roller coaster adrenaline high of spending time alone with a girl he thought was the most beautiful person in existence, but the kind that came from hearing your father had been questioned by police in a previous murder case having similarities too coincidental to ignore.

"We don't need to talk about it. In fact, let's not. I don't like thinking of her on the beach like that, just discarded," Anya visibly shivered.

"Sure, yeah, agreed. It's not a great topic," Noble said, pulling his tablet from his backpack. "But, yeah, let's finish our chat about what I found. Let's, um, let's talk about Raymond LaRange."

Anya pushed her notebook aside. "Let's!"

Noble picked up his chair and brought it closer. "I added the searches on here so we could look them over. So, these two," he said, tapping on the tabs to display two different articles. "They are the ones with specific mention of the phrase 'Papa LaRange.'"

Anya admired Noble's lips as he spoke, before shifting her focus to the tablet he was tilting her way, expecting her to look at. She noted how he didn't have a distinct smell. No aftershave, cologne, or body spray. There was a hint of his surroundings, a touch of perfume from a masculine body wash and shampoo, but nothing forward and aggressive like most teenage boys in the halls of Lost Grove High. "And what is 'Papa LaRange'?"

He tapped on the first tab and scrolled down, skimming the words.

"Here," he said, pointing it out and turning the tablet for her.

Anya skimmed through it for reason and relevance. "This is about…?"

"The nickname 'Papa LaRange' was mentioned in the testimony of a young girl who says a twenty-something man molested her while she was supposed to be having piano lessons with the man's mother. The guy's name was Raymond LaRange."

She tilted her head down to read. "Jesus, I don't think I want to read this."

"No, why would you?"

"Did you?" Anya asked.

"Well, yeah," he admitted with a snicker.

Anya giggled.

"I think it's kind of strange that a kid you say isn't all there says, well, *maybe* says, Papa LaRange, a nickname this sicko told these girls to use—"

"Girls? As in plural?" Anya interrupted.

Noble cringed in response.

Anya blinked multiple times. "So what happened? Who was he?"

"Basically, the case was against him and his mother. They charged him with molesting two girls. They charged her with a lot more."

"His mom?"

"Yeah. I only saw a few mentions and didn't go much deeper into her case, but she was kind of the mastermind. She told the girls they were going to play house and that Raymond was going to be Papa."

Anya winced. "How old were the girls?"

"Twelve and thirteen."

"Oh my God." Anya brought a hand to her face, contorted in disgust.

"Tell me about it! I'm sitting here reading this shit, thinking about Zoe. Or even Cheshire—"

"Oh shit. I'm sorry, Noble." Anya grasped his forearm. "I'm awful for asking you to do this."

Her cool fingers sparked his heart once more and made his skin prickle with goosebumps, a pleasant sensation that crept into his abdomen. "You didn't ask me. I volunteered, remember?"

Anya shrugged. "Still."

"It's cool. I mean, as dark as this is, it was kind of fun to trawl through the internet in search of clues." Noble left the tablet on the table, sitting back in the chair. His long legs stretched out, his knee bumped into hers. He noticed how she didn't move it out of the way.

Anya smiled. "Okay. So, what happened to Raymond LaRange?

This was in, what…" She leaned forward and looked at the article before saying, "Ohio, 1992?"

"Well, he had a really low IQ. As in, he was incapable of standing trial. He displayed a lack of remorse, no understanding of the charges they had brought him up on. He couldn't conceive of the seriousness. Shit, in one of these, which was it?" Noble skimmed the tabs and articles. "Doesn't matter. In one of them, a reporter says he smiled at the girls. He waved! He waved at one of them."

"Oh, man. So it was all his mother?" Anya asked.

"Well, no, not *all* his mother. She may have been the ringleader, or whatever, but he still, like, did stuff to them."

Anya squinted. "Jesus. That's just so…ugh. What happened to the mother, though?"

Noble shrugged. "I didn't really go too far into her part of the case because what happened with him jumped out first, and that…well."

"Well, what?"

Noble sighed. "So, he ended up being sentenced to rehabilitation and placed in psychiatric care. Turns out, one of his relatives, like his grandfather, I think, is some well-to-do guy, I don't know. Anyhow, he gets him transferred to the best psychiatric facility in the country—"

"Shut up!" Anya gasped, reaching out again and grabbing his forearm, already knowing the answer.

"Yeah…so, yeah." Noble looked into her excited eyes, such a vibrant green. He was kicking himself again over how he'd failed to notice just how stunning she was before.

Anya carefully chewed her thumbnail. "Tell me you're joking, please?"

"I wish I could. They moved him to the Orbriallis Institute. And even though it's been, what, two decades, I didn't come across anything about him leaving there," Noble said. "So, is it possible that Nettie's brother had…met Raymond?"

"I freakin' hope not!" Anya proclaimed.

"No, definitely. But it just seems…"

"Possible?"

Noble let out a slow exhale. "I mean, like you, I hope not. But how would we know?"

"Wait," she said, narrowing her eyes. "Was there a picture of this guy?"

Noble nodded, immediately recalling the strange photo of the man, who looked older than what he was, with a disconcerting smile. "Yeah, there was definitely at least one."

"Well, that settles it. We show Nettie the picture." Anya held her hands up like that settled everything.

"Why? I mean, because you think she may have seen him at the Institute when she's been there for family therapy?"

"That and also from before, when she saw the Green Man as a kid."

"As a kid?" Noble's eyes flicked to her tongue as it flicked out and wet her pastel lips. "Wait, you think this could be the Green Man?"

Anya shrugged. "I mean, it could be, no? When he came to their house at night and tried to lure George outside, to steal him? Nettie always saw him. What if Orbriallis released this molester creep and now he's hanging around like some hermit in the area?"

Noble's eyebrows shot up, uncertain how to form the many thoughts that sprang to mind.

"Or she could have seen him at the Institute during one of her many visits. Either way, maybe she can tell us more or maybe she'll recognize him." She set her cheek against her fist, her elbow on the tabletop, and lifted her eyebrows. "We can find out if what Not-George was trying to say was 'Papa LaRange.'"

Noble ran his hand through his hair. "Oh, man. Yeah, I think either way, maybe Nettie can shed more light on it."

Anya shuffled her feet, coming to rest against the heel of Noble's shoe. She liked that the touch didn't cause him to move his leg away. "This took a lot of effort from the sound of it. You really committed. So, thank you."

Noble shrugged, his eyes glancing down to his feet under the table, the color of her washed-out jeans against his dark ones. "Like I said, it kind of became a puzzle to solve. It drew me in."

"Sure. You've never shown much interest…in Nettie before…"

"Nettie?" Noble half laughed, then quickly adjusted. "Sorry, no, I didn't mean it like… She's… I'm fine with her. I know a lot of people think she's a little…off, but I, no, it's not her. I mean, it's not that or anything."

"You just like a good puzzle, then?" Anya asked. The hidden meaning in his words made her grin.

"Yeah, I like puzzles," Noble said, grinning back.

"Thought of becoming a detective?" Anya asked, purely out of interest.

Noble laughed. "No, that's all Nate. He thinks he's going to become a hotshot homicide detective. Me? I...I have no idea what I'm going to do."

"No?"

He shook his head.

Finally, Anya shifted her weight to her side and lifted her legs up and under her. Her knee came down, touching his knee again under the table. "Sorry."

"It's fine," he quickly responded, not wanting her to remove that subtle weight on his knee that made his stomach flutter.

"So, why not? Not sure if you're going to college or right into a career?"

"Yeah, I just don't know yet. I assume you have a plan. Know exactly what you want to be?" Noble threw the question back at her.

Anya took a deep breath. "Actually, no. There's so many things I think I might want to be. I'll just be a perpetual student, just not in any organized schooling system."

"Okay, the first question that comes to mind is, what did you want to be when you were ten?"

"A physicist."

"A what?" Noble laughed out loud.

Anya laughed along with him. "I wanted to be Meg from *A Wrinkle in Time*. Well, I wanted to be Meg, or her genius brother, Charles. But mostly Meg. Then later, when I was like twelve or thirteen maybe, I wanted to be like Adam Eddington, a marine biologist. Another Madeline L'Engle character."

"Damn. I clearly don't read enough."

Anya picked at the edge of the table. "Okay, you. What did you want to be when you were ten?"

Noble was not as quick with his response, but eventually, he replied, "A farmer."

Anya's gentle smile lit up her face. "That suits you."

"Does it?"

She nodded. "My father would be happy to hear me say that. 'I'd like to take over the farm, Pa.'" She snorted with laughter.

Noble did too. "Pa?"

Anya shrugged. "It's not that I don't like the farm. I love the farm. I don't think I need a degree to farm, but I'm going to Cal Poly Humboldt for environmental ethics."

"Already decided. That's awesome."

"Well, I'll just say I got accepted. Part of me still just wants to stay here on the farm. But I'm sure I'll end up going."

"That's cool. That your parents would be okay either way."

Anya cocked her head to the side. "I wouldn't say that. I think they would both be very disappointed if I didn't go to college at all. But they wouldn't force me. I don't think," she added with a giggle.

Noble smiled, wondering how upset his mother would be if he didn't go. She never pressured him, but he sensed that was what she wanted for him.

"So you haven't decided on a college yet?"

Noble bobbed his head from side to side. "Sort of. I could go to the University of Tennessee. My mom's parents live close by there. They have this major breeding program for racehorses, a huge ranch. I'd be going to school for veterinary medicine, but I'd mostly be learning from what happens on the farm there."

"That's cool. You're great with horses, as I recall."

"I love them. But the years of schooling? I kind of wish I could just learn a trade."

"Yeah," Anya enthused. "So you were accepted to Tennessee, or…?"

"I was, yeah."

Tennessee seemed like it was very far away, and Anya pondered him leaving, of being so far away. She felt the disappointment like a lead weight drop into her stomach.

The bell for the period jarred them out of their private reverie.

"Shit." Noble stood, tossing his tablet inside his bag and zipping it up. He helped Anya collect her things. Flipping closed her notebook of pretty highlighted headings and penmanship that he was sure only existed in the 1800s.

"I like calligraphy," she said, noticing his eyes hanging on to the open book.

Noble closed it and handed it to her. "It's gorgeous."

"Thanks," she replied, shuffling her backpack onto her shoulders, blushing again. "Meet me after school out front, then? We can show Nettie this guy's photo."

Noble paused and took a deep breath. He felt like he'd run 10K the way his heart hammered in his chest. Who knew two words, *meet me*, could incite such a thrilling bodily reaction. "Okay, then. I'll be waiting."

Chapter 27

Their Shit Doesn't Add Up

Seth sat in his personal 2017 Mercedes Benz C-Class, parked down the street from the Grahams home, not wanting to be spotted in his police-issue Bronco. He had been nursing his third cup of coffee that morning, thoughts of anger stirring as he'd watched Bess enter the house just fifteen minutes earlier. His gaze was still fixed on the door when movement in the rearview mirror caught his eye—it was Bill, walking up to the car. Seth had asked him to stay out of sight, so as not to arouse suspicion from Richard and Bess coming home from work. Seth's time patrolling the peaceful streets of Lost Grove had tempered his hard edge, but it hadn't taken away his determination for justice; he knew the Grahamses were lying to him, and he wouldn't leave until he found out what they were hiding.

Bill opened the passenger door and slid in, holding his travel mug of coffee, instantly spotting the deep scowl on Seth's face.

"Shut the door," Seth said without taking his eyes off the Grahams home.

Bill obliged and then shifted around in his seat to get comfortable. "What's the status?"

"Bess got home at 5:17 p.m. No action since."

Bill looked at his watch. "Hope Richard doesn't get caught working late."

"You got someplace else to be?" Seth asked, his tone low.

"Nope. Just gotta take a piss."

The corner of Seth's mouth curled up.

"You really think they would make a mad dash to their car if they saw us?"

Seth chuckled, a smile reluctantly showing itself.

"Get into a high-speed chase down the 101?"

Seth laughed as he placed his coffee in the cup holder. He didn't envy Bill's need to answer nature's call. "No, I just don't want them calling anyone or hiding anything they may have unburied or brought home."

"Unburied?" Bill asked, eyes trained on the Grahams home.

"So to speak." Seth glanced over at Bill. "You get a hold of Peter Andalusian?"

Bill shook his head. "Nope. I talked to Jolie, and she said she would try to get a hold of him."

"Why didn't you just get the number and call him yourself?"

"You heard the interview about Kelly Fulson. I think we'll have a better chance getting a hold of him through Jolie. She didn't sound too happy with him, I'll tell you that."

"You tell her what it's about?" Seth asked, checking the rearview mirror.

Bill chuckled. "Didn't even have to. I told her I needed to get in touch with him, and she said, 'Let me guess, this is about the Grahams girl.'"

Seth glared at Bill.

"She's not stupid. She sure as hell didn't forget about him being questioned about Kelly's death, and she knows that he just left town. Doesn't take much to put those pieces together."

"So, did she give you any indication of when she thinks we'll hear from him?"

Bill sighed. "She said she'll make sure he knows it's urgent, but that sometimes she doesn't hear from him for weeks."

"Shit. Because he's crab fishing in Alaska? I just—"

Bill turned to Seth. "It checked out."

Seth narrowed his eyes.

"Sasha got a hold of a company in Dutch Harbor that verified Peter's name was registered for a vessel that went out to sea on Saturday."

"Did they verify he actually showed up?"

"Couldn't say. But the vessel isn't due back for three weeks."

"Jesus Christ," Seth muttered and looked back toward the Grahams residence.

Bill took a swig of coffee. "So, how are we going to play this? Good cop, bad cop?"

Seth glared at Bill. "There's no good or bad here. It needs to be two cops who've heard enough lies from the parents of a girl who was fucking mutilated."

Bill's heart started racing. He could feel the steam emanating from Seth. "I'm not sure we're going to get very far if we both charge in there guns ablaze—"

"I'm done pandering to them and their bullshit, Bill. We can't hold back that there's a missing baby out there any longer. The fact that the whole town doesn't already know is a clear sign they're hiding shit. Oh, and by the way, something we both missed during our final interview with the two of them," Seth said, his eyes wild.

"What?" Bill said.

"I listened to all the interviews again throughout the day. Bess said, 'If you're telling me that I might have a grandchild out there alive, then you better find her.'"

Bill nodded a moment before it hit him. "She said 'her'? Are you sure? I mean, obviously you heard it."

"I think that's why I didn't buy her concern. Because she's not concerned. I think she knows damn well where that baby is, and they're not saying a word to anyone. You know what else is incriminating? I went to see their pastor—"

"Yeah, you said."

"And guess what? He knew nothing about Sarah dying giving birth or a potential lost infant."

Bill's jaw fell open.

"That's right, the one person they could trust the most. And he spent half the day with them yesterday. In fact, they straight up lied to him and told them they were still waiting to hear from our medical examiner. The one person you'd think they'd tell they possibly had a grandchild the police were looking for. Bess sure as shit acted outraged that we were wasting time questioning her and her husband when we should be looking for a child, but then she doesn't even tell their pastor, their friends? I mean, why not tell the whole congregation and organize a search party?"

"Like she doesn't actually want the baby to be found," Bill said offhand, understanding the thoughts percolating in Seth's mind.

"You should have seen the look on his face when I told him all of this."

"You told him? I thought you wanted to keep it under wraps."

"I may not be religious, but I think I can trust Pastor Todd Marquette to not go blurting it all over town. Plus, I wanted to gauge his reaction."

"In what way?"

"Well, someone fathered that child, and as we discussed, it's likely someone that would be frowned upon."

Bill raised an eyebrow. "And you thought her pastor might be—"

Seth huffed. "Really? You need me to pull up some articles about Catholic priests? But it's not him. He was shocked and visibly hurt that they didn't confide in him."

"Did you ask about anyone in the—"

"Of course. I got the names of three kids around her age. All off at different colleges, so not likely. The only other person he mentioned, though denied seeing anything suggestive, was Will Bernthal."

"Her principal in high school?"

"You know another Will Bernthal in Lost Grove?"

"Well, no."

"I spoke with him again today, and I would have to agree with Pastor Marquette's assessment. I sensed nothing raising a red flag. But these fuckers," Seth said, pointing down the street at the Grahams residence, "have been pulling our pud for days now."

Bill gazed downward and pursed his lips.

"They are clearly hiding something. Their shit doesn't add up." Seth glanced from the Grahamses' house to his chief. "You okay?"

Bill nodded imperceptibly. "Just trying to remove myself from… from knowing them as I do."

Seth took in a slow, deep breath and watched Bill's jaw clench and unclench. He turned his attention back to the house, a manner of giving Bill some space and privacy. Seth caught movement in the rearview mirror. The white Lexus he'd been waiting for. When he looked back to the chief of police, he saw a hardened Bill Richards. Seth straightened, the leather creaking as his weight shifted.

"Get ready to go break this case wide fucking open."

Richard heard the heavy pounding of fists on his front door and quickly rushed to answer. His tie was undone, but he had yet to take off his blazer. When he opened the door, he locked eyes with Seth and Bill, who stood solemnly on the doorstep. A lump rose in his throat as he saw the icy expressions on their faces. "What is it? Did you find something?"

Seth could see in Richard's eyes that his resolve was wearing thin. "I would say so." He motioned for Richard to open the door.

Bill didn't wait for the door to open before pushing past into the house. "I gotta use the restroom."

Richard snarled. "Sure, yeah…"

Seth stepped through the doorway, and his gaze locked with Bess standing in the kitchen. Her chin was cocked at an angle, her arms folded across her chest, radiating a smugness Seth had seen before—but this time she'd gone too far. He could feel the tension in the air between them, like a charged wire.

Bess raised an eyebrow. "Well, have you finally made some progress in—"

"Both of you, in here," Seth cut her off, walking into their sitting room. The house smelled like lemon furniture polish. "Now," he demanded, with the unquestionable authority befitting his career. It wasn't a tone you learned, it just somehow became a skill, and some were better at it than others. Seth excelled at harnessing that melody of an authority figure.

Richard shut the door. "Now, look here—"

Bess blew past her husband, following the sergeant into the front sitting room. "You can't just come into my house and order—"

"Enough of the act, Mrs. Grahams," Seth sternly said, taking a stance in front of the fireplace with a mantel all decorated with family photos and a cross on a stand.

Bess took a spot just inside the room, a safe distance from Seth, whose attention was laser focused solely on her. "What act?"

"Like you're the one in control."

"Sit down, Bess," Bill ordered as he walked past her to join Seth. "Both of you."

Richard hesitated, glancing at his wife as he stepped past her and sat down in an armchair. He fiddled with his tie, adjusted the legs of his pants, then folded his hands in his lap, keeping his gaze on his fingers.

Bess moved further into the room to stand next to her husband but refused to be seated.

"We have, in fact, made some major progress in the case," Seth started, his gaze still steady on Bess.

"Good," Bess said with a toss of her head. "It's about time."

"It's progress we could have made four days ago."

Richard looked up, eyes moving between Bill and Seth. "What do you mean?"

"Your daughter," Seth started and looked at Richard, then back to Bess, "never returned to Baylor after that winter break. Not for a single day."

"What?" Bess exclaimed. "Why wouldn't they have told us?"

"You're saying the school didn't inform you of her absence?" Seth asked. His jaw tightened along with every muscle in his body.

"We never even got—"

"Bess," Bill chimed in, "I've got two daughters, one who graduated college, the other will graduate this year. I have a hard time believing they didn't call, not just once, but many times. And they surely had to have sent you a massive amount of mail, especially considering the circumstances. Hell, the amount we get from Vanderbilt because of her basketball scholarship. And Sarah was a full ride, if I'm not mistaken."

"Well, I don't know about the school your daughter goes to, but Baylor didn't," Bess said defiantly.

"I think they did," Seth stated, casting a hard, knowing look across the room at Sarah's mother.

Bess shook her head and threw her hands up in the air as she started to pace.

Seth took a step forward and crouched down to grab Richard's attention, who had remained conspicuously quiet and was currently staring down at the ground. "Here's the thing, Richard. You told us you and your wife brought Sarah to the airport to return to college on January 2nd, and that you were driving."

Bess stopped pacing, her hand glued to her forehead.

"Yes," Richard muttered as he looked up at Seth.

"But your wife said she drove her."

Richard's wild eyes danced up to look at his wife, only to find the back of her head.

Seth stood back up. "You said you never once talked about going to Waco to see your daughter, whereas Bess over here said you talked about it all the time."

Bess dropped her hand to her hip and continued shaking her head.

Seth's voice rose. "You two couldn't even keep your stories straight about what you did the night before we found your daughter's corpse on the beach. Bank records are coming in, her cell phone history, we've got calls lined up with her college counselor, her roommate, and every instructor she had. I've spoken with your pastor, who says you didn't even bother to mention that your daughter died during childbirth and that you might have a missing grandchild out there."

Bess turned toward Seth, her face red and eyes wet.

"I could have chalked up your multiple blunders in your interviews to heightened emotion, grief, or whatever other horseshit you might try to use as an excuse. There's a reason your stories have holes in them. It's because you didn't fucking take her to the goddamn airport! I already have you on obstruction charges. In a matter of hours, I'll have enough evidence to charge you with conspiracy to conceal evidence, so do yourselves a favor now and tell us the fucking truth."

"Bess?" Richard whimpered, looking up at his wife.

Bess stared at Seth, her face red, her body trembling. She balled her hands into fists and grit her teeth. "You can't threaten us like this."

"This isn't a threat, Bess," Bill said, gravel in his voice. "You need to tell us what went on with your daughter, now!"

"We have told you," Bess snarled.

"Bess," Richard pleaded.

She scoffed at him. "No, they can't treat us this way. They're taking a few minor details, some slipups, some faulty memories," she snorted, her assurance and ego rising as she continued her diatribe, "and throwing them in our faces like, like leading the witness or—"

"You said 'her,'" Seth interrupted.

Bess gawped at the police sergeant, her interrogator. "What?" she asked with a screwed-up face, still high on the momentum of her blundering act of outrage.

"When Bill and I brought you both together in the interview room and explained that you had a grandchild, you threw a fake tantrum and said, 'you better find *her*.'"

Bess glanced down at her husband, who stared, wide-mouthed, at her.

Seth watched her chin begin to tremble, the way her eyes darted around the room as if it held some response, an answer, an excuse.

"We all did what we thought was best for Sarah, you assholes!" she screamed and then stormed out of the room, shortly followed by a door slamming shut and the subtle click of a lock.

"And there it is," Seth said, shaking his head, his lip twitching up.

He looked down at Richard, still sitting motionless in the armchair. Panic seeped into the room through the man's wide eyes. Through his parted mouth, Richard released a strained, pitiful sound.

"Goddamnit," Bill fumed, joining Seth so they both now hovered over Richard. "What the hell, Richard?"

"Yes, Richard, what the hell?" Seth asked. "Looks like your wife has left you here to explain what it is you thought was best for Sarah Elizabeth."

Richard dropped his face into his shaking hands and sniffled. "We brought her to the Orbriallis Institute."

Bill's head jutted back. "What?"

"You brought her to the Orbriallis Institute," Seth repeated slowly, his words dripping like thick maple syrup. A hundred scenarios shuffled through his brain, trying to connect the pieces.

Richard sighed, and his whole body sagged. "She was having a hard time—"

"Remove your hands from over your mouth so we can hear you," Seth ordered.

Richard dropped his hands, revealing tears on his cheeks. He kept his gaze fixed on the ground. "Sarah was having a hard time adapting to life in college. She was sick. She wasn't eating. Sometimes she would go days without sleep. I guess…I guess she had a nervous breakdown. I just can't believe she's gone."

Richard began sobbing.

Seth ran his hand down his face. "We had you in the station for hours on Friday. Why in blue fuck wouldn't you have told us this in the first place, Richard?" Seth shouted.

Richard shook his head repeatedly, his right leg jostling up and down. "I don't, I don't, I don't know. It's just…the story we've been telling for so long."

"That makes no sense whatsoever. Do you not want us to solve the case? Don't you want to find your potential grandchild?"

"No, no. Yes, I want to, I mean, that's not…"

"What was the endgame of you telling us this bullshit, Richard? Make us understand."

Richard slumped over as if folding in half and continued weeping, once again lifting his hands to cover his face.

"What are you hiding? Who are you trying to protect?" Seth asked in a calm, measured manner.

"No one."

"Are you in danger?" Seth pressed.

Richard savagely shook his head.

"Is someone coercing you into these lies? Blackmailing you? Threatening you?"

Richard hiccupped, his shoulders seizing with sobs.

Seth bent at the waist to lean closer to Richard. "If you're being threatened, I'm the person to tell. We're the ones who can protect you."

"I'm not. It's…it's our fault," Richard garbled through spittle, snot, and tears.

Seth rubbed his fingers over his forehead to release some tension and exchanged a skeptical glance with Bill from under his hand. There was a definite spark when he asked if they were being threatened.

"It's our fault," Richard repeated with dismal despair.

Seth took a deep breath through his nose to keep his composure. "Okay, Richard, when was this? When did Sarah have a nervous breakdown?"

Richard took a stuttering breath, lifting himself upright a fraction, and dropped his hands limply to his lap. "Over Christmas break. She said she kept hearing voices and seeing things. She thought she was losing her mind."

"What sort of things was she seeing and hearing?" Bill asked.

Richard sniffled and brushed his forearm across his nose. "I don't know. She…she thought she was having visions of the future…or the past. I don't know."

A chill rippled down Seth's spine. Sarah Elizabeth's body on the beach flashed in his mind. He blinked it away and shook his head. "Okay, were the voices from the visions, or did she hear them on their own without the visions?"

Richard flipped his hand in the air. "I don't know. They may have been one and the same? Sometimes, when we were sitting at the dinner table or watching TV, we'd notice her talking to herself, trancelike, and then she'd snap out of it. We asked her about it, like we told you," he said, glancing up at them with a red face. "That was true, I promise. We were trying to get her to tell us if she was on drugs, or we kept asking, you know, and she'd snap at us. Scream at us, saying she didn't want to talk about it, that we couldn't understand. That we never understood."

"What had you never understood? She'd had these visions before?"

Richard nodded. "As a child. She told us they'd gone away," he sobbed, again falling in half and pressing his face into his hands.

Seth squatted down next to the chair; antagonizing Richard would not do them any good. The man was a wreck, racked by guilt and secrets and mourning for his daughter, possibly living in paralyzing fear from something threatening them. "That had to have been incredibly difficult to see her go through. Watching someone you love struggle and not be able to help themselves is excruciating. So, she'd told you these visions had gone away when she was a child still?"

Richard nodded. "Yeah, when she was about eight or nine."

"Okay. Now she heads off to college, so you can't see that the visions are back or have gotten worse. You can't see the way they start affecting her, not physically, but what about over the phone? I know you've said she was distancing herself. Did you see this nervous breakdown coming?"

Richard shook his head. "Not before that winter break. It wouldn't have even crossed my mind. Everything we said about how she had changed when she came back was true. We could hardly even recognize her as the same daughter."

Bill nudged Seth's shoulder and motioned to the bathroom to see if he should go check on Bess. Seth shook him off, so Bill grabbed the armchair on the other side of the room, slid it closer, then sat. "I'm truly sorry, Richard. I can't imagine."

Richard worked up a meager smile and nodded at him.

Part of Bill wanted to reach past Seth and grab Richard by his jacket collar and shake him silly until he spit out just what in the hell happened to Sarah Elizabeth, but he knew it took supreme patience to let a suspect work through their admission.

"So, you brought her to the Orbriallis for psychological treatment?" Seth asked.

Richard let out a long, trembling sigh, trying to regain his composure. "Yes. And believe it or not, she was relieved. It was almost like she was waiting for us to suggest it. She wanted help. She wanted to sleep and for the visions to go away."

"When did this discussion between you and her take place? That you wanted to take her to seek professional help?"

"It happened a couple of times. Well, we asked if she wanted us to help, if she wanted to see someone, if she'd go see her pediatrician, you know, Dr. Lancaster. Then one day we said we were going to admit her, that we believed she was doing harm to herself, even if it wasn't outwardly, like cutting or… and she broke down. She just started crying. It was a new reaction, not the screaming and denial."

"She was worn down," Bill suggested, nodding as if they had a fatherly understanding between them.

Richard nodded back. "And then she told us that she had visions, that they hadn't gone away, but they'd become uncontrollable and she was starting to think it was something more. She thought they were a mental illness."

Seth understood Sarah better, probably better than anyone ever would have or could have. If he had been in thrall to moments such as the vision he had of Sarah Elizabeth, he might think he was mentally ill as well. Yet there was a disconnect, and he needed answers. Seth leaned down to grab Richard's attention. "So, how do we get from her being admitted for treatment at a renowned hospital to where we are now?"

Richard made eye contact with Seth for the first time. "I don't know."

Seth felt the presence of the acorn in his pocket, and for whatever reason, it stopped him from grabbing Richard's head and slamming it into the side table next to him. Sometimes the questions are too broad and the interviewee, who's already in duress, can't formulate a response. It's too hard for them to connect the dots. As a detective, he had to have patience, and he couldn't lead a suspect. It came down to asking the right questions.

"You're going to have to do better than that if you want to avoid us putting you in handcuffs."

Richard held out his hands, pleading. "I'm telling you the truth. She was at the Orbriallis Institute for almost two years. Dr. Jane Bajorek, the head of the psychology department, treated her. She was getting better. So much better. We visited her all the time. She said it was the first time she felt stable in as long as she could remember."

"What about her phone?" Bill asked.

"That was Sarah's idea," Richard admitted. "She didn't want anyone to know she was there. She didn't want her friends to worry, and she didn't want the whole town to think she was crazy. The idea of the new number was hers."

Seth stood up. "So she never disconnected her phone from your family plan. You did. Was it you or Bess who removed her number from the plan?"

"Bess handles those things."

"And money. You said you were putting money in her account so she wouldn't have to work while going to school. When we find your bank statements, are we going to see that's a lie, too?"

"Yes. We stopped putting money in her account once we admitted her. Anything she needed, if she needed toiletries, we bought them or someone at the Institute purchased them for her."

"Mm-hmm. Where were you last Thursday night between the hours of eight p.m. and midnight?"

Richard looked up and pleaded. "We…I told you. We were home, watching TV."

"What were you watching?"

"A show, I…some kind of home improvement show."

"You were watching this show?"

"My wife was."

"And what were you doing?"

"I told you, I was reading. Why are you asking me all of this again?"

"Why do you think? What were you reading?"

"My John Grisham book. *A Time for Mercy*."

"That's not what your wife said."

"What?"

Bill jumped in. "She said you were both watching *Downton Abbey*."

"Well, she's wrong. We watched that earlier in the week, but not last Thursday."

Seth decided to drop that line of inquiry. Richard was sticking to his story. "So, Sarah was at the Orbriallis Institute for almost two years, and then what?"

Richard reached over to the side table, grabbed two tissues, and blew his nose. He slowly dropped his hand. The shaking had returned. "About a year ago, Sarah had progressed to a point where they wanted her to work her way back into society, to reestablish what it was like to be around other people who weren't doctors or other patients before reconnecting with friends. The Orbriallis found a place for her to stay, a women's safe house. Bess and I sat with her and the doctors to talk it over. We wanted her to come back home, of course, but Sarah wanted to do it on her own. She said it was the only way she would know that she was cured and could have a normal life. Or at least improved to a point where she felt comfortable being around her friends, the people at church." Richard paused, and his lip quivered. "She wanted to go back to college, to become a doctor so she could help people like the doctors at the Orbriallis helped her."

Seth scratched his chin and glanced over at Bill to gauge his impression. Bill lifted an eyebrow and tilted his head to the side, showing that he believed Richard. Or at least that he wanted to believe him. The defeat in Richard from the moment they entered the house to the onslaught of information that Seth could verify within the hour pointed heavily toward him finally telling the truth. For the first time since they found Sarah Elizabeth's body, Seth thought he was finally getting the answers they'd need to put this case to bed. He looked back at Richard, who was staring down at his crumpled tissues. "Richard," Seth prompted.

Richard looked up and met Seth's eyes. "Yeah?"

"Assuming we believe you and that we can verify all of this with the Orbriallis, how do you explain Sarah getting pregnant?"

"We never knew that," Richard stated with as much conviction as he could muster.

"How?" Seth exclaimed. "How do you expect us to believe that?"

"We hadn't seen her since she went to the safe house. She told us she didn't want us to know where it was and asked the doctors to respect that decision. We got updates from Dr. Bajorek, who was in touch with the manager at the safe house, but no one knew she was pregnant. I still can't believe it. We never should have agreed to the stupid…safe house with no contact. It's all our fault." Richard broke off into a fit of sobs.

Seth let out an audible exhale as he stood up. "Okay, Richard, I'm sure you know that we're going to have to bring you down to the station to take official statements."

Richard simply nodded without protestation.

Bill stood and moved the chair back into place and waited for Seth to walk over to join him. "How you wanna do this?" he asked under his breath.

Seth looked at his watch and spoke softly. "It's late, but I'm gonna swing by the Orbriallis Institute and see if I can get lucky; catch Sarah's doctor or talk to anyone who can verify any of this. You bring them down to the station and put them in separate rooms. Keep Richard in the front passenger seat and don't let them talk to each other."

"Roger that."

Seth turned around. "Richard," he called out.

Richard looked up at him, beaten and deflated.

Seth pointed toward the bathroom. "Go to your wife and get her ass out of that bathroom, or Bill will kick down the fucking door. Got it?"

Richard nodded. "I'll get her out," he said, pushing himself up and heading toward the bathroom.

Seth walked toward the front door and looked back at Bill. "I won't be long. Let them sit until I get back."

Bill joined him at the door. "You think this is all true?"

Seth opened the front door and considered for a moment. "At least part of it, yeah. He's not stupid enough to make up everything about the

Orbriallis when he knows we'll be able to verify it in no time."

"I was thinking the same thing."

A soft knock on the bathroom door grabbed Seth and Bill's attention. They looked to see Richard leaning up against the door, turning the knob. "Bess, honey, you need to come out," he urged.

"I hate you!" Her voice echoed from behind the door.

Seth looked back at Bill. "Well, she's going to be a treat to deal with."

"Yep." Bill drew the word out.

"I'll see you back at the station."

"Hey." Bill stopped Seth, who had reached the front doorstep, and motioned with his thumb down the street. "My car is…"

Seth grinned. "You enjoy that walk."

Retrospective No.6: Sarah Elizabeth—Adult

Sarah Elizabeth stood in front of the full-length mirror, finding her gaze unwavering and peaceful as she surveyed the woman who had emerged in the course of the past months. Her fair skin, which had become so pale and dull, now looked pearlescent. She was still slim, but it was a mature sleekness instead of a gangly awkwardness. Hazel eyes studied her reflection carefully, taking in the elegant shape of her nose, the dusting of freckles across her cheeks, sprouting back up after a long hiatus. A rose blush had returned to her cheeks, giving some color to her otherwise alabaster complexion. Her hair, which seemed to have thinned and darkened to an oak brown during her breakdown, was a vibrant light auburn, and it curled softly around her face. The steady thudding of her heart pulsed through her veins as she finally found contentment with whom she had become—an adult, secure in her identity and confident in her path.

The timing of Dr. Owens's visit yesterday was no coincidence. He must have noticed her serenity and the clarity in her eyes, inquisitive and sharp. The doctor told her originally he wasn't planning on having this conversation with her for some time yet, but things had changed. He asked her to accompany Dr. Bajorek to speak with him in his private office the following day. Did he believe she was already fit enough to leave? Sarah thought that notion premature. She was just beginning to build a relationship with herself and feel at ease in her own flesh.

And there was still so much to learn and uncover about her visions: how to manage them and avoid being caught off guard. Dr. Bajorek didn't give off the impression that their work was finished. On the contrary, she spoke of the start of a journey. It appeared Sarah's feet were firmly planted and her mind was as clear as it had ever been, but she was in no way cured. And she knew she could be. If the Orbriallis could cure, or at least control, the affliction suffered by Dr. Bajorek's mothers, then it was just a matter of time before Sarah would be healed and could return to pursuing her dreams.

Sarah looked down at her dresser, a mid-century modern dresser that came with the upscale, furnished private apartments within the Orbriallis Institute. It wasn't her style; she preferred something more elegant, perhaps feminine, but they furnished the apartment with beautifully fabricated pieces. The impression the apartment gave her was that someone had handpicked everything specifically, from the calming shade of dusty blue to the heavy linen curtains hanging from floor to ceiling over the windows. Taking pride of place on the dresser was a Polaroid photo of her and Tommy that his brother Clint had taken a week before she left for Baylor. She brushed her fingers over it.

Last night she lay awake, not because of visions but a flood of memories that levied her with an immense weight of sadness. She missed her friends. Not a day passed without enduring the guilt of leaving Brigette and Jeremy in the dark. But she thought it was a decision that had to be made. Not just because she didn't want them to worry about her but also because Sarah knew she couldn't concentrate on curing herself while holding on to their concerns. She'd inevitably be compelled to update them on her progress.

But Tommy. Sarah's heart broke every time she imagined what he was going through, the abandonment he was surely experiencing by her unexplained absence. She ached to see him again, the desire to hold him, to be held, to look into his eyes, to feel his breath on her lips, was almost paralyzing. They hadn't broken up, but what would he think of her when she returned, when she could explain? Would he listen? Would he still love her? That question hurt the most.

She'd held the Polaroid against her chest all night, focusing all of her energy on sending him a sense of peace. She tried and failed to visit him from her bed. Sarah was certain that if she gained enough understanding and control over her visions that she could, in fact, communicate to the person she was visiting. She would ask Dr. Bajorek about it during their next session.

She grabbed a small bottle of perfume off the top of the dresser. It was the only perfume she'd ever owned, purchased when she and Tommy first started talking. She'd bought it from Christopher Wolfe, the owner of the town pharmacy, praying that he wouldn't mention anything to her parents. Or anyone else. She would put a drop or two on her neck the nights she and Tommy met and then wash it off when she got back home.

Sarah removed the cap and held the bottle upside down on her index finger. She lifted the bottle to her nose, breathing in memories of sweet kisses and long talks in the dead of night. She set the bottle down, then pulled her hair to one side with her other hand as she dabbed the perfume on the back of her neck, wanting to feel Tommy near her. Sarah was wearing her favorite juniper-colored sleeveless blouse, her beige linen pants, and brown vegan leather ankle boots. The first time she wore this outfit, home for her Christmas break from Baylor, she felt like an imposter, a crazed girl in someone else's clothes. Today, everything felt right.

Sarah moved to the apartment window, pulled open the curtains, and looked over the town she'd spent all but four months of her life in. Her room was on the twenty-third floor of the Institute and the view was as breathtaking as it was terrifying. It was quiet. It was always quiet on her floor, which was a stark contrast to many floors of the Orbriallis. Despite all the issues she had with her parents, all the years they pressured her to speak to God on their behalf, she was thankful they had taken mercy on her and brought her here.

Sarah knew it was ultimately her father's voice that swayed her mother to agree to have her admitted. Her mother was more concerned that the town would find out and think that Bess Grahams's only daughter was crazy. They wouldn't have been that far off. Sarah had been an unhinged disaster when her father walked her through the front doors of the Institute. She had completely lost control of reality, not able to separate her visions from her daily life, often the two becoming intertwined. That was the crux of the problem. Her experiences inside the visions were so real, the emotional and psychological impacts were the same.

Each month she spent at Baylor grew progressively worse. Sleep lasted two hours at best. Her visions came on in the middle of classes. They also became vicious. It only took one incident of her becoming catatonic in class, speaking to the person she was seeing with her eyes closed, for word to spread around like the black plague. It seemed like every one of the over 14,000 students knew about the "crazy, possessed girl." Thankfully, the very worst vision she ever had in her life happened on a Saturday night toward the end of the semester when her roommate was at a party.

The girl in the vision, her name was Sofie McAllister. Sarah knew her from the Anatomy and Physiology course they shared, though they had never spoken. During that first semester, Sarah's visions had become increasingly intense. Often the person in her vision was in danger or being harmed. Her most recent vision before this one involved a tense and frightening scene of two men fighting. The brawl spread across an entire living room in the dark of night, culminating in one holding the other out a broken window, not unlike the one Sarah stood at now, trying to throw him out. Sarah screamed at the top of her lungs to stop it, but snapped out of the vision before seeing what happened. That vision had felt like déjà vu, though she couldn't pinpoint when or where she had experienced it before.

Her vision of Sofie was worse. Much worse. On only one previous occasion had Sarah slipped inside the person she was visiting, seeing through their eyes. The first time had been the young boy who got lost in Devil's Cradle State Park, crying, searching for his parents. After seeing the nearby landmarks through the boy's eyes, Sarah discovered the boy unhurt and brought him back to his parents.

This time, Sarah had slipped inside of Sofie McAllister's body in the middle of a tumultuous and confusing ordeal. A young man had Sofie pinned up against a wall, kissing her neck, hands on her breasts. She sensed that Sofie desperately didn't want this to be happening. When she made it known by trying to push the boy away, he reacted by throwing her on the bed and tearing off her clothes, piece by piece, as Sofie feebly fought against it. In retrospect, Sarah assumed that Sofie had been drunk because her movements were weak and her vision cloudy.

When the young man inserted himself into her, Sarah tried desperately to pull herself out of Sofie's body, away from the terrorizing vision. No matter how hard she tried, how hard Sofie fought, they both had to endure the assault to the end. When Sarah broke out of the vision, she immediately bent over her bed and wretched on the floor. She was inconsolable for the next three days. She felt so violated that she believed in some part of her mind she was no longer a virgin.

On the third day, her second in a row of missing classes, she realized who the girl was. She'd heard the young man say the name Sofie frequently during the grotesque desecration, but it was the memory of seeing the girl's distinctive handmade bracelets adorning her wrist that put the pieces together.

Sarah made the ill-advised and sleep-deprived decision to approach Sofie McAllister the following day after class. Sarah told her she knew what happened the previous Saturday night, and that it wasn't okay, and she needed to report it to the authorities. Sofie looked in disbelief and horror at the crazy, possessed girl standing across from her. After telling her to fuck off and to never talk to her again, Sarah never returned to class. She booked a flight home and left school a week early.

With past visions haunting her, coming home offered her no reprieve. Everyone bothered her about the way she looked, her parents, her friends, people on the street, the congregation. So what, she got a piercing and a tattoo, two things she had wanted for years. What right did any of them have, including her parents, to judge her? And what was the big deal? It was like she had time-traveled backward for once, into a generation prior to her own where such things were, incomprehensibly, taboo. She thought the small town would provide solace; instead it weighed on her.

And the visions kept up. To get them to stop, to pause, was impossible. It was like there was a hole in her that allowed them all to come through whenever they wanted. She couldn't keep living that way. All her hopes of becoming a doctor, getting married to Tommy, providing a loving home to his little brother Clint, helping people. None of that would be possible.

All of that changed the day she came to the Orbriallis Institute. The first meeting she had with Dr. Jane Bajorek was a watershed moment. She taught Sarah strategies to keep the panic attacks at bay, practices that lowered her anxiety and stress. Sarah was going to do all the things she dreamed of, but she still needed more time with Dr. Bajorek. They couldn't be asking her to leave yet.

A tingle fluttered up Sarah's spine. She turned from the window and walked to her door, opening it as Dr. Bajorek was stepping up, fist rising to knock.

"Oh!" Jane gasped, stumbling back before laughing. "You scared the lights out of me."

"Sorry," Sarah offered with a smile.

Jane wrapped her arms around Sarah. "Quite alright."

Sarah's heart filled with warmth at the show of affection from the doctor who had changed her life. Perhaps saved it. "What was that for?" she asked as Jane stepped back.

Jane smiled. A conflicted smile, Sarah observed. "Oh, nothing really. I apologize."

"No!" Sarah protested, grabbing hold of her doctor's shoulders and pulling her in close. "You can hug me as much as you want. I'll actually probably never stop hugging you now that you've opened that door."

They both laughed.

"I just know this is a big deal," Jane said. "I mean, not that you would. But it's rare to be invited into Dr. Owens's personal living quarters."

Sarah's tranquil state of mind became mildly disrupted. "Living quarters? I thought—"

"No, no," Jane jumped in. "Of course I'm going to be there with you. And his living quarters are also his office, his lab, his…everything."

"Here?" Sarah asked, brow furrowed.

"The top two floors are all his," Jane explained. "Anyhow, I didn't mean to startle you. After startling me." She laughed.

"It's fine," Sarah said, smiling.

"You look lovely," Jane said. "The green blouse makes your eyes pop and your hair seem more vividly red than usual."

Sarah blushed. "Thanks." She wished she could ever look as beautiful as Dr. Bajorek. From the moment she first met her, Sarah was in awe. She had the most luscious long black hair she had ever seen in her life. The doctor usually wore it up, but the times when she let it down, it fell past her breasts, almost reaching her waist. And her eyes, Dr. Bajorek's eyes were as wide as saucers and were a rich brown that almost seemed to shimmer. Her high cheekbones reminded Sarah of a young Angelina Jolie, and her lips were so pink and full that Sarah consistently felt compelled to touch them.

"You look happy, too," Jane said. "I'm so impressed with how far you've come. The work you've put in is inspiring."

Sarah playfully pushed Dr. Bajorek's arm. "My life would be in ruins without you."

"You keep saying that."

"It's true."

Jane rolled her eyes with a smile. "Should we go, then? Are you ready?"

"I'm ready."

"Come in, come in. Make yourselves comfortable, both of you," Dr. Owens chirped as he held open the door to his home at the top of Orbriallis. The doctor was five feet six, the same height as Sarah, and had a lean physique that matched his boundless energy. His dark brown hair, slightly greying at the temples, and tanned skin gave him the appearance of being in his early fifties, though it was rumored that he was in his late seventies, some said eighties. He was wearing a neatly tailored suit of complementary colors of yellow and brown, with a white satin scarf around his neck.

Sarah entered with her mouth open in awe of the vast and opulent setting. She had never observed Dr. Owens to be so upbeat, which was saying something. During her stay here, he had dropped by once a week to see how she was doing. Hopefully, he wasn't in such a chipper mood because he was getting rid of her.

"Anywhere, anywhere, sit wherever you like," Dr. Owens offered, his arms spread wide. "Can I get either of you something to drink? Water, seltzer, tea, soda?"

"I'll have chamomile tea," Jane said, a grin teasing the corner of her mouth.

Dr. Owens looked put out for the briefest of moments before smiling even wider than he had been. "Yes, yes, of course. Sarah?"

Sarah turned back toward him, meandering into the middle of the room, taking in the grand piano, the library, and massive atlas globes. "Um…"

"Don't be shy. Please, anything you want."

"Okay. A vodka tonic then."

Dr. Owens froze. "Oh…I…"

"Sarah," Jane started, "for starters, you're not—"

"I'm joking. Look at both of you. I'll have a Coke, please."

Dr. Owens let out an uproarious laugh. "My goodness!"

Jane brought a hand to her chest and giggled. "Vodka tonic. You had me in the midst of a moral conundrum for a moment."

Sarah shrugged and smiled as she turned back to take in the rest of the room, approaching the wall of books. She questioned whether she would have actually followed through with it and taken her first drink if the doctors hadn't reacted with such shock. Something about the day had her feeling rather audacious.

"Lina!" Dr. Owens called out as he opened a door. "A chamomile tea and a Coca-Cola on ice, please. Thank you," he said, shutting the door.

Jane had taken a seat in a large Victorian chair at the head of a sitting circle, a couch on both sides and a smaller leather armchair across from her.

"Jane, I see you're making yourself comfortable," Dr. Owens commented.

She crossed her legs, holding a steadfast gaze on him. "You said to, did you not?"

"I did indeed," Dr. Owens said under his breath as he turned his attention to Sarah Elizabeth. "Feel free to explore, Sarah. Grab a book. Play the piano. It's not a museum."

"Thanks," Sarah replied over her shoulder as she ran her fingers over the spines of the books at eye level. She paused, catching the word *sleep*. "*The Psychological Study of Sleep Patterns and Paralysis,*" she muttered to herself.

Sarah pulled the book from the shelves and tucked it under her arm. She'd return it when she was done. Continuing down the row, she listened to the hushed words being spoken by Dr. Owens and Dr. Bajorek. She could sense the tension in both of their voices the moment they started speaking to one another. Did they disagree on the reason they had asked Sarah to come here? Would they openly disagree in front of her?

A soft feminine voice preceded the crack of a door opening. "I have all your drinks, Neil. Shall I set them over here?"

Sarah spun around to see a woman with a scarf wrapped around her head and a black veil over her face. Her brain caught up to the moment as she recalled Dr. Owens shouting for a woman named Lina. Could this be Lina Orbriallis? Was she actually alive? Did she live here with Dr. Owens?

Dr. Owens walked over to the sitting area, motioning to the stone table with a glass top. "Yes, right here is fine."

"Hello, Jane," Lina said as she approached the table. "The tea, I presume?"

"Yes, thank you, Lina." Jane grabbed the saucer and cup from her outstretched hand.

Lina looked up at the young girl approaching them, her eyes wide with interest. "You must be Sarah Elizabeth."

"Lina," Dr. Owens sighed.

Sarah stuttered and stepped around the corner of the first couch. "Hi. Yeah, I'm Sarah."

"The Coca-Cola?"

Sarah nodded as she reached out to grab the heavy glass. "Thank you so much. Are you—"

"Lina is my niece, and she's just leaving," Dr. Owens said as he casually sat down in the leather armchair.

"Well, here. I brought you your cognac," Lina said, holding out the glass to him.

Dr. Owens laughed. "Cognac?" He looked over at Sarah and shook his head like his niece was out of her mind. "I didn't ask for—"

"But you always have—"

"Thank you, Lina." Dr. Owens glared at his niece, his eyebrows raised.

"It was nice meeting you," Sarah said as the meek woman walked through the doorway, shutting it behind her.

"Well!" Dr. Owens clapped his hands. "Thank you for coming to see me, Sarah."

Sarah took a sip of Coke and then set it on her lap. "Thank you for everything you and your staff have done for me. Honestly. I was…in a terrible way."

Dr. Owens nodded. "That is why we're here. To help people. Not just here within the Orbriallis, but all over the world."

"I know. My parents talk about the Institute a lot. And, of course, I was here before," Sarah said, dropping her head.

"Nothing to be ashamed about. You were eighteen and had every right to come to us on your own."

"I thought for sure they were going to find out," Sarah said, lifting her eyes. During the summer before she left for Baylor, Sarah, at the urging of Tommy, had come to the Orbriallis for her sleep issues, which paled in comparison at the time to where they would get months later. She only had three visits but was so impressed by the doctors and facility that when she had her breakdown, she had begged her parents to take her there.

"Patient confidentiality is a principle of the medical field. It's one we take as seriously as anything we do here," Dr. Owens said, his voice dropping to a more somber, level tone. "Many of the patients who seek treatment with us suffer from severe afflictions. We're able to do our research because of these brave people. Research that no one else is doing. Research that others are afraid to do, or think us mad for doing."

"Like with me?"

Dr. Owens nodded. "Yes, like you. And others. Others who have diseases and afflictions you have never heard of."

Sarah glanced over at Jane, quickly returning her eyes to Dr. Owens.

"Or perhaps you have." Dr. Owens looked over at Jane.

Jane sipped her tea. "It's fine," she breathed.

"Either way…" Dr. Owens looked back at Sarah, slapping his knee. "Our goal, our mission, is to make this world a better place. A safer place. Happier, healthier. That is the goal of every doctor and researcher that steps through these doors. They have all dedicated their lives to curing illnesses that have yet to be cured. Cancer, Alzheimer's, lung, heart, and kidney failure. Making the blind see and the deaf hear. We believe there is a cure for psychopathy and sociopathy. A way to rid the world of those most likely to kill. And one area we pride ourselves on most is our research on children and fertility. We will find a cure for childhood cancer. We will ensure every parent who wants a child can bear one without complications."

"Like my mother," Sarah interjected.

"That's exactly right. Like your mother." Dr. Owens shifted to the edge of his chair. "Jane tells me you want to study medicine."

Sarah quickly swallowed the sip of cola she'd been in the middle of. "Yes. And I was for a quick spell before, well, before I came here. I want to help people, as you said. Even more so now."

"Why is that?" Dr. Owens asked.

"What you've done for me, it's life changing. Life saving. I've always wanted to do that for someone. Maybe even someone like me."

Dr. Owens nodded along. "Yes. The feeling is, well, it's like a drug, almost. Don't you think, Jane?"

Jane tried to gauge what game Neil was playing. "It can be fulfilling."

"Oh, come on," Dr. Owens goaded. "Seeing Sarah here, you must be more than fulfilled?"

"No," Jane corrected. "I'd say that's spot on." Then to Sarah she said, "There's an overwhelming joy that comes with helping someone and seeing that work out. There's also the conflict, the regret, the blame when you can't help."

Sarah nodded.

"Yes, but when it goes right!" Dr. Neil Owens enthused. "Which more often than not, it does, especially here at the Orbriallis Institute… my goodness, what a rush that is."

Sarah smiled at his joy and candid conversation.

"What is it you plan to focus on, Sarah?" he asked.

"In medicine?"

He nodded.

"Well, I'm very interested in my condition. Insomnia, um, how the brain works." She held up the book she'd pulled from his shelf. "Sleep paralysis is very interesting."

"That's good, very good!" Dr. Owens nodded with his whole body. "What do you think about, well, the distinctive abilities someone like you has?"

Sarah looked from Dr. Owens to Jane. Jane blinked and nodded reassuringly.

"My visions, you mean. Not just psychosis, like many would believe?"

Dr. Owens leaned forward and pointed at her. "I mean exactly that."

"I think it's astonishing. We've all heard stories about people having visions. Well, Joan of Arc, Saint Thérèse of Lisieux, Florence Nightingale. She's the mother of modern nursing, and she said God called her to that duty," Sarah explained. "Jane Goodall even has said she had an experience that showed her the compatibility between science and spirituality."

Neil laughed. "My goodness, you do know a lot of mystics."

Sarah looked down at the glass in her lap.

"All a part of your studies, I'm sure, in trying to understand yourself," Dr. Owens quickly said.

"Yes. I mean, those are the only people I seem to be able to find information on. Mystics, you call them?"

Dr. Owens swatted the word away. "The name given to them because people can't believe they're actually gifted. So they say, let's call them something silly, like mystics. Or witches!" He laughed.

Jane choked on her tea.

Sarah laughed a little as well. "Oh, are you alright?"

"Fine," Jane said as she glared at Dr. Owens.

Neil smiled back at her like they were sharing a joke. He looked back at Sarah. "So you see yourself in all these other people of the past, yes?"

"I do. In a way," Sarah answered.

"Yes, and who knows how many others are out there. Other young girls just like yourself, trying to understand why they are different. Teenage girls who can't cope, who have no one to rely on, nowhere to go," Dr. Owens's tone turned somber. "Young people, taking their lives because they're different and no one will believe they're not suffering from psychosis. What they have, a doctor cannot diagnose."

Sarah nodded, her attention drifting toward Jane and back again as a moment of silence hung amidst their conversation.

Dr. Owens clasped his hands and leaned forward. "Sarah, you've come to us at a very serendipitous time in our research. The human body, the DNA that makes up who we are, has been mutated, compromised over centuries through inbreeding, disease, chemicals, and toxins. Children born today suffer a tremendous disadvantage because of this. Quite simply, the humans being born now are not the same as the ones God created."

Jane set her saucer down on the glass table, drawing both of their attention. "My apologies," she said as she laid a stern glare at Dr. Owens. "Please, continue."

Sarah returned her attention to Dr. Owens, knowing why Dr. Bajorek had interrupted. He didn't need to appeal to her beliefs to interest her in what he was saying.

Dr. Owens let the moment go and looked back at Sarah. "What we've been working on for decades now is to bring us back to that. To give parents the opportunity to bear a child free of disease. Not only that, but a child immune to disease. A child with advanced learning capabilities, stronger bones and muscles to protect our delicate organs, a superhuman, if you will."

Sarah held up her hand. "Just a moment." She turned her body to face Dr. Bajorek. "Is this all true? Children born immune to disease? And you're helping with that research?"

Jane slowly nodded. "I am a part of this research and, yes, it is true."

The conviction behind her response was unmistakable. Sarah felt her heart rate drastically increase for the first time in weeks.

Sarah turned back toward Dr. Owens. "I'm sorry for interrupting."

Dr. Owens waved the notion off. "Not at all. I would be disappointed if you didn't question what I'm telling you. You're an incredibly smart person, Sarah. Your gifts are…truly original. This is why I've asked you to come here today. I want to explain to you what we're doing. But more than that, I want to tell you what we need to get past our last hurdles."

"Okay."

"Not only are we going to make sure children are born immune to all diseases, we're taking it a step further. There are other gifts, ones different from yours. You clearly know about the conditions of Jane's mothers," he said with a pained smile, letting that hang in the air a moment. "Imagine what other marvels lie outside of what science, to this day, continues to ignore. We've collected samples of DNA from willing donors of many gifted people with unique abilities such as your own. Some would call these mutations, I call them miracles, marvels to behold, conditions that can advance humanity to new heights. We have contained and extracted these miracles from the DNA and added them to the overall equation. I know you see your visions as a curse at times, but haven't you saved a little boy from getting lost in the woods? Possibly dying alone, cold, lost, without his parents? I know you can see, with practice and control, your visions are a blessing that could save someone's life."

Sarah felt tears building in her eyes as his words alluded to her very thoughts and feelings.

"You've truly graced us with your presence here. And I genuinely mean that. I believe you're here for a reason much bigger than what you came here seeking."

Sarah could feel her hands trembling, gooseflesh rising on her arms and back. Her armpits grew damp, her legs tensed as if she would be called to spring from the couch at any moment. These words felt familiar.

"Do not be afraid, Sarah Elizabeth. What I'm going to—"

Sarah gasped, her eyes springing to the size of saucers.

Dr. Owens stopped mid-sentence.

Sarah looked at Dr. Bajorek. "I've been here."

Jane sat up and reached across to grab Sarah's hand. "This moment?"

Sarah nodded.

"Do you want to leave? We can come back another time."

Dr. Owens offered an immediate scowl at his colleague, thinking of a way to protest, but he needn't have bothered.

Sarah shook her head and turned back to Dr. Owens. She set her glass down on the table. "You need me to carry a child."

Dr. Owens's mouth dropped open, working to form words.

"Sarah," Jane gasped. "What are you—"

"I know this. All of this. This was my first vision."

"From when you were seven?"

Sarah nodded. "The one that came back to me in fragments multiple times throughout my life."

"Unbelievable," Neil mused.

Sarah felt a touch of pride seeing the look of pure amazement on his face.

"This…this moment right here, right now?"

"Yes. I've been here. And you need me to carry a child. A child of immense importance."

"Yes," Dr. Owens said slowly. "That is what I was going to speak to you about."

Jane had never seen Neil so awestruck in her entire career. "Sarah, it's quite complicated, and I—"

"It's okay, Dr. Bajorek." Sarah glanced back at her and then returned her gaze to Dr. Owens. "Please, continue."

Neil straightened his posture, having leaned in toward this remarkable girl. "Yes. I must say, before we continue, I've been in the presence of some remarkable people, adults and children alike, and seen some things that would fracture most people's minds. But…I've never seen or experienced anything quite like this. I mean, if I'm understanding correctly, and I believe that I am, you've already met me. Many years ago, as a child. But it was now."

Sarah nodded. "Yes."

Jane felt her heart pounding in her chest. The whoosh of it seemed to fill her ears. It truly was remarkable.

"Please, go on," Sarah urged Dr. Owens.

Neil rubbed his hands down his pant legs. "Right. Well, our efforts have brought us this far, but there have been failures. An embryo is a delicate thing, no matter how strong the DNA it's composed of. We need a viable egg and a real womb. Science can accomplish so many things, Sarah, but the miracle of growing a child is not one of them. That spark cannot happen in a petri dish or in some simulation. Now, I know I'm asking a lot and I'm sure you have many questions. I'll answer all of them. Then you'll probably need time to—"

"I'll do it."

"Sarah," Jane said, reaching across and squeezing her hand. "You don't need to decide anything now."

Sarah squeezed her hand back. "Please don't worry. I've never felt more sure of anything in my life. I've seen this, over and over, like so many other visions. Visions that didn't make sense to me at the time. But this one finally does. All I've wanted to do since I got to an age where I understood having a life's purpose is to help people. That's why I'm going to be a doctor. But this means something, too. If I can help a woman like my mother, who suffered through years of pain, not able to conceive another child, or the mother who gives birth only to spend a few precious hours before the baby dies, or the suffering children lying in hospital beds the globe over, suffering from diseases, viruses, cancers, then I'll have already done a deed greater than I ever imagined, more than I could do within the confines of my career."

"Yes, but at what cost, Sarah?" Jane asked. Her eyes darted briefly over to where Neil was sitting. She felt him wanting her to be silent.

"You mean school?"

"School, yes. You want to help. You can become a doctor like you planned."

"And I will." Sarah smiled.

"Sarah, carrying a child comes with risks," Jane explained. "You should know them."

"Okay, tell me what they are," Sarah urged.

Jane looked at Neil, foolishly. As if he would bother explaining the risks of pregnancy. "There's the possibility of a miscarriage. Depression, anxiety, preeclampsia, gestational diabetes, anemia, stillbirth, preterm labor—"

"Jane, don't frighten the young woman," Neil urged.

Jane turned to him. "She needs to know all the risks."

Sarah took in a deep breath, a smile lifting her face. "Dr. Bajorek, I understand what you're saying. I know there may be risks, and we can go over all of them. But I know this. I've had this conversation and seen it before. And not just this."

"What do you mean?" Jane asked.

"I've had visions of myself with a child. *My* child."

Jane's eyes widened. Sarah hadn't shared this vision with her before. She argued back, "How do you know that isn't sometime in the future? With Tommy?" Jane asked.

"This is the future, Dr. Bajorek. Right now is the future I've been seeing. The visions of this moment, and the one with the child I mentioned, are connected. I can't describe it, something in the color, the tone, the aura. I associate them with blush and the smell of powder. When both visions leave me, that's what I recall. That's a link, like what you've been teaching me about the connections." Sarah said.

"Yes, but the interpretation could be wrong. It's like tarot, like palm reading," Jane argued.

Sarah recalled the time she went to the town librarian and asked her to read her palm. The librarian, Story was her name, hadn't read her palm like there was some way to interpret it other than what she saw. There was conviction in what she'd said lay within the lines gracing Sarah's palm. Sarah felt that way about her visions and it was funny how this one little moment and turn of phrase from Dr. Bajorek made her see that.

She shook her head and smiled. "No, it's not like that."

"Alright. I understand your conviction—"

Sarah interrupted her doctor. "And doing this doesn't mean Tommy won't be a father to the child."

Jane opened her mouth to respond, to argue, but found that she couldn't. There was no argument she could give to a young woman who had visions of her own future, who had instincts to decipher those visions that time had yet to reveal. Jane hated having to hope that she was right. To hope that the way Sarah read her visions was correct, and this path wasn't a giant misstep in her young, adult life.

Sarah scooted forward a little, still holding Jane's hands. "You're part of the research, right?"

Jane nodded.

"You must believe in it. Do you believe this is possible?"

Jane closed her eyes for a moment. She opened them back up and looked Sarah directly in the eyes. "I do," she admitted reluctantly, but honestly.

"With your belief and my visions, I know this is what I should do," Sarah assured her.

Jane gave an imperceptible nod. "I'll be here with you every step of the way."

Sarah let go of her hands and reached out, wrapping her arms around Dr. Bajorek. Her heart was beating with pride, relief, and love. She let go and looked back at Dr. Owens, who appeared to be genuinely moved. "I agree. I'm ready."

DON'T MISS IT!

WANT A SNEAK PEEK OF LOST GROVE: PART TWO

SCAN THE QR CODE TO FIND OUT WHAT IS HAPPENING IN LOST GROVE

Acknowledgments

First and foremost, we'd like to thank the city of Ferndale, CA for inspiring our fictional town of Lost Grove. I (Charlotte) first stumbled upon the city on a West Coast trip, starting in San Francisco and heading north to Ferndale. I found a Bed & Breakfast online and fell in love with the Victorian design of not only the Inn but the entire town. During this visit, I had a writer's inspiration for interconnected characters in this small town, all quite peculiar: Mary the vampire, Story the witch, Leith the…you haven't met her yet, and the Green Man. This was the genesis of Lost Grove. Flash forward twelve years when Amazon announced their creation of Kindle Vella, an online platform to share a serialized story. I pontificated on what sort of story I could launch and shared a handful of ideas with my husband, Alex.

Upon hearing the bare-bones idea of Lost Grove, I (Alex) slammed the door on the rest. Lost Grove tickled that prime detective story nerve in my soul, which is my favorite subgenre to read and write. From there, we embarked on a two-year journey, accompanied by another visit to Ferndale (my first), plotting, researching, and writing this story.

We'd like to give a massive thanks to our greatest inspirations, our fellow authors: Jane Casey, Paul Doiron, Stephen King, Shea Ernshaw, Eric Rickstad, Ken Bruen, Sarah Pinborough, Douglas Lindsay, Ania Ahlborn, Joanna Schaffhausen, Adam Nevill, Kate Atkinson, Tana French, Paul Tremblay, and the late Mo Hayder (we'll never stop missing you).

Thank you to our copy editor, Lisa Gilliam, for catching boundless silly mistakes

Thank you to our fellow indie authors Wofford Lee Jones, Elise Kova, Seán O'Connor, Emmaline Harris, Mark Stay, Kenneth Baldwin for your support, both in your constant cheerleading of our work and your own fantastic work.

We'd also like to thank all of our Instagram followers for their constant support; special shoutouts to Kevin Buck, Annie Buck, Phoebe, Lucy and Charlotte, Bassetude_boys_w_olive_garnish, and Malena.

All the readers, booksellers, librarians, reviewers, and bloggers who have supported us on this journey. We are honored you moved our book to the top of your massive TBR piles.

We'd like to thank our longtime friends for their love and support: Shannon Lucio, Shannon Sadecki, John Myers, Brian Harrer, Mallory Lovings, Charlie Hofheimer, Tim Christensen, Tim Hoagland, Forrest Brandt, the Chomsky family, Marty Taylor, Joel Pike, Morgan Strauss, Bobby Hart, Gary Poux, Geli Duoos Ulku, Rich and Doug DesCombaz.

Thank you to the Minnesota Timberwolves, the WWE, and all horror filmmakers for supplying us with a weekly escape from the constant grind.

Our families, who never bat an eye when we call them to ask insane theoretical medical questions, float random deliveries into the inbox demanding they read the abysmal first drafts we concocted and embarrass us by blurting out to anyone present that their son, daughter, brother or sister has "recently written a book! You should buy a copy!" We are eternally grateful.

About the Authors

Charlotte Zang

From the moment her mother started reading her bedtime stories, Charlotte has cherished literature. The first stories introduced to her were fairy tails and folklore, and these weren't the kind you'd find the princess living happily ever after. Thanks to one oddly placed door in a friend's basement, her first novel, Satan's In Your Kitchen, sprang to life in all its glorious comedy. She also wrote a fairy tale of her own, a dark retelling known as Consuming Beauty. Blooding is her third novel.

She is an author of fantasy, horror and magic, master of her garden, queen of delicious recipes and mother of basset hounds. She lives in the Pacific northwest with her three hounds and adoring husband.

You can follow her on Intagram @charlottezang and TikTok @charlottelzang and visit her website www.charlottezang.com.

Alex J. Knudsen

ALEX J. KNUDSEN was born in Minneapolis, Minnesota, and attended the University of Southern California. He first started writing in the third grade when he created the short story, Mr. Raquetball. He went on to write numerous unpublished short stories and a bevy of screenplays. Knudsen is the founder of Gantry Productions and is the writer-director of numerous films, including the Independent award nominated feature film, Autopilot and the award nominated short horror film, Consuming Beauty, which was adapted from his wife's novel of the same name. Knudsen is a self-taught mixologist and devourer of horror films. Alex currently lives in Oregon with his wife and three Basset Hounds. The Nawie is his first novel.

You can follow him on Instagram @knutzauthor and visit his website www.alexjknudsen.com.

Printed in Great Britain
by Amazon